A Tapestry of Lives

A variation on Jane Austen's
Pride & Prejudice

by

Jean Sims

~Book I~

ISBN: 1490468056
ISBN-13: 978-1490468051

This book is dedicated to my father, William Riley Sims, Jr.

CONTENTS

ACKNOWLEDGMENTS

This book was inspired by Jane Austen but would never have been written (much less published) without the camaraderie and support of the Derbyshire Writers' Guild. Nikita Ghandi kindly proofread the manuscript and provided much needed encouragement when I could no longer face reading it again. The characters and events portrayed in this book are fictitious or are used fictitiously. Any similarity to real persons, living or dead, is purely coincidental and not intended by the author.

1 MR. BENNET IS SURPRISED

Mr. Thomas Bennet sat silently at his desk as his favorite daughter stalked out of his study, shutting the door soundly behind her. He had dismissed Elizabeth's plea to stop her youngest sister's trip to Brighton more out of habit than for any particular reason. However, he easily perceived Lizzy's heightened emotions—she had not come to him lightly nor due to envy of Lydia's opportunity to travel.

What had she said? "Our importance, our respectability in the world, must be affected by the wild volatility, the assurance and disdain of all restraint which mark Lydia's character." If any female but his Lizzy had uttered such words he would have disregarded them as missish diatribe and returned to his beloved Plato. But his second eldest was no temperamental miss.

Mr. Bennet stood and went to his window, looking out across the yard to the stables. He firmly believed that children should be allowed to live and explore—not dressed up as miniature adults and forced to sit stiffly, never speaking unless spoken to. Elizabeth and Jane had enjoyed such freedom as children and were both growing into lovely, interesting young ladies (he shuddered to think of any of his girls growing up). Why would Lizzy be so adamant that a child like Lydia could do something that would, how had she put it? "Bring censure and disgrace upon the family."

He shook his head and sighed, ready to dismiss the issue, when he caught sight of his second eldest striding through the garden toward a copse that had allowed to grow wild. He could not dismiss the unhappiness in her posture and eventually, after some internal debate, forced himself to walk out and continue their discussion.

Shutting the door to his study behind him, Mr. Bennet turned down the hall only to collide with a young lady in such a sudden fashion that he was knocked to one knee. As he rose, Thomas could not avoid noticing an impressively buxom figure framed by a low cut bodice. Then Thomas received quite a shock when, expecting to look into the face of a visitor, he was instead presented with the laughing eyes of his youngest daughter.

"Papa! Oh Lord, I'm in such a rush—we're walking into Meryton to see Mrs. Forster and the officers!" And in a rustle of petticoats and lace she was off skipping up the stairs.

Mr. Bennet remained stationary for some moments in the hall, mind reeling. His baby girl was quite a well-developed young woman. How old was Lydia? After some rapid calculations his feet began moving, as swiftly as his second eldest's and in the same direction. Elizabeth was not concerned over the potential antics of a little girl on her first trip to the seaside but the very real danger that a lively but naïve young lady could get into while living largely unchaperoned amidst an entire camp full of soldiers. He groaned and very nearly slapped his own forehead.

Thomas Bennet might be inclined toward solitude and scholarship but he did care about his family and, once awakened to his own obliviousness, applied his native intelligence to the matter. The longer he considered, the more disturbed he became.

When he reached the copse into which his daughter had disappeared, he paused for a moment by an ancient oak planted by one of his own ancestors. Elizabeth appeared to have calmed and was sitting on a stone bench reading. As his eyes adjusted to the shade, Mr. Bennet noted first that it appeared to be a letter and second, that his daughter seemed to be staring through the pages rather than reading.

"Lizzy, I apologize for disturbing you but after further consideration I believe it necessary to continue our discussion."

The sound of her father's voice wrought an unexpected change upon his favorite's face. Elizabeth started violently and blushed violently. In doing so, her fingers loosened and the letter went fluttering in the breeze. She moved quickly to catch one page but the other drifted to her father's feet. Reaching down to retrieve it for her, Mr. Bennet could not help but notice that the writing was very close and in a distinctly masculine hand. Glancing at the salutation his concern deepened.

Be not alarmed, Madam, on receiving this letter, by the apprehension of its containing any repetition of those sentiments, or renewal of those offers, which were last night so disgusting to you.

"Good heavens, Lizzy! What is this? What man is writing to you in such a manner?" Bennet's emotions, already heightened by his revelation over his youngest daughter, were rapidly deteriorating. This was not helped when the usually steady Elizabeth lowered her face to her hands and burst into tears.

Though not normally a demonstrative man, Mr. Bennet cautiously gathered his weeping daughter into his arms. Eventually her tears slowed and he was relieved when she finally raised her head from his shoulder and accepted his handkerchief with a watery smile. Patting his now dampened shoulder she attempted a tease; "Mr. Mabberly shall not be pleased with me for mussing your coat, Papa."

Happy to see the reemergence of his normally even-tempered daughter, Mr. Bennet smiled back. "Well, I shall take care of my manservant. Perhaps I shall venture into the stables before returning to dress for dinner. Old Nelly has a cold and might be convinced to sneeze upon me. Although I suspect Mabberly has long since come to accept my tendency to return my wardrobe in a less than pristine condition. As has your own maid, might I conjecture?"

Seeing his daughter smile wanly he continued in a more serious tone, "But Lizzy, you must tell me about this letter. Does it have something to do with your concern over Lydia?"

Elizabeth took a deep breath to steady herself. "Oh Papa! I do not know what to think about anything— I certainly do not know myself anymore!" Unsure of how to begin, she thrust the second page of her letter at him and stood to pace. "You remember Mr. Bingley and his party from last autumn?"

Mr. Bennet nodded, though still confused. "Of course."

"You may not recall but I was quite decided in my dislike of one of his guests, a Mr. Darcy." After noting her father's nod of assent, she seemed to retreat further into herself before continuing. "I suppose I should not have been so quick to judge a new acquaintance, but he was so silent, and his looks were so severe… and the things he said…"

When his daughter trailed off, Mr. Bennet waited a moment before prompting, "What exactly did he say, child?"

"Oh, it sounds so silly now, but at that first assembly where we all met, I overheard Mr. Bingley trying to convince Mr. Darcy to ask me to dance. Mr. Darcy was quite blunt in his refusal. I laughed about his incivility to Charlotte but I must admit that he hurt my feelings." She looked up at her father who was smirking slightly. "Well, Papa? I am expecting some suitably educational proverb on the evils of eavesdropping."

Mr. Bennet chuckled. "Actually my dear, I was thinking of the one that goes, 'Do not speak unless you can improve on the silence.'"

"Hmmm… and bees with honey in their mouths have stingers in their tails." Elizabeth stilled for a moment, looking off across the oat field that adjoined the copse. After a minute she roused herself and turned back to her father. "Charlotte told me on several occasions that she thought Mr.

Darcy admired me." Seeing her father's look of surprise, she added, "I judged her to be quite fanciful… I did notice that he stared at me a great deal but I believed he only looked to find fault… to criticize a girl he considered 'not handsome enough to tempt him' at an unimportant country dance. I was quite impertinent to him, Papa.

"And then, of course, there was Lieutenant Wickham and his stories. His father had been the steward at Pemberley, the Darcy family's estate in Derbyshire. Mr. Darcy's father gave young Mr. Wickham the benefits of a gentleman's education and the assurance of a comfortable living if he took orders, but the Lieutenant claimed that Mr. Darcy had refused to honor the promise after his father's death. Oh Papa, I was so eager to believe every ill word he spun and they were all half-truths and lies."

Elizabeth picked up a long stem of grass and began using it to prod a clump of daffodils whose only fault was to grow along her path. Mr. Bennet watched her for a moment. He remembered Lieutenant Wickham vaguely— the young man was fair of face but his silver tongue covered for a mind with no depth of understanding. "And how did you discover these truths, Lizzy?"

Elizabeth stopped abusing the flowers, shut her eyes and sighed, then turned back to her father. "I went to Kent in March to visit Charlotte and Mr. Collins, you remember Papa?" After waiting for her father's nod, she continued, "Lady Catherine de Bourgh is Mr. Darcy's aunt— his mother's sister. He and his cousin, a Colonel Fitzwilliam, came to visit Rosings Park for Easter and, as our own cousin is so fond of telling us, the parsonage is separated from that great estate by just a lane.

"Mr. Darcy still stared at me a great deal and I met him unexpectedly walking in the park, but truly Papa, I thought nothing of it except how unpleasant he was. I truly believed that he desired my company as little as I wished for his. And his own aunt let it be known that he was to marry her daughter!"

While Elizabeth paused to sort her thoughts, Mr. Bennet rubbed his chin and worked very hard to control the chuckle rising in his chest. He well knew the scathing wit that his daughter could unleash upon anyone who irritated her. His vague memory of Mr. Darcy was of a tall, serious, young man who had appeared distinctly ill at ease in the drawing rooms of Hertfordshire. Another memory tugged at him.

"Didn't you dance with him at the Netherfield ball, Lizzy?" His daughter returned to sit beside him and hid her face in her hands. This did not, however, completely hide the rosy blush that had risen on her cheeks.

"Yes, Papa."

"Well, well. Continue your story. We were in Kent, I believe."

"Yes, Papa." She studied the grass stem in her hands and began to wind it around her finger. "One evening, I remained at the parsonage while

Charlotte, Maria and Mr. Collins went to Rosings for dinner. I had been invited as well but begged off claiming a headache. It was not entirely untrue. In a conversation with Colonel Fitzwilliam— Mr. Darcy's cousin had accompanied him, you remember? He mentioned that Mr. Darcy congratulated himself on having recently saved a friend from a 'most imprudent marriage.' The Colonel did not know any of the particulars but I knew it must be Jane and Mr. Bingley. I knew she was still heartbroken and here was evidence that not only had Mr. Darcy purposefully caused her misery, but he had then boasted about it to someone wholly unconnected to the situation."

Thomas sighed and, to himself, admitted that he had not noticed his eldest's true feelings. Mrs. Bennet had been plotting matches since Jane turned fifteen and he had always ignored her. For the second time that day he did some quick arithmetic in his head and realized that his firstborn was almost twenty-three, an age when most young ladies of her station were married or at least affianced. Putting that fact aside for future consideration, Mr. Bennet turned his attention back to Elizabeth when she resumed her story.

"So I gave myself over to an evening of solitude, re-reading Jane's letters and seething over the arrogant, high-handed... interference of Mr. Bingley's so-called friend. And then, who should have the misfortune to come calling on me curing my fit of pique but Mr. Darcy himself."

Lizzy covered her eyes as if attempting to block out the memory. "Oh Papa, I was already so vexed... and then he proposed and I was so surprised and then so angry. And I said so many things and he was so angry to be refused. Well, that is not entirely true. He was surprised to be refused. He only became angry after asking me why I had refused him. Oh, Papa, the things I accused him of..."

By now, Mr. Bennet's head was spinning with new information. Mr. Darcy had not only separated Jane from her beau but had proposed to his Lizzy? And been refused? And she seemed to regret it? "Well my dear, I don't know quite what to say. Am I to understand that this letter is from Mr. Darcy, then?"

Elizabeth nodded weakly. "We parted in anger that evening, as you can imagine. I did not sleep well and when I awoke in the morning, I could not face Mr. Collins over the breakfast table so I went for a walk to clear my head. If nothing else, Rosings Park does have some lovely old groves. I met Mr. Darcy—entirely unexpectedly on my part— though he did say he had been looking for me. He put that letter in my hands and asked me to do him the honor of reading it. In hindsight, he looked as exhausted as I felt." She sighed and rolled her shoulders, attempting to release some of the tension she felt.

Motioning to the pages in her father's hands, she finished, "Please read it, Papa. I think I should like to know what you think."

Mr. Bennet took his time reading the closely written missive but as Elizabeth had it nearly committed to memory, she could easily track her father's progress by his changing expressions.

When he reached the charitable adieu, he sighed heavily and rubbed his eyes. Not for the first time, Thomas wished that his wife was a source of sensible advice for their daughters or that there was a rational female relative living nearby. He thought wistfully of his sister-in-law, Mrs. Gardiner, in London but knew that he would have to deal with his daughter's worries by himself, for now.

"Well, my dear, this is quite a letter that your young man has written to you."

"Oh heavens, Papa; he is not my young man. After the hateful things I said to him I should be surprised if he does not positively despise me! If by some chance I ever see him again, I am quite sure he will do everything possible to avoid me."

"Hmmm. Does that bother you? You said you have always disliked him."

"I barely know myself anymore. It would be the height of silliness for me to become jealous of his esteem after I have abused him so horribly to his face."

Mr. Bennet considered his daughter for a moment and then chided her gently. "You are avoiding my question."

She sighed. "I once read that one may feel uncommonly clever in taking so decided a dislike of someone. It is such a spur to one's genius, such an opening for wit to have a dislike of that kind."

Chuckling, her father folded his arms in the manner of a stern school master. "Miss Lizzy, you will answer the question."

Elizabeth groaned in defeat and, if it must be admitted, embarrassment. After pausing for a minute to collect her thoughts, she eventually responded, "I believe that he is a good man in essentials. He is intelligent, well-educated, and I appreciate the way that he listened to me and my pert opinions and was not averse to engaging me in discussions of books, philosophy, politics and…. oh, everything and nothing."

Mr. Bennet's eyebrows rose at this bit of fancy but he remained silent, encouraging her to continue.

"I believe he is a good elder brother and guardian to his sister—he truly cares for her education and well-being. He is also handsome, which a young man ought likewise to be, if he possibly can." She smirked, needing to lighten the atmosphere.

"I sense a 'but' coming…"

Elizabeth sighed. "But… he should not have delivered his sentiments in a manner so ill-suited to recommend them. Between my prejudice and his assurance of success there was little chance of civility being maintained for long.

"I forgive him for separating his friend from my sister. Even Charlotte noted that Jane's admiration was wholly concealed from the world in general. I understand how someone with no understanding of her nature could, after hearing Mama gossiping, assume that Jane would enter into a marriage of unequal affection to secure the financial security of her family. If anything, knowing the truth has lowered my opinion of Mr. Bingley; that he so depends on the opinions of his friend and did not have the fortitude to believe in his own knowledge of Jane's affections is no great compliment to his character."

"Well, that is for Jane to decide if it ever comes to it. I might point out that you have shown no qualms in turning your sister's head from admirers you determined to be wanting. But let us continue on the subject of the young man from Derbyshire," admonished her father gently.

Elizabeth paused, thinking back. "Once, in Kent, I teased Mr. Darcy about his poor showing in Meryton society and he responded by saying that 'he had not the talent which some people possess of conversing easily with those he had never seen before.' He said that he could not 'catch their tone of conversation, or appear interested in their concerns.' I am afraid I was quite impertinent and told him that he should try practicing more." She sighed and then continued firmly.

"I do not regret refusing Mr. Darcy's proposal. His words showed that he had feelings which would have made marriage between us insupportable. He is an intelligent, educated man but I cannot agree with the significance he places on a person's inherited wealth and position in society rather than their character. Of course I know the importance of such things in our world, such as it is, but I cannot agree that such attributes constitute the innate value of a man… or of a woman for that matter. If such are his principles, then I cannot approve of him."

Mr. Bennet cleared his throat to relieve the tightness that had gathered there. "Well, my dear, I am proud of you. There are few ladies (or gentlemen for that matter) who could sort through such an emotional subject and produce such a well-reasoned conclusion."

They sat quietly for a minute until finally Mr. Bennet stood and offered his arm. "Come, I feel the need to walk. Perhaps we could go up to Oakham Mount?" Lizzy agreed and the pair proceeded along a well-worn path.

After some time, Elizabeth made the effort to form her confused feelings into words. "It is just that, although I have seemingly spent much time in Mr. Darcy's company over the last year, I suddenly feel as if I have never actually met him. The man I believed he was turns out to be a figment of my imagination."

"And do you wish to know the true Mr. Darcy?"

"I doubt I will ever have a chance to do so… I would be mortified to see him again and he… well, he must hate me for the things I accused him of… really of the way I've treated him since the day we met."

This time Mr. Bennet made no effort to restrain his laughter. "Lizzy, the man certainly does not hate you. Your letter is proof enough of that." At her look of disbelief, he shook his head in amusement.

"My dear girl, he cared enough about what you thought of him to write an exceedingly detailed letter explaining himself. Few men who had just been refused in such an… unambiguous fashion as you have described would make such an effort."

His daughter still looked unconvinced. "My dear, I cannot say that I know Mr. Darcy any better than you. For myself, my own indolence kept me from making more of an acquaintance that I now believe would have provided me with some intelligent conversation. I have gotten too much in the habit of complaining about any society rather than looking to see any good." To himself, Thomas admitted that he had become especially harsh toward those within his own family circle.

After helping each other over a stile, father and daughter continued to walk in silence for some time until Elizabeth spoke. "I still cannot fit together the different aspects of the man. I have been thinking over our interactions and though there are many instances when I now believe I misinterpreted him and others when my misapprehension prompted him to respond in such a way that affirmed my notions… there were times when he was at the very least impolite and often quite rude. And yet, he seems to be in fundamentals a very good man."

After a few moments of consideration, her father responded. "At the risk of sounding like our dear, saintly Jane, I believe that the gentleman has been misunderstood. Or perhaps it would be more accurate to say that he makes it difficult to be understood. He clearly feels deeply but masks his emotions as much as possible. Quite like our Jane, in fact, which is a bit of irony worthy of Mr. Shakespeare given how Mr. Darcy appears to have misread your sister."

After the pair walked some way further, Mr. Bennet stirred himself to speak. "Like Mr. Darcy, I lost my mother at a young age. I do not know much about his father, but my own was exceedingly retiring and had little use for society. My elder sister was married even before I started university so I received little guidance from her.

"I remember attending my first private ball—I was visiting the family of a university friend in Bath. I walked in and was awash with fear that I had worn the wrong sort of waistcoat and everyone would turn and stare at me. I do not consider myself shy by any means, but in such a sea of strangers I found myself barely capable of speaking coherently to my companions, let alone requesting an introduction to anyone. My friends were all more accustomed to society than I and found great amusement laughing at my stupidity."

Father and daughter paused to move a fallen tree branch off the path before continuing on to climb the hill, both lost in thought. Eventually Mr. Bennet roused himself again. "Do you remember that young curate who visited Meryton a few years back? He gave a few sermons when Mr. Grant was getting ready to retire and we were interviewing candidates for his living. What was his name, Channing? Banning?"

"Mr. Manning. Mr. Frederick Manning," said Elizabeth decidedly and then blushed when her father began chuckling.

"You were fifteen, I believe, and gave him such sighs and blushes as I would never have believed could come from my most sensible daughter."

"Oh Papa…"

"I'm sorry, my dear. I don't remind you of this solely for my own amusement but to make a point. First, while in the throes of your infatuation there were several occasions when you quite snubbed old Mr. Grant in your eagerness to speak with the young curate." Seeing her look of mortification, he continued, "You must not worry about having offended him; Grant had seen it all before and we had quite a laugh over it. Poor, young Manning hadn't a clue, however. After one of your conversations with him, he came to me and expressed concern over your lack of theological understanding."

Seeing how disconcerted his daughter appeared, Mr. Bennet couldn't help but chuckle. "Never fear, Lizzy. Although your diligence may never match Mary's, I am confident that your understanding is at least as good. My point is that such emotions often leave the best of us less than articulate."

Elizabeth considered her father's words for some time as they climbed. "But Papa, even if I begin to understand Mr. Darcy better, there remains the fact that I insulted him most grievously and with little provocation. I still believe he must despise me. Even were I to ever see him again (which itself is most unlikely), I doubt that he would ever acknowledge me, let alone speak to me."

"Well, if he acts in such a manner then he is not worth your concern. However, his letter suggests to me that he cares a great deal about what you think of him. If anything, I would say that he sounds rather stunned at the level of misunderstanding between the two of you."

"But Papa, he is not some callow youth who has never lived beyond his home village. I cannot comprehend how he came to so misunderstand me; I suppose my spirits must have misled him."

Mr. Bennet chuckled. "Well, my dear, your teasing manner may well camouflage your irritation to all but those who know you best, though I cannot believe it to be the worst fault to have." He thought for a moment. "But remember, Lizzy, that though Mr. Darcy may be experienced with London high society, it does not necessarily translate that he is well-prepared to understand a lady such as yourself."

Seeing that his daughter was listening intently but not catching his meaning, he elaborated, "Our culture makes it exceedingly difficult for a gentleman to spend significant time getting to know any young lady who is not a close relation. And remember, Mr. Darcy has not had a mother since he was a child himself and his sister is so much younger as to look to him for a father figure, not a confidant.

"We gentlemen are educated by our tutors, sent to school with other boys, and then spend some years at university with other young men. We are encouraged to spend our hours out riding and shooting or equivalent gentlemanly pursuits indoors—billiards, cards, fencing and the like. Although I suspect Mr. Darcy spent most of his time learning to run an estate and manage the family's business affairs from a young age.

"It may not be your favorite activity, Elizabeth, but you are comfortable making drawing room conversation and navigating a crowded ballroom. Those are not habitats in which a gentleman is schooled until he reaches an age when... well, when he becomes the invited prey at such gatherings.

"Now, for a young man such as Mr. Darcy, whose connections and inheritance would have made him a catch on the marriage market even if he did not cut such a fine figure..."

Mr. Bennet chuckled at the look on his daughter's face. "I *was* young, once, Lizzy. But to continue, I suspect that many of Mr. Darcy's poor manners might be better explained by *defensiveness* rather than *offensiveness*. You observed how Miss Bingley chased him. Consider that such is what he has come to expect from ladies in social situations. Some attempting to gain his favor through overt flattery and flirtation, while others are trying to trick him into a situation in which he would be honor bound to marry them. I would hypothesize that he has learned through sheer self-preservation to be on guard against everyone."

Seeing that his daughter's expression had turned to shock, Mr. Bennet smiled grimly. "I am being blunt, my dear, because it is the only way I can think of to help you understand. In spite of your mother's desires, I have kept you girls away from the ton precisely because the society there is so savage. Longbourn may be nothing to Pemberley but I know a little about what it is like to be a young heir pursued by ladies and their match-making parents. I cannot even imagine enduring the attention that Mr. Darcy must receive."

Bennet turned to his daughter with a sudden clarity forming in his mind. "In fact, I would be willing to wager a great deal that your impertinence and lack of attention to Mr. Darcy may be precisely what attracted his notice in the first place. After years of being fêted for his wealth and connections, to be dismissed by a pretty, intelligent young lady must have been quite a novel sensation."

Elizabeth opened her mouth but closed it again when she couldn't think of what to say.

Her father continued, "And indeed, to have his proposal rejected and your refusal couched in terms of his failings (whether real or perceived) as a gentleman rather than as a figure of high society must have been thoroughly strange. In terms of money and connections, you had everything to gain by accepting him. I suspect that you have given young Mr. Darcy a great deal to consider."

Seeing that his daughter still appeared skeptical, Mr. Bennet attempted to summarize his point. "In short, you have treated Mr. Darcy as a man rather than solely the sum of his wealth and connections. I suspect that that is what he has always desired in theory, but he has had little experience with such relationships in reality and thus made a complete hash of it. If he has the sense to look beyond his bruised ego then he should realize that if you ever were to accept him, it would be for his own merit. You have proven beyond a doubt that you are no fortune hunter."

They soon reached the peak of Oakham Mount and settled side by side on a large boulder. For some time, father and daughter looked out over the Bennet lands and enjoyed the afternoon sunlight in silence. A boy and dog followed a herd of grazing cows, moving them from one pasture to another. In the far distance, Mr. Goulding and his son were riding along the hedgerows that separated their land from Longbourn.

While Elizabeth contemplated more recent events, Mr. Bennet's thoughts drifted further into the past. He roused himself and began to speak. "As you may know, I started at university when I was sixteen. As you can probably imagine, I was soon determined to focus my studies on the classical philosophers, particularly the Greeks. That is where I met your Uncle Gardiner and, as he will attest, I did little else but immerse myself in my studies, though I did emerge occasionally for debates." He quirked an eyebrow. "And the chess club, I will admit."

Elizabeth smiled, easily picturing her father in such behavior.

"At the time, I wished never to leave. I received my degree in three years but convinced my father to allow me to stay on and continue my research. At times I let myself dream that Father would live forever, leaving me to pursue an academic career. You never knew him but he was not terribly concerned with intellectual pursuits. He had some interest in politics but no desire to participate in them. Really, the only time I remember him leaving the boundaries of Longbourn was for the hunting parties."

Mr. Bennet sighed and focused his memories. "In short, I had very little in common with him and no great friends among the neighbors. With my mother long dead and my sister married and living in London, I could see little attraction in returning to Hertfordshire.

"At Oxford, one of the professors took me under his wing, Mr. Burbidge. I met him in my first semester and he became a mentor… even a father figure, if you will, for I certainly felt more comfortable talking to him than I ever had with my own. He and his wife invited me to visit quite often for dinner and such."

Mr. Bennet removed his spectacles and rubbed his eyes before absent-mindedly cleaning the lenses with a handkerchief. "The Burbidges had a daughter, Olympia. She was away at school for several years, but returned when she was eighteen and I was twenty. She was very pretty and, because of her father I suppose, very comfortable with scholarly gentlemen carrying on the sort of academic discussions I found fascinating. In short, I became infatuated without taking the time to actually get to know the girl. Sound familiar?" He smiled crookedly.

Elizabeth returned his smile but found that she could not laugh at him.

"One Sunday afternoon, we all went for a picnic along the river. It was a lovely day and Olympia agreed to go out in a punt with me. Somewhere in the course of our conversation, I suggested that if we were to marry, we could repeat such idyllic days for the rest of our lives."

Thomas Bennet sighed. He might be nearing fifty, but he could still feel the mortification he had experienced as a young man. "She laughed—it did not even occur to her that I might be serious. She explained that she had no intention of spending her life wasting away in the dullness of the university community. She had returned to Oxford only because it gave her the perfect opportunity to meet some rich, well-connected gentleman, preferably titled, who would sweep her away into the glitter of London society."

"Oh Papa, I'm sorry."

"Don't be. I was young and self-centered; It never occurred to me that she would not jump at the opportunity to join my life… never occurred to me that she might have hopes and dreams of her own. I observed her but never bothered to get to know her." He shrugged. "Some months later she got herself engaged to a rich baronet's only son and was, by all reports, deliriously happy."

Not certain how she should respond to such a disclosure, Elizabeth remained silent.

Remembering the point of his confession, Mr. Bennet turned to her. "For me, the hurt did not last long. I was enamored with the dream of escaping my responsibilities and imitating my mentor's life, not with the lady herself. It would never have occurred to me to write a letter such as your young man has done."

He paused before continuing. "To be honest, I have no idea what happened to Olympia, or Lady Cobb, as I suppose she is now. She departed (for London, I assume) and within a year, your grandfather passed on and all my energies were consumed by Longbourn."

Father and daughter sat quietly for some time, each lost in their thoughts as a lark filled the air with his songs. Finally, Elizabeth stirred herself and asked a question that she had long wondered about but never dared to raise.

"Papa? How did you and my mother come to marry?"

Thomas sighed. It was a question that he had hoped never to receive from his children, but he supposed that he should not be surprised that his disclosures that day had prompted it.

He stood, leaving his hat and walking stick on the ground. After making a brief circuit around the peak, he returned to look his daughter straight in the eye. "I will answer, but this is in the strictest of confidence, Lizzy. You will not even speak of it to Jane, you understand?" At her earnest nod, he attempted to lighten the mood. "Although I suppose you may share it with Mr. Darcy if you find yourself scrounging for family secrets with which to repay him."

When she rolled her eyes, Thomas smiled. Fanny Gardiner might not have been the ideal he once dreamed of marrying, but she had gifted him five beautiful daughters that he prized above all the jewels in the Kingdom.

"After the debacle with Olympia, I plunged myself into my studies. Really, what were girls to Plato and Aristotle? My only social outings, if they might be termed such, were to the chess club. I had met your Uncle Gardiner over a chessboard and we became friends, which is odd, I suppose, given the disparity of our academic interests. His course work might have appeared haphazard but he was always very focused— every lecture or laboratory he took had a reason, educating him to take on a larger role in his father's business. He studied modern languages so that he wouldn't have to rely on translators. He was interested in politics and economics so that he might predict the market. I remember once he even took some geology courses so that he might better understand why certain gems and ores were found where they were.

"We were an odd pair, I suppose. I, heir of a modest country estate and trying to forget the responsibilities that would someday drag me from my beloved books. He was the only son of a gentleman's younger son with a good head for business and a disdain for frittering away his time in society's useless nothings. Old Emmet Gardiner had taken a small inheritance and bought a share in a brig headed for the Orient. That was the start of his import business and he grew an excellent income at it. Edward planned to continue with his father and had no qualms with making his living through honest work, even if the ton spurned him as a tradesman.

"Anyway, we roomed together at Oxford and kept in touch when he left to join his father's business. It was a friendship that meant a great deal to me particularly when, only a few years later, I received word that my own father was deathly ill. I returned to Hertfordshire and immediately discovered that all my Greek and Latin were of absolutely no help in managing an estate."

After a lengthy pause, Elizabeth's father finally continued; "I muddled along for some months until Father finally passed away. I used the funeral as an excuse to beg Gardiner to come out and apply his keen business sense to Longbourn's ledgers. And he came, bless his heart."

Thomas sighed, having arrived at the difficult part of his story. "Gardiner also brought his younger sister with him. Their own father had died the previous year and Edward became Fanny's guardian; he did not like to leave her in London without his supervision."

"She was barely seventeen, as beautiful as Jane is now, but lively… effervescent. I don't know how else to describe it. She said nothing particularly witty or intelligent but a room was warmer with her in it, somehow."

Lizzy nodded, beginning to see her mother in a new light.

Mr. Bennet continued, "Gardiner and I spent most of our time buried in the study— my father had not been a particularly attentive record keeper and I have never been any sort of correspondent. My elder sister Jane (your sister's namesake) came to help me with the house and funeral. Unfortunately, she was attended by her husband."

Elizabeth's eyes widened at the venom in her father's voice.

"Wilberforce Collins was not a moral man and I rue the day my sister met him, let alone married him. I realize that I should have some affection for young William Collins as my sister's only child and I do have sympathy that he grew up in the house of such a domineering, unprincipled miscreant… but the son looks so much like his father that I find it hard to forget."

Mr. Bennet shook himself. The man had died, quite miserably if Gardiner's information was correct. There was no need to hold on to such anger. "In short, Collins enticed Fanny into a compromising situation. Although Gardiner and I interrupted them before anything… err… *serious* had happened, they had been seen and Fanny recognized."

He sighed, feeling very, very old. "Luckily, Collins was not. She was in need of a respectable husband and I was in need of a wife and helpmate. So I proposed, and once our engagement was announced everyone assumed that it was I whom she had been seen embracing."

Thomas could see in his daughter's eyes that she was listening intently. "She was not a brilliant wit but she was pretty and affectionate and knew how to run a household."

He saw that Lizzy was unhappy by such a brusque summary and tried to explain. "It was not the sort of understanding that I hope you girls establish before you marry, but I had a sincere affection for her." He quirked his eyebrow in an effort to lighten the atmosphere. "And she was far more beautiful than an old bookworm such as myself could ever have hoped to attract."

Pleased to see his daughter smile a little, he wound up the story. "And so we were married. It was a quiet ceremony because of my father's death. I suspect that is why Fanny dreams of lavish weddings for her daughters." They both chuckled.

"But seriously, Lizzy. I cannot imagine Longbourn without her, especially in those early years. I have never been lively and I was overwhelmed with estate work. Fanny brought light into the house; she bustled around re-arranging the furniture and redecorating; she had people over for dinners and jollied me out to socialize with the neighbors. And then, a year later, she gave me the gift of a beautiful baby girl. We named her Jane for my sister who had died not long after my father. Over the years, she was followed by four more girls to whom, for all of my teasing, I am quite attached."

Father and daughter shared a fond smile. After some minutes of contemplation, Mr. Bennet clapped his hands together. "Well, I need to go sort out this business of Lydia going to Brighton. Shall we walk back by the pond, Lizzy?"

"Thank you, Papa, but I should like to sit here a bit longer." She smiled up at him. "I have a great deal to think on. Thank you for talking to me."

Her father picked up his walking stick and waved farewell. "Yes, yes. I will inform your mother that you may miss tea. Just be certain you are back before dinner or I shall not be responsible for all the tremblings and flutterings!"

Thomas Bennet might live a quiet life as a country squire, but he was well aware of the evils abounding in the world. Longbourn provided a rural sanctuary for his family and he was beginning to realize how far he had allowed himself to drift into lethargy. The information from Mr. Darcy had provided a rude awakening. For a moment, he considered what might have happened if he had ignored Elizabeth and never read that man's astonishing letter but soon pushed such thoughts aside. There were more important plans to work out. Foremost was how to deal with his wife and youngest daughter without breaking up all his peace.

Fortunately, the walk was long enough that Thomas was able to work out a plan that had some hope of succeeding with a minimum of feminine angst. He arrived at the house in time for tea and, after informing his wife that he had given Elizabeth permission to absent herself, he sat and observed.

Such was his usual mien that none of the Bennet ladies detected anything amiss. He, however, schooled himself to use that brain of which he was so proud to assess his family. Instead of looking upon their silliness as his own private comedic performance (as had been his habit in the past), he observed his daughters, sternly reminding himself of their ages. Finally, he listened to his wife and gradually realized that living at Longbourn had left her just as out of touch with the dangers of the world as it had him. Setting down his teacup, he stood. He had found a place to begin.

"Mrs. Bennet? Please come to my study—there is a matter I must discuss with you."

That lady looked startled—surely he knew that Lizzy handled all the household accounts? But she stood and followed him to his sanctuary. The girls barely noticed. Mary had her nose in a book while Kitty and Lydia spread out scraps of ribbon and lace and began arguing over how best to re-trim an old bonnet. Jane was sitting by the window, placidly hemming baby clothes for a poor tenant.

When his wife entered, Mr. Bennet shut the thick door of his study and guided her to a comfortable pair of chairs by the fire. Once they were seated, he spoke, taking care to modulate his voice in a calm tone with none of the sarcasm and censure that he used so often of late.

"Mrs. Bennet, I am in need of your advice. I am deeply concerned for our Lydia. I have heard from an acquaintance who, upon hearing that our dear girl was to go to Brighton, has cautioned me with some disturbing stories. I have decided it best to relay the unvarnished facts, for though unpleasant to you, for I believe them necessary to help her. In short, I am told that it is not uncommon for young ladies, particularly those of our Lydia's beauty and liveliness, to be enticed into compromising situations soon after they arrive in Brighton. The girls are lured by promises of marriage but then left in unwedded disgrace."

Thomas was glad to hear his wife's exclamations of horror (although slightly ashamed by his own dramatics). "Yes, my dear, it is in every way horrible. These girls are shunned by all society, their only recourse to be sent to a distant farm in Scotland, never to be married or seen by their family again."

"Oh, Mr. Bennet!"

Thomas did not like to frighten his wife so, but it was necessary for Fanny to understand the consequences. "And worse, their entire families are also shunned. No decent gentleman would marry the sister of such a girl, and all of their former friends cut them direct."

"Oh, Mr. Bennet! What a terrible thing for our girls!" By now, Fanny was in tears, her imagination full of horrible visions.

"Yes, my dear. But you must remember that this has not yet happened to us. However, you see why I have sought your advice on how best to protect our girls? My acquaintance said that it was the most gentlemanly of officers, one who had all the goodness in his countenance and the kindest of manners who was caught trying to seduce a fifteen year old girl."

By now Mrs. Bennet was frightened to silence, her eyes round in shock. Thomas did not like to confront her with such unpleasant thoughts, but it was necessary for her to understand. "What do you think, my dear? Lydia so desires to go to Brighton but I fear that Mrs. Forster, with a similar liveliness as our girl, may not know enough to look out for her."

Bennet waited, praying that his wife's mean understanding of the world, added to her genuine love of their daughters, would lead her to the correct conclusion. He was not certain that he would be able to save Lydia from herself without the help of her mother. Thus, he was deeply relieved when Mrs. Bennet spoke in a calmer, more decisive tone than he had heard in a very long time.

"Lydia must not go to Brighton! There are no two ways about it— she and Mrs. Forster would have had wonderful fun and I am sorry for her to miss it, but that lady would not watch over her properly in such a dangerous place!"

Fanny looked up at her husband with fear in her eyes. "Thomas, do you think that there are such men in the regiment at Meryton?"

She blanched when her husband nodded emphatically. "I am afraid I do, my dear. In fact, tomorrow I shall be making the rounds of the shopkeepers to see that Colonel Forster is informed of any accounts that his soldiers have not settled. It is the Colonel's responsibility to make sure that debts of honor are managed within his regiment, but it is our duty to be sure that our tradesmen are not cheated. I will take Sir William Lucas and Mr. Goulding with me. Perhaps your brother, Mr. Phillips as well— it never hurts to have a good solicitor at our back, after all."

For all of her pretensions, Miss Fanny Gardiner had grown up the daughter of a merchant and understood the implications of unpaid debts. She looked up to her husband and, for the first time in many years, they were in complete understanding. "I shall speak to Lydia. Kitty as well, now that I think on it. I have encouraged them to make merry with the officers, but our girls are still full young and do not understand the dangers, I fear."

Mr. Bennet touched his wife's arm and the genuine approval in the gesture prompted tears to form in her eyes. Stepping away, she patted her eyes dry before gathering herself like a general going forth to discipline her troops. "Well then! I shall go see to them now. Dinner will be at seven as usual. Don't be late— Cook found a lovely piece of fish this morning at the market."

Mr. Bennet smiled briefly as his wife bustled out of his study with her usual energy. Then he moved back to his desk and penned brief notes to his foremost neighbors and brother-in-law, asking them to call upon him the next morning on a matter of some importance. After sending a servant off to deliver the notes, Thomas settled back in his favorite chair and poured a glass of wine that he considered well-earned. The afternoon had been nothing short of astonishing. He was especially pleased with this new understanding with his wife and hoped it boded well for their future. He was beginning to see that their daughters might be leaving soon and surmised that in the not too distant future it might be just himself and Fanny left at Longbourn. It was rather like a chess game, he thought to himself. Groundwork laid now could pay dividends in the future.

Later, Mr. Bennet settled back in his most comfortable chair and allowed his mind to wander into memories. He thought of the story he had told Elizabeth and all the details that he had left out. Details that he had observed himself and details that he had pieced together from his sister, father, and others.

2 MR. BENNET'S STORY

Reading Mr. Darcy's letter to Elizabeth had startled Thomas Bennet into some action. After speaking with Mrs. Bennet he had rescinded permission for Lydia to accompany Colonel Forster's wife to Brighton, provoking no small outburst. Fighting his natural inclination, he kept to his plan and attended his family through dinner and then sat with them for two hours complete, allowing himself to retreat to his study only when all five girls had retired for the night.

Once safely barricaded behind the solid oak door, Thomas poured himself a generous snifter of brandy, slumped bonelessly into his most comfortable chair, and took a long sip. He could still hear his family moving around upstairs preparing for bed but at least they were separated from him by the thick walls of the Bennet ancestral home. His ears were still ringing from Lydia's tantrum over her lost trip to Brighton. Now that he had realized his baby girl's true age (fifteen!), he was stunned by her childish behavior.

Lydia had been a beautiful baby—quite as pretty as Jane—but with a liveliness that reminded Thomas of his wife. It was easy to see how she had grown up as the spoiled baby of their family, effortlessly wrapping her mother around her little finger. When on Earth had he agreed that she was old enough to be out in society? He suspected that he had not— 'coming out' was not such an event in small town Hertfordshire as it was in London. Children were often brought to gatherings and would gradually make the transition from the youngsters' play-dancing in the corner to joining the adults in their more formal sets on the dance floor.

Thomas could still remember his perturbation when one of the lads from the village had invited Jane to dance in the adult circle for the first time. When had he ceased to care? Mary had shown little talent for dancing; he suspected that this was why she pretended to dislike the activity so much and regularly disappeared into a corner with a book at such events. Although he knew it was selfish, he could admit to himself that, as a father of beautiful daughters, Mary's attitude had been a relief.

His two youngest were another matter entirely. After an evening spent attending to them, Mr. Bennet was beginning to think that Catherine might not be quite as silly as he had labeled her. Rather, it seemed that she had lost herself between Lydia's bold bullying and her own craving for some crumb of attention. Kitty's stunned response when he had attempted to speak with her had spoken volumes to him. When she had finally responded there had been more than a hint of hurt sarcasm in her voice; 'Why don't you ask Lizzy, as you always do?' Mr. Bennet was man enough to recognize an arrow well-aimed, but determined that he would try again after contemplating how to reach his second youngest.

Lydia's wildness was the most disturbing. Her clothes were nothing like the modest garments that he expected to see on a fifteen-year-old daughter of a country squire. Mrs. Bennet had always dressed her daughters well (often exceeding her allowance) and it had once amused him to see how she outfitted their beautiful little girls like porcelain dolls. Lizzy's habit of muddying her clothes during her energetic forays outdoors had left her mother with little choice but to amend their second daughter's wardrobe with more practical outfits.

Jane's serene countenance concealed a firm grip on the elegant styles she preferred; Mr. Bennet had often heard Mrs. Bennet fretting that she remembered a dress being ordered with more lace or trimmings than it finally appeared on Jane, only to catch a hidden smile between his two eldest daughters. He would not be at all surprised if much of the lace that Mrs. Bennet remembered demanding from the seamstress ended up in the scrap bag that Lydia and Kitty used to re-trim bonnets.

Mr. Bennet picked up his glass to take another sip and found that it had left a ring marring his great-grandfather's old oak desk. He grunted to himself. How had it come to this? Was he really sitting alone in his book room, worrying about the lace and bonnets of his womenfolk? Was he so desperate to avoid the true issue at hand? How was he to correct his family's behavior after years of leniency?

Thomas released a great sigh. After inheriting Longbourn, he had begun his adult life with the best of intentions; determined to be a fair and liberal master, a good neighbor, and above all, a kind and attentive husband and father. When had all his good intentions gone so awry? He had five wonderful daughters and a wife who, though not the most intelligent or educated of her sex, was a warm and generous hostess and mother.

In the minutes immediately after reading Mr. Darcy's letter, Bennet had focused on Elizabeth's turbulent emotions and the dangers posed by Lieutenant Wickham. Now freed of that crisis, Thomas' mind circulated back to the gentleman's other points. He had long dismissed the poor behavior of his wife and youngest daughters as silliness to be laughed at. To have it summarized in such stark terms by a relative stranger and to have himself included in the list of improper conduct was startling.

After Mr. Bennet quelled his first impulse to laugh it all off and forced himself to consider Mr. Darcy's depiction more seriously, his indignation swelled rapidly into anger. How dare the young whippersnapper speak of him so! And to his favorite daughter, of all people! Certainly his own behavior was nothing like that of his wife and younger daughters...

Thomas sighed again and drained his glass, the fury leaching out of him. That was the material point, was it not? He was the head of the Bennet family and therefore any improprieties committed by them were his fault... his responsibility. He was struck by the rightness of Elizabeth's words when she had come to his office earlier in the day and begged him not to allow Lydia to go to Brighton, arguing that the behavior of the youngest reflected poorly upon her sisters and could materially affect all of their prospects in life. In the end, he was the head of the family and any faults of behavior or education were his responsibility to correct.

Suddenly wishing desperately that he might hide away in his book room for the remainder of his natural life, Thomas allowed himself the extravagance of a second glass of brandy before firmly turning his mind to more practical considerations. The day's revelations had made it clear to him that his eldest daughters (and perhaps all his daughters) would be marrying in the next few years. None of them had dowries to speak of, nor had he laid by any significant sum to supplement their provisions after his death.

His own father, a devout misogynist by the end of his life, had written an iron-clad clause into the title of Longbourn. First, the Bennet estate could never be split up among multiple heirs. Second, only males could inherit— if the master died without male issue then his sister's son would inherit, provided that that man adopt the Bennet surname as his own. Because of this, Thomas Bennet's five daughters would inherit nothing but what their mother had brought to the marriage and the little that their father had set aside or invested in business ventures with Mr. Gardiner.

Thomas ground his teeth. Because of his father's determination to keep the estate whole and in the family, Longbourn was set to pass to the halfwit offspring of the despicable Wilberforce Collins.

Thomas Bennet sipped some brandy and his eyes came to rest on the Bennet family bible. He idly flipped it open to the record of births, deaths, and marriages inscribed on its opening pages. As his eyes read the names of his dead relations, his mind filled in their stories and he let his current troubles fade from his consciousness for a moment, in favor of memories.

In 1759, the heir of Longbourn, Mr. Horatio Bennet, had married Miss

Elizabeth Smythe to the great joy of his elderly parents. The couple had lived quietly in the country and had one daughter, Jane, and one son, Thomas. Mrs. Bennet died when her son was barely six but Horatio never remarried, being a solitary man by nature and well satisfied with the care of his housekeeper and cook. The son was sent off to school but, having little understanding of females, Mr. Bennet paid scant attention to his daughter other than to ascertain that she was properly clothed and fed and, when the vicar mentioned that the girl had a pleasant singing voice, to arrange that she might join a neighbor's daughters at their lessons on the pianoforte.

Thus, Miss Jane Bennet had grown up in an odd sort of genteel neglect. Since her mother had passed on when the girl was but twelve, she had been expected to act as hostess on the rare occasion that her father had visitors. She learned to sit quietly and see to the guests' needs. As the conversation was generally beyond her limited experiences and education, she became adept at asking such questions as would lead others into conversing. However, as her father rarely attended social occasions in the neighborhood, she herself spent little time with other young people her own age.

As neither of her parents had had siblings and all of her grandparents were dead, Miss Bennet turned to Longbourn's housekeeper, Mrs. Wagner, and spent more time in the kitchens than most gently born ladies might. Fortunately, the Wagner family had served the Bennets for generations and that good woman made certain that none of the servants took advantage of the poor motherless girl while she attempted to fulfill the mistresses' duties.

Some females might have been jealous of a younger brother given so much attention as the estate's next heir, but Jane had always adored her little brother and took on many of the duties of a mother— putting him to bed, reading stories or telling him of their mother when he was home from school. Thomas was a quiet, thoughtful boy with an underlying wit that became more apparent as he grew older. He was never loud or boisterous but a twinkle in his eye would often give him away when the object of his joke became aware of it. Like his father, he had little interest in girls except for his sister and preferred to spend his time with his books, studying dutifully as his tutor directed him.

Although Thomas wrote his sister occasionally, he was no great correspondent and Jane felt the loneliness of her existence at Longbourn where their father sequestered himself in his study or rode out to see to the estate but rarely entertained company. Perhaps because of this neglect, Jane married young and perhaps unwisely, to a much older gentleman named Collins who, though a gentleman by birth, later showed himself to be one of those perennially disappointed by his allotment in life. In visiting Longbourn to conduct some business with old Mr. Bennet, Mr. Collins noted the quiet daughter who, it seemed to him, was well-trained in serving the men and running a household. After confirming that her dowry was adequate to his needs, it took little effort on his part to flatter a girl unused to a man's attentions into believing herself in love and beloved.

Mr. Bennet was rapidly applied to and, though knowing little of Collins except through their recent business association, assumed that it was the natural course of things—girls grew up and left their father's home for a husband's. Although he had felt a sincere affection for his late wife, he did not consider himself a romantic and his years as a widower had made him more cynical than most. "Happiness in marriage is largely a matter of chance," he thought to himself before giving the couple his consent.

Thomas Bennet did not meet the fiancé of his beloved sister until he traveled from school to Hertfordshire for the wedding. Despite his best efforts, he could not like Collins, finding the man condescending and peevish but without the quickness or even the social standing to support his attitudes. Even so, Thomas kept his thoughts to himself as his sister appeared happier than he had ever seen her. He was somewhat concerned when his father mentioned that the business venture with Mr. Collins had failed but the financial loss to the estate was not great and, at fourteen, Thomas was not confident enough to question his parent's decisions.

The sky was grey and dull on the February morning that Miss Jane Bennet wed Wilberforce Collins. Although the bride was blissful and the groom appeared pleased with himself, the morning's festivities were marred when it began to sleet and the groom insisted that the couple depart early for his London house. Jane was saddened to leave the wedding breakfast so soon after it had begun, particularly after Longbourn's servants had made such an effort to please their young mistress. However, after a lifetime's habit of submitting to her father's will she never thought to question the demands of her new husband. After a tight hug and a few tears with her brother and a more formal acknowledgement from her father, Mrs. Jane Collins entered her husband's carriage and set off for her new life. Later, Thomas would remember the bleak weather of the day and wonder if the Fates were signaling the future of his sister's match.

The siblings would not see each other until their father's funeral eight years later, although they corresponded with some regularity. In 1791, Thomas was called away from his studies at Oxford with word that his father had been thrown from his horse and was seriously ill. For some weeks, the son struggled to comprehend the estate's ledgers and planting schedules even as the father struggled against death. For nearly a month, Thomas allowed himself to believe that his father would recover and release him back to his university position until, finally, the doctor and the vicar took the young man aside and forced him to face the facts.

After a long night spent in Longbourn's study emptying a bottle of brandy, Thomas Bennet rose the next morning and never mentioned his desire to return to Oxford again. He wrote to his sister, suggesting that if she wished to farewell their father she should journey into Hertfordshire immediately. Jane arrived two days before their father breathed his last and, though she spent every moment by his bedside, he never uttered any final words of affection for her to hear.

Young Mr. Bennet (as he was now known) also wrote a letter to an old acquaintance, Mr. Edward Gardiner, with whom he had roomed at university. Edward's own father had died two years previously and Thomas dearly hoped that his friend's experience with the legal intricacies of inheritance, combined with his excellent business sense, could help Bennet from what currently felt like a quicksand of accounting.

After his own father's passing, Edward Gardiner had assumed control of the family business and tried to look after his sisters as best he could. His elder sister, Alice, had recently married a young solicitor named Phillips, but Fanny remained at home with increasingly wild expectations of her own prospects. During one of her sister's parties, Edward found Fanny flirting with a leering captain in an unoccupied room, oblivious that she was nearly to the point of being compromised. Although he repeatedly tried to restrain her, her vivacity continued to override her common sense.

Edward Gardiner's father had been a good man but extremely strict with his household, keeping his daughters carefully guarded. He had enjoyed Fanny's exceptional beauty and lively nature at his table, but paid little attention to her education or understanding, believing that his rules would keep her safe until he passed the duty on to her husband.

Unwilling to leave Fanny to her own devices while he traveled to Hertfordshire for the Bennet funeral, Edward made the fateful decision to bring her with him. During the weeks that the Gardiners spent at Longbourn, Fanny appeared even more lively than usual but Edward shrugged off the observation as his sister's normal spirits made more noticeable by the somber mood of a house in mourning. He spent much of his time in the study with Bennet, helping his friend work through the estate's ledgers and paperwork. It was an assumption that would make him shake his head for many years.

One afternoon, the two gentlemen decided to take a break from business and, noting the time, moved toward the drawing room where the family was accustomed to taking afternoon tea. Bennet was turning his head to speak to Gardiner as he opened the parlor door but stopped at the stunned look on his friend's face. He snapped back to the room and felt his jaw drop.

"Collins!"

"Fanny!"

Wilberforce Collins had become bored while accompanying his wife to her father's funeral and resentful after learning that he gained little from the deceased man's will. He was hoping to soon have an armful very lovely Fanny Gardiner, whether or not she was aware of it. Having discarded his coat, he had begged the young lady to assist him in retying his cravat. While Fanny's hands were occupied in unwinding the linen, he amused himself by making a great show of brushing off some crumbs along the neckline of her gown. Upon the entrance of Bennet and Gardiner, the so-called gentleman ceased his groping but was clearly more irritated at the interruption than embarrassed by his actions. Fanny's complete incomprehension of the potential consequences was immediately obvious. "Eddy! Wilber has invited me to visit him in London!"

At his brother-in-law's searing look, Collins rapidly extracted himself from the settee and, jerking on his coat, strode out the other door without a word. "Oh! Well," said Fanny, adjusting her gown to a more ladylike arrangement (though with little change to her demeanor).

"Oh, Fanny," said Edward, sinking into the nearest chair with his head in his hands. Just then a maid arrived with the tea, her curiosity aroused by Mr. Collins' brusque manner passing her in the hall. Miss Gardiner moved to pour for the gentleman, fussing over the pretty china and generally oblivious to her brother's consternation.

Edward and Thomas remained silent as they took their first sips and collected their thoughts. "Perhaps Miss Gardiner might like to rest in her room after tea," suggested Bennet, doing his best to speak delicately. "My housekeeper's niece, Sara, is training to be a lady's maid and would be happy to assist her. Perhaps her hair...?" At this point Thomas ran out of words and waved his hand vaguely at his own brown locks, having little experience or interest in ladies' coiffures except to know that they could take hours to fuss over.

Edward recognized the suggestion for what it was—a ploy to keep Fanny occupied and out of the way with a trusted servant, preventing her from seeking out Collins again, or worse, spreading stories of their 'friendship.'" He agreed immediately and with a little encouragement his sister was off to her room with the maid to try out new hairstyles, although this amusement was delayed for some time as her brother lectured her sternly on proper behavior.

After nearly an hour with his sister, Gardiner was certain that Mr. Collins had overstepped the bounds of propriety on several occasions and neither he nor Fanny had cared much over being observed. Edward's only hope was that, given that both Collins and Fanny were strangers in Meryton, they might not have been recognized. Finally, Gardiner left his sister cooing over hair ribbons with the maid and made his way downstairs to Bennet's study, feeling decades older than his years yet wishing mightily for the wisdom that would come with those decades.

The two men spent the afternoon in a very different mood than they had begun it. Bennet had quietly questioned Longbourn's trusted housekeeper and was forced to tell his younger friend that a rumor was circulating among the Meryton servants that Miss Gardiner had been seen embracing a man in the garden, although no one was certain of her lover's identity.

The next morning, Wilberforce Collins bullied his wife into their rented carriage well before breakfast, ignoring her quiet pleas that she wished to remain for some days more to mourn with her family. After seeing his sister off with barely a glance to her husband, Thomas noted the sun just peeking above the horizon and took himself off for a long, solitary walk across land that Bennets had lived on for centuries. After some hours, he returned to the house and calmly sat down to break his fast with Edward and Fanny.

Steady to his purpose, Thomas paid more attention to his friend's sister than ever before. Although unread, she was well versed in acting as hostess and had a happy, unpracticed demeanor that pleased him. After an hour, during which Edward became increasingly concerned by his friend's behavior, the gentlemen retreated to Longbourn's study.

The two friends sat, remaining silent for some minutes until Bennet roused himself to speak. "Gardiner, I would like to ask your permission to court your sister with the intention of asking for her hand in marriage."

Although he had been expecting something of the sort, Edward was still stunned. "Thomas... I don't know what to say."

"Then say yes."

"I appreciate your offer; it would certainly solve the rumors of my sister's compromise, but it is not your responsibility."

"Her reputation was tainted while she was a guest in my house, by one of my own relations. Therefore, it *is* my responsibility and so shall be the solution. What would you have me do—challenge Collins to a duel? He may be a worthless excuse for a man, but I cannot see myself coming off well regardless of whether he chose pistols or sabers."

"Bennet, you take too much upon yourself. Since my father passed on and our sister married, Fanny has become as silly a creature as I have ever seen. *Her* thoughtless flirtation is not *your* fault. She... she is certainly not the sort of lady you might hope to marry."

Thomas sighed. Edward knew a bit about his failed infatuation with his mentor's daughter at Oxford. "While it is true that I do not yet feel a passionate regard for her, I do feel an affection already and I have every hope that time together would cause it to grow."

"She knows nothing of books, much less philosophy— our father did not believe in educating females except for their household duties," said Edward, weakening.

"I have no need of a fellow student to debate Plato and Aristotle— that is my past life. I need a companion, someone who can run this household."

Thomas sighed and rubbed his eyes for a moment before continuing. "Edward, I am aware that your sister is not the most brilliant or educated of her sex, but she has a liveliness about her that Longbourn and, in truth I, am in need of. There is little society in this neighborhood and I fear being the prey of every matchmaking mother in the county. You know me well— what do you suggest? Would you send me to Almack's in search of a wife? I would be a disaster."

Gardiner couldn't help but laugh at the thought of his bookish friend thrust among the London popinjays and debutants. It was the turning point of the argument and by dinner, Edward had agreed that they would discuss it with his sister.

Miss Fanny Gardiner might be a silly, vain young woman but she had a mean understanding of society's structure and was well aware that marriage to a gentleman with his own estate was a clear step up in the world for the daughter of a tradesman. Thomas Bennet might not be as flashy as some of the officers she had flirted with but he was handsome in a serious sort of way and life as mistress of his estate would be far more comfortable than that of a soldier's wife. The final satisfaction in her new situation came when her sister, Mrs. Phillips, wrote that her own husband had just taken a partnership in the largest law office in Meryton, a village just a mile from Longbourn. Thus assured of her every happiness, Fanny accepted Thomas Bennet's offer of marriage and assured her brother that her contentment was certain.

Mrs. Collins died less than a year later, supposedly of a fever but her brother often thought it more likely that she had willed herself to death out of sheer misery. Her husband had written to offer his regrets that they would not be able to return to Hertfordshire for Bennet's wedding due to "business." Thomas had been more relieved than he cared to admit.

The early years of their marriage were happy. A year after her wedding, Mrs. Fanny Bennet presented her husband with a beautiful baby girl who looked up at him with a serene smile and his own blue eyes. Thomas insisted that she be christened Jane and promised himself that she would have a better chance for happiness in life than his poor sister. It was not until the birth of her third daughter that Fanny learned of the nature of the estate's entailment should she not produce a male heir and her nerves began to fray.

Some weeks after Jane's death, Thomas had received a letter addressed to him in a strange hand. The writing was feminine but not the loopy copperplate taught to gentile young ladies. Upon breaking the seal, he found a short note and a second letter enclosed within the first, this one clearly in his sister's handwriting. In an effort to control his sudden emotions at the sight of his dear sister's hand, Thomas forced himself to read the outer note first.

To Mr. Thomas Bennet, Longbourn, Hertfordshire:

Please accept my sincere condolences on the loss of your sister. Forgive me if I speak out of place, sir, but I served as housekeeper for the Collinses since she arrived as a new bride and, if I might be as bold to say so, she will be dearly missed.

Two days before she passed, Mrs. Collins had a good morning when the sickness lifted a bit. She asked for her writing desk and spent a couple hours composing letters. I'd hoped she was finally recovering and tried keep her from overdoing it but she refused to stop until she was finished. Now I can see she knew her end was coming up and wanted to write some last words to those she cared for most. She gave the letters to me and asked me to be sure they got sent should the worst come to pass. Here's the letter she left for you. She often called you her dear little brother and you could just see the love shining in her face.

Your servant,
Martha Hill

Thomas took a moment to slouch back in his chair, closing his eyes tightly to prevent any tears from escaping. Some of his station might have found such a letter from a servant to be a presumption, but as Thomas Bennet had always found the study of characters fascinating regardless of rank, he saw only what it was: the sharing of sorrow between two people over the loss of a loved one.

With a sigh, young Mr. Bennet set down the opened letter and picked up the second, running a thumb over his sister's familiar handwriting. With a quick brush at his eyes, he broke the seal and read.

11 February 1793

My dear brother Thomas,

I've been unwell enough this last week to retreat to my bed. You know me well enough to perceive that this sort of idleness is not to my taste, but it has given me much time to think and ponder. I was very disappointed that we missed your wedding last month, both because we have so little family left, you and I, but also because you have always been so dear to me... even when you would follow me around, tugging on my skirts and asking "why?" all the time! Goodness, you did drive Cook half mad the way you got underfoot in her kitchen, do you remember? Those are good memories.

Though you have never said anything, I think you know that my life with Mr. Collins has not always been the happiest. And yet, even with the sorrows and frustrations, I do not regret that I left our father's house for this life. It has given me the chance to see and do things, to meet people I never would have crossed paths with in Meryton, however dear.

Would you believe that Mrs. Hill and I went to hear Mary Wollstonecraft read excerpts from her treatise on the education of women last autumn? It was our great secret expedition. Thomas, you may tease that I am turning into a blue stocking in my old age, but I find that I agree with much of what she says on the education of females. We are not mentally feeble by nature... or rather, there is just as great a range in intelligence among beings of my gender as those of yours (I'm sure we can both think of examples at the extremes!). It saddens me to see young ladies raised to believe their value lies in their figure, their ability to embroider cushions and decorate screens, and perhaps worst, the ability to carry on <u>hours</u> of conversation without saying anything of substance!

A few months ago, I attended a dinner party at the home of one of my husband's business associates. After dinner, while the men were at their port and cigars, I began talking with the second daughter of the house—a pretty young lady of about 17 or 18, with the dowry and connections to expect a reasonably excellent match in her future. She had recently read a play that I had seen and we began to discuss it. In her enthusiasm, she dropped that proper façade for a few minutes and let me see her brilliance. She cited lines, dissected subtext, and identified allusions to other works that I had completely missed. She would have easily held her own with even you, I believe! But it only lasted for a few minutes. One sharp look from her mother and the light in her eyes was shuttered. It was as though a life-size talking doll had taken her place. The play was "lovely" and then she began talking about whether the weather would be fair for the Creightons' garden party later that week. Ever the proper and ladylike topic, but, oh Thomas, that such intelligence and wit should be so suppressed!

William is an obedient little boy but I will admit to you that I have wished for a baby girl, although I fear it is not to be. Dearest Thomas, if you should be so lucky as to have a daughter, teach her to value herself—her intelligence, her character, her abilities. Educate her! I have heard so many young brides dismissed by their husbands as stupid because they could not keep the housekeeping accounts without assistance. Yet when ever were they supposed to practice their arithmetic when throughout their girlhood they were told that mathematics is too much for the female mind! Gentlemen (and you are as guilty of this as any, my dear Thomas) complain of women's silliness, that all we talk about is lace and bonnets and balls, and yet is that not what we are encouraged to focus on from a young age, really from birth?

Dear Thomas, I did not intend this letter to be any sort of sermon, but the thoughts that have been stewing in my mind appear to be flooding out of my pen. I loved our father as you did, but with all my heart I believe you have the potential to become a greater master, husband, and father. I hope you have many children, and you invite their laughter into your book room, as you call it (even the girls—perhaps one of them will even learn to beat you at chess!) There will be sorrows and disappointments in your life, much as your big sister might wish she could protect you from them. Do not let these become the focus of your life. I see in you a wit that could descend into cynicism and misanthropy if you allow yourself to focus on the ill in life. Remember the joys, the beauties, the amusements, however inconsequential they might seem at the time.

Perhaps that old chestnut says it best—Think of the past only as it brings you pleasure. You will say that these are very deep thoughts for your ever practical big sister! Always remember that you are in my heart.

Your loving sister,
Jane Bennet Collins

P.S. My dear brother—if this illness takes me to our Lord, I have asked Mrs. Hill to send you this letter, maudlin as it is. As you have probably guessed from my letters, Hill has been my closest confidant and steadiest supporter throughout my years in London. It is nothing improper—she keeps her manner as befitting a servant and respects me as mistress, but I do not think I could ever have had a dearer friend. I have left her a letter of recommendation written in as glowing terms as I could make it, but I have just recalled a thought I had after reading your last letter. You mentioned that dear Mrs. Wagner's arthritis and sight were worsening rapidly and you might be looking for a new housekeeper soon, particularly as your marriage will necessitate a livelier household than Longbourn has seen in many years. In the case that I no longer have need of her, I would like to recommend Mrs. Hill to you. She has a story which is hers to tell, but I am certain that you would find no more respectable, capable, and loyal servant should you search across England.

-jbc

After reading his sister's letter for the first time, Mr. Bennet set it down carefully on his desk, lifted his shaking hands to his face and wept as he had not since he was a young lad.

Some twenty years later, the harsh truths relayed in a letter to his daughter from a young gentleman he had barely noticed reminded Mr. Bennet of his sister's final letter. Unlocking a hidden lockbox that contained all his most important papers, Thomas retrieved the yellowed pages and carefully unfolded them. Reading his sister's script again brought tears to his eyes, but also reminded him of the ideals that he had striven for as a younger man, ideals which his sister had suggested he might attain as a master, husband, and father.

3 THE MORNING AFTER

Mr. Bennet had not yet risen from his bed when his manservant arrived to help him shave, but the appearance of Mabberly was enough to convince him that it was time to face the day. There was much to be done, however little he was looking forward to it. In short order, the Bennet patriarch was seated at the breakfast table with his wife and daughters, wishing that he had not indulged in a second glass of brandy the night before.

After two cups of strong coffee, Mr. Bennet squared his shoulders and told himself to get on with it. "Well, girls. What shall you be doing with yourselves today?"

The question was so unexpected that the table fell silent for a moment before Lydia turned her attention back to Kitty and continued babbling about one of the officers—something about dressing in women's clothes and passing unnoticed among his fellows at a card party. Mr. Bennet sighed.

Before he could become wholly frustrated, however, Jane spoke softly at his elbow. "I shall be visiting the Wagners this morning, Papa. Young Annie just had her baby last week and we have a basket of clothes and food for them."

Mr. Bennet nodded, pleased. To be perfectly honest, he hadn't been aware that his daughters were visiting Longbourn's tenants and continuing the tradition of charity baskets. He was mildly ashamed but quickly brushed this feeling aside. Turning to his left, he queried, "Lizzy? Shall you be accompanying Jane on her mission of mercy?" To himself, he grimaced; it was too easy to fall into his old habits of sarcasm even when the situation did not merit it.

Elizabeth did not seem to notice her father's tone—it was what she was accustomed to, after all. She was merely happy that he appeared to be making some effort to inquire into his daughters' activities. "No, Papa. Hill and I must go over the month's housekeeping accounts this morning."

Her father nodded, something of his sister's letter on the importance of educating girls in matters other than embroidery and useless conversation coming back to him. He turned to his next daughter, tucked between Elizabeth and Kitty at the table and obviously not expecting to be addressed by her father. "Mary?" When she did not respond, Elizabeth poked her sister with her elbow and Mr. Bennet realized that his middle daughter had been reading from a book hidden in her lap.

When her startled eyes met his, he repeated his query. "Mary? What shall you be doing today?"

After opening and closing her mouth several times in surprise, Mary eventually managed two words. "Studying, Papa."

Bennet smiled—he might be able to reach this daughter. Unfortunately, Mary took his smile as one of derision and tucked her chin so that all he could see was a slightly crooked part in her soft brown hair.

"Mary?" He attempted to gentle his voice and was rewarded by a pair of eyes peeking up at him from under a thick fringe. "What are you reading, my child?"

"Fordyce's instructions on the importance of charity," she squeaked, obviously expecting to be mocked.

Bennet sighed, sorry to see how his sharp tongue had affected the poor girl. He was struck by an idea. "Mary, I would be pleased if you would take some time from your studies this morning to accompany your sister on her visit to Longbourn's tenants." Seeing that she was about to argue, he continued in a firmer tone, "Charity is indeed a virtue, daughter. However, we must remember that it is the *practice* of charity that is virtuous, not merely its exposition."

He looked Mary straight in the eye until she nodded slightly before relenting. "It is a worthy subject for your consideration, my dear. Bring your Fordyce to my book room this afternoon and we shall discuss it further; I should like to hear your thoughts. Did you know that charity is one of the Five Pillars of Islam? According to their holy book, Muslims believe that each year a percentage of their possessions must be given to the poor and deprived." Mr. Bennet noted that his daughter was looking at him wide-eyed.

"Muslims, Papa?" Mary's curiosity overcame the caution she had learned to practice around her father.

"Muslims—followers of the Islamic religion. Sometimes called Mohammedans or Mahometans, although that is incorrect; they do not worship Mohammed but consider him a prophet, just as we Christians believe Jesus of Nazareth to be the Messiah and the son of God." Thomas observed that he was well beyond his daughter's knowledge but was encouraged by her obvious interest. "Well, well. I have some business to attend to this morning but come into my study this afternoon after tea and we shall discuss it. At university I came to know a man from Jerusalem; he was translating various ancient texts and studying the intersections between the Christian, Islamic, and Jewish faiths. Quite fascinating—I shall see if I can find the notes I took on his lectures."

Not much later, Mr. Bennet retired to his study, pleased that he had made some progress with at least one of his daughters. His hope for a bit of quiet before meeting with his neighbors and seeing to the safety of the local shopkeepers' pocketbooks was not to be, however. Within minutes, there came a great pounding on his door accompanied by the sounds of his wife and youngest daughter in high dudgeon.

Thomas groaned but rose and went to his door, allowing his sanctuary to be invaded by his high-strung wife and the daughter he feared was most like her.

"Mr. Bennet! You must tell her— she will not listen and is determined to ruin us all!" wailed Mrs. Bennet, waiving a lacy handkerchief in the air like a white flag.

Simultaneously, Lydia was stamping her foot and snarling. "Papa— I must have new clothes for Brighton, for there shall be ever so many balls and parties and I've *nothing* to wear! Mama promised but now she won't take me..."

Mrs. Bennet turned on her spoiled daughter. "You most certainly are not going to Brighton— such a dangerous place! I've half a mind to keep you away from Meryton until the regiment leaves!"

"But you *promised!* I'm to be Mrs. Forster's particular companion! And make merry with all the officers! I can't miss the parties or I'll just die— I *must* go to Brighton!"

The spat continued on for some minutes at such a decibel that Mr. Bennet could not catch their attention long enough to get a word in. Rolling his eyes, he moved to shut the door and then picked up an old straight-backed chair from the corner and set it behind Lydia. Neither female took any notice of his activity until he picked up a very heavy atlas from a shelf and dropped it on the floor with a satisfying "THUMP!"

Before Lydia had a chance to wind up her tongue again, he spoke sternly, "Sit down and be silent, child."

Lydia sat in the uncomfortable chair, crossed her arms over her chest and pouted. Thomas nodded severely and moved to stand before her. "Lydia. You are fifteen years old, yet you act like a child of five— a spoiled, reckless little girl who should still be on leading strings."

Seeing that she was about to argue, Mr. Bennet pointed at her sternly. "Silence, I said. You *will* listen even if I have to gag you with my handkerchief." Lydia humphed and kicked the chair rungs but at least she held her tongue.

"It is *because* of your poor behavior that your mother and I have decided you are not mature enough to travel without one of us to look after you. You will not be going to Brighton, much less ordering any new gowns. I shall explain the change in plans to Colonel Forster when I see him later today."

Red in the face, Lydia leapt to her feet and shrieked at her parents. "But you promised! I want to go to Brighton—the balls! The officers! You said I could!"

Mr. Bennet put his hand on Lydia's shoulder and pressed her back into the chair. "Quiet! This is precisely the type of behavior that prompted our decision, child. In fact, if you continue as such, you will force me to reconsider whether you are truly mature enough to be 'out' in Meryton society."

Lydia's jaw fell open and her eyes goggled, too stunned to speak for a moment. For the first time in her young life she saw her parents united— Mrs. Bennet was standing beside her husband nodding in agreement, even to his last statement! Lydia snapped her jaw shut; clearly a different tactic was necessary.

Her father watched with increasing disgust as his youngest daughter's expression shifted from fury to cunning to wretchedness, crocodile tears dribbling down her cheeks.

"But Papa... Mrs. Forster is depending on me... You don't want me to let her down, do you?" she whimpered, patting at her cheeks with a hanky.

Mr. Bennet snorted. "Lydia Bennet. You are a fifteen year old girl with little education and no sense that I can see. Mrs. Forster is a married woman full-grown. If she needs assistance, she should turn to her husband or the other officers' wives. She has a household to run; she will not be spending her days trimming bonnets and her nights gadding about at balls and parties. And if she *is* spending all her time on such frivolities then she is not a lady whom we would wish you to model yourself upon!"

Most of what Mr. Bennet said passed straight over Lydia's head; she was not interested in reasons, just approval. Seeing that her father was unmoved, she turned her watery eyes upon mother with an expression that had never failed before. "But Mama... if I go to Brighton, one of the officers is sure to fall in love with me! Denny and Carter like me a great deal already, and now that Wickham is no longer engaged to Mary King, he has begun to pay attention to me as well!" Her begging voice began to gain enthusiasm as she repeated her favorites' names, but her mother was already shaking her head.

"Oh no, my dear! It is too dangerous! I admire a handsome officer in a red coat as much as the next girl, but we do not know anything about these militiamen. Who knows what sort of trouble they might get you into, and then we would all be ruined!"

"But Mama..." Lydia's voice returned to a wail.

"Lydia..." remonstrated her father.

"But you *promised*!"

"Lydia."

"BUT I WANT TO GO TO BRIGHTON!!!"

"SILENCE!!!" Mr. Bennet had finally had enough. "For heaven's sake! This is not a discussion. You are *not* going anywhere near Brighton and that is final. In fact, you will not be attending *any* assemblies or parties for the next month, at least. At the end of that period, I shall review your behavior and decide if you have shown adequate improvement to be allowed out into company."

"But..."

"No buts. For now, you will go to your room until you are calm enough to act like a sensible little girl, as it is quite obvious that the proper behavior of a young lady is well beyond your current capacity." Thoroughly disgusted, Thomas rang the bell for a servant and motioned for his daughter to stand.

Fortunately, it was the housekeeper herself who answered Mr. Bennet's summons. "Mrs. Hill— excellent. Miss Lydia shall not be going to Brighton or anyplace else for the next month, so you may tell Sarah that she need not see to any packing, regardless of what my daughter claims."

Hill's eyebrows rose at the sight of Mr. and Mrs. Bennet united and taking their spoiled child in hand. Wisely, she simply nodded and said nothing. Mr. Bennet continued in a stern tone, "For now, she will be going to her room."

Lydia couldn't stand it anymore and flounced to the door, crying over her shoulder. "I hate you! I *want* to go to my room! I don't want to see you ever again!" And with a last huff, she swept from the room, whipping the door open so hard that it slammed into the wall.

Mr. Bennet sighed and turned to his wife who had burst into tears upon her favorite's spiteful words. Patting her on the shoulder, he said gruffly, "There, there Fanny. It had to be done; it is for her own good. She cannot go on like this and it is our responsibility—yours and mine—to see to her." He offered his handkerchief in place of her damp one and then turned to their patient housekeeper.

"Mrs. Hill? As you have no doubt guessed, we have come to the conclusion that our youngest daughter needs to... err... modify her behavior." Mrs. Hill met his eye and nodded in such a way that Mr. Bennet understood that she considered such a statement to be long overdue. He cleared his throat with some discomfort. "Please tell the other servants; I would not be surprised if Lydia becomes more difficult for a time. If she causes you or the others any trouble, come to me immediately."

Hill nodded and left the study, privately wondering if Mr. and Mrs. Bennet had any hope of reforming their wayward daughter. On the way to the kitchens, she sighed and rolled her shoulders. She was really getting too old for this but was determined to see all the Bennet girls off and married before she retired to the pensioner's cottage that Mr. Bennet had promised her. She sighed again and reminded herself that she had worked for far worse masters.

While Mrs. Hill was reporting the startling turn of events to those in the kitchen, Mr. Bennet spent some minutes comforting his wife. He was pleased to see that her eyes appeared to be opened to Lydia's poor behavior.

"Fanny, I have a difficult time comprehending that our babies are growing into young ladies. It seems just yesterday that Jane was put in my arms for the first time."

"Oh Thomas, I know, I know."

"But, just as we had to be on guard when they were toddling about on leading strings, so we must do now that they are young ladies. Do you remember when Lizzy was almost run over by that cart in Meryton?"

"Oh Thomas, how could I forget? I took my eyes off her for one second and she was out of the shop and halfway across the street!"

"Yes, my dear; we were lucky that day... and many others I suspect."

Mrs. Bennet nodded, lapsing into memories of her children's escapades until Mr. Bennet spoke again. "I have been trying to think of how best to make Lydia behave in a way that she will be safe in the world... safe from men who are not gentlemanly, let us say. I can only guess that it is like teaching her not to run into the road when a cart is barreling down on her; a combination of clear rules backed up by punishment for breaking them and praise when she obeys." He paused. "We must be united in this, my dear."

A determined glint appeared in Mrs. Bennet's eyes. "Yes, Thomas—you are perfectly right. Indeed, I believe I shall go check that Lydia did indeed go to her room—it would be just like her to sneak off."

Once Mr. Bennet had approved her plan, Fanny rose and prepared to deal with her youngest daughter. She paused with her hand on the door and spoke haltingly, unable to meet his eye. "Thomas, I've never thanked you for what you did... marrying me, I mean. But I want you to know that I do understand how a proper gentleman's daughter should act, even if I don't always manage it myself. I'll do everything I can to set Lydia to rights."

Thomas Bennet felt tears forming in his own eyes and moved forward to take his wife of twenty-odd years in his arms. "Oh, my dear Fanny, you are a good woman with a good heart. Neither of us would measure up to the ton's caricature of perfect behavior, if strictly examined." He paused, disliking to speak of his emotions, but forced himself to go on. "Though I may not show it very well, I firmly believe that *I* was the lucky one. Longbourn came to life the day you became my wife."

"Oh, Mr. Bennet… God has been very good to us."

"Yes, my dear, He has."

And with that, the Bennets parted in far better spirits than one might have expected, given the cause of their meeting.

Not much later, Mr. Bennet convened with his neighbors to explain his concern that Meryton's shopkeepers had been extending credit to the soldiers but that some individuals might be tempted to depart without settling their debts. As the regiment was set to march within the week, the gentlemen readily agreed to accompany him into the village, assemble a list of debtors and then share it with Colonel Forster.

Mr. Bennet's neighbors were surprised to see the usually retiring gentleman taking on such activity but easily agreed to follow his direction. The Bennets had been the leading family of the district for generations and it was something of a relief to see the current patriarch finally step up to his role in the community.

Mr. Wickham was probably less pleased, although the gentlemen never saw him. The Lieutenant's name figured prominently on the lists of unpaid debts produced by Meryton's merchants. Colonel Forster was displeased to see the extent of his new officer's expenses, but his face had brightened when he recalled hearing that Wickham had had an excellent run at cards on the previous night. When the regiment departed for Brighton later that week, the shopkeeper's ledgers were balanced and George Wickham's pockets were quite empty; a situation that old Mr. Darcy's godson was not at all pleased with.

Needing a bit of solitude after so much unaccustomed activity, Mr. Bennet took a roundabout way back to Longbourn, finally handing his gelding's reins over to the stable boy not long before tea.

"How is it around the house, Davey?" inquired Mr. Bennet. The young man was Mrs. Hill's son and, though somewhat simple, he usually had a good idea of the comings and goings of the family.

"All's well that I know of, sir. Miss Bennet and Miss Mary went out earlier with a basket. I asked 'em if they wanted the carriage, but Miss Jane said they'd rather walk."

Mr. Bennet nodded with approval. A long walk outdoors would do Mary good, not to mention time in company with Jane's good sense.

After he had washed and changed to clean clothes, Mr. Bennet descended to his study and asked for a tray to be sent to him. In the course of his activities in Meryton, he had missed luncheon and now his stomach was rumbling in protest. He allowed himself a half hour to eat and read a favorite chapter of *Tom Jones* before settling down to the tedious duty of checking over Longbourn's ledgers and calculating the annual taxes. Thus, when Mary tapped tentatively on his door, clutching Mr. Fordyce's *Sermons* to her chest, it was a relief.

"Ah, yes. Come in Mary, come in. You needn't look so frightened, child; come, let us sit by the windows where the light is best." After they settled themselves, Mr. Bennet prompted her; "So, how was your morning?" He was pleased to see Mary's expression brighten.

"Very well, Papa. Jane and I visited the Wagners and gave them the basket. They were very thankful— even for the smallest things." Mary paused before adding softly, "I would never have known what to bring but Jane seemed to know just what they needed."

Thomas nodded approvingly— to himself he noted that his eldest daughters probably knew what went on in his tenants' lives far better than he did himself. "She knows because she has taken the trouble to learn; by visiting them regularly, she understands their lives better and they are more comfortable telling her what they are lacking."

After a few minutes discussing Longbourn's tenants and the obligations of the Bennet family to their servants, Mr. Bennet turned the conversation to what he knew of the beliefs of charity in other cultures—the Muslims, the Jews, the Greeks, the Romans—and the pair spent an enjoyable hour in discussion. When Mary departed, she was clutching several books in addition to the Scottish clergyman's manual on proper behavior and her father had hope that he had broadened her mind just a bit and possibly gained himself a new student.

He returned to his chair and heaved a sigh. Now, what to do about Kitty and Lydia? His eyes drifted around the room until they alighted on a chessboard given to him by Mr. Gardiner as a wedding present long ago. For the day-to-day matches that he played with Lizzy or against himself, he preferred the older, plainer chessboard that had belonged to his grandfather with its worn pieces and polished wood.

Mr. Gardiner's set had come from the Orient. The pieces were individually painted in a rainbow of bright enamels, each with such detail that one could see the long, lacquered fingernails on the Queen's hands and individual feathers in the plumes on the Knight's helmet. Thomas had always kept them in a box on a high shelf, protected from little fingers that might break the fragile figurines. However, now he considered that they might be just the thing to capture a young lady's attention and so he eased the box off the shelf and spent the remainder of the afternoon cleaning the pieces.

That evening after dinner, Mr. Bennet brought the chess set into the drawing room to many "ooohs" and aaaahs." Lydia had been sent to her room halfway through dinner so the family gathering was already somewhat calmer than usual. Mary's attention soon returned to her new books but Catherine was quite entranced by the exquisitely painted enamel figurines.

In short order, Mr. Bennet was showing Kitty how to set up the board and the remainder of the evening was spent teaching her about each piece and the moves it was allowed to make. Elizabeth retreated to the corner with Jane, allowing Kitty the pleasure of their father's uninterrupted attention.

Later that evening, after his family had retired, Thomas poured himself a glass of claret (he was off brandy) and sat alone in his book room, well-pleased with himself. He had no illusions that Catherine would grow into any sort of chess prodigy—she was not nearly as quick as Lizzy had been to pick up the moves and strategies. However, his second youngest had shown an honest interest that he was glad to encourage. In truth, he was willing to latch on to anything that would exercise her mind.

It was not for several days that Thomas unearthed his second youngest's real passion.

After a windy ride around Longbourn's fields, Mr. Bennet unexpectedly came across Kitty standing in the front hall with her nose nearly touching a framed painting. The Bennets had never been great art collectors, but Thomas had always enjoyed this particular painting of a girl in a white dress, running through a field of wildflowers with her hair blown loose and bonnet trailing behind her.

Catherine was so focused on the brushwork of the painting that she positively jumped when her father spoke. "Lovely, isn't it?" Seeing his daughter flush, Thomas realized that he had surprised her. "I apologize for startling you, my child. I did not mean to interrupt your study."

Kitty smiled apologetically. Her father had paid her more attention in the last few days than he had for years previously but she did not yet wholly trust his kinder, gentler manner. "I'm sorry, Papa. I didn't mean to hurt it."

"Looking at it will do no harm; that is what it is here for. If you wish to examine it more closely, we can even take it down from the wall and bring it where there is better light." He paused but continued when his daughter remained silent. "What about it intrigues you so?"

Kitty looked at her father carefully and decided that he was truly interested. She turned back to the painting and gestured with a finger. "I was out watching the wind blow across the hay field this morning—the grass stems roll, almost like waves on water? I think it is the undersides of the leaves showing that also changes the color as they bend in the wind. I was trying to see how the painter captured the wind so perfectly, do you see? There is a blue sky and a few puffy white clouds, but the moment you look at the painting you know there is a big, breezy wind blowing right across the meadow."

Kitty recalled herself and peeked at her father out of the corner of her eye. "It probably sounds silly…" she began.

"Absolutely not!" reassured her father, placing his hand on her shoulder and looking at the painting more closely than he ever had before. "I'd never noticed it but you are quite correct. And I believe you are correct about the colors—the bent stems are just a bit lighter than those upright, unbent by the wind—a hint of pink, perhaps. And I suppose that adds to the story it tells—why the girl's hair has blown loose and her bonnet won't stay on."

Father and daughter stood in silence studying the painting for a few more minutes until Mr. Bennet stirred himself. "Catherine, have you ever tried drawing yourself?"

Kitty looked flustered. "A little, but Mama got angry with me for ruining so much paper…"

Her father nodded, clearly pleased. "What you need is your own sketch book and perhaps a set of charcoals or watercolors. I can't claim to have any talent myself beyond some basic drafting skills but I do have a book or two on drawing in my library. Basic figures, perspective, composition and such. Come along and I'll see if I can't find them. Then this afternoon we shall go on an expedition and see if there are any art supplies to be found in Meryton. I suspect that Culter's should have something, but if not I shall write to your Uncle Gardiner and he can send them from London."

Pleased but still rather amazed by his behavior, Kitty quietly followed her father into his study. When he began climbing a ladder in order to poke around the contents of a high shelf in the corner, disturbing clouds of dust in the process, she couldn't repress a grin. "Is your answer for everything in a book, Papa?"

4 WOUNDED EGO, BROKEN HEART

As the carriage left the village of Hunsford and turned on to the main road toward London, Fitzwilliam Darcy allowed his eyes to close and rested his aching head back into the cushions. He had not slept well in weeks and barely at all on the two nights since his failed marriage proposal to Miss Elizabeth Bennet.

Elizabeth. The very thought of her name made his stomach clench. He had returned from the parsonage that evening full of wounded fury. How dare such an impertinent, ungrateful slip of a girl refuse *him*! His insulted ego had kept him energized through the night, writing a letter he was determined would expose the truth and thus shame her with his innocence. In hindsight he could only marvel at how blinded he had been to his own bitterness.

Darcy's fury had lasted until the moment he had placed his letter in her hand the next morning. He had stalked through his aunt's groves for nearly an hour, irritation mounting at being made to wait (entirely neglecting the fact that they had no appointment). When he had finally sighted her, he had marched up with all the hauteur which the young Master of Pemberley, nephew of the Earl of Matlock, could muster.

Darcy cringed in memory of the arrogant tone he had used to demand that she read his letter, leaving her no way to defend herself from such an impropriety. Gentleman, indeed! More like the actions of a spoiled, petulant child denied a new toy for the first time in his life.

He had practically shoved the letter into her hands, he remembered. But the next moment she had looked up at him and, in the warm light of an otherwise insignificant Thursday morning, all his self-righteous anger and hurt pride had melted away, leaving only a great, aching sorrow that threatened to collapse his chest.

Feeling the overwhelming need to hide himself away and weep for the first time since the death of his mother, Darcy forced himself to make a deep bow, took one last look at the lady who had stolen his unwilling heart, and then turned to walk stiffly away. He strode swiftly with little idea where he was heading except that it was away from Elizabeth and away from his aunt's house. Eventually, he found himself descending a rocky outcrop to a ledge jutting out over a creek.

Discarding coat and cravat, Will leaned back against the large willow whose draping branches formed a protective green curtain between him and the world. He pressed the heels of his hands against his face, but no amount of his father's strictures on the effeminate nature of tears could stop them from coming, leaking silently from his eyes. How could it possibly have gone so wrong?

Some hours passed before Darcy's sense of duty nudged him hard enough that he felt it over the pain of his broken heart. Although he wished for nothing more than to remain alone in his peaceful green grotto, he knew that the longer he remained away from Rosings, the more strident would be his aunt's demands when he returned.

Sighing, he stood and, after donning his coat and setting himself to rights, climbed up and re-entered the world, feeling exhausted. Taking the most direct route back to the main house, every field and flower seemed to remind him of some delightfully witty comment or arch look by Miss Elizabeth Bennet.

Darcy had just reached the paved courtyard at the rear of the house when the door opened and his cousin exited, clattering down the steps.

Seeing his younger relative, Colonel Fitzwilliam hailed him. "There you are, Darce! I was just coming in search of you, to make sure you didn't miss luncheon." He stiffened his features so as to mimic their aunt. "Had you done so, your future mother-in-law would be most displeased."

The cousins rarely mentioned Lady Catherine's matrimonial plans for her daughter between them. Darcy had only the energy to give Richard a pained look. Did even his cousin—as close as any brother—understand him so little?

Genuinely concerned by his cousin's ill appearance, Richard drew him off to a more private corner in the courtyard. "What has happened? Did you talk to Anne? I've wondered if she even wants to marry, given her poor health. Certainly she wouldn't *refuse* you, given her mother's attitude."

The irony that Fitzwilliam could come so close to the cause of his misery and yet simultaneously be so far off the mark struck Darcy forcibly. Fighting back the grief that had plagued him earlier, he let out a mirthless laugh and forced himself to speak before his cousin might make another guess.

"No, Richard. Such a thing never occurred to me." Leaving his cousin to wonder if he was referring to asking Anne de Bourgh to marry him or to the possibility of being refused, Darcy continued; "Come, let us repair to the dining room before we are missed."

Richard made a last attempt. "Darce, are you certain you are well? Truly, you are exceedingly pale. If you are ill, we can put off our departure again. Is that why you missed dinner last night?"

Darcy waved him off and started up the steps. With no desire to explain his absence the previous evening, he concentrated on the present. "I slept poorly and skipped breakfast to get some fresh air. We shall depart tomorrow morning as planned."

"Very well. We can visit the parsonage after luncheon to farewell the Collinses and their guests." As the Colonel had followed Darcy into the house, this last was uttered as he entered the room where their aunt waited.

"Why ever would you be visiting the parsonage on your last afternoon at Rosings?" demanded Lady Catherine, turning from one nephew to the other. "Certainly you had much better spend your remaining time with Anne." She waved in the direction of her daughter, missing how the girl shrank back into her wool shawl.

Seeing that Darcy was not planning to respond, Richard applied his most charming manner. "Ah, but we must farewell our new acquaintances before leaving Kent, for we would not wish our poor manners to reflect badly upon yourselves."

Even Lady Catherine could find no fault with his logic and so she was forced to adopt the idea as her own. "Very well— you shall visit the parsonage this afternoon. I am certain that Mr. and Mrs. Collins shall appreciate your condescension."

The Colonel nodded obediently and managed to hide his smirk in a glass of wine.

After allowing a footman to serve her, Lady Catherine continued. "Miss Lucas has little to recommend herself other than being a quiet little thing, but Miss Bennet has a bit of wit about her. I believe I shall have her extend her visit. Certainly she is nothing to Anne, but she is a genteel, pretty sort of girl even if her unfortunate connections and lack of fortune make it impossible that she shall marry anyone of consequence."

Darcy started at how close his aunt's words came to those in his head when he had met the young lady in question.

Oblivious to her nephew's discomfort, Lady Catherine continued, "Indeed, she has managed to gain herself a reasonable education despite the lack of governess or masters. Though such independence in a lady would be deplorable at *our* level of society, of course, I believe she has done well to raise herself within the sphere in which she was born."

Darcy could not restrain his desire to defend Elizabeth. "Miss Bennet is the daughter of a respectable gentleman."

His aunt dismissed the comment with a flick of her hand. "Do not be simple, Fitzwilliam. Who is her mother? Who are her uncles and aunts? If I imagined myself to be ignorant of their condition, I might admit that she had virtues enough but without the advantages of a more advantageous birth, she has little hope other than to throw herself at any available gentleman. She should have snapped up Mr. Collins when she had the chance."

To say that his aunt's pronouncement made Darcy queasy was an understatement. And yet, there was more.

"Her mother must be beside herself— five daughters and an estate entailed away to a distant cousin. I remember the Countess of Waverly suffered much the same fate, although in her case, she had three daughters and the estate was inherited by a stepson who threw them all from their home less than a month after the death of the old Earl. The last I heard, she had the eldest girl married to a clergyman and the second to a retired army officer. As best as could be hoped for, I suppose, and she has some reassurance of a home in her dotage."

Darcy's stomach continued to roil and his attention wandered as his aunt began to expound her uninformed yet strident opinions on entailments. He needed some quiet solitude to consider why her words so upset him. It was a similar feeling that he had felt when, at university, he had been confronted by a mathematical equation that appeared to be solved but some inner sense told him that further exploration would reveal a fatal error in the logic.

Though inelegantly phrased, Lady Catherine's words about the Bennet family's circumstances were little different from the rules that had been imprinted upon him since birth. Had he not used similar words to discourage Bingley from pursuing Miss Bennet? He cringed—perhaps that was not the best example. As he considered his aunt's statement, what struck him most clearly were her final words. He had never considered why Mrs. Bennet's nerves might be so frayed… why she was so desperate to put her daughters forward.

Darcy knew from managing his sister's interests that, although Georgiana had 30,000 pounds in name, in truth he was in full control of her inheritance and would continue to be so until he turned it over to her husband. After Ramsgate, he had had his solicitor tie her inheritance up with so many strings that she could not touch it without the agreement of her guardians or the man Darcy approved to marry her. After hearing Lady Catherine's astonishing commiseration with Mrs. Bennet's nerves, his thoughts wandered into previously unexplored realms. What would it be like, he wondered, to be so completely dependent on another?

Meanwhile, Colonel Fitzwilliam was growing increasingly irritated with his cousin. They planned these annual visits together so that neither would have to bear the uninterrupted focus of Lady Catherine for any length of time. However, after skipping two meals, Darcy was making no effort to take his turn engaging their aunt. By dessert, Richard had had enough of deflecting his aunt from noticing Darcy's inattention. Anne was silent as always—even when she was in good health she could not be relied on to speak more than monosyllables.

Somewhere in the dim recesses of Darcy's mind, he registered an expectant silence at the table and was dismayed to see his aunt looking at him imperiously, obviously expecting a response. Seeing that his cousin had no idea what their aunt was demanding of him, Richard allowed the silence to hang for just a moment longer until he was assured that Darcy felt the embarrassment before stepping in.

"Thank you for the kind offer, Aunt Catherine, but I must return to London tomorrow—my duties to the army require it, you understand. However, if my cousin wishes to accept your invitation and extend his visit, I can very easily find an alternate means of transportation."

Thankful for his cousin's rescue, Darcy spoke at once. "I appreciate your hospitality, Aunt, but I have business in town that cannot be delayed. We must leave tomorrow morning, as planned."

Lady Catherine spent the remainder of the meal expounding her displeasure at their departure while simultaneously admonishing the two young men to be mindful of their responsibilities, entirely unaware of the contradiction inherent in her words.

When the meal finally concluded, the participants dispersed to different parts of the house. After sending her ever-submissive daughter to her apartment for a nap, Lady Catherine took herself to her study to review the housekeeping accounts. Darcy climbed the stairs and sequestered himself in his own rooms, desperate for a bit of quiet to calm his emotions before facing the occupants of the parsonage. Colonel Fitzwilliam hid himself in the library and treated himself to a well-earned whiskey.

An hour later, the two cousins met in the front hall and, with few words, departed for their visit. Although both gentlemen were too deep in thought to notice, they walked toward Hunsford with measured, resolute steps in near synchrony. As they neared the lane that separated Rosings from the parsonage, Darcy stopped abruptly. The Colonel had taken several steps before he noticed and turned to his cousin, raising his eyebrows in question.

"Richard... I should have spoken to you earlier. I had something of an... argument with Miss Bennet."

"Yes, well, that is not unexpected, is it? She's made it quite clear that your behavior in Hertfordshire didn't impress her, and certainly your stupid manner here in Kent hasn't improved her opinion."

After snapping his jaw shut—it would not do to present the appearance of a gaping trout to his cousin—Darcy forced his mind back to the point he needed to convey. "Whatever my behavior and manners have been, Miss

Bennet's opinion has been poisoned by another source— George Wickham."

Fitzwilliam's irritation with his cousin was immediately set aside in favor of boiling temper. "Wickham! Has he finally crawled out of whatever foul hole he hid away in last year? We must do something immediately—that cretin mustn't be allowed to prey on any more innocent young ladies! I am as protective of Georgiana's reputation as you, but enough time has passed that we can have him punished without endangering her!"

A wave of guilt swept over Darcy— Richard's reaction was that of a true gentleman. *He* would not have departed Hertfordshire without warning the populace that they harbored a viper in their midst. After a moment, he forced the guilt into a corner of his mind with all the other emotions that threatened to overwhelm him, to be dealt with later.

"I agree, cousin. But for now, I need your help with Miss Bennet. Wickham has told her his favorite sob story— that my father educated George for a position in the church, but upon Father's death I refused his godson an inheritance because of jealousy over my parent's affection."

Richard snorted and Darcy continued, "Her words made me aware of how far he has wormed his way back into polite society. I... I have told her... the *whole* story."

"You told her about Georgiana?" Richard was startled. Even in his greatest fury he would not have revealed Georgiana's near elopement to anyone and until this moment he would have sworn that his cousin would do the same. Indeed, it was Darcy who had kept Richard from challenging Wickham to a duel before the vermin had gone to ground in London, leaving poor Georgiana a miserable, sobbing wreck. In his mind, Richard had known his cousin to be correct—any hint of retribution (not to mention a duel) would have brought them unwanted attention and most likely a blemish to their charge's reputation. However, the memory still had his hand reaching unconsciously for the sword that hung at his side in battle.

Darcy shut his eyes tightly for a moment before responding in a level tone. "Yes. There was no other way to convince her and I would not leave her unprotected."

The Colonel was looking at him oddly. "You trust Miss Bennet that much?"

"Yes," answered his cousin succinctly. "And I suggested that she refer to you for confirmation," he finished hollowly and began to walk toward the parsonage again.

Fitzwilliam matched his step automatically, still reeling over the trust his cousin had placed in this impertinent country miss. "Of course I'll reaffirm everything you've said. But Darce... I'm certain that she believed you— she's known you much longer, after all. I can only claim a casual acquaintance of these past few weeks, most of which has been in the company of our exceedingly intrusive aunt."

When the other man did no more than grunt in response, Richard continued, "Really, Darce. Wickham might have charmed her into believing him for a time, but when confronted with the facts by a respectable gentleman such as yourself, I'm certain that an intelligent woman such as Miss Bennet would know who to believe. Why just yesterday we were speaking of how honorably you care for your friends."

That was enough to stop his cousin dead in his tracks. "What?!"

The Colonel knit his brows in consternation over his cousin's odd behavior. "I met her walking near the grove yesterday while making my annual tour of the park. It was nothing improper, I assure you. She asked if I knew the Bingleys and we discussed what good care you take of your friends." Richard attempted to lighten the mood; "I even attempted to raise her opinion of you by telling her of how you had lately saved young Charles from the misery of a most imprudent marriage!"

Observing Darcy's complexion blanch, the Colonel was thoroughly confused. "Really Wills. She is not the sort who will repeat it as gossip—I made it clear that I wasn't even sure that it was Bingley, just that he was the type to get into a scrape of that sort. You removed him before he could be accused of jilting the foolish chit, didn't you?"

Will leaned against a tree solid enough to keep him upright, despite suddenly weakened knees. "Is that truly how I sounded?" he muttered softly.

The Colonel was uncertain if Darcy was speaking to himself or required an answer, so he followed the cardinal rule of any good soldier and kept his mouth shut. After a few minutes, his silence was rewarded.

"Richard, the lady in question was Miss Elizabeth Bennet's most beloved, elder sister," said Darcy through gritted teeth.

"Oh Lord," breathed his cousin, immediately contrite. "Bloody hell, Darce. I'm sorry—she said something about how you enjoyed the power of arranging things as you liked and I just wanted to make her understand that you take your responsibilities toward your friends very seriously. It was the first example that came to mind."

This thought was followed by others. "She said she had a headache, but it must have been from being upset, not the sun as she claimed. That explains why she didn't come to dinner last night." He turned to Darcy with pity on his face. "You must have met her this morning on her walk. My God, man. I am sorry—she must have been furious, and I would wager that once sparked, Miss Bennet's temper is even sharper than her wit."

Darcy worked for a moment to regain his control before forcing himself back on the path to the parsonage. "Don't worry about it, Richard. I made a poor enough impression on Miss Elizabeth that she was well-prepared to believe me guilty of most anything."

The Colonel was disturbed to hear the bone-deep melancholy in his cousin's voice but was unable to come up with anything suitable to say before they reached the steps of the parsonage. If nothing else, Darcy's problems were enough to make him forget his own issues for a time, he thought.

It was perhaps beneficial to the equilibrium of both cousins that Miss Bennet was absent when they were shown into the parlor. They managed not to sigh in relief when Mrs. Collins explained that her friend had left after luncheon to run an errand in the village. Mr. Darcy quickly made his farewells in his usual sedate manner and then departed, leaving Richard behind.

Darcy breathed an immense sigh of relief upon entering the relative safety of his own rooms at Rosings. That he had not been forced to face another round of Elizabeth's righteous anger seemed no small blessing. After advising his valet that he wished to be left alone until it was time to dress for dinner, Will removed his coat, loosened his cravat, and settled into a chair by the fire. Like everything at Rosings, it had been chosen to impress rather than comfort, so it was not long before he stood, moving to the side table to poor himself a brandy. It was a short glass, but combined with the heavy lunch, he suddenly felt all the exhaustion of his sleepless nights.

Some time later, the rumble of thunder woke Darcy. Checking his pocket watch, he noted that he had dozed for less than an hour but the light had dimmed dramatically. Though not yet six o'clock, a blanket of dark clouds had rolled across the sky, hiding the sun. Wary of how such weather might affect his travel plans, Darcy left his rooms and moved quietly through the house to a little used sitting room with windows facing full west.

Standing at the windows, Fitzwilliam Darcy watched the storm front. Thunder continued to rumble but the only lightning he could see was well to the south. Counting the seconds as one of Pemberley's stewards had taught him as a boy, he estimated the main storm to be some twenty miles distant. The London road might get a bit of rain, he guessed, but not the brunt of the storm. For some minutes, he admired the power of the natural world and let himself be reminded of the insignificance of his own problems. Then, a distinctly human noise caused him to turn back to the room.

"Anne?" he said with some surprise, having believed himself alone. His cousin was across the room, huddled in an armchair that had been turned so as to catch the light from a side window.

The sound that had drawn his attention was a book that, forgotten, had slipped from her lap to the floor. Clearly embarrassed to be noticed, Anne loosened the thick blanket that was wrapped around her in order to reach for it. "Hello, Cousin," she murmured, not quite meeting his eye.

Without a thought, Darcy moved to retrieve the small volume. After handing it to her, he stood considering for a moment and then pulled a second chair over to where she sat. Perhaps he could begin to rectify one of his errors immediately. "May I speak with you for a few minutes, Anne?"

This time Darcy's cousin looked him full in the face, but her expression reminded him disturbingly of a frightened rabbit caught in a snare. Adding another portion of guilt to that already weighing upon him, Fitzwilliam realized just how unfair he had been to his cousin. By never directly contradicting Lady Catherine's dreams of a Darcy-de Bourgh union, he had provided himself with a buffer from some of the husband-hunting ton (at least, those who listened Lady Catherine). However, he had left his poor cousin to bear her mother's whims and fancies while never considering that he held the keys to Anne's prison as firmly as did his aunt.

Settling himself, Darcy gathered his thoughts before speaking. "Anne, your mother has often spoken of her desire for a match between us, but we two have never discussed it ourselves."

"Oh!" she squeaked, red spots blooming in her sallow cheeks. Pressing herself as far back into her chair as she could, Anne peeked up at her intimidating cousin. Glad to see that he appeared more startled than angered, she murmured softly "I apologize, Cousin… I was only surprised that you would want to talk about… that," she ended weakly.

Darcy spent a few moments studying his cousin, realizing that although their family often spoke *of* her, he could not think of a time when he had actually spoken *with* her, beyond the usual courtesies. Elizabeth's words echoed in his head, "…your arrogance, your conceit, and your selfish disdain of the feelings of others…" Well, this was one error in behavior that he could correct. He decided that it would be best to be direct.

"Anne, I will be honest. I care for you as a cousin, almost a sister, but I am not at all sure that I could ever feel for you as a husband care for his wife."

Miss de Bourgh looked at him in astonishment, having spent a lifetime with a mother who dismissed love as the stuff of childish fairytales; certainly nothing to do with the business of marriage. To hear her serious, ever-dutiful cousin speak of such feelings as important left her stunned.

Darcy forged ahead. "I also worry for your health. Being Mistress of Pemberley is not an easy duty for the most fit of women." Forcing his mind away from a vision of Elizabeth's healthy pink cheeks and sparkling eyes, he considered how to speak on a subject important to him but most sensitive to his sickly cousin. "Lately, I have been thinking a great deal on what I want from marriage. Although Richard would probably laugh at my saying such a thing, I should dearly like to see Pemberley's nursery full of children again."

Anne could not help but squirm. Most of what she knew about marriage and the production of children came from her mother, whose own marriage had been a wholly miserable ordeal. Anne's more recent observations of the newly wedded Collinses had done nothing to change her distaste for the institution.

She was not certain how a man might go about "planting his seed" in her, as she had read about in her novels, but it seemed to involve a great deal of petting (which she had no desire for) and pain (according to her mother). A tenant had once presented a newborn babe, only hours old, to Miss de Bourgh for blessing. The thought that such an enormous thing would grow inside a woman and then force its way out terrified her. Anne still recalled the pain of passing a stone when she was sixteen with a shiver and it had been barely the size of a pea.

In short, Miss de Bourgh was uncomfortable around men in general and her tall, serious cousin in particular. She had no interest in children and, to be honest, no desire for any physical contact of any kind. Lady Catherine might believe herself to have educated her daughter on the running of an estate, but Anne had paid as little attention to her mother's poorly conceived lectures as to the lengthy monologues that lady considered conversation. Although Anne occasionally would have liked to have some time away from her overbearing parent, she held no real aspirations to run an estate or even a household. It all sounded so very... exhausting.

Seeing that Darcy was looking at her expectantly, Anne realized that her cousin was still waiting for a response. Deciding that he might not appreciate it if she told him that she would prefer a quiet cottage somewhere in a warm climate with unlimited supplies of novels and confections, she decided to see how he would react to a smidgeon of truth.

"I fear I don't I have the energy for such things. I do not believe that I wish to marry at all. Please don't take it personally, Cousin."

Considering her cousin's face for a moment, Miss de Bourgh finally identified the dominant emotion in his eyes as relief. She was not certain that she should allow such a feeling in her suitor as her mother had made it quite clear that any gentleman, the Prince of Wales included, would be honored should the heiress of Rosings Park deign to give him her hand. However, mustering the appropriate indignation seemed like too much effort to bother with.

Darcy reminded himself that he was speaking to the daughter of Lady Catherine and quelled all thoughts of humor over such a statement. "Do not worry about offending me, Anne. If you are certain, then I shall speak to Aunt Catherine tonight after dinner."

Anne nodded slightly, but enough that Darcy was satisfied his plan met with her approval. "Is there anything you *do* wish for? Something that I could suggest to your mother when I speak with her? Perhaps a trip to London or Derbyshire?"

Anne shook her head. "I think not, but I shall consider it, Cousin." His expression had brought back a long forgotten memory of young Fitzwilliam Darcy earnestly insisting that she take the last biscuit at a tea party the girls had hosted in the Pemberley nursery. "It has been a long time since I visited Pemberley," she added softly.

"It has been a long time since we have had a family gathering of any sort at Pemberley," Will responded seriously.

"I remember visiting Derbyshire when we were children," offered Anne after a moment. "Mother would complain about how far north it was, but I liked it. The house always seemed so warm and... and happy." Unspoken was the comparison to the wretchedness that had pervaded Rosings. "Uncle Darcy was so jolly, and Aunt Anne was always playing the piano or the harp. Except for the last visit, of course," she trailed off weakly.

Both cousins bowed their heads, their thoughts turning to the terrible summer of 1800 when a pox epidemic had swept through Derbyshire, leaving the cemeteries full and many a family decimated, including the Darcys and de Bourghs. Ten year old Fitzwilliam had traveled with his father to visit his uncle's estate, leaving his mother and baby sister behind. Darcy remembered being eager to go as he greatly preferred his Fitzwilliam cousins to those de Bourgh relations who were soon to descend upon Pemberley.

After news of the epidemic reached them, George Darcy and his son had been forced to remain at Matlock for several weeks until the sickness had burnt itself out. When they returned, baby Georgiana and her grandmother were the only Darcys still alive at Pemberley. Lady Catherine had survived through sheer willpower but buried her sister, her husband and two sons, leaving only her daughter, Anne, whose constitution was permanently weakened. The number of deaths among the household staff, tenants, and villagers in Lambton and Kympton was horrific.

The sound of boots alerted Anne and Will that their solitude was soon to be interrupted. "Ho there," called the Colonel as he strode in. "Why are you two hiding in here? I had to ask the butler for directions when he said you were in the striped sitting room!"

Seeing that Anne looked frightened, Richard instantly regretted his teasing manner. "Not to worry, Anne. I am exaggerating, as always." Trying for a lighter tone, he added, "Our King's army spent a great deal of time teaching me to gather information and track my prey silently but with deadly accuracy." He waggled his eyebrows and succeeded in drawing a soft giggle from Miss de Bourgh.

"Our cousin exaggerates, as always," commented Darcy drily. Seeing that Richard was about to repeat his demand for an explanation, he continued, "Anne and I have been discussing our mutual desire *not* to marry and how best to apprise Aunt Catherine of that fact."

"Ahhhhhha. *Well.*" Colonel Fitzwilliam had just spent a delightful hour chatting with Mrs. Collins and, to be honest, his mind was still at the parsonage. Until his cousin's startling announcement, that was.

Darcy, however, had noticed that Richard was dressed for dinner. Checking his watch, he stood. "I must go now and dress if I am to keep to our aunt's schedule. Anne?"

Miss de Bourgh rose as well but shook her head. "I don't need to change. I'll just wait for you in the red drawing room, as usual." With barely a whisper of sound, she left the room and disappeared down the hall, still muffled in her thick shawl.

After watching his cousin retreat, Darcy turned to go opposite, climbing the stairs to the suite of rooms that his aunt always assigned him. It took Richard some minutes to sort out what had just occurred, but then he followed in Darcy's footsteps. If he understood correctly, there would be fireworks tonight and he needed more information if he was to avoid getting burned.

And so it was that the party gathered only a few minutes before the butler announced that dinner was served. During the meal, Darcy was even quieter than usual. His manner went unnoticed by their hostess as Lady Catherine was quite content to have her monologue run uninterrupted. In truth, he felt oddly removed from the group, as though observing them all for the first time. He was forcibly struck by his aunt's ornate gown, jewels and turban, ridiculous for a small, family meal (although perfectly in line with the heavy decorations evidenced throughout the house). Her references to wealth and connections as a woman's primary virtues made him feel vaguely ill.

Darcy had not quite worked out how best to approach the subject of marriage so it was perhaps lucky that he was not the only one who wished to discuss it. Once the meal was over and the four removed to the drawing room, Lady Catherine seated herself in her favorite chair and directed her nephew to the settee to her right, beside her daughter. She had noticed that Darcy admired Miss Bennet and had decided that it was high time for him to marry Anne before he was trapped by some fortune hunter.

With more determination than subtlety, Lady Catherine dismissed the servants from the room and spoke exactly what was on her mind. "Fitzwilliam." (It was important to remind him of his obligations to his mother's family; she would never countenance the use of such common nicknames as William or, heaven forbid, Fitz.) "It is high time that we formalize your engagement to Anne. I have been thinking that the family will be gathering at Matlock this August for my brother's birthday; it would be an excellent venue for a wedding of this magnitude."

Richard made an odd noise in his throat but Lady Catherine chose to ignore it.

Darcy squared his shoulders before speaking in a calm voice; "Aunt, while I respect your wishes, I am afraid that this one shall not come true. Anne and I have discussed it and decided that we do *not* wish to marry." Even the portraits on the walls seemed to hold their breath in the moments before her Ladyship responded. They were not disappointed.

"Of what are you speaking? Certainly you shall marry! I have told you for years— your mother and I planned the union while you were in your cradles! From your infancy, you have been intended for each other! It was the favorite wish of your mother, as well as of hers."

"That may be so, Aunt Catherine, but your wish does not confine me to my cousin by either duty or honor if such is not my inclination."

"Obstinate, headstrong boy! I am ashamed of you! Is this your gratitude for my attentions to you? Is nothing due to me on that score?" cried the lady.

Darcy took a deep breath and counted to ten in Greek in an effort to control his rising temper. "I do understand your concerns, Aunt, but Anne will not be left unprotected, even if she decides to never marry. All of her cousins care for her and her fortune provides her with security to live as she wishes."

Lady Catherine surged to her feet, her face turning a florid crimson. Unfortunately, this flush highlighted the thick powder that her maid applied to mask her aging features. "Never marry!" she sputtered.

"Aunt Catherine, it seems probable that my cousin's poor health shall prevent her from assuming the responsibilities of running a household or acting as hostess in society."

"Anne's health shall be perfectly well by the time she marries! And if there are duties she must refrain from, then I shall assume those responsibilities for her… just as I should have been allowed to do when my sister died!!!" Lady Catherine's voice rose to a shriek.

Darcy felt as if he had been punched in the gut. He knew that his father had had little contact with his aunt after Lady Anne's death; each year Will had travelled with his Uncle Henry's family to visit Rosings. Now that he thought on it, his father had never accompanied the Fitzwilliams, and Lady Catherine and her daughter had not visited Pemberley since the epidemic. Even so, it had never occurred to him that there had been a conscious break between the two. He glanced to Richard but it was clear from his cousin's expression that he was shocked as well.

Darcy forced himself to set aside the questions raised by his aunt's unguarded words and return to his primary point. "Aunt, I have tried to be delicate, but surely you understand that I must have an heir, and Anne's health makes it uncertain she could survive a pregnancy."

By now, Lady Catherine's fury had grown beyond all sense. She stood and shook her walking stick inches from Darcy's nose. "You are just like your father—all men are alike. Fools! Hypocritical, weak fools! Acting all moral and noble and gentlemanly, but in the end, you're all unreliable, untrustworthy… good for nothing, every last one of you!"

Uncomfortable with his aunt's aggressive posture, Darcy rose to his full height. Faced with her nephew looming over her, Catherine took a step back and shook her head as if trying to awaken from a nightmare. Looking around the room, she saw no support in the faces of either her daughter or her other nephew. She turned back to Darcy and spat, "You have no idea what I've suffered!" before sweeping from the room.

5 LADY CATHERINE RESENTS

Lord John Fitzwilliam, the third Earl of Matlock, wed Lady Alice Pettigrew in the year 1752. Although the marriage had been arranged by their fathers for reasons of finance and connection, the pair proved quite compatible and were known throughout their circle as a relatively happy couple. They divided their time between London and Matlock, the primary Fitzwilliam estate in southern Derbyshire, although they spent more time in the country as the years passed and their three children were born.

As the eldest Fitzwilliam child, Lady Catherine thoroughly resented the fuss that was made over her younger brother (anointed Viscount Ashbourne and the heir to the Earldom) and spent a great deal of time and thought attempting to make her parents (and everyone else) acknowledge her own superiority. Perhaps because of his elder sister's constant desire to outdo him, young Lord Henry learned early to get his way through steady, reasoning stubbornness rather than tantrums. His skills at mediation would later aid him when he took his place in the House of Lords.

Lady Anne was younger than Henry by six years and vastly different from her elder sister in both looks and personality. Blond and pretty where Catherine was dark and angular, musical and artistic where her sister was direct and tactless, Anne was a quiet child with a natural warmth and desire to please. Lord John and Lady Alice spent little time with their children, leaving them in the care of nurses and governesses as was customary. However, when the family did gather together, the parents would laugh to themselves that three more different children could not exist in a single family.

According to the Fitzwilliam family tradition, their son spent time working on different parts of the estate to gain a better sense of what the tenants and staff did. Catherine, being only a year older than Henry and exceedingly strong-willed, often managed to insert herself into whatever he was doing. Although Lady Alice drew the line at any manual labor, she did not think it so bad for a ten-year old girl to spend some time in the barns, learning to milk a cow or feed the hens. Like her husband, the Countess believed that it was important for her children to understand the responsibilities that came with their birth, not solely the advantages of wealth and position.

This upbringing would serve Lady Catherine well when she married Sir Lewis de Bourgh at twenty-one (he was thirty-four). Despite her pedigree and dowry, few suitors had shown any lingering interest in the Earl's eldest daughter over her first two seasons. Lady Catherine was flattered by Sir Lewis' attention, even if he was only the second son of Lord Maxwell de Bourgh, Baron Ramsey. She reassured herself that his status as second son was redeemed by the de Bourghs' great wealth. Sir Lewis courted her assiduously in the salons and ballrooms of London and they married at the end of the Season. Unfortunately, the bloom of her newly wedded state wore off quickly.

Sir Lewis moved his new wife to his estate in Kent and set about his marital duties with great pertinacity if not finesse. Upon ascertaining that she was with child, he returned himself to London for "business." At first the young bride believed him but as weeks went by with little or no communication from her husband, Lady Catherine's opinion plummeted. As the months passed, the lackadaisical management of the estate also became clear to her. Sir Lewis de Bourgh had no interest in the property except that it continued to fund the lifestyle to which he was accustomed and occasionally served to host a country house party for his friends.

Catherine's family, had they known of the situation (she was too proud to tell anyone), could have predicted what happened next. Despite being several months pregnant, the young wife began to take the reins of the estate herself. It required every ounce of her formidable will to browbeat the servants and tenants into acknowledging her directives after being accustomed to the freedom of an absentee landlord. The steward, a Mr. Gibbs, was nearing fifty and, having been born at Rosings Park where *his* father had served as steward, fully intended his own son to follow in his place. As the de Bourgh family had paid little interest to the management except that its rents continued to fill their coffers, the Gibbses were accustomed to carry on as they deemed best.

In spring of 1777, Catherine gave birth to a healthy boy and her husband returned in time to christen the babe Frederick Alexander Montgomery de Bourgh. Sir Lewis paid little attention to his wife when she attempted to discuss her concerns over the estate. Under the guise of celebrating the birth of his heir, he assembled a large house party, although more gambling and drinking occurred than fishing or hunting. Soon Catherine was pregnant again and de Bourgh departed Kent, feeling that he had fulfilled his duties as husband and landlord and was justified in enjoying the benefits of his position far away from his disagreeable wife.

Lady Catherine's life followed a similar pattern several some years but as Frederick was followed by another boy (Herbert Malcolm Godfrey de Bourgh), she felt justified in barring Sir Lewis from her bedchamber. For the most part, that gentleman preferred the more compliant opera girls and courtesans he frequented in town, but on the rare occasion that he found himself in Kent he would demand his rights as a husband out of principle. One of those occasions resulted in the birth of Miss Anne de Bourgh, nearly ten years younger than her eldest brother.

Unfortunately for the new babe, neither of her parents saw much use in female offspring, particularly one that seemed to cry constantly and in such a shrill tone that the nursery was removed to a distant wing, far from the family apartments. Anne's wet nurse was hired just as she was weaning her own child, so even that woman had little affection to spare for her Ladyship's colicky baby.

As Anne grew, she progressed from a noisy babe to a nearly silent child, often hiding from her loud, jolly brothers and critical mother. Of her father she knew nothing at all except for a portrait in the gallery—that gentleman had not even bothered to attend her christening. Although Lady Catherine attempted to instill what she considered to be Fitzwilliam family values in her sons (to varying degrees of success), she largely ignored her daughter.

Even as her brothers were educated by a series of tutors and then sent off to school, Miss de Bourgh grew up with the same woman who was first hired with the title of governess and later promoted to companion. A young widow, Mrs. Jenkinson was a good woman but any spirit she arrived with was rapidly crushed by Lady Catherine. She did her best to educate her charge but lessons were frequently interrupted by Anne's many childhood illnesses.

After much tribulation, reading was mastered once Mrs. Jenkinson discovered Anne's taste for fairy stories and romantic poetry. Lady Catherine would have been scandalized by most of the books purchased under the guise of "school texts" but it was a well-kept secret between student and teacher. The collection of penny dreadfuls and trite romance stories squirreled away in Anne's bedroom was never brought to the notice of her mother, who much preferred to call the girl to wait on her than to visit the nursery.

Mrs. Jenkinson did have some talent for music and had brought her small pianoforte with her to Kent after selling off all the other furnishings of her dead husband's house in order to pay his debts. In her rare free moments, the widow would closet herself with her old instrument and play songs that reminded her of a happier time. To that woman's credit, she made a valiant attempt to teach the young lady but it was soon clear that in addition to a weak voice, Anne was entirely tone deaf and without any sense of rhythm. Thus singing and playing were given up, though they explained to Lady Catherine that it was on account of her daughter's poor health.

All of this changed in the summer of 1800.

In 1787, Lady Anne Fitzwilliam had married an untitled but tremendously wealthy and well-connected gentleman named Mr. George Darcy. The match was shockingly advantageous for the Fitzwilliam family and Lady Catherine was extremely displeased that her younger sister had surpassed her. Despite her elder sister's sniping, the new Mrs. Darcy settled in Derbyshire and enjoyed what appeared to be a happy alliance. Before her second wedding anniversary, Lady Anne bore her husband a healthy boy, the heir to Pemberley, christened Fitzwilliam in honor of his mother's family.

Sadly, subsequent years brought a series of miscarriages until the year of young Fitzwilliam Darcy's tenth birthday. Lady Anne had not told her husband of her failures; they had occurred so early that he had not noticed any change to her figure and she was uncomfortable speaking with him on such intimate subjects. Thus, the continuation of this last pregnancy through those uncertain early months to the point that she felt the babe quicken made her alternately euphoric and fearful.

Mrs. Darcy went into labor more than a month early and so it was that after breakfast on his tenth birthday, young Fitzwilliam was brought to his mother's bedchamber and introduced to his new baby sister, Georgiana; it was a precious memory that he would treasure for the rest of his life.

It had been a difficult delivery and Lady Anne had been attended by only her mother-in-law, the midwife, and her friend, Rebecca, the vicar's wife. Her sister had been present for her previous confinement but because of the premature labor, Lady Catherine did not arrive at Pemberley until baby Georgiana was nearly four weeks old.

In truth, Lady Catherine had missed the express informing her that her sister needed her immediately. It had arrived at Rosings after her departure but due to the conflicting orders given to her housekeeper, the letter was returned to Derbyshire with a larger packet of mail to await her arrival at Pemberley. Lady Catherine herself took a more circuitous route, stopping in London to shop, pick up her two sons and, unfortunately, her husband.

Sir Lewis' decision to accompany his family to Derbyshire was due to politics rather than any affection. His latest affair in London had resulted in something of a scandal and his own father had ordered him to spend a bit of time in the country with the rather staid and respectable Darcys while his reputation recovered. Whether by luck or providence, the de Bourghs traveled north to Derbyshire with Lady Catherine, Anne and Mrs. Jenkinson in one carriage while Sir Lewis and his two sons occupied the other.

That gentleman's lethargy on the last days of the trip was dismissed as a preference to pass the dull time on the road by napping. Certainly his activities at the taverns each night kept him up late and required a goodly amount of energy. Unfortunately, one of the scullery maids with whom he spent several hours had a bit of a fever but chose to ignore it in her desire to pocket a few extra shillings. Not three days after the de Bourgh carriages left the inn with a fresh set of horses, the village would be quarantined for the pox.

By the time the de Bourghs arrived at Pemberley, Sir Lewis was so ill that he nearly fell out of the carriage and both Frederick and Herbert had fevers. Being the warm, caring hostess that she was, Lady Anne welcomed them all into her house without complaint and set her servants to tending her sister's family. Her only precaution was to send a note to the dower house asking if her mother-in-law might keep baby Georgiana and her wet nurse until the de Bourgh's illness had passed.

Mr. Darcy and his son had traveled to Matlock only days before the de Bourgh's arrival. When George Darcy had decided to visit the newly minted Earl's estate, he could never have known the devastation he would return to, although guilt would haunt him for the rest of his days. Lady Anne's husband had received a letter from his brother-in-law requesting advice on a drainage issue in several wheat fields that were often too boggy by autumn to harvest.

Darcy decided it best to travel the thirty miles to Matlock to study the situation himself and announced that his son Fitzwilliam would be joining him, along with his steward, Mr. Wickham. John Wickham asked and received permission to bring along his own son, George. Master and steward both hoped that such time together would encourage as steady a friendship between the boys as existed between their fathers.

Fitzwilliam was happy to be leaving his governess behind to spend a joyful week with his father and cousins. After a few days at Matlock, a plan for the drainage issue was worked out but Mr. Darcy was tempted by his brother-in-law to remain another week for a bit of course fishing. Not being particularly fond of Sir Lewis de Bourgh's company (or Lady Catherine's, for that matter), he was tempted. His wife wrote, encouraging him to remain, understanding her husband's temperament and liking to encourage his friendship with her own brother as well as her son's friendship with his Fitzwilliam cousins.

Lady Anne wrote that Pemberley was quiet— Sir Lewis had arrived with a bit of a fever but otherwise all was well. When Mr. Darcy decided to extend his stay, Mr. Wickham allowed his own son to remain with the Darcys at Matlock while he himself rode back to Pemberley alone.

When Wickham reached the estate, he was shocked. Although Lady Anne had written of a fever, the illness was not identified as the pox until after that good man's return. The fever had spread quickly from the family to the servants at Pemberley House, the tenant families, and then the nearby villages of Lambton and Kympton. The doctor, though skilled, was at his wit's end and had begun to fall ill himself.

Deaths began to be reported the day the loyal steward arrived and, although he worked tirelessly, it never seemed to be enough. Stunned by the extent of the suffering, when Wickham himself awoke with a fever his only consolation was that his own boy was safely away with his master.

It is understandable that Lady Catherine's sanity suffered as she watched her sister, husband, and both sons all die miserably over less than a fortnight. Georgiana and her grandmother were the only Darcys left at Pemberley and, as they were restricted to the dower house, Lady Catherine resolutely took charge. It was not a pleasant charge as the pox took its toll on all the neighborhood.

Both the housekeeper and butler at Pemberley succumbed to the fever early and were laid to rest even before Lady Anne. Young Susan Reynolds, previously of the home dairy and then promoted to the kitchens, stepped into the void and worked tirelessly to manage the house. Her practical, forthright nature might not have endeared her to Lady Catherine in a different situation (that lady preferring the cowering, obsequious style of servant), but her organizational ability and familiarity with Pemberley (in addition to her continued health) made her indispensible.

For the next three weeks, Lady Catherine came to rely on the vicar and his wife who worked day and night to support the healthy and see to the sick. Even as the cemeteries filled, many lives were saved due to their efforts. Sadly, their generous nature did not grant them immunity to the disease and they passed within hours of each other.

Through all of this, Lady Catherine persevered. She organized the healthy to see to those most fundamental tasks that kept all fed and clean. She sent several expresses to her brother, ordering that Mr. Darcy and his son be kept away until the danger was past. Pemberley's master was extremely unhappy, feeling that it was his duty to be with his people at such a time but he was forced to agree after much pressure from the Earl. Eventually, as the fever burnt itself out and left behind a tattered remnant of the population, it was also Lady Catherine who wrote to Mr. Darcy and the Fitzwilliams with news of the deaths.

After so much misery, Lady Catherine was very nearly mad by the time Mr. Darcy returned to Pemberley, more than a month after he had left. When the carriage stopped at the front steps, there was an odd moment of hesitation when no footmen darted out from the house or stable and no butler appeared at the door. Even the birds seemed quiet. Mr. Darcy had just opened the carriage door himself and stepped down when a strange woman appeared at the front door. He only recognized the thin, grey-haired crone as his sister-in-law when she looked past him and cried to his son in a harsh but unmistakable voice.

"Fitzwilliam! You must not be here! Return to Matlock, or go to the dower house." She turned on Mr. Darcy and her urgency was replaced by bitter anger. "Fool! What are you thinking, bringing him to this death house? Have you no care for my sister's only son?!"

Father and son stood for some moments, stunned to silence, even after Lady Catherine retreated indoors and slammed the door of Pemberley House behind her. Eventually, Mr. Darcy gathered some wits about him.

"Son, she is correct. You will go to your grandmother until I am certain it is safe."

Fitzwilliam rarely argued with his parent but an innate sense of duty was already pushing him to put his responsibilities before himself. "But Father…"

"No," interrupted Mr. Darcy curtly. He sighed before continuing in a calmer tone, "You must go to the dower house and look after Georgiana and your grandmother while I see what needs to be done here. Will you do that for me?"

The boy nodded seriously, accepting the responsibility and turned to climb back into the carriage by himself. Mr. Darcy gave his instructions to the driver but did not think to farewell his son as the carriage crunched down the gravel drive. His whole attention was focused on the house that his forefathers had built and maintained for hundreds of years. Feeling centuries older than his forty-two years, George forced himself up the steps and through the door.

After standing for a minute to allow his eyes to adjust to the dimmer light, he noticed a young woman moving to meet him. Clearly not his sister-in-law, yet she moved with a sense of confidence and authority.

"Mr. Darcy," she curtseyed.

"Err, yes…"

Seeing that the master was overwhelmed and did not recognize her, the servant spoke; "Mrs. Reynolds, sir. I've been filling in as housekeeper since Mrs. Thompkins and Mr. Briggs passed."

Darcy forced his mind to focus and was reassured with the recognition that followed. "Of course— Mr. Moore's daughter, Susan. You married John Reynolds in March, did you not?"

The woman nodded. "Yes, sir. My husband died early in the fever, but my father is still at work in the stables here." Her eyes betrayed her grief for a moment before she drew herself up and continued, "I'm sorry if no one met your carriage, sir, but we didn't know to expect it and I'm afraid that hands are mighty short at the moment."

Her master was already shaking his head. "Not a problem. Lady Catherine met us." Seeing the servant look toward the window, he added,

"I sent my son and the carriage along to the dower house until I was certain that the main house was… was…" He trailed off but Mrs. Reynolds was already nodding.

"That was wise, sir. There's been no sickness at old Mrs. Darcy's house and they're provisioned well enough that they could last a few more weeks at least without having to venture out, even feeding a few more mouths. There's been no new sick at Pemberley House in a week, but it's better safe than sorry with the young ones, I'd say."

Mr. Darcy was relieved by these facts but remembering his surviving son led to thoughts on the fate of others. He turned his mind to more immediate issues. "Mrs. Reynolds, please come to my study. There is a great deal I must know."

Though widely known as a jolly, social man, from that day forward George Darcy fought a melancholy that seemed to overwhelm him more often than not. Even as he worked to bury the dead and rebuild his estate, he mourned his wife, denied even the comfort of attending her funeral as the bodies had been interred within hours of death for fear of contagion.

His mood was not aided by Lady Catherine's attitude. Years married to Sir Lewis had left that lady with a bitter antipathy toward the power of men. In her mental and physical exhaustion, she had become convinced that only she could run the estate successfully. When she was not ignoring Mr. George Darcy, she was haranguing him, blaming the epidemic on his neglectful management and her sister's death on that lady's marriage.

Weighed down by his own guilt, Mr. Darcy could only think that he somehow deserved such reproofs. Such was the situation when old Mrs. Darcy finally returned to the main house with the two Darcy children. Lady Edna was a force unto herself and Lady Catherine soon found herself waging a losing battle for control. She was even more furious when her own brother arrived, having been summoned by Lady Edna.

Finding that his sister had commandeered the mistress' study for herself, Lord Henry settled in a nearby chair and waited until she dismissed the maid whom she had been lecturing. When the door closed, Lady Catherine turned to him.

"Yes, Henry? What is it?"

The Earl reminded himself to keep his voice gentle despite his irritation at her tone. "I came to see how you are, Cathy."

His sister gave him a look that expressed all of her impatience with her younger sibling.

Henry tried again. "Catherine, you have been working very hard. You must not forget to take care of yourself. You have lost as much as any of us; you must take time to mourn."

"Must! *MUST!* I shall be the judge of what I *must* do, just as I have been for some time!"

He sighed. "Sister, you have held the place together, no one is disregarding your efforts. But Darcy is here now; it is time to step back and allow the Darcys to rebuild their lives."

"Step back! This is my sister's estate! Her son's legacy! How can you possibly suggest that I just leave it to ruin?!"

Henry closed his eyes for a moment before leaning forward and taking his sister's hand, only to have it snatched back. "Catherine, you must listen to me. I loved our sister as much as you and I swear to God that I shall look after her children as if they were my own. However, we must remember that Anne's husband *lives*. George Darcy is the head of the Darcy family and master of Pemberley. We may *offer* him our help but we must respect his position."

"His position!" sputtered Catherine.

She was gathering breath for a diatribe on why everything was George Darcy's fault when her brother tried a different tact. "What about Rosings? With your sons gone, is Sir Lewis' daughter his heir?"

"What?! Whatever can you mean?!?" Lady Catherine had never considered that she might lose Rosings Park.

"Sister, I was not involved in negotiating the settlement for your marriage; Father dealt with Lord Maxwell and barely mentioned it in his letters to me. The only thing I know for sure is that the de Bourghs like to keep their land and money in the family and preferably the male line. Do you know anything about Sir Lewis' will?"

Lady Catherine de Bourgh gaped like a fish. Had the circumstances been different, Henry might have found it amusing to see his sister speechless for the first time in her life. Before she could recover, however, there was a knock on the door.

Henry tensed, knowing what was to come. He had arranged for Catherine's daughter to be brought down, hoping to remind his sister that she still had a living child. Into this charged atmosphere came little Anne de Bourgh escorted by her very solemn cousin. Fitzwilliam Darcy might have been slightly shorter and a few years younger than his female relative but he was clearly taking his duty as host of the nursery very seriously.

In all the turmoil, Catherine had largely forgotten her daughter. Upon arriving at Pemberley, the girl had been assigned rooms in the family wing. However, Mrs. Jenkinson had seen the pox before and had acted quickly to isolate herself and her charge in a far wing at the first mention of a fever.

Still reeling from the idea of losing her home, Catherine focused on the two children standing uncomfortably before her. "Anne..."

For the first time that the girl could remember, her mother reached out a hand to touch her. They did not embrace; that would have been too much for either. The touch alone was enough to bring tears to Anne's eyes.

"Anne... Are you well?" Catherine cleared her throat and gathered her wits about her. "Has Mrs. Jenkinson been caring for you properly?"

"Yes, Mother," Miss de Bourgh spoke barely above a whisper.

"You are too thin. Have you not been eating properly?"

Having never received so much focused attention from her parent before, Anne could only mumble again, "Yes, Mother."

Lady Catherine turned her sharp eyes upon her nephew. "And you, Fitzwilliam. You have returned to Pemberley House. Have you and Anne been spending time together?"

Something in Catherine's voice vaguely worried Lord Henry but he was so relieved to see his sister showing interest in her daughter that he brushed it aside. He watched his nephew answer her questions gravely, foreshadowing the serious, responsible man he was growing to be. The Earl had spent quite a bit of time with the lad over the last month while Mr. Darcy and his son had been forced to remain at Matlock. Although he would never admit it to anyone, Henry Fitzwilliam wished his own heir showed half as much promise as his nephew.

Lord Henry's attention was brought back to the present when his sister stood abruptly and directed her most imperious expression at her brother. "Henry— pay attention! I have determined that I and the children must return to Kent immediately. I have done all I can here; inform Mr. Darcy that I shall spend the afternoon overseeing our packing and depart in the morning. He may write to me at Rosings with his questions regarding the management of the estate and household."

With that, Lady Catherine de Bourgh swept from the room with the two children trailing along in her wake. Henry grimaced. He might be the Earl of Matlock, head of the wealthy and well-connected Fitzwilliam family and honored in the House of Lords, but his elder sister would always treat him like an errand boy. Chuckling for the first time in weeks, he left the room and headed to Darcy's study to pass on the news.

From that day on, Lady Catherine was assiduously protective of her daughter's health. Her brother tried not to spend much time thinking about whether that care was due to its implications for her own position rather than maternal feelings. To his widow's horror, Sir Lewis' will stated that if all of his children died without issue, Rosings Park would go to one of his brothers.

Unfortunately, Lady Catherine's form of cosseting consisted of keeping Anne indoors, wrapped in thick blankets and dosed with every sort of physic that her apothecary might recommend. Within a year, Miss de Bourgh could not sleep without a generous dose of laudanum and spent most of her days in an opiate-induced haze. This detail did not deter her mother's new crusade; to marry the heiress of Rosings Park to the heir of Pemberley.

6 THE VIPER ROOM

When Fitzwilliam Darcy returned to London from Kent, he threw himself into work—estate matters, business investments, charity requests, household accounts; nothing was too minor to merit his attention. He avoided his sister and took most of his meals in his study. Unfortunately, his efforts only served to worry her, irritate his staff and eventually to exhaust himself.

After nearly a fortnight of such activities, he finally succumbed to his melancholy and spent an evening locked in the library, drinking an unaccustomed quantity of fine brandy and staring morosely into the fire. The only benefit was that, for the first time in months, he slept without dreaming of Elizabeth.

Or at least, he couldn't remember the dreams.

When Darcy woke the next morning (much later than his norm), he felt as if he had been put through a laundry mangle. More than anything, he wished he could take a long, bruising gallop through the countryside to blow the cobwebs out of his mind, but this was London and he had no desire to prance down Rotten Row with the fashionable crowd. Instead, he took himself to his fencing club, hoping that the physical exertion would yield a similar result. Unfortunately, his sleepless nights combined with a distracted mind led to poor concentration and he was soundly thrashed by the master.

Leaving the building, Will waved off his carriage and walked home. He must conquer this obsession! Elizabeth Bennet had turned him down in no uncertain terms. She positively despised him and not even his wealth and connections could overcome her poor estimation of his character.

Darcy slapped his stick against his leg forcefully. If she could not see his value, then clearly *she* was the one who was lacking. He was an honorable gentleman, an excellent master, and a good brother (he quickly squashed a flash of guilt over how little time he had spent with Georgiana since his return from Rosings).

By the time Darcy returned home to Derwent House, he had concluded that the best way to convince himself of Elizabeth's inferiority was to throw himself into the Season. After checking his schedule and the pile of invitations that had accumulated over the past month, he found an invitation for a ball being held that very evening by Lord and Lady Carlisle in honor of their daughter's coming out. It was still early enough in the Season that all the new debutants would be fresh and relatively untarnished, he thought cynically.

Darcy's determination wavered when he read a note from Bingley indicating that the younger man was extending his annual visit to his Yorkshire relations. Could he face the madding crowd without the buffer of his more outgoing friend to ease the way?

As Fitzwilliam sat at his desk, he was unnerved at how easy it was to slip into his old habit of daydreaming that Elizabeth was there with him. Before he could stop himself, he had imagined her curled up in the armchair by the window, reading letters of her own, and occasionally turning to relay some tidbit she thought might interest or amuse him.

What would Elizabeth say if he confessed he was uncomfortable attending a ball alone? The answer came to him immediately, coupled with a vision of the lady herself seated at his aunt's pianoforte with one eyebrow raised. *"Why Mr. Darcy, you must take the trouble to practice!"* Without daring to think much on the course of his reasoning, he notified the butler of his plans and retreated to his rooms to bathe and dress.

Within minutes of entering the grand ball, Darcy had retreated to a corner and begun to seriously question why he had voluntarily inserted himself into a situation so at odds with his temperament. As his countenance stiffened into his best imitation of a forbidding statue, he could not help but overhear the conversation among a countess and several other noble matrons regarding the attentions of a gentleman to her daughter.

"Such a charming young man, and so rich!"

"And his estate is such an easy distance to your own!"

"I always knew that my dear Mary could not be so beautiful for nothing!"

"And has he asked for her hand yet?"

"Oh, I am certain it shall be any day now. I have already instructed the butler to 'accidently' leave them alone in the drawing room for a few minutes, the next time he calls."

The ladies dissolved into satisfied titters before the Countess continued, "And of course, once Mary is married, she shall be able to introduce her sisters to other such young men. Really, their brother has been no help at all. Good heavens— the friends he brings home from university! I don't understand a word they say—it's all Greek and Latin and philosophy, and that's when they're not spending hours staring at a chessboard without speaking a word. Do you know he was upset with me when I asked what sort of income one young man could expect?"

"Upset?"

"Most certainly! He gave me some interminable lecture on the value of a man not being measured by his income or inheritance. As though I should not protect my girls from the attentions of an inappropriate suitor!" The lady paused to take a breath (a fortunate occurrence as it allowed the bobbing feathers attached to her turban a chance to settle back into their natural position).

"The boy turned out to be the son of some country squire, no connections to speak of; his father's estate brings in barely four thousand a year and he was paying attentions to *my* daughter, can you imagine?"

The other ladies bobbed their own turbans in like-minded commiseration before moving away like a flock of oddly colored birds. Darcy continued to stand very still with his punch cup, doing his best not to attract any attention. His mind was not still, however, and he searched his memory for why the conversation had sounded so very familiar. He did not recognize the words as reminiscent of those which he had once so condemned from Mrs. Bennet until he overheard a second conversation, this one between the Countess' two daughters.

"Oh, dear Mama. Why must she speak of such things so…"

"Loudly? Callously? Unthinkingly?" laughed the younger sister.

"I am sure that she means well."

"She may *mean* well but that does not give her leave to disregard every rule of propriety." The two sisters sighed together with a sense of long-suffering. "Though it *has* taught us a valuable lesson; good breeding has absolutely nothing to do with one's birth."

"Eva, you must not say such things," remonstrated the elder sister even as she could barely restrain her own giggles. "And you know that I would never…"

The other voice became more serious. "I know you will never marry a man you cannot respect, Mary."

"But Eva… I would wish… I would so much prefer to marry where there is some chance at affection."

"And so you shall, my dear. Simply take care that you fall in love with a gentleman of large fortune and a title … and preferably an estate far away from Dorset, if you can manage it."

"Oh Eva…." The two young ladies moved away, hiding their giggles behind fans.

The famous Darcy mask was firmly in place but Fitzwilliam was laughing on the inside. In his mind's eye, he could perfectly imagine Elizabeth and her elder sister having a similar conversation after their mother embarrassed them with a flight of wild volubility.

Suddenly Darcy blinked and couldn't stop himself from scratching his head. Had he truly just compared Mrs. Bennet of Longbourn to the Countess of Dorchester? *Focus, man!* he commanded himself.

Looking for answers, Darcy ran his eyes over the room. Just entering were a fashionable couple, the man jovial and vaguely familiar and the wife happily greeting friends with hugs and kisses before naturally gravitating back to her husband's arm. The affection between the pair was obvious and with a pang, Will recognized the intense desire within himself to be part of such a relationship.

He turned away quickly and was faced with the polar opposite. Mask firmly in place, he bowed. "Ashbourne, Lady Alameda," he greeted his eldest cousin, the Earl of Matlock's heir (and one of the most immoral, profligate men of his acquaintance) and that man's wife (a self-centered, manipulative, society maven who made Caroline Bingley look like a saint). The Viscount barely grunted at the younger cousin whom he considered to be an uptight, straight-laced prig before departing for the card tables.

Unsurprised, Darcy barely controlled a shiver when he felt a pair of claws take possession of his arm. "Darcy, dearest. Aren't you going to ask me to dance?" Lady Alameda had never quite forgiven the tall, handsome, and above all, exceedingly wealthy gentleman for not falling to her feet when she was first introduced to Society.

Recognizing that he had no recourse, Darcy resigned himself. At least Alameda was already married and would not be trying to entrap him in *that* way. He led her to the next room where a dance was just forming and asked after her son, hoping to introduce a neutral topic for conversation.

"Oh, my darling Reggie is wonderful, a perfect angel. You must come visit us in Essex. Ashbourne is so often away, we could have a lovely visit." Just in case he had missed her invitation, she brushed her hand across the fall of his trousers as she circled him in the dance.

Gritting his teeth in disgust, Darcy only barely kept himself from stalking away and leaving her standing alone on the dance floor. However, he knew from experience that Lady Alameda would find a way to punish him, probably by telling the gossips that *he* had suggested a *rendez vous* and had walked away when *she* refused.

Focus, man! he reminded himself again. "How old is he? It seems as though your wedding was only months ago."

Alameda laughed but allowed him the diversion. "Oh Darcy, you charmer. My dear boy has just turned four, the very image of his grandfather."

"The Earl?"

There was a flicker in the Lady's eyes that Fitzwilliam could not interpret. "Oh… I hadn't thought of that, but perhaps he does have a bit of Lord Matlock about the eyes. No, I meant my own father, the late Baron Asbury."

Darcy wondered at her response while they were separated by the dance but knew he should not let her take control of the conversation again for fear her next invitation was not as easily deflected. "Of course. It must be delightful to watch your child growing up on the same estate where you yourself spent your youth."

The set came to an end and as they made their final obeisance she looked him full in the face. "Yes. Yes, it is." The Viscountess looked oddly vulnerable for a moment before her eyes focused over Darcy's shoulder and any softness instantly disappeared. "Thank you for such a lovely dance, Mr. Darcy," she cooed, holding out her hand for him to kiss before moving off to several of her cronies, leaving Fitzwilliam to wonder if he had imagined her reaction.

What on Earth am I doing here? he wondered as he worked his way through the crowd to find a place along the wall, his stony visage an expression that Hertfordshire's society would have recognized instantly. The ball was already a crush and he could see that people were still arriving. There were entire rooms into which he had not yet ventured. Even if by some ridiculous twist of fate, Elizabeth appeared at the ball, he doubted they would meet in the swirl of silks and glitter of jewels.

Not that he was looking for her, he assured himself.

Although he desperately wished to escape the function, Darcy forced himself to maneuver through the mob into one of the rooms in which a light buffet had been set. Seeing several of his more agreeable Fitzwilliam cousins, he joined them at a table and ate quietly while they chatted about the evening.

"Darcy, where have you been?" asked Lady Ellen. The second eldest of the Fitzwilliam children, she was more than five years older than her cousin and saw it as her duty to regularly step in as the elder sister he lacked.

Will relaxed his mask enough to venture a weak smile. "I arrived a bit late, but I did have the honor of dancing a set with Lady Alameda."

Ellen had a similarly low opinion of her sister-in-law and patted his arm comfortingly. "Poor Wills. Did she leave any claw marks? There must be a doctor about if you require stitches." She was pleased to coax a chuckle (camouflaged as a cough) from her very serious cousin. "Not to worry; just stay close to Olivia and me and we shall protect you from the vipers." She turned to respond to a question asked on her other side, leaving Darcy to his thoughts.

Watching the young (and not so young) ladies titter and flirt with the gentlemen, Darcy was struck by a revelation. Jane Bennet had acted the perfect example of proper, ladylike behavior. He had informed Bingley that he had seen no evidence of affection but really, if he had, would he not have condemned her as too forward? A flirt no better than these supposedly well-bred Society ladies he despised? Which would he want Georgiana to emulate, Lady Alameda or Miss Bennet? Why had he been so determined to condemn the Bennets?

Not much later, Darcy excused himself and began the exhausting process of working his way toward the mansion's entrance (or, in his case, its exit). In the next to last room, a husband and wife known to Darcy greeted him and then asked leave to introduce their niece, Miss Elizabeth Barnett. Having only caught a glimpse of a dark-haired young lady in yellow standing behind them, Darcy started upon hearing her name and turned to her with an intent look that descended rapidly into a frown when he realized that it was not *her.*

Luckily, Colonel Fitzwilliam had appeared at his elbow at just that moment and, after charmingly begging an introduction, swept the young lady off for a set. Darcy spent some minutes speaking with the couple (pleasant but dull) although most of his attention remained focused on his cousin. Richard spoke easily, smiling and flirting, and soon the young lady had recovered her spirits from the odd reaction of the handsome Darcy heir.

Will had just collected his coat and hat when Richard appeared at his side again. "Darce! Are you off? Mind if I beg a ride? I've had quite enough of this crush." Darcy agreed and indicated that he would wait outside while the Colonel collected his coat.

When Richard emerged, he trotted down the pink marble steps but came to a halt when he noticed his cousin. Darcy had stepped off the street into the front garden, a lilac bush hiding him from most passers by. He had removed his hat and was staring up at the stars with a nearly desperate look of melancholy etched upon his face.

A moment later, the spell was broken. A boy ran up the sidewalk and called, "Mr. Darcy, sir. Your man's just pulling the coach around."

Firmly resettling his beaver, Mr. Darcy turned toward the voice. "Thank you, lad." Tossing a copper to the urchin, he nodded at Fitzwilliam and the two men moved toward the carriage.

Richard watched his cousin's mask descend. His own duties had been keeping him so busy that he had not seen Darcy since their return from Kent. He recalled that that carriage ride had been mostly silent but he had assumed his cousin was unsettled after confronting Lady Catherine. Now Richard was not so sure and he had a sneaking suspicion as to what, or rather *who*, was the cause of his cousin's angst.

As the two men settled back into the cushioned seats, Richard stretched his legs out and sighed. "'Tis a beautiful evening. Almost seems a waste to take a carriage instead of walking."

Darcy managed a smirk. "Dancing yourself to exhaustion?"

Richard was pleased to see a spark of liveliness in his cousin. "I'll have you know I've been up since five, drilling a new batch of recruits. Bloody fools, the lot of them! By God, how I wish, just once, these families would consider their sons' aptitudes when buying their commission instead of which uniform looks most impressive, or matches the boy's eyes or… Oh, Hell's bells, I don't know… I swear, one of the lads doesn't know one end of a horse from the other but he can swim like a fish. And why was he sent into the cavalry instead of the navy? His mother likes red coats better than blue. Bloody fools, may God help them."

Darcy had listened to his cousin's grievances before. Although he had no first-hand knowledge of military life, he could understand the frustration of working with underlings whose talents were not best matched to their tasks. With his households and estates, Pemberley's master had a certain freedom to transfer people to positions for which they were best suited. He could easily comprehend the Colonel's frustration at not being able to do so.

When the carriage pulled up at the Darcy townhouse, Richard accepted an invitation to come in for a nightcap. "Although if you have any more of that excellent brandy, you may have to lend me a bed for the night."

Darcy chuckled warily, knowing from painful experience that his older cousin had a much better head for liquor than he himself did.

The two men left their coats and hats with the butler and Richard headed to his cousin's library while Darcy checked for messages. Smiling to himself when he found a nearly full decanter of fine French brandy, the Colonel poured out two generous snifters. He sniffed and tasted it out of habit. However, rather than savoring the brandy (however excellent), the majority of his thoughts focused on how best to tease out the cause of his favorite cousin's melancholy.

When Darcy entered, he received the snifter with a nod of appreciation and both men settled into the comfortable armchairs arranged by the fire.

"Did you see that Miss Elizabeth Bennet was at the ball?" inquired Richard with a studied insouciance even as he watched his cousin out of the corner of his eye.

"Barnett, not Bennet. And of course I saw her; I was the one who made the introduction before you asked her to dance," answered Darcy grumpily.

"Oh no, it was Miss Elizabeth *Bennet* from Kent. Or rather, Hertfordshire, I suppose. I wasn't able to get to her in the crush—just caught a glimpse across the room. She arrived with a couple, slightly older, very fashionable. Didn't Miss Bennet have an aunt and uncle in London?"

By now, Will's heart was pounding and his mouth was dry. "Yes; the Gardiners."

"Perhaps we should call on them. Do you know their address?" Richard probed.

"Gracechurch Street. Near Cheapside." Darcy was barely able to unlock his jaw enough to choke out the words and unconsciously leaned away from his cousin, dreading his response. When it came, he was stunned.

"Hmmm... that makes sense. They were fashionable and obviously well-known but I didn't recognize them from Father's set. Do you know where on Gracechurch Street?" Richard was increasingly certain of his suspicion that his cousin had developed a *tendre* for Miss Bennet.

"Fashionable and well-known?" Darcy couldn't hide all of his shock. "It was common knowledge in Hertfordshire that Elizabeth's uncle is in trade. Since when is Cheapside fashionable?" He did not even notice his slip in calling her by her first name.

Bull's eye! Richard took a sip of his brandy to hide his amusement. "Gracechurch Street is *near* Cheapside certainly, but some of the houses there are quite fine. Surely you've been through that neighborhood? It runs somewhere between the East India House on Leadenhall and the Bank of England on Threadneedle. Really, Cousin, I had not realized that you were so provincial as to know nothing of London beyond Grosvenor Square!"

Seeing that Darcy still appeared confused, Richard tried again. "Well, you *do* know where the new London Bridge is being built? At the end of King William Street? Or at least you still remember where Christopher Wren's monument to the Great Fire is, yes?"

Darcy rolled his eyes at his cousin's sarcasm.

"Well, if you go north on King William and veer right at the Monument... *et voila!* You are on Gracechurch Street. Further north it turns into Bishopsgate, after you cross Leadenhall."

He smiled at Darcy's expression. Another suspicion clicked into place. Was his cousin resisting his feelings for Miss Bennet because he believed her to be socially inferior? "Trade or not, some of the families that live along there are wealthier than any of the cash-strapped peers in Bloomsbury... or Mayfair for that matter. Many with excellent connections, as well— younger sons finding an honest way to support their families and so forth."

Darcy remained silent, staring into the fire and looking thoughtful. Richard decided that he had given his younger cousin enough to think about on that subject for the moment.

"By the way, are you going to John Cookson's wedding tomorrow? It's at Saint Paul's, although I can't imagine he has enough family left to fill his side of the pews."

Will forced his mind away from the Gardiners' condition in life long enough to formulate a coherent response. "I saw the invitation, but didn't realize it was tomorrow," he admitted. "I hadn't even realized that he was

73

engaged. Who is the bride?"

Richard rolled his eyes. "Miss Cecily Rickles, Heaven help him."

Darcy couldn't help but groan. Miss Rickles had come out the previous season. Her beauty, wealth, and connections all made her popularity in Society a certainty. Darcy's aunt, the Countess of Matlock, had hosted a dinner party and made certain that her favorite nephew was seated beside the young lady. Darcy himself had approached the introduction with a certain eagerness. At twenty-six, he had been increasingly tired of bachelorhood and all that he had heard suggested that Miss Rickles was just what he had been taught to look for in a wife.

Unfortunately, it had taken less than one course for him to realize that the pretty face hid a vapid and poorly educated mind. He had rapidly given up any discussion of literature or current events. She agreed that she had recently seen a play and he was able to piece together that it had probably been Hamlet only after Miss Rickles commented on the color of the curtain (blue with gold tassels), which he recognized as being unique to one theatre on Drury Lane. The acting had been "nice," the staging had been "pretty," and the plot had been beyond her ability to describe, quite literally.

"I suppose some men might prefer a silly wife," said Darcy without thinking, then pressed one hand over his mouth.

Richard roared with laughter at his cousin's loosened tongue. "Well said, my boy, well said! I'm glad to see that wicked sense of humor hasn't become entirely atrophied while I was away."

Darcy tried to cover his embarrassment by taking a sip of wine. He couldn't quite contain his curiosity, however. "How did Cookson... When did they..." Will trailed off, not quite able to phrase his question without speaking poorly of the lady.

Richard chuckled again. "How did he get himself shackled to the dullest, stupidest girl of our acquaintance? Family dynasties, of course. Mother and Ellen were talking about it at breakfast this morning. It sounded as if the fathers had the marriage contracts drawn up before the bride and groom had even met."

Even with his own recent disappointment, Darcy couldn't help but ask, "Are you serious? Was no account taken for affection?"

Richard snorted. "Old Mr. Cookson desires a connection to the Duke of Northumberland, which the Rickles possess. And apparently there is some possibility that John has a claim to the Earl of Ailesbury's title when old Brudenell finally dies... or something like that. I have to admit, I wasn't particularly interested after I'd established the bare facts of the matter."

Darcy shook his head. John Cookson was a few years younger but they were part of the same circle and met socially on occasion. His wasn't a particularly brilliant mind but Darcy would never have called him stupid. He found himself wondering what he would have done in the same situation, if his parents had lived and arranged his marriage to a woman with whom he had nothing in common.

Darcy sat lost in thought for some minutes until he went to take a drink and found his glass empty. He stood and refilled his glass and then did the same for his companion's after silently gesturing with the decanter.

Sipping his brandy, Richard leaned further back in the comfortable armchair and stared into the fire. He spoke thoughtfully. "It has been very interesting, being back in Society this last month after so long in the trenches."

Darcy blinked and looked over to his cousin. Richard rarely spoke of his time in war. Other noblemen's sons might have purchased a uniform but avoided any active service. The Right Honorable Richard Fitzwilliam, however, had earned every advancement with sweat and blood, his most recent promotion coming on the battlefield after his squadron's previous commander had been literally shot off his horse by a sniper.

"This is a strange world we live in, you know. So much time and money spent on such frivolous nothings. And the angst! I was born into this life, believing that the only thing that mattered was money and consequence. I may have laughed at it but I never really questioned it; remember how I always said that I could only ever marry a wealthy woman?" Richard paused for another sip of brandy.

Darcy's attention was now fully engaged. "And that has changed?"

The Colonel gave a harsh bark of a laugh. "I feel like I am observing some strange, foreign culture that I once read about in a book. I can still remember the dance steps—I can flirt and charm with the best of them—but it feels like a charade I am forced to play when the situation demands it."

Richard sighed and tossed off the remainder of his brandy. "Bah... I need something stronger than this." Standing in order to better examine the options, he chose a whiskey that he judged would have the bite he needed. As he poured, he continued speaking softly.

"All those primped and powdered dandies. I found myself imagining what Dunn would say... probably how many of them could dress themselves without help!" Richard chuckled.

Not quite knowing what to think (and wondering how long it had been since he had tied his own cravat), Darcy ventured a quiet question. "Dunn?"

Richard looked at him owlishly as if he had just been asked what water was. "Dunn. Bertie Dunn. Ah, right... of course you wouldn't know. He was my batman; not an officer, but the entire company would have fallen apart in a day if he hadn't been there, myself included. Food, supplies, horses. Once we were camped in a bog for days—pinned down by artillery on two sides. Rats would chew on our boot leather while we slept, even as

we wore them. So, there we were, bitter cold with holes in our boots…
even stuffing them with rags didn't help— just left us with cold, wet feet
that felt like lead weights. Then, two days before we were supposed to
sneak out, Dunn appeared with a sack full of shoe leather and an awl. We
spent the day sewing new soles on our boots with horse hair and then
everyone marched out with dry feet."

Richard took a swig of whiskey and enjoyed the burn down his throat.
"There is nothing in this world quite so wonderful as dry feet."

"How did he manage it?"

The Colonel shrugged with a weary chuckle. "I have no idea and he
would never tell us. Had some of the younger lads convinced he was Merlin
reborn. Dunn came from a big family—fourteen children in some little
fishing village near Ipswich—and said it was something he'd picked up
from minding the young ones. Always kept some candies or peppermints
hidden in a secret pocket so he could produce them with a flourish. After
that, the kiddies would follow him anywhere."

"He sounds like a good man."

Richard smiled fondly. "He is the very best of men, the very best of
friends." His voice became rough. "Darce, I don't think I would have made
it back this last time without him."

Sensing that his cousin needed someone to confide in, Will stood
silently to refill Richard's glass. The Colonel nodded his thanks, but his eyes
remained unfocused, looking beyond the fire into those nightmares only he
could see.

"We were sneaking out through the artillery, a few hours before dawn—
that's when the enemy's sentries are usually least alert. Only five miles but it
took hours, mostly on our bellies. We went single file, spaced out with
Dunn in the lead as he'd scouted the route, and me bringing up the rear so
we didn't lose any stragglers."

Richard closed his eyes. "We made it through the worst and were about
a mile from where our regiment was dug in when some fool of a lieutenant
saw us coming. Later I heard that he and his mate had been drinking
bootleg all night instead of watching their posts." He threw down the
remainder of his whiskey.

"And of course, word that we were coming hadn't made it down to the
rank and file, so they thought they were seeing a band of enemy infiltrators.
In their inebriated condition, it seemed eminently logical to use the
cannon."

Darcy was stunned. "Are you saying that you were fired upon by your
own side?"

Richard tried to smile. "And I have the scars to prove it. For better or
worse, their aim was off; they overshot us by a fair bit."

"And thus you were closest."

"I was indeed. Tried to jump into a ditch but as I went in headfirst, it protected my handsome face, but not much else."

"I knew you returned because you had been wounded, but never heard any specifics."

Richard smirked. "Ah, yes. Let us just say that I spent most of my time in the hospital lying on my belly, shall we? So there I was, stretched out in a muddy, Portuguese ditch, bleeding from my backside, when whose ugly face should pop up like some nefarious chipmunk?"

Darcy was so lost in imagining the nightmarish scene that he didn't respond.

"It was Dunn, of course. After realizing that I wasn't going to be able to walk out, he started dragging me. Unfortunately, the cannon blast had woken up the enemy sentries and one of them came poking around in my ditch. Before we knew what was happening, Dunn had a bayonet stuck through his shoulder."

Richard stood and looked into his whiskey as if it held the answers to all the world's questions.

"But what happened? How did you get away?"

"I shot him," responded the Colonel plainly. "When I first received my commission, Father gave me a little pocket pistol, really too small to do any good except at point blank range. The lads used to tease me about it but I always kept it dry and primed. As soon as I saw that bayonet go into Dunn, I twisted around and fired."

Richard took a swig of whiskey, wishing it could numb the memory. "He was just a boy, Darce. Somehow I'd fired into his open mouth, blew the back of his head off, but when he fell, it looked like he was just lying in the grass, staring up at the sky. He could have been any of the lads we'd ever played with growing up." He bit his lip; lately too much whiskey made him maudlin.

They were quiet for some minutes until Darcy finally spoke; "Did Dunn survive?" He was surprised to hear Richard chuckle.

"Oh, nothing could kill that old rat catcher. I pulled out the bayonet and we did our best to wrap up the wound. Then we set about getting ourselves back to camp. Used the bayonet as a cane; I had two good arms and shoulders, but my bottom half was a right mess. He had two good legs but couldn't use his arm. We made a sorry pair, carrying each other. I suppose that's why the sentries didn't shoot us when we dragged our sorry asses into camp. But the way we were giggling like a couple of schoolgirls might have been a contributing factor."

"What on Earth did you have to laugh about?"

Richard actually smiled at the memory. "We were both nearly bled out, so just about anything seemed amusing." Seeing his cousin was dumbfounded, he explained, "We'd been in some tight spots over the years but neither of us had ever gotten much more than a scratch. Now here we were— I'd been blasted by my own side and Dunn had been stuck by some beardless drummer boy with a pigsticker. I remember telling the surgeon that we had just about enough working parts between us to make one good man."

"But you both made it back."

"More or less. Dunn didn't lose his arm but it doesn't work all that well. I may not need a cane forever but I won't be winning any footraces." Richard stopped there. His pride made it impossible to speak of all his injuries, even to the cousin he loved more than a brother.

"What will you do now? Have you thought of resigning your commission?"

Richard shrugged. "Not just yet. I'm due for another promotion in about six months and until then they have me trying to dribble a bit of common sense into these striplings with their morning milk. I was able to keep Dunn with me, at least, and he's got the barracks humming in rare form."

The Colonel stood and the effort it took made him decide that he had had enough for the night. "After that, who knows? Obviously I don't have an estate to settle down on... and though they'd take me in, we both know I'd go crazy cooped up with *Mater et Pater*, trying to be a proper social accoutrement."

After their chuckles subsided, Richard continued. "Actually, Dunn and I have been talking about going into a partnership."

"A business?"

Richard smiled crookedly. "No, politics. I'd be the front man—second son of an Earl, decorated officer, all that rubbish. And Dunn would be my manager—the puppet master. Make sure I'm always in the right place at the right time. Remind me who's who and keep me from offending them. Make sure a crowd shows up and cheers whenever I'm to give a speech. The usual."

Richard shrugged off the serious tone and waggled his eyebrows at his cousin. "But then again, someone from the War Office has been sniffing around. Can you see your old cousin in military intelligence?"

Darcy laughed but there was an edge of worry in his eye. Not wanting to deal with his cousin's concerns that night, Richard herded them both off to bed.

Will awoke gradually the next morning feeling warm and fuzzy. He couldn't quite remember how he had made it to his bed but his aching head was enough to remind him vaguely of the evening before. Then the sun peeked from between the drapes and sent a bolt of pain into his skull.

"When will I learn? Never, never drink with Richard," he moaned. Fortunately, his valet had anticipated him and there was already a glass of water and a packet of headache powder on the bedside table. "Bless you, Hawkins."

Darcy forced himself to sit up and, leaning against the headboard, drank the concoction. After several minutes he began to feel more like himself and ventured to open his eyes again. Almost immediately he made the embarrassing observation that, although he did have his nightshirt on, it had been pushed up above his waist while he slept and he had spent the night wrapped around one of the large pillows that his head normally laid upon.

Added to this were several other observations equally mortifying. Bits of a dream came back to him, remarkable in its vividness and, glancing down at the pillow that was still resting by his knee, he noted a damp stain that was no doubt the cause (or rather, the result) of his warm and fuzzy feeling.

Darcy groaned and slumped back down onto his (clean) pillow. He hadn't lost control of himself in such a way since adolescence. What was happening to him? And yet, he could already feel himself stiffening again as he recalled the dream of Elizabeth.

He had been riding through a meadow and fallen. Elizabeth, with her sparkling eyes and amused expression had come upon him and helped him up. He had barely made it to a standing position and wrapped his arms around her when he had seen Elizabeth's expression change. Turning, he had been confronted with George Wickham in full regimentals and charging at them with a bayonet. Without a thought, Darcy had pulled a small pistol from his pocket and shot Wickham in the heart. Elizabeth had been grateful and appreciative... and they had made love there, out of doors in the sunny meadow, for hours.

Will groaned again and, after retrieving an old handkerchief from his nightstand, covered his eyes with his arm and went about relieving an almost painful tumescence.

When Darcy finally made it downstairs, he was irritated to see Richard already seated, attacking a mountain of eggs, kippers, and toast as if it were any other day. His uniform looked clean and pressed and his boots were polished to such a sheen that his cousin thought he might get another headache.

Selecting some dry toast and a large mug of coffee, Will seated himself with only a mild glare at his cousin. Richard chuckled. "Ah, civilians. Forgot you were such a lightweight, Wills, my boy. I should have cut you off earlier."

Unable to come up with anything suitably abusive, Darcy responded with only a grunt.

Finishing his plate, Richard watched his cousin carefully for several minutes before speaking again. "Well then. Are we still going to this wedding?" At Darcy's short nod, he continued, "Capital! If we leave at eleven we should arrive in plenty of time to get good seats for the performance."

Darcy rolled his eyes but remained silent. Putting his napkin aside and standing, Richard chose his words carefully. "You are still coming to Mother's dinner party tomorrow evening, yes? It should be fairly small— just the family, more or less. I spoke with Georgiana earlier and she seemed eager to attend." He did not repeat what else his youngest cousin had intimated about how little she had seen of her brother in the weeks since his return from Kent.

When Fitzwilliam mumbled his agreement but did not appear to note the implied reproof, the Colonel squared his shoulders and allowed the force of command to trickle into his voice.

"And Darcy— if you continue to ignore your sister as you have recently, I shall be forced to take her to stay with Mother for the indefinite future." Richard was pleased to see Darcy's head jerk up from his coffee. "She is lonely and miserable, and worse, she believes that you are angry and disappointed with her because of the Ramsgate affair. In short, she is worrying herself sick and I will not stand by if you continue to mistreat her."

Satisfied by the stunned look on his cousin's face, Richard moved to the door. Before leaving, he couldn't resist one last dig. "You should introduce Georgie to Miss Elizabeth Bennet. She is just the sort of young lady who could help our girl build up the confidence to face Society." And with that, he ducked out the door and chuckled all the way up to his room.

When the two men met again at the front door, Richard was pleased to see his cousin looking better. Darcy was still very quiet as they traveled to the church but it was a thoughtful silence rather than the melancholy of before. After the service, Darcy declined an invitation to the wedding feast and farewelled his family. Richard helped his mother into the Fitzwilliam carriage and, just climbing up after her, glanced down the street. He was pleased to see his cousin wave off his carriage and begin walking east along Cannon Street.

In truth, Darcy had been struck by the words of the wedding vows as much as those of his cousin.

"I, John, take thee, Cecily, to be my wedded Wife, to have and to hold from this day forward, for better for worse, for richer for poorer, in sickness and in health, to love and to cherish, till death do us part, according to God's holy ordinance."

Only the Christian names were used, emphasizing the union between those two individuals before God. Marriage was meant to bond man and woman in mutual support, through good times and bad, for life; not just for the acquisition of wealth and connections. In considering the words, Will was finally struck by how right Elizabeth had been to reject him. He might love her but he had never demonstrated that he cherished her; he had not even considered her need to be respected as well as adored.

Darcy sent his carriage ahead, telling the driver to meet him in two hours at Wren's monument to the Great Fire. He took a circuitous route that eventually had him walking south along Gracechurch Street. He did not see Elizabeth but he did take note that the neighborhood was perfectly respectable. Although the houses were certainly not as large as his own, they were clean and well-kept, and the neighborhood had a sense of vitality. Children played in a small public park, nurses pushed prams along the walk and a well-dressed young man was expounding his philosophy to a group of listeners in a speaker's corner.

That evening, Darcy made a point of dining with his sister and then joining her in the music room where she exhibited a new piece on the pianoforte. He was still quiet and thoughtful, but Georgiana was somewhat comforted by Richard's reassurances that her brother's behavior did not reflect some error of hers. It was a beginning.

7 DARCY'S REVELATIONS

Two days after his conversation with Richard, Darcy attended a dinner party at the Earl of Matlock's London home. Will's Aunt Eleanor was one of the most revered hostesses in High Society and he was looking forward to an enjoyable evening. On this occasion, five of the six Fitzwilliam offspring would be in attendance and so Darcy arrived early with Georgiana, hoping to spend some pleasant time with their extended family.

Instead, he was treated to several adult siblings bickering like spoilt children, the Earl sitting by the fire with his daughter's father-in-law making sport of their offspring (the two had started drinking before lunch at their club and were already well-sauced), and his normally imperturbable aunt standing in the hall screaming at a maid and the housekeeper like a fishwife.

Later, when the men gathered for port after supper, the Colonel's elder brother asked about their trip to visit the "Kentish witch." For nearly twenty minutes, Ashbourne, Richard, and their father argued over appropriate nicknames for Lady Catherine. The battle-ax was finally voted most popular, although harridan, gorgon and Medusa were close seconds. Darcy stood by the fireplace cringing as three of his closest male kinsmen openly disparaged their relation as entertainment for the other guests.

When the men finally returned to the ladies in the drawing room, Lady Lucy, the youngest of the Fitzwilliam clan, jumped up to greet her favorite brother. "Richard, you will never guess what we've just heard— it's just the funniest thing! You remember Lady Mayberry? The Earl of Malmesbury's eldest daughter? Nasty freckled little thing but with such a dowry and connections she's being sold as the greatest beauty of the season."

Richard chuckled. "Would that be the lady with the... distinctive laugh?"

"Like a horse!" contributed Lady Ellen.

Lucy bounced and clapped her hands in glee. "The very one! Well, Lady

Sackett said that…"

Darcy closed his eyes and sighed, trying to block out the story which appeared to involve the Earl's young daughter drinking too much rum punch at a ball and then loudly demanding that the orchestra play a waltz, while neither of her parents did anything to check her behavior. He sighed again and looked to his sister. Georgiana was sitting next to her Aunt Eleanor, looking as if she wished to hide behind the settee or barring that, at least plug her ears.

It was not very long before Darcy decided that there did not seem to be much hope of his own family providing him with evidence to support his predetermined superiority over the Bennets. Making his way to his sister's side, he asked quietly, "Georgie? Are you ready to return home?" His sister had not the courage to whisper a word but relief left her eyes shiny with unshed tears. After performing his goodbyes and deflecting some off-color remarks by his Cousin Edward (now well in his cups) regarding Darcy's plans for later in the evening, he was vastly relieved to take Georgiana's hand and depart.

As the Darcy siblings walked across the square to their own house, he pondered whether the Fitzwilliams had always been so rowdy or if he had simply never acknowledged it. He was rather relieved to drop this line of introspection when he felt his sister's small, gloved hand squeeze his arm slightly.

"Brother?" asked a whispery voice.

"Yes Georgie? Did you enjoy the evening?" Darcy asked, concerned.

"Oh… yes. It is so… *lively* when all of our cousins are at home. I used to think it was the holiday spirit when we went to Matlock for Christmas and it seemed so much more… jolly … than Pemberley, but it isn't, is it? It's just their natural state when such a big family gets together."

"And loves each other, warts and all," murmured Darcy, half to himself.

Georgiana giggled softly, thinking that he was referring to the discussion of nicknames for their Aunt Catherine.

As the two climbed the front steps of their own house, Will bent and lightly kissed his little sister on her forehead. "Well poppet, what shall it be? Shall we bang the keys in the music room or perhaps go sliding around in our stocking feet in the ball room?"

"Oh Wills, *you* would never do such things. I know you must be tired and have business to attend. Shall you have time to take breakfast with me tomorrow?" Georgiana was handing her coat to the butler and peeked up at her brother for just a moment, but in that moment he was staggered by how eager his sister was for just a few moments of his time.

"Yes, yes, of course. Nine o'clock?"

"Oh thank you, Brother!"

"It would be an honor and a pleasure," he replied solemnly with a deep bow. Then more softly, "Good night, Georgie. Sweet dreams."

"Good night, Wills."

As Georgiana climbed the stairs to her apartment, Darcy watched her for a moment before dismissing the servants for the night and making his way to the library. After pouring himself a glass of wine (he was off brandy since the evening with Richard), Fitzwilliam settled into the large wing chair with his feet stretched out to the fire. He felt off balance.

Looking into his sister's eyes that evening, Will had seen an upwelling of emotion that his own heart easily recognized—loneliness. He took a sip of the wine and considered it. He worked hard to make sure that Georgiana had all the accoutrements appropriate for a young lady of her station. He had conferred with his aunts and female cousins regarding masters and schools, dress makers and dance instructors. But what were those but things?

Who did his sister spend time with? Paid companions and servants? Their cousins were kind to her but even the youngest Fitzwilliam cousin was almost a decade older. He knew Georgiana occasionally had callers for tea but those were almost universally ladies of the Miss Bingley variety who were attempting to capture *his* attention by ingratiating themselves with his sister.

Darcy groaned, took another sip from his glass and toed off his shoes. What friends had he had when he was sixteen? Within two years of his mother's death, he had been sent off to school and his overarching memory was of deep, aching homesickness for Pemberley. But when he thought more carefully, he realized that that was where he had met Bingley and his other close friends. He had joined various clubs—fencing, athletics, chess— and they had given him a sense of tribe. How did young ladies make friends, he wondered. Exchange embroidery secrets?

Darcy sighed again and wiggled his stocking-clad toes in the firelight. If Elizabeth were here, she would have taken up his notion and jollied him and Georgiana to slide around the ballroom in their stockings. He could almost hear her laughter, like the peal of silver bells. A sudden pain wracked his heart and he clenched his jaw. She had *refused* him. She would never meet Georgiana and help his sister learn to laugh again. They would never sit by the fire after an evening out and chat over their impressions of the other guests. He must overcome this!

Yet, when Fitzwilliam Darcy took the last sip from his glass and rested his head back into the cushions, it was but a moment before he was immersed in another dream of Elizabeth. Over the last six months, he had dreamt that he had seduced her, that she had seduced him, that they had danced together, and that they had made love in a distant sunny meadow at Pemberley, but this dream was altogether new.

That night, in his exhaustion and loneliness, he dreamt that Elizabeth welcomed him into the bosom of *her* family. He dreamt that Georgiana sat on the settee in the Longbourn drawing room between Jane and Catherine Bennet, glowing with happiness while Mrs. Bennet bustled around mothering her. He dreamt of himself on the other side of the room, playing chess with Mr. Bennet while debating philosophy and trading witticisms with him and his second daughter. He dreamt of being happy.

The next morning, it was only the deeply ingrained habit of rising with the sun that had Darcy leaving the warm cocoon of his bed in time to dress and meet his sister for breakfast. He found her in the family's breakfast parlor, already drinking her tea. After their greetings, he filled his own plate and cup from the buffet laid out on a sideboard and sat at the small table.

The siblings ate quietly for some minutes, the only sound being the clink of silver on china. Once he had eaten his fill, Darcy refilled his coffee cup and sipped thoughtfully, observing his sister out of the corner of his eye. She had been upset the previous evening and he sensed that the tension remained. After his contemplations the night before, he had resolved to encourage his sister to open up to him; he would try to aid her in making her own resolutions rather than making the decisions for her as was his habit. He could almost imagine Elizabeth's whisper in his ear, encouraging him to treat Miss Darcy as the young lady she was growing into rather than the baby sister he still saw in his mind's eye.

Seeing that Georgiana appeared to be at a loss over how to begin, he again consulted his imaginary Elizabeth. She rolled her eyes, arched a brow, and reminded him to take the trouble of practicing his conversational skills. Taking another sip of his coffee, he thought for a moment and then spoke.

"I don't know if you remember, Georgie, but this breakfast room was the first thing I feel I did on my own after Father's death… For so long I was trying to do what I thought he would have done… to maintain things just as they were. Then one morning, I sat down in the large dining room and was struck by how ridiculous all the formality was for just the two of us."

Georgiana smiled softly. "I remember. The footmen always served me too much porridge but I was afraid Cook would be upset if I didn't finish it all."

Will smiled back. "There were more servants than Darcys in the room. And that was before we installed the dumbwaiter so they were always rushing up and down the back stairs with trays. Although I fear the overabundance of porridge is a rite of passage; I remember Mrs. Reynolds pressing large bowls of it on me as well. Perhaps someday we shall do the same to our own children."

A sad look flickered across Georgiana's face and her eyes dropped to her lap. Unsure of what had affected her, Fitzwilliam forged ahead. "I went looking for a new family breakfast room that very morning. This room was set up as some sort of small parlor but hadn't been used for as long as I can remember, probably because of its place at the back of the house and near the kitchens. It was horribly dark for most of the day and the decoration didn't help much—dark greens and grays and heavy oak furniture. But it looked out over the garden and once we removed the heavy drapery the morning sun lit it up. Do you remember helping me pick the yellow paper for the walls?"

Georgiana smiled faintly at him in response but her brother could tell that her heart wasn't in it. He remained quiet for a moment, hoping that she would speak her mind.

"Brother? I wanted to speak to you... I... Oh Wills, must I have my debut next year?" Her eyes were glassy with tears.

Darcy moved to his sister's side and took her hands in his. "Of course not, dearest; not if it causes you so much anxiety. I would never force you to do something that upsets you so. But Georgie, it is months away. Why are you suddenly so concerned about it now?"

For some moments, Darcy worried that his sister's behavior was a new symptom of continued self-loathing after her experience with Wickham. Thankfully, Georgiana's next words reassured him otherwise.

The Lady Mayberry whom the Fitzwilliams had jeered at on the previous evening had been a school chum of Georgiana's. They were nearly the same age and had shared a love of music and a dislike of French grammar. Together, they had giggled over their dreams of coming out and being presented to the Queen, imagining it would be like a fairy tale with themselves the beautiful, poised princesses, each with a cadre of handsome, charming knights begging to dance the night away with them. Hearing her dear friend dissected and sneered at by her own family, to the amusement of guests no less, left Georgiana in tears and desperate to avoid similar attentions.

Darcy was able to reassure his sister somewhat but he again felt his imaginary Elizabeth nudging him to go further. "Georgie... I know that we tend to focus on the great responsibility that our family and connections demand... maintaining our place in Society and so forth. But it was recently pointed out to me that such things are not what is truly important. Our principles—how we treat others, how we live our lives is what matters, not our attendance at high society events or knowledge of gossip. Our wealth gives us the option to live as we wish."

Darcy paused, rather surprised by his own speech. Georgiana, on the other hand, was fascinated. Her elder brother usually treated her almost as a father; he had never before shared so much of his inner feelings.

"But Wills, you go to so many balls and parties, even though they make you miserable."

Brother and sister shared a fond smile; she had heard him teased by their cousins over his lack of enthusiasm for such social events all too often. Darcy was tempted to shrug off her question, but realized that he owed her (and perhaps himself) a truthful answer.

"My first impulse is to say that I attend because it is what is expected of me—a gentleman of my position. But in truth, I think it is a way for me to escape being alone... which is ironic given that the moment I enter a ball I am determined to disapprove of everyone and everything around me." Darcy sighed, looking into the distance. "It was easier in school... between lectures and discussions and athletics, making friends and having things to talk about was much simpler."

He looked over to Georgiana's wide eyes. "That is why I sent you to school, you know. I was overwhelmed trying to manage Pemberley and I didn't want you to be lonely, but I had absolutely no idea how to introduce you to other girls of your own age."

For the first time in her life, Georgiana saw her brother as a young man, saddled with immense responsibilities at a young age. He tried very, very hard but he was not omniscient. "I may not have seemed happy at school but I am glad I went. I still correspond with many of the girls that I made friends with there. It was the right thing to do."

Darcy considered her for a moment. The only ladies he ever saw visit Georgiana were those of the Miss Bingley variety, attempting to curry favor with him by befriending his sister. "Are any of your friends in London? Do you visit with them?"

The pink in his sister's cheeks led him to believe that her shyness prevented such invitations, but her next words contradicted this conclusion. "I would not... that is... Aunt Catherine..." she trailed off.

"What on Earth does Aunt Catherine have to do with it?" roared Darcy before realizing that such a forceful manner would not help encourage confidences from his timid sister.

"Georgie, dearest, I apologize for my tone." He sighed and tried again. "You must know my opinion of our most revered Aunt's advice." This drew a small smile.

"Aunt Catherine told me that I must not invite any unmarried ladies to the house until you and Cousin Anne were wed, as they might try to compromise you," she summarized weakly.

Darcy slumped back into his chair with such a petulant look that Georgiana couldn't help but giggle. He looked up at her and grinned. "My dear sister, Lady Catherine de Bourgh is our mother's sister and as an elder relation deserves our respect. However..." Will smirked. "She has no sense and even less knowledge of the world. She has isolated herself at Rosings, established total dominion there, and assumes that her power extends all the way to London and Derbyshire. Treat her respectfully but under no circumstances are you to do what she says... unless by some accident she stumbles onto something sensible, of course," he ended in a rush and was happy to see his sister smiling brightly.

"Georgie, this is your home as well as mine, regardless of whether I am single or married. As a single lady, you should have someone with you if you entertain gentlemen callers..." He smiled when Georgiana blushed, pleased that his tease was successful. "But you should feel free to invite female friends to visit at any time... although I would appreciate some warning so that they don't catch me wandering about in my robe and slippers."

The siblings grinned at each other and Georgiana suddenly jumped up and threw her arms around her brother. "Oh Wills, it is so good to really talk to you!" As he hugged his sister, Darcy felt his imaginary Elizabeth smile at him proudly. She was right—it helped to practice.

The moment ended, as such moments do, and Miss Darcy moved back to her own chair after freshening both of their cups. She ventured a look at her brother who was sipping his coffee while staring vacantly out of the window. He had a soft look on his face and she decided to venture a personal question.

"Wills? Are you going to marry Cousin Anne?" she asked softly.

Fitzwilliam had been contemplating a pleasant vision of Elizabeth sitting with them at the sunny breakfast table and was shocked out of his daydream into near incivility. "No! Absolutely not!" Seeing his sister's raised eyebrows, he added more quietly, "Another example of why you should *never* listen to Aunt Catherine."

"Is there someone else?" observing her brother's disoriented look, she added hurriedly, "It is only that... well, Miss Bingley is always speaking of you as though... as if..." She trailed off at her brother's horrified look.

"Good God, no! Again, absolutely not. I would rather remain a bachelor all of my life than have to share it with the likes of Caroline Bingley!" He paused. "Does she actually say such things to you, Georgie?"

"Not exactly. But the ladies who visit me... Well, you *are* their favorite topic of conversation. I'm careful not to gossip, of course, but it's so hard to get them to speak of anything else... other than redecorating Derwent House and Pemberley, of course."

To say that Darcy was embarrassed was an understatement but he soon moved on to sympathy for his sister. "Oh poppet, I'm so sorry." He looked her in the eye. "You do not need to accept such visitors. I know that my friendship with Charles gives Miss Bingley the opportunity to insinuate herself but I will not be offended if you keep her at arm's length... and nor would Charles, for that matter."

Seeing the relief on his sister's face, he added, "You should invite your own friends to visit; young ladies who share your interests. You are an intelligent, sensible girl and you should not be restricted to spending time with the worst that the ton has to offer." He was just thinking of how much he would have liked to encourage a friendship between Georgiana and the two eldest Bennet sisters when he realized that her smile had melted into tears.

"But Wills... I don't! I *don't* have any sense about people at all! I was completely misled by Mrs. Younge and Mr. Wickham. If you had not come to Ramsgate in time..."

Darcy felt the familiar flash of anger toward Wickham but this time it was tempered by the certain knowledge that he needed to comfort his sister rather than wallow in his own hurt pride. He moved to kneel by her chair and took her hands in his own.

"Georgie, listen to me. You were the victim of two experienced fraudsters. You were assured by me that you could trust your companion and *I* failed in *my* duty there. I should have checked Mrs. Younge's background more carefully. She had excellent references but I found out later that they were acquired through blackmail and other nefarious schemes. And Wickham..." Darcy rocked back on his heels and ran a hand through his hair.

"He and I... we played together as boys but even then I suppose I was aware of his lack of morals. He was always spying or plotting, and he felt no guilt if the blame fell on someone else." Fitzwilliam felt his throat tighten but forced himself to continue.

"I remember once when I was eight and he was ten, George boasted to me about sneaking into the home orchard to pick some early cherries. He nearly got caught but somehow managed to shift blame onto one of the tenant's sons." He drew a breath. "Wickham found it amusing that the boy received a whipping for thievery that he did not commit."

"Oh Wills... how horrible! What did you do?"

"I went to Father. I fear he did not put much credence in the story of an eight-year-old."

"Oh Wills..."

Darcy shrugged. "George's manners around our father were always very engaging. He was always careful to maintain his high opinion." Will glanced to his sister. "Do you remember Mrs. Wickham at all? I sometimes think that she coached her son from his earliest days to insinuate himself with Father; pushing 'dear Mr. Darcy' to do this or that for his godson... Well, regardless, George could not hide his want of principles from another boy with whom he spent so much unguarded time. By the time we were at university, he stopped bothering with even the pretence of hiding his immoral tendencies from me."

Darcy hesitated again but glancing up at his sister, he reminded himself that her best protection might lie in knowing the truth. "He drank and gambled... ignored his studies whenever he could charm his tutor or another student into doing his work. He... he frequented brothels... and he would boast of seducing other men's wives."

Hearing his sister's sharp intake of breath, he looked up at her widened eyes. "Ignorant as you previously were of everything, detection could not be in your power, and suspicion certainly not in your inclination. I wish I could protect you from knowing such things, Georgie, but... well, I've learned recently how important knowing the truth is for a woman to protect herself. Just because Father wouldn't listen to me, doesn't mean that no one else will."

Her brother sighed and stared into the distance while Georgiana considered his words. "Wills? Have you seen Mr. Wickham since Ramsgate? I wonder where he is, sometimes. I... I quite dread that I might meet him on the street some day..."

"Georgiana—if you ever see that bastard again, you are to tell me *immediately*. Or Richard. Wickham knows that he is never to come near you again; if he does, we will take care of him once and for all."

"But Brother, I don't want to lose you or Richard to a duel... or to prison for murder!"

Seeing how distraught his sister had become, Darcy took a deep breath and settled himself back in his chair. He needed to reassure her, he reminded himself, not rant like some irresponsible youth ready to fling himself into battle.

He purposefully lightened his tone. "It would not come to that, my dear. You see, George has done something very stupid— he has entered the Hertfordshire militia as a lieutenant. He is currently stationed in Meryton under the command of one Colonel Forster, a gentleman who happens to be well-known to our own Colonel Fitzwilliam."

Pleased to see his sister relax a bit and even smile slightly, Darcy continued, "*Lieutenant* Wickham is now subject to military regulations and punishments and, as you know, Richard is in a position to make certain that they are enforced."

Georgiana clapped her hands together in a mixture of pleasure and relief. "So he can never do this to any other girl?" She was surprised to see her brother's face fall. "Wills? Has he hurt someone already? Is it anyone I know?"

"I don't believe that he managed a seduction... she is too intelligent and proper to fall for that... but he certainly managed to turn her head... and whisper enough lies in her ear that she quite despised me..." This last was said quietly, almost to himself as his memory spun him back to that fateful evening at the Hunsford parsonage.

"Wills?" His sister's curious voice brought him back to the present. He hesitated for a moment and then decided that, just as he knew all the details of her failed romance, perhaps it would help her to know of his own recent heartbreak.

He stared into his empty teacup for a moment. "Last autumn, while you were staying with our aunt and uncle at Matlock, you know that I spent some time in the country with Bingley, helping him learn to run the estate he has leased."

"It was in Hertfordshire!" exclaimed his sister with growing concern. "Is that how you found out that Mr. Wickham was in the militia?"

"Yes, although he was careful to avoid me once he realized I was in the neighborhood. He had no compunction about spreading rumors behind my back, though." Darcy was quiet for a moment, gathering his thoughts, until he noticed his sister's ashen face.

"No! Not about you, dearest… He said nothing about you. You must understand—his resentment, his desire for revenge, it is all focused on me. He worked very hard to maintain Father's high opinion but that was all made useless upon his death because I was the heir and George could not fool me. Wickham resents my birthright and looks for any way to take his revenge. At Ramsgate, his chief object was unquestionably your fortune but I cannot help supposing that the hope of revenging himself on me was a strong inducement."

Georgiana relaxed somewhat over his words, but remained concerned. "But Wills… what lies did he spread? And why would anyone believe them of you?"

Darcy sighed. Would his sister's good opinion of him survive the story of his so-called courtship of Miss Elizabeth Bennet? "That, my dear, is quite a long story which I will tell you if you truly wish to hear it. However, may I suggest that we move to the library so that the servants may begin clearing the breakfast dishes?" Upon gaining his sister's agreement, he offered his arm and the two Darcys walked quietly through the halls of their big, empty house, feeling for once that it was a little less lonely.

As they settled into the comfortable chairs on either side of the fireplace, Darcy was wondering where to begin and how much to tell when Georgiana spoke up. "Was it Miss Bennet?" Seeing the look of shock on her brother's face, she gathered her courage to continue. "You spoke of Miss Elizabeth Bennet several times in your letters from Hertfordshire and then from Kent, yet you haven't mentioned her once since you returned from Rosings. Was she the lady who believed Wickham's lies?"

To say that Darcy was surprised was an understatement. Thinking that Richard might have been talking out of turn, he queried. "How do you know about Miss Bennet?"

Georgiana stifled a giggle. Her Aunt Eleanor was right—sometimes men were completely obtuse. Her brother truly had no idea how often he spoke of the lady. "From your letters, Wills. And you mentioned her a few times over Christmas." Seeing that her brother still looked perplexed, she explained further. "Usually when you mention ladies it is in such an ironic tone that I can almost see them fussing over you."

She mimicked his deep voice. "Miss Bingley bids me send her greetings, as she cannot be bothered to write herself, and hopes to exchange table designs or some such nonsense when next she hunts you to ground in London."

Darcy could not help but be amused at how well his sister mimicked him and waved his hands in mock defeat.

Encouraged, Georgiana continued, "With Miss Bennet, it was different. You spoke of her preference for Milton over cards and how it shocked Mr. Hurst. And of how she loves to walk in the mornings and appreciates nature... and how she beat Mr. Bingley at chess!" Seeing a soft smile grow on her brother's face at this recitation of memories, Georgiana decided to take a chance. "Might I meet her? She sounds wonderful." She started at the flash of pain that ripped across her brother's face. "Oh Wills, what have I said? I am so sorry! What has hurt you so?"

Darcy looked down into his sister's dear face where she had come to kneel at his feet. Her eyes, so like their mother's, were full of concern and compassion. He squeezed her hands in reassurance. "Miss Elizabeth is all that is lovely... and kind... and I don't know that either of us will ever have the opportunity of meeting her again."

He sighed deeply. "Georgie, you might as well know that your big brother is an arrogant dunderhead."

Seeing that her brother had recovered somewhat, Georgiana stood and, mimicking the stance and tone so often taken by their cousin the Colonel, responded with far more spirit than she had lately displayed; "I shall be the judge of that, sir! The facts, if you please... leaving nothing out or there will be a cross-examination!" She then sat down in a comfortable armchair opposite her brother and, toeing off her slippers, tucked her feet up under her skirts.

Unable to do anything but laugh, Darcy gave her a mock salute and began his side of the story.

8 HIS SIDE OF THE STORY

Fitzwilliam Darcy had never been much of a lady's man by any stretch of the imagination. As a child, he had adored his mother before her death and still thought of her with a wistful longing. He had felt an intense, protective love for his sister since she had been placed in his arms as a newborn on his tenth birthday. Growing up, he had spent some time with his Fitzwilliam cousins, but more often he spent long, solitary hours exploring Pemberley's woods and peaks, often pretending that he was one of those great explorers he read about, discovering new continents or scaling the impossibly high mountains of India.

His time at Eton and later Cambridge had been spent almost entirely in masculine company. He had divided his time between his studies, his bookish, intellectual friends debating philosophy and playing chess, and athletic compatriots serious in their training for various sport.

Darcy knew that most young men spent time during their university years practicing other sports with the local ladies but he had steadfastly avoided such outings. In hindsight, he recognized that this was due in no small part to his disgust with the antics of which George Wickham boasted when that man returned to their shared rooms in the wee small hours of the mornings, in addition to the near constant teasing by his boyhood playmate over what he considered Darcy's prudery.

In the privacy of his own mind, Fitzwilliam knew that he had been tempted like any other man but his childhood in the idyllic wilds of Derbyshire left him with a greater desire to mimic Malory's King Arthur than Radcliffe's Signor Montoni. The fundamental problem was that such a youth had left him singularly inept at understanding women.

He was a fine dancer—it was much like the intricate footwork of fencing—but he was uncomfortable making conversation with strangers, not to mention the feeling of being on display. This had become worse after his father passed away and he inherited sole control of the Darcy family's vast wealth, properties and connections. He knew the rules of propriety—what constituted "too much" interest in a lady, how to avoid being tricked into a compromising situation, and so forth. Unlike many gentlemen he knew who regarded it as a great game, Darcy was left with a fundamental distrust of people in general and Society ladies in particular.

Darcy's years of schooling had not prepared him to converse easily with strange females. He could not catch their tone of conversation or appear interested in their concerns as he saw other men do. He could debate Socrates and Voltaire with Oxford dons, discuss the economic implications of the war with members of Parliament, and talk about sheep breeding with a tenant farmer, but he had not a clue as to how (or why) to appear interested in the newest fashion of sleeves or the latest lace pattern from Belgium. He despised gossip of all types and, perhaps worst of all, the subtle flick of fans and eyelashes that ladies used to convey their interest was as obscure a language as Mandarin to him.

In short, the advance of a flirtatious lady created in Fitzwilliam the desperate urge to flee. However, the knowledge that a gentleman (and particularly a Darcy) must not run from a drawing room like a frightened fawn when faced with an approaching matron and her unmarried daughter was deeply ingrained and so Darcy had developed a mask, locking himself in place and speaking as little as possible until he might politely excuse himself.

It was not until Miss Elizabeth Bennet had admonished him in her delightfully arch manner that it occurred to Darcy that by participating in a conversation and introducing topics *he* found interesting, such interactions with strangers might be tolerable and possibly even enjoyable. He might even discover new people with whom he wished to further an acquaintance!

Elizabeth. He remembered the first time he had really seen her. Upon stepping into the small, stuffy public assembly hall at Meryton, he had immediately stiffened as a sea of strangers turned to study him. In truth, he had spent the first half hour fighting his every instinct to sprint from the country inn's great room as greedy eyes followed him around the room and he caught whispers of his name and estimates of his wealth from behind fans. He vaguely remembered being introduced to some of the locals but although his habitual manners had him bow and nod at the appropriate moments, he recalled neither face nor name.

Eventually, Darcy was able to retreat to a corner and hide behind a trio of half-drunk, elderly gentlemen who were deep in a discussion of horse breeding and paid him no attention. Fitzwilliam took several deep breaths, discretely wiped his sweaty palms on his coat and rolled his shoulders in an attempt to release some of the tension that locked his neck. He was a Darcy, he berated himself, and a Darcy had no reason to fear a roomful of strangers. "*Countrified rustics! Not a one with any connections!*" Even the Bingleys and Hursts were far below him in Society, for all of Miss Bingley's pretensions.

Darcy's thoughts continued in this vein for some minutes, reassuring himself of his own superiority in order to break through his overwhelming self-consciousness. As his emotions settled, he began to notice faces and individuals. The ladies of his own party swept by, Mrs. Hurst dancing with her husband and Miss Bingley with one of the local gentlemen—a Mr. Goulding, Darcy remembered. Both wore an overabundance of jewels, lace, and feathers in an obvious attempt to assert their superiority over the local populace. Bingley appeared as the dancers moved through their forms. Will smirked to himself—Charles had, as always, immediately attached himself to the prettiest girl in the room.

The dance ended and Bingley led his partner to a younger girl sitting along the wall not far from Darcy's corner. The ladies' interaction suggested that they were close relatives but the two could not have been more different in appearance. Where Bingley's partner was a classic beauty with her symmetrical figure and serene visage, the younger girl appeared sullen, spotted, and slumped over what Darcy supposed was a pocket novel, removing her spectacles only when addressed directly.

At that moment, the horse-obsessed gentlemen screening Darcy moved away and Bingley's face brightened at the sight of his friend. Without hesitation, Charles and his enthusiasm invaded Darcy's quiet corner. "Come Darcy," said he, "I must have you dance. I hate to see you standing about by yourself in this stupid manner. You had much better dance."

Darcy very nearly groaned aloud. He had only just barely regained his equilibrium. Partnering some unknown female with whom he had nothing in common could only constitute the worst of tortures. "I certainly shall not. You know how I detest it, unless I am particularly acquainted with my partner. At such an assembly as this, it would be insupportable. Your sisters are engaged at present, and there is not another woman in the room whom it would not be a punishment to me to stand up with." To himself, he added, "*There! If that won't make Charles back off, nothing will.*"

"I would not be so fastidious as you are," cried Bingley, "for a kingdom! Upon my honor I never met with so many pleasant girls in my life, as I have this evening; and several of them, you see, uncommonly pretty." His eyes drifted back to the blonde he had last partnered.

Darcy allowed himself a smile. It was good to see Charles happy again. The death of his parents and elder brother in a carriage accident two years prior had deposited a heavy load of unexpected responsibility on his friend's shoulders.

"You are dancing with the only handsome girl in the room," said Mr. Darcy, looking at the eldest Miss Bennet.

"Oh! She is the most beautiful creature I ever beheld! But there is one of her sisters sitting down just behind you, who is very pretty, and I dare say very agreeable. Do let me ask my partner to introduce you."

Without bothering to look, Darcy assumed that Bingley was indicating the unappealing creature seated by Miss Bennet, which fired a spark of indignation within his ego. He might not wish to dance, but he was distinctly irked that Bingley would push him toward such an unattractive girl when the younger man was dancing with such a beauty.

Darcy replied coldly, "She is tolerable, but not handsome enough to tempt me; and I am in no humor at present to give consequence to young ladies who are slighted by other men. You had much better return to your partner and enjoy her smiles, for you are wasting your time with me."

Recognizing that his old friend's foul mood was unlikely to be worked around, Mr. Bingley was forced to follow the advice and turned to greet a local squire and his wife. Darcy was afforded but a minute to fume over the perceived insult to himself before the rustle of skirts alerted him to a presence moving in from the balcony just beyond his corner. Then all thought was driven from his mind as a pair of sparkling eyes laughed up at him from beneath long, dark lashes. Darcy was left breathing in the faint scent of lavender and gazing at dark chestnut curls bouncing above a slender neck and an elegantly simple rose-colored gown, accenting fair skin and an appealing figure. Will swallowed and very nearly followed in her wake like a puppy.

Locking his feet in place, Darcy could not stop his eyes following the lady as she moved through the room. She greeted a plain-faced young woman—one of the Lucas offspring, he remembered vaguely—with the familiarity of an old friend, and the pair was soon joined by Bingley's partner. With twinkling eyes and expressive hands, she pantomimed a story at the end of which, three pairs of female eyes turned to stare directly at Darcy, making little effort to hide their giggles. In an instant of mortifying clarity, he realized that this intriguing beauty was the sister Bingley had recommended to him as a dance partner, and that she had heard every word of his insufferably rude refusal.

Darcy had once had the opportunity to stand upon a stage where university friends were rehearsing a student production of Hamlet. He had been shown the clever trapdoor in the stage floor that allowed one of the actors to seemingly disappear into thin air during the production. Now, in this moment of personal ignominy at a country assembly in Hertfordshire, he wondered inconsequently why ballroom floors were not equipped similarly with escape hatches for gentlemen who needed a bit of privacy in which to remove foot from mouth. What irony was it that he had finally noticed a lady whose features and manner attracted him, but whom he had managed to insult in such a way as to make him appear worse than ridiculous?

He had thought things could not possibly get worse when a set of talons raked his back before settling around his arm like a pair of iron shackles. "Oh, Mr. Darcy. What was my brother thinking to drag us to this dreadful backwater? I am quite certain that we shall all catch some horrible disease." Somehow, Miss Caroline Bingley's voice managed to carry an irritating shrillness even at a whisper.

When the object of her attentions did not respond, Caroline felt this was reasonable encouragement to continue. "I have never seen anything so ridiculous; all these countrified rustics prancing about as if they belonged to the first circles of Society. And the fashion! I have seen sleeves two years out of date, at least."

It was only with the greatest effort that Darcy managed to control a noise that combined snort and sneeze, the latter prompted by the once towering feathers that now drooped from his unwanted companion's turban and tickled his nose. He desperately hoped that they were dyed for it did not bear considering that such a violent hue of orange might exist in nature.

"And I cannot imagine what other so-called amusements these people shall force upon us. Perhaps a costume party for their swine?"

This time Darcy could not control the slight twitch of his lips, though not for a reason that would have pleased Miss Bingley. Once when he was about twelve, he had visited his Uncle James, an odd character to be sure, but always great fun. After securing an earnest promise that Will would never tell his father, Uncle James had spirited him off to a country fair on the outskirts of London where one of the events had indeed been a porcine costume contest. There had been ballerina pigs, bird pigs (complete with wings), court jester pigs, and Fitzwilliam's personal favorite, a particularly large Chester White transformed into a fire-breathing dragon.

"What I would give to hear your strictures on them!" Caroline finally paused long enough to take a breath, causing Darcy to remember his position. Luckily for him, though he might not know how to deal with pretty country misses with sparkling eyes who laughed at him (*laughed at him!*), he was well practiced at dealing with the likes of Miss Bingley.

"Miss Bingley, you appear upset. Allow me to fetch you some punch." With the ease of long practice, he turned toward Miss Bingley so that she was forced to break her clench on his arm and he could move to the refreshment table. There, he proceeded to receive a cup with punch and direct a few biscuits be placed on a plate. Handing both to Miss Bingley (it was critical to fill both of her hands so that she could not resume her possessive grip of his arm), he motioned toward Mrs. Hurst who had just finished a dance.

"I am sure that you will wish to speak with your sister. If you will excuse me, there is something to which I must see." And with that, Darcy made his escape. Unfortunately, his pleasure over a successful disentanglement was punctured when he noticed that he was being laughed at again.

Miss Elizabeth Bennet, currently known to Darcy only as the pretty country miss with sparkling eyes who laughed at him (!!!), had noticed the one-sided conversation. While she harbored no friendly feelings toward the gentleman, she could certainly recognize an aggressive husband-hunter and a most unhappy target. While Miss Bennet continued her dance with a pleasant but dull partner, she considered how best to tell her father of the amusing portrait formed by Mr. Darcy and Miss Bingley. Meanwhile, Mr. Darcy very nearly groaned aloud before turning desperate eyes around the room for a safe potted plant behind which he might hide for the remainder of the evening.

Months later, Fitzwilliam found that his melancholy was lightened immeasurably by telling the story to Georgiana. Even when she laughed, the soft look in her eye soothed some of his pain. To his surprise, he found himself telling her of his failed marriage proposal to Miss Elizabeth Bennet as well. When he finished, his sister moved to sit beside him, head on his shoulder and arms around his chest.

"Oh, Wills. I am so very sorry. You have been hurting so."

"She was right to refuse me, Georgie. I loved her but gave no thought to respect. If a man ever proposed to you in such a way, I'd toss him out on his ear."

Georgie giggled. "We are a sorry pair, are we not? But her opinion of you must be improved by your explanation, don't you think?"

Fitzwilliam sighed. "Perhaps. But the way I forced my letter upon her… it was just one more act proving me less than a gentleman."

Georgiana leaned away and crossed her arms seriously. "Fitzwilliam Darcy. If *you* are not a gentleman then I do not know what the term means. You are caring and honorable." She smirked. "If a bit awkward in expressing yourself to strange ladies."

Darcy couldn't help but chuckle. "Well, Miss Elizabeth did tell me that I must practice more in order to become proficient."

The clock tolled the hour and they realized that it was nearly time for luncheon. After dining together amiably, the siblings parted ways. Georgiana spent the afternoon practicing a new piece on the harp and Darcy went to his study. It took him some hours, but by the time the dinner bell was rung, he had sorted through all the papers and ledgers he had been muddling over for the past month and sent them along to his secretary and stewards as he should have done weeks before.

After a pleasant dinner and some quiet conversation, the Darcys retired for the night after agreeing on a time to meet the next morning for breakfast before attending services. Georgiana was obviously pleased when her brother suggested that the pair spend Sunday afternoon together taking a walk in Hyde Park. That night, Will slept better than he had in months and woke eager to face the new day.

9 A WELCOME INTERUPTION

Although spring was usually her favorite season, Elizabeth found that her spirits remained low that year, even after her father read Mr. Darcy's letter and made some changes in how he interacted with his family. When Mr. Bennet informed Lydia that she would not be going to Brighton, the youngest Miss Bennet threw a tantrum that lasted for weeks. She guessed correctly that Lizzy had something to do with their father's change of mind and directed at her all the vitriol that a spoiled child could muster.

Exceptionally cold, rainy weather kept Elizabeth housebound for days on end. At Longbourn, there was the inescapable cacophony of Lydia's complaints (echoed by Kitty), Mary's pedantic playing at all hours, and Mrs. Bennet's continued moaning over the dismal expectations of her five unmarried daughters. She continued to blame Lizzy for rejecting Mr. Collins, fret over Mr. Bingley's disappearance, and gossip with her sister Mrs. Phillips about everything under the sun.

There seemed a greater distance between Lizzy and her father, as though Mr. Bennet's confidences had made him slightly uncomfortable around her. She was pleased to notice that he was gentler toward her mother and younger sisters. Although his sarcasm could never be wholly discarded, he attempted to direct it at people or events outside their family circle more often than before. In general he seemed to spend a great deal more time watching them, as if trying to understand these people with whom he had lived for years but only just noticed.

Elizabeth was most saddened by the turn her relationship with Jane had taken. Immediately after returning from London, they had discussed Mr. Darcy's proposal and the revelations over Mr. Wickham, agreeing that the information should not be shared beyond their father. Jane had spoken little of Miss Bingley, saying only that she had given Lizzy all the details of their encounters in her letters. Of Mr. Bingley, she spoke not at all. To anyone less familiar than Elizabeth, Jane might have seemed unconcerned but her heartbreak was palpable to her closest sister.

While Elizabeth craved a confidant with whom to vent, Jane turned inward. She went through the normal motions of her life but her gentle smiles never turned into real laughter as in times past. When Elizabeth attempted to tease her into displaying her true feelings, Jane would simply wave her off, saying only "I am perfectly well, Lizzy," and leave to attend to some household duty.

Some of Elizabeth's despondency was due to the weight of the many secrets she was charged with keeping. She was relieved when the militia left for Brighton but Lydia and Kitty spoke of the officers so often that she was constantly reminded of her own mistakes and the truth revealed by Mr. Darcy's letter. She told no one except her father of what she knew about Mr. Bingley's absence and that weighed on her every time Mrs. Bennet wailed over the loss of Netherfield's master or she caught a glimpse of melancholy in Jane's eyes. And then there were her father's confidences that she could share with no one.

Elizabeth wished for a confidante and it amused her to no end that the one person with whom she could see herself trusting with it all and understanding her feelings was Mr. Darcy. She had not come to regret her refusal; his offer had been worded in such a way that she could not have been assured of his respect. However, the longer that she thought upon their unconventional acquaintance, the more she recognized that they had shared a unique honesty in their interactions that was rare between ladies and gentlemen in polite society.

Elizabeth often wondered what might have happened, had he been less proud of his wealth and connections and she been less prejudiced by his rude words at the Meryton Assembly. She found herself having imaginary conversations with him, peppered with phrases that she remembered from their various exchanges. As she gradually lost her habitual irritation at the very thought of the man, other more pleasant memories began to surface.

Mr. Darcy had not been intimidated by her intellectual bent; indeed, if she now understood his words at Netherfield correctly, he had openly praised her extensive reading habits. The memory of Miss Bingley yawning over a volume with little interest other than the desire to gain a certain gentleman's attention made Lizzy smirk even now, months later. Although she still squirmed with discomfort over *her* words to *him* during their dance at the Netherfield ball, his suggestion that they converse about books now made her smile softly.

Even if Mrs. Bennet did not regularly remind her, Elizabeth had long learned to conceal her quick mind and broad education from their general acquaintance. Gentlemen, in particular, did not appreciate being corrected by some slip of a girl. One evening when she was but fifteen, she had been driven to a fury close to tears after she had contributed to the gentlemen's conversation over why the French commoners had rallied to Napoleon. Her comment had been brushed aside by Mr. Lucas (soon to become Sir William).

Young Evan Goulding, of an age with her but unable to locate Paris on a map, had laughed aloud at her. "Don't be silly, Miss Lizzy! Everyone knows that ladies can't understand matters of politics or the military!"

It was probably fortunate that dinner was announced before Elizabeth could respond. She found herself beside the ever-serene Jane and managed to absorb some of her elder sister's composure for the remainder of the evening. Later she had poured out her woes to her father but he had had no good solution for her. "You have a good mind, Lizzy. Don't let the opinions of those dolts impede your pursuit of knowledge. A well-stocked mind shall always be a good companion, even when you are surrounded by fools." Then he had given her a copy of Mary Wollstonecraft's treatise on the education of women and retreated to the well-worn caverns of his own well-stocked mind.

Now, in these days of self-study, Elizabeth took out that book and read it again, although with somewhat different feelings. At fifteen, she had been struck by all the inequalities of the world and had instantly resolved to become a bluestocking. The phase had not lasted long for as much as Lizzy enjoyed learning about that which interested her, she was not given to constant study and Longbourn's bustle was certainly not supportive of such.

Now enlightened by her father's revelations, Elizabeth found her memories colored in a new light. In truth, she had always felt somewhat ashamed by her lack of focused study. Certainly she was the best-educated among the ladies of her acquaintance, but she had never had any desire to closet herself away for days on end studying the minutia of a single essay as she saw her father do. Now, having heard her father's description of how Mrs. Bennet had brought a certain liveliness into the house upon their marriage, Elizabeth began to realize that she had inherited aspects of her mother in addition to her father, and that that was not a wholly bad thing.

Rather than seeing her own ease and enjoyment of society as a fault, she began to allow herself the freedom to be herself rather than a poor replica of her studious, cynical father. Indeed, she realized that, although she had always belittled her own lack of accomplishments, she had never really had the desire to alter her true self, perhaps knowing unconsciously that she had inherited too much of her mother's warmth and energy to ever fully take on her father's misanthropic demeanor.

Through all of this introspection, Elizabeth cheered herself with the thought that her upcoming trip to the Lake District with the Gardiners would soon provide a pleasant distraction. However, on the first day of

May, Elizabeth received a letter from her aunt indicating that their trip to the northern counties would be delayed and abbreviated. Her disappointed mood was raised slightly by the letter's hint that, although the public explanation to be given out was her uncle's business, the reality was a temporary illness of her aunt that they hoped signaled a new addition to the Gardiner family.

Mr. Bennet needed to consult with his brother-in-law on a business matter that could not be delayed, so it was arranged that Elizabeth and her father would travel to London. When he returned to Hertfordshire, she would remain with the Gardiners for several weeks to assist while her aunt was indisposed. Although Lizzy might prefer the country, she looked forward to whatever entertainments they might partake of in town while being of use to her favorite relatives.

The change of scenery improved Elizabeth's mood a great deal. She was adored by her young cousins for her stories, games, and fearless nature when they went to explore the parks. Although her Aunt Madeleine's sickness often kept that lady bedridden in the mornings, she spent her afternoons and evenings with as much energy as ever. One afternoon, after seeing Lizzy return from the park with her skirts six inches deep in mud and children's dirty hand prints scattered about the rest of the fabric, Mrs. Gardiner insisted on taking her niece on a shopping expedition.

"It is the least I can do after my own children ruined your dress!" Mrs. Gardiner exclaimed. "Truly Lizzy, I am well aware of how quickly a lady's clothes wear out with four little ones; half get stained and the others are ripped or stretched beyond imagining!" Seeing that her niece was not yet convinced, she tried a different tactic. "Oh, come now, Elizabeth. You must allow me the pleasure of shopping with a young lady; Edward is no fun at all!"

"Why do I feel my ears burning?" came a deep voice from the doorway. The ladies dissolved into giggles while Mr. Gardiner moved to settle himself by his wife. When she had explained the situation, he turned to his niece.

"Yes, you should certainly have some new dresses. Anything to save me from spending hours at the milliner, never knowing whether I am supposed to respond that I like or dislike a pattern!" They all chuckled at this, knowing that Madeleine Gardiner was far more efficient in her shopping than most ladies.

"But seriously, Lizzy— you must have a new evening gown for the Carlisles' ball next week; it is going to be quite the event and your aunt is having one made up especially as well."

Madeleine added, "And a new morning dress, as well, to replace the one my little hoodlums destroyed when you took them out to the park to fly their kites."

She chose to ignore the furtive looks between her husband and niece and the pleased grin that flashed across that gentleman's face when Lizzy whispered, "They flew! Even Amelia's!"

Clearing her voice in mock disapproval, Mrs. Gardiner's eyes twinkled. "Perhaps we can work out a trade. You shall have a new gown, but in return you must fashion a dress for Rebecca's dolly from the remains of your kite-flying dress. She has been twitting Jonathan constantly for tripping you into that mud puddle and announced to me that when she is grown up, she shall never wear any other color—your blue sprigged muslin is simply the most beautiful fabric in the world."

Laughing at her aunt's overly dramatic testimonial, Elizabeth agreed and it was decided that they would venture out to the shops the very next day.

The Gardiners were well known among the London intelligentsia and evenings were often spent at poetry readings or scientific demonstrations. Their dinner guests ran the gamut from politicians to artists, a countess determined to improve hospital conditions and university dons fond of intelligent conversation. In short, life at the Gardiners' was never dull and fed Lizzy's mind in a way that she had not even recognized she was missing.

Elizabeth's moments of melancholy came primarily from her sister's letters. Jane wrote of happenings in the village and the estate, but there was little of herself in her notes and Lizzy knew it was because of her sister's continuing despondency over Mr. Bingley. However, her guilt did not let her refuse the Gardiners' invitations and they kept her busy in a swirl of doings and seeings. The plethora of entertainments was in part purposeful; Mr. Bennet had spoken to his brother and sister and, without giving many specifics, let them know that Lizzy suffered from an argument with an admirer.

Deciding that her niece needed to be exposed to a broader circle than the four and twenty families with whom the Bennets usually socialized, Mrs. Gardiner had even accepted an invitation to a grand ball that was being hosted by an old family friend to celebrate the debut of an earl's niece. The ball was certain to be well-attended and the Gardiners were determined that Lizzy would be admired.

Although Elizabeth was not prone to the love of shopping often attributed to elegant females, she freely admitted to having a most excellent day with her aunt. That lady was in her mid-thirties and her vitality made it easy for Lizzy to consider her as a friend rather than an elder relation of her mother's generation. After visiting Mrs. Gardiner's modiste and choosing styles and fabrics, they adjourned to a popular chocolate house for a bit of refreshment.

"I cannot wait to see you in that rose silk that you chose for your ball gown, Lizzy. It truly makes your skin glow."

"Thank you, Aunt." Elizabeth pulled a small swatch of the fabric from her reticule and rubbed it between finger and thumb fondly. "At the risk of sounding vain, I will admit that I am looking forward to it as well."

"There is nothing wrong in taking enjoyment from looking our best. I dare say that the world is a much prettier place with ladies wearing silks than it would be if we all appeared in sackcloth. And I should know, as my own husband's warehouse is filled with a rainbow of those fine fabrics!"

After some laughter, Elizabeth fingered the silk in her hand and said wistfully, "I was only thinking on how beautiful Jane would look in this. I feel rather ashamed to have something so exquisite made up just for me. I am just enough taller and thinner than Jane that we can remake her dresses to fit me, but with the bust already taken in, I shall never see her wear it."

Mrs. Gardiner considered the younger woman for a minute. Although Madeleine had been the eldest child in her own family, the deaths of her parents and siblings had left her dependent on the charity of relatives when she was barely eighteen. Her cousins had all been very kind and embraced her like a sister, but Madeleine had an inkling of what the second Bennet daughter was feeling.

"Elizabeth. You are a beautiful young lady; just as lovely as Jane."

Her niece was already shaking her head. "Aunt..."

"No, Lizzy. Listen to me for a moment. Your mother does you a disservice, always praising Jane's beauty and dismissing your own."

Slightly pink with embarrassment, Elizabeth protested, "Aunt, this is really not necessary. I am well aware of my looks."

"No, Lizzy— you are not; that is just what I am trying to tell you. You must know that your mother was a truly beautiful woman when she was young. I can only guess that she favors Jane because your sister looks so much like Fanny did at that age. Although their personalities could not be more different," added Madeleine wryly.

Elizabeth did not bother to stifle her giggle. It was good to spend time with a sensible relative.

Mrs. Gardiner tried again. "Jane is all that is sweet and serene. However, the point I am trying to make is that you undervalue yourself. You know that you are intelligent and well-educated, thanks to your father, but you have also grown into a beautiful young lady. I want you to remember that when you walk into the Carlisles' ball. Do not dismiss your own attractions, Lizzy; not every gentleman desires a sweet and serene wife!"

Elizabeth smiled weakly; her aunt's words reminded her forcibly of Mr. Darcy's preference among the Bennet sisters. Seeing that Mrs. Gardiner was about to speak again, Lizzy was quick to interject. "Thank you, Aunt. I understand what you are trying to tell me and I promise to consider it carefully."

The two women regarded each other fondly. Finishing her hot chocolate, Mrs. Gardiner straightened her cup and folded her napkin. "Well, shall we take a last look for ribbons and slippers to match our new gowns before we go home?"

Several hours later, the two ladies returned to Gracechurch Street, tired but well-pleased. Mr. Gardiner was given to understand that their expedition had been successful and his purse not *too* greatly damaged. After some teasing that he would have to visit his own tailor if he was to escort two such lovely ladies to a ball, conversation drifted to other topics. A noted poet and his wife were expected for dinner, so Elizabeth excused herself early to dress. In her room, she reviewed several of the author's published works, hoping that she would not embarrass herself in conversation.

She need not have worried. While the poet was shy and serious, his wife was merry and pleasing. Side by side, the couple was an inspiring example of a relationship based on mutual affection and respect, in which differences in temperament complimented rather than grated.

After farewelling the guests, Lizzy climbed the stairs to her room but paused at the landing to peek out the window. Parting the curtains so that she might look up at the moon in the clear night sky, a movement below caught her eye. Leaning slightly to the left, she saw the poet and his wife walking down the sidewalk. For just a moment, they paused before the gentleman made a deep bow to his wife and the lady curtsied. When she was spun around in an impromptu waltz on the quiet street, the lady tipped her head back and laughed with pure joy and abandon.

Feeling as if she had intruded on a most intimate moment, Elizabeth allowed the curtains to fall and skipped up the stairs to her room. She was blushing slightly and did not care to share the reason, even with her dearest aunt and uncle. Without bothering to call the maid, she quickly changed into a nightgown and brushed out her long hair, binding it into a braid even as her mind was far away.

When Elizabeth had finally blown out the candles and curled up under the blankets, she gave herself over to the deep feelings that the impromptu dancers had stirred within her. Why should it affect her so? She knew any number of people who might act in such a way; she could easily imagine Mr. Lucas or young Mr. Goulding engaging one of her sisters so. Well, perhaps not Mary unless the middle Bennet sister had been truly struck by an affection.

It was then that Elizabeth realized why she had found the scene so moving. Such actions by a quiet, serious man spoke of a profound affection and trust. He was not one to display his deepest feelings for all the world to see, making the gift of such openness that much more precious.

Watching the moonlight filter through her aunt's curtains, Elizabeth could no longer deny that Mr. Darcy had always affected her. She had immediately perceived that he was an exceptionally handsome man and it was that admiration that had left her so hurt by his rude dismissal of her own person at the Meryton assembly. Had he not intrigued her, she would have easily brushed aside his slight. Instead, she had turned the entire scenario into a great joke and spread the story among her neighbors, unconsciously attempting to hurt his feelings as much as he had hurt hers.

Lizzy hugged her pillow and sighed. She wished that she and Mr. Darcy might start afresh, but it did not seem possible. First, it was unlikely that she would ever meet that gentleman again, and second, there was surely too much between them to form an indifferent acquaintance (much less a friendship). Not given to melancholy, Elizabeth told herself sternly that she would remember the past only as it gave her pleasure. Certainly her acquaintance with Mr. Darcy had taught her a great deal about herself.

Not much later, Elizabeth drifted off to sleep. If she dreamt of dancing on a moonlit sidewalk with a quiet gentleman from Derbyshire, she did not allow herself to dwell upon it extensively in the morning.

Several days later, Mrs. Gardiner and Elizabeth went for their final fittings at the dressmaker's. The two older women watched with pleasure as Elizabeth modeled her ball gown. The style was simpler than the current high fashions and Lizzy entertained them with an imitation of her mother demanding "more lace, more feathers!"

However, it was easy to see that the young lady was well-pleased. The color brought a glow to her skin and the classic, elegant lines of the style complimented her figure without making her feel exposed. Although Mrs. Bennet always made sure that all of her daughters were well-dressed, for reasons of economy Lizzy often forwent new dresses to remake one of Jane's. By combining their allowances, the sisters were able to purchase more expensive fabrics and notions.

Although she had never complained, Elizabeth was struck by how nice it was to have a gown made just for her; to choose colors and fabrics that complimented her dark hair rather than Jane's light tresses. Although she was not ready to admit it aloud, Lizzy had considered some of her aunt's advice. She still considered her sister to be one of the most beautiful women of her acquaintance, but away from their mother's constant criticisms Elizabeth began to think that beauty might not be the sole property of the golden-haired folk.

It was in this mood of self-reevaluation that Elizabeth arrived at the Carlisles' ball. On her uncle's arm, she was introduced to the host and hostess as they moved through the receiving line. In short order, her attention was drawn to the glittering throng filling a seemingly endless series of rooms. Her focus was recaptured when her uncle's arm drew her forward and in short order she was introduced to several of the Gardiners' acquaintances.

Not wishing to be lost in the crush, Elizabeth attempted to keep one eye on her aunt and uncle while making conversation with two gentlemen and a lady. Though she attempted to remain open-minded, Elizabeth rapidly found herself bored with the exchange. The gentlemen seemed only interested in discussing a recent horse race and the lady did nothing but agree with every word they said.

It was with some relief that Lizzy watched a tall, dark-haired gentleman join their group. When he was introduced as Lord Edward Fitzwilliam, Viscount Ashbourne and eldest son of the Earl of Matlock, she realized that she had unconsciously recognized a similarity in his features to others she knew.

"Lord Ashbourne, I believe I met several of your relations recently; Colonel Fitzwilliam and Mr. Darcy," she offered after her curtsy.

The dark eyes that focused on her were like Mr. Darcy's in color but the different feeling in them nearly made her gasp out loud. Where Mr. Darcy's eyes always left her curious as to what was going on behind them, Lord Ashbourne's orbs were like hard stones.

With little attempt at civility, the gentleman replied coldly, "Is that so, Miss... err... Bennet." Moments later, however, his gaze swept down her figure with enough attentiveness that it left her feeling unclean.

With no immediate excuse to politely detach herself from the group, Elizabeth attempted to distract his roving eye with conversation. "Yes; we met several times in Kent. I understood that they were visiting your aunt, Lady Catherine de Bourgh."

Lord Ashbourne eyed her with a bit more interest. "Indeed. And are you from that part of the country, Miss Bennet?"

In this instance, Elizabeth had no qualms with trusting her instincts. She had no wish for this man to know anything about her (particularly where she might live), peer's son or not. "No, sir. I was visiting my cousin and his new wife. She is a dear friend of mine, and they only recently settled into the Hunsford parsonage."

The gentleman's eyes rose from his study of her bosom and Lizzy was only barely able to restrain herself from crossing her arms over her chest. "Your cousin is Aunt Catherine's curate?" he inquired without attempting to disguise a sneer.

Though she had no great respect for Mr. Collins, Elizabeth felt her courage rising to defend him and her family. It is perhaps lucky that she was *interrupted* before she *erupted.*

Mrs. Emma Watson, cousin and close friend of Mrs. Gardiner, appeared at Elizabeth's elbow. Greeting the others with the ease of a veteran of London Society, she gently detached her friend's niece and guided her through the crush to another room that was only slightly less full.

When they joined Mr. and Mrs. Gardiner, Elizabeth managed to squeeze the lady's hand in gratitude. "Thank you, Mrs. Watson. I was having difficulty making a polite exit."

The older lady smiled and patted the girl's hand. "Not at all." Lowering her voice, she spoke so that only Elizabeth could hear. "Lord Ashbourne is not someone with whom you would wish to be acquainted. He may be the Earl of Matlock's heir, but he is nothing like the rest of the family." She paused, clearly trying to find a delicate way to word her warning, and then spoke even more softly in Elizabeth's ear. "Suffice it to say that all the money and connections of the Fitzwilliam family can only cover up so many of his... activities."

Elizabeth nodded thoughtfully and soon Mrs. Watson was involved in conversation with the Gardiners and several acquaintances. Lizzy remained quiet for some minutes as she considered the lady's warning. Although she was saddened to hear such a thing of Colonel Fitzwilliam's brother (and, if she were honest, Mr. Darcy's close relation), she was somewhat relieved that her instincts against a gentleman appeared to be well-founded for once. It also occurred to her that where one Fitzwilliam had appeared, a brother might be in attendance (and perhaps also a cousin). However, the ball was spread out among a seemingly endless series of rooms and soon she was distracted by the entreaties of several gentlemen to dance.

The remainder of the night passed in a swirl of dancing and new acquaintances such that it was nearly dawn before Elizabeth finally fell into her bed. When she awoke later that morning, her feet were still sore (not all the gentlemen had been as adept as Sir William Lucas would have expected, regardless of how much time they spent at St. James), but she felt happier than she had in weeks. Lying in bed, she contemplated the reasons for her raised spirits.

Elizabeth had never attended such a grand ball nor mixed with the first circles so intimately. The Bennets were old and established members of the gentry, but they had never been ones to strive for connections or advancement into the peerage. Indeed, Mr. Thomas Bennet had actively avoided London Society for much of his life, although he did allow his eldest daughters to participate in events when they visited the Gardiners.

In a moment of insight, Elizabeth realized that part of her elation after the ball was relief. She had felt comfortable circulating among those people. She had not been intimidated, overwhelmed, or embarrassed. She had felt beautiful and admired but had maintained the irreverent view of the world that she had learned at her father's knee, taking nothing too seriously. They were just people, after all. Some had been ridiculous in their pursuit of high fashion, ladies with their feathered and bejeweled turbans and the gentlemen with their intricately knotted cravats and wildly hued coats. A few, such as Lord Ashbourne, had seemed positively predatory in their proclivities, but she had eased away from them without much fuss. She had met several ladies that she would like to know better, having sensed kindred spirits during their brief exchanges between dances.

Smiling, Elizabeth allowed herself one last moment in bed to reflect. She had not realized that the thought of being introduced to Mr. Darcy's circle in Society had worried her. Truly, it had never even crossed her mind that they were not of the same sphere; he was a gentleman and she was a gentleman's daughter. However, her father's reminiscences of his own time before marriage and suppositions on Mr. Darcy's life away from Hertfordshire must have stirred some insecurity deep within her. He might be a mere "Mister" like her father, but in hindsight it was obvious that his family's vast landholdings and ancient lineage probably traced back to some Norman d'Arcy who had fought beside William the Conqueror. Truly, his very name was as good as some paltry titles granted more recently.

The sound of a maid moving out in the hall drew Lizzy from her musings. She rose and dressed quickly, hoping to head off the Gardiner children before they woke their parents. In short order, she and the nurse had fed them breakfast and were herding Jonathan, Rebecca, Tommy, and Amelia off to the neighboring park.

Elizabeth did not consider her thoughts on the previous evening's ball to be any great revelation, but she walked with a bit more assurance than she had known on any previous visits to London. She still preferred country life but she began to have confidence that she could handle the ton without losing her sense of self.

The next day was Sunday and so, after services, Mr. and Mrs. Gardiner, their children, the nurse, and Elizabeth all crowded into the carriage to spend the afternoon in Hyde Park. The two ladies spread blankets and unpacked the picnic lunch while the others fed stale bread to the ducks. When it was determined that the fowls' appetites were temporarily sated, everyone settled on the blankets and enjoyed the delicacies that their cook had packed.

Cutting an apple into slices for her young cousins, Elizabeth smiled at her aunt and uncle, leaning against the trunk of an enormous beech. "This park is wonderful. It satisfies even my need for trees and wilderness!"

Her uncle nodded. "Yes, old Queen Caroline did well by us, keeping some of the woods wild while landscaping the park."

Mrs. Gardiner stroked the hair of her youngest child, asleep in her lap. "It is hard to believe how London has grown in the last decades. I remember my grandfather ranting on about the Grosvenor estate being broken up and developed into houses, however grand their architecture."

Mr. Gardiner grinned and nipped a slice of apple from his niece's hand. "Ah, but wouldn't we all be poorer if we did not have the architectural marvels of Mayfair and Park Lane?" They all laughed for, though some of the houses were lovely, the facades of many had clearly been designed to impress rather than please the eye.

"Papa, come and play catch with us!" Nine-year-old Tommy Gardiner was never still for long. When his father collapsed backward in mock exhaustion, Jonathan took charge of his younger brother and soon they were daring each other to toss the ball higher and farther between them. When it rolled a bit too close to the duck pond, Lizzy and Rebecca joined them for a game of keep-away, after moving to a safer area.

When Jonathan overthrew their ball into a little bit of wilderness beyond the pond, Lizzy waved off the others and ventured into the shadows to retrieve the ball herself. While the children were distracted by a troupe of ducklings, she found her prize lying on a faint path. Grinning over what Miss Caroline Bingley would say of her now, Elizabeth couldn't resist following the trail a bit to see where it led.

For once, Miss Bingley's attitude would have been justified.

Ducking beneath a low hanging branch and around an azalea bush, Elizabeth was startled to find that she was no longer alone. Unbeknownst to her, she had blundered into a favored staging area for local pickpockets. Two rough men, neither very sober, were counting out their take from the Sunday crowds. They were not at all displeased to discover an unprotected female stumble into their midst, particularly one who would not require payment to share her pleasures.

The lady in question froze until the men dropped their prizes and moved for her with evil intentions clear in their eyes.

Elizabeth was able to twist away when the first man grabbed at her. She ran but had no sense of which direction she was going. After stumbling through the undergrowth, she had just managed to break through the brush onto a wide trail when the other thief caught up to her.

Lizzy's hope that she had escaped was lost when the ribbons of her bonnet tightened around her neck and jerked her backwards. Shrieking, her hands went to her throat, leaving her unable to break her fall. She landed hard but fear overcame any pain as a pair of mean eyes leered down at her and dirty hands grabbed at her wrists before she could fend him off.

The second man appeared at her feet and she had just managed to kick him between his legs, causing him to a turn away with a howl of pain, when she heard quick footsteps from another direction.

"Unhand her, you devils!"

The man holding her wrists was jerked away. Finally free to loosen the bonnet ribbons about her neck, Elizabeth turned onto her side and took several gasping breaths before she was able to look around. Meanwhile, her attacker received a sharp punch to the chin and gut before stumbling away to his comrade who was still bent over, nursing his own pain.

Elizabeth felt strong hands brush her shoulder and heard a concerned voice, gruff with worry; one she had never expected to hear again. "My God— Elizabeth? Are you hurt?"

She looked up to see none other than Mr. Darcy kneeling beside her, his eyes full of tenderness and shock. Too overcome to form any words, she managed to smile wanly and move a hand from her throat to cover his hand and squeeze it in reassurance. It seemed completely natural to lean into his shoulder and for his arm to come up behind her and gather her to his chest.

The sound of bodies crashing through the bushes caused both to look back in the direction of her attackers, just in time to see the two ruffians retreating into the inky shadows. At the same time, Elizabeth's uncle appeared along the main path, calling "Lizzy! My dear girl— what on Earth happened? Are you all right?"

Before he reached her, she smiled wanly. "It's all right, Uncle. I'm only a bit shaken, not hurt." Feeling the arm around her tense slightly, she turned back to her rescuer. "Thank you, Mr. Darcy. I... I don't know what to say... or how to thank you enough."

By now, her uncle was also kneeling at her side and, with one hand steadied by each man, she was gently assisted to her feet. Without thinking, she removed her left hand from Mr. Gardiner's and began brushing leaves off her dress.

Her uncle was still deeply concerned that his niece had been attacked while under his care. Taking a moment to look her over, he noticed her scraped elbow and handed her a handkerchief that was larger and more practical than the small square of embroidered linen that she was using. "Lizzy, I can see that your arm is hurt; is there anything else that pains you?"

"My side aches a bit where I fell, and my neck—he grabbed my bonnet and jerked the ribbons backward— but nothing lasting, I believe." Lizzy's spirits were beginning to rise again and her smile was a bit more believable.

"That is a relief, my dear, but tell me what on Earth happened? One moment you were playing with the boys, and the next you had disappeared and I heard a shout." Mr. Gardiner's fear had begun to recede and he took more notice of the tall, serious young man who was still standing with a hand hovering at Elizabeth's back and intense eyes watching her every movement. "And you, sir. I'm not certain what exactly has occurred but clearly I must thank you for your protection of my niece." He was not sure whether to be concerned or amused when both young people blushed.

Although every fiber in his being screamed to do just the opposite, Darcy forced himself to release the lady's hand and take a step back. He felt oddly gratified when she swayed toward him involuntarily before straightening and looked discomposed for an instant.

With Mr. Darcy standing at a slightly more proper distance, Elizabeth forced her mind to steady and turned back to her uncle and his question. "Tommy overthrew the ball into the little wilderness there. I was closest and believed I could find it easily. Unfortunately, I was not far in when I stumbled upon two men in a clearing. They tried to grab me and I ran without paying attention to the direction. I was fortunate enough to break through to this path, where Mr. Darcy rescued me. Mr. Darcy, may I present my uncle to you?" At that gentleman's nod, she made the proper introductions. "And Uncle Edward, this is Mr. Darcy. We met when he visited his friend, Mr. Bingley, at Netherfield in the autumn."

Mr. Gardiner was nodding in recognition of the names and the two men shook hands, Darcy rather stunned at how easily Elizabeth had just handled the social niceties at a moment when most women (and many men) would be in hysterics, or worse. At that moment he felt a soft touch on his elbow and, glancing back, was astonished to realize that he had entirely forgotten about his own sister.

Squeezing Georgiana's hand to his arm, Darcy couldn't help but kiss her forehead as he drew her foreword. "Mr. Gardiner, I am honored to meet you, although I wish the circumstances were different. May I introduce my sister, Miss Darcy, to you both? Georgiana, this is Mr. Gardiner and his niece." Darcy couldn't help but take a breath before making the introduction he had long desired between the two most beloved females in his life. "Miss Elizabeth Bennet, this is my sister, Georgiana."

For once, Georgiana Darcy felt none of the timidity that normally froze her when faced with a new acquaintance. Instead, she stepped forward with hands outstretched to take the other lady's in her own. "Miss Bennet, I am so happy to meet you at last! You were so brave! But are you hurt?"

As the two young ladies checked Elizabeth's dress for rips and repaired a loose hairpin, the two gentlemen turned to assess each other.

"Again, sir, I must thank you for your assistance…"

Darcy couldn't help but interrupt, barely able to remove his eyes from Elizabeth. "Truly, Mr. Gardiner, I thank God I was here. I only wish that I had been able to reach her before those scum could touch her."

Lizzy's uncle could barely restrain a smile at the younger man's fervor. "Yes, well, let us thank Providence for what we do have."

Upon Darcy's agreement, Edward continued, "Do you have any idea who they might have been? This area is usually quite safe—I wouldn't bring my family here after dark, but on a Sunday afternoon in broad daylight I would never have expected such a thing!"

Darcy shook his head. "As you see—I brought my sister here myself."

"Brother?" Both men turned to Miss Darcy. "We must take Miss Bennet home to clean up and have a cup of tea."

Elizabeth couldn't help but quirk an eyebrow—it sounded rather as though Miss Darcy was informing her brother that she was bringing home a stray kitten.

Mr. Darcy, however, was immediately nodding. "Yes, please come. We live but a few minutes' walk from here, just beyond the Brook Street Gate."

His dark eyes were so earnest that Elizabeth was agreeing before she could think.

Her uncle answered more carefully; "That is very kind of you, sir, and I would like to accept, but my wife and children will be concerned if we don't return soon..."

"Oh, dear Aunt Maddy... We mustn't worry her..." Lizzy was torn between a feeling of responsibility toward her relations and her unconscious desire to remain with Mr. Darcy.

Georgiana looked to her brother and was amused to see him shift from one foot to another, staring rather desperately at Miss Bennet. She had never seen him look less like the Master of Pemberley... more like a mooncalf. She decided to speak before her brother simply picked up the young lady and carried her off like some sort of American savage. "Mr. Gardiner? Is your family far?"

The gentleman waved back up the path from whence he had come. "Just around the bend a bit. We were picnicking under the big copper beech by the duck pond."

Just then, a burly manservant came jogging along the path and seemed relieved to see Mr. Gardiner.

"Ah, Burt. Did my wife send you to track us down?" At the man's nod, Mr. Gardiner turned to the Darcys and made a quick decision. "Why don't the three of you go on to Brook Street. Burt shall accompany you, if you don't mind. I will go collect my brood and be along in a few minutes." He looked carefully at Elizabeth to see if she had any qualms with this plan, but she was already nodding.

"Thank you, Uncle."

Trying not to look as eager as he felt, Darcy replied with every shred of gravitas he could recover. "Excellent, sir. We are at number seventeen; just up Brook Street, about center of the square on the north side."

Mr. Gardiner smiled at such precise directions and thanked him, then turned to his niece and couldn't resist hugging her. "I've a feeling that you were very lucky today, my dear. Now run along for a nice cup of tea. I'll bring your aunt to fuss over you as quick as I can."

And so, the group parted with smiles. When Mr. Gardiner looked back over his shoulder for a moment before rounding the corner, he was pleased to see that the Darcys had arranged themselves protectively on either side of his niece, each taking her arm. He rather suspected that he might need to become accustomed to such a view.

10 ENTER THE JUDGE

Fitzwilliam Darcy desperately wished to speak but could not think of a single word to say. How was it possible, he wondered, that he was walking along Brook Street with Miss Elizabeth Bennet on his arm? And on her other side was Georgiana, dearest of sisters. Even dearer than before, he thought as he watched the shy girl exert herself to chat with Elizabeth about the age and architecture of the various houses they passed, just as if they were old acquaintances. And *she* was coming to his home!

"Ahoy, the Darcys!" called a powerful voice, distinctive by its strength and timbre.

Fitzwilliam turned and immediately smiled with pleasure. "Hello, Uncle James."

Elizabeth stood back and watched the two Darcy siblings move to greet an elderly man, their affection obvious. She could not help but be amused by the character to whom Mr. Darcy had referred as "Uncle James."

Although he was as tall as his nephew and resembled him in coloring, the similarity ended there. Where Mr. Darcy was dressed immaculately in a black coat, buff breeches and polished hessians, "Uncle James" looked rather like he had dressed himself from a charity grab bag. His tweed coat was patched at the elbows and darned at the cuffs but still managed to look tattered, his shirt had not seen an iron in recent memory and, though he did wear what once might have been a cravat, that strip of linen hung limply about his neck and appeared to have been used more recently as a handkerchief.

Luckily, Elizabeth noticed the object of her study when he turned to look at her, intelligence and wit sparkling in his eyes, just as Mr. Darcy returned to her side.

"Uncle, please allow me to introduce you to our friend, Miss Elizabeth Bennet, who is visiting from Hertfordshire. Miss Bennet, may I present my

115

uncle, Sir James Darcy. Despite his currently disreputable appearance, he is a respectable judge at Westminster."

Elizabeth was pleased with the open affection she saw in Darcy's face as he introduced her to his relation. However, her attention was soon taken up by the relation himself.

"Wills, you know very well that I spend all week in that stuffy old barn, wearing black robes and a powdered wig… a wig in this day and age, I tell you! You have no idea how hot and itchy the things get in summer! I retain the right to dress as I wish on my days off… and if it is not possible for me to flee to the countryside to do it, then I shall do so here, Society be damned!"

The sternness of his remonstrance was dispelled by the twinkling of his eyes. Seeing that he had made all three young people laugh, Sir James nodded with approval before reaching out to shake Elizabeth's hand.

"Well met, Miss Elizabeth Bennet. Always good to find a young lady who still knows how to laugh. We're all born with a sense of humor, you know, but I swear that they school it out of girls these days. Why, the last time I saw these two, they were accompanied by a young lady who looked like she was going to faint at the very sight of me, though her brother appeared pleasant enough! The only interesting thing about her was her hat—it had an entire, stuffed oriole perched amid some fake leaves. I suppose its orange feathers matched her dress well enough, but it made it difficult to look at her face when those beady black eyes were staring down at you."

Lizzy burst into most unladylike peals of laughter, particularly when Mr. Darcy leaned over and whispered, "Miss Bingley!"

She squeezed the older gentleman's hand. "I've never been particularly fond of taxidermied headgear, myself. I once met a very grand lady whose very serious advice could not keep my attention away from the stuffed kestrel perched upon her head!"

The laughter only increased when Darcy whispered to his relatives, "Lady Catherine!"

Elizabeth's cheeks turned rosy at being caught out but her sparkling eyes and good-natured grin gave full evidence that amusement outweighed her embarrassment. Choosing to alter the direction of the conversation before she said something that she might later regret, Lizzy nodded toward the satchel and binoculars that the older gentleman wore on a leather strap about his neck.

"And you, sir; have you been out bird-watching? The live variety, I hope?"

Sir James was well pleased that this young lady might know something of his passion. "Indeed I have been! You would be amazed at the number of rare species that pause to rest in Hyde Park before continuing their spring migration northward. I've just been down to the Thames to watch the waterfowl." He turned to his nephew. "Saw a bittern, *Botaurus stellaris*. The lads are going to be madly jealous!" He referred to the other gentlemen of his birding club, all of whom had passed the half century mark.

Sir James turned back to Lizzy. "But it is nothing compared to a good stomp through the countryside, of course. You are from Hertfordshire, I understand? Beautiful county, that."

Elizabeth's eyes made it clear how much she enjoyed her new acquaintance. "Indeed, sir. My father quite detests town and so I have enjoyed an idyllic childhood scampering about the countryside." She looked sideways upon hearing a snort coming from the direction of Mr. Darcy but saw no disapproval in his eyes. Quite the opposite, in fact. Reassured, she teased, "Some might say that I have never grown out of it."

Sir James was not shy in voicing his approval. "And take care that you never do. There is nothing better for your health than a brisk ramble through wood and dale; I don't know why these two spend so much time in town when they could be in Derbyshire. But what is this, my dear girl?" He had caught sight of the bloody scrape on Elizabeth's elbow. "Have you been climbing trees and taken a fall?"

"It is nothing, sir." Elizabeth tried to dismiss her injury but Darcy's attention had been refocused.

"It is *not* nothing; we must stop dawdling and get you to the house where your injuries can be seen to properly." Suddenly feeling tired and achy, Lizzy nodded without argument, a response that Fitzwilliam took correctly as a sign that she was indeed worse than she had claimed.

He turned to the older gentleman who had caught his nephew's serious tone. "Uncle, would you accompany us to Derwent House? Your assistance would be invaluable in this case and the details would be best discussed in privacy."

"Yes, of course, Wills. Lead on." Turning to his niece, he offered his arm. "And how are you, my dear? Found any lost kittens lately?" As a girl, Georgiana had once brought home two bedraggled kittens that she had found starving in the mews. She and her brother had been visiting with Sir James at the time and although he never missed a chance to tease her, he still had the cats.

Georgiana gladly took his arm, asking after the health of Hansel and Gretel as the pair happily headed toward home.

Fitzwilliam stood beside Elizabeth and suddenly all that had passed between them in Kent rushed at him. He was reassured by the amused look she was directing at his relations but still stopped breathing for a moment when those intelligent eyes turned to meet his own.

He hesitantly offered his arm, a flicker of hope breaking through his certainty that she must still despise him. When Elizabeth shyly tucked her own hand around his arm, he couldn't help but cover it with his left.

When she peeked up at him from under the brim of her bonnet, he took a deep breath and it seemed like the first in months. "Shall we?" he asked softly. She gave him a small nod and they followed Miss Darcy and her uncle. Both felt too much to speak but it was not a wholly uncomfortable silence.

When the foursome reached the grey stone building where the Darcys lived, Elizabeth was leaning heavily on Will's arm. Even before he turned his hat and walking stick over to the butler, he began giving orders to see to her comfort. In no time, Georgiana and the housekeeper were taking Elizabeth up to a guest room and a footman was running for the family's physician.

Darcy's directions were carried out so rapidly that he suddenly found himself standing quite alone in the foyer of his own house. For just a moment, he shut his eyes. *Elizabeth was in his home!* Then he took a deep breath, squared his shoulders and set about doing what needed to be done.

Sir James had made his way to the library and was found bent over a notebook, updating his birding observations. When his nephew entered, he efficiently tucked his pencil away and turned to face the young man. "Miss Bennet is a lovely young lady, Wills. If she had been out when I was a younger man, I might have been tempted to suffer some of Society's idiocies for the gift of her company."

Darcy chuckled. "You would like her father. Mr. Bennet detests London and I begin to believe he did right by raising his daughters exclusively in the country."

Sir James studied his nephew with a speculative gleam in his eye but turned the subject. "What happened this afternoon? You mentioned that you might need my assistance?"

Fitzwilliam nodded and proceeded to explain what he knew about the attack. Within minutes, the older gentleman was transformed from eccentric ornithologist to formidable magistrate and another footman was sent running to Bow Street. Darcy voiced some concern for Miss Bennet's reputation but his uncle brushed aside his concerns.

"This is not such a crime that would garner the interest of the scandal sheets. In fact, Miss Bennet's name may not even need to be entered into the report."

Seeing that his nephew was confused, Sir James grunted. "I fear I've skipped ahead without explaining properly. I would recommend that you not pursue any charges for the attack itself. Rather, Miss Bennet's discovery of the men is likely to be of great interest to the constabulary and may very well lead to the arrest of several known felons. Last autumn there was a disturbing increase in petty thievery in the large public parks, particularly Hyde Park. People are at their ease and there are plenty of places for hoodlums to hide so I suppose it is easy pickings for the criminal element. The Runners have deduced that there was a well-organized ring preying on visitors. First, pickpockets (often children) lift wallets, watches, jewelry, and the like. They hand off the takings to go-betweens; we think they may have been women posing as nurses with prams. Those blinds transport the valuables to a location where another would sort through them and arrange for them to be sold out of a back door or melted down."

Sir James watched Darcy sit down heavily on the settee, clearly stunned. The judge smiled sardonically; most of the ton had no idea how closely London's underbelly brushed up against them. "The thievery quieted down over the winter but appears to be heating up again with the weather. If I am correct, Miss Bennet may have just stumbled upon one of their staging areas. With any luck, they won't bother to move it just because some random young lady interrupted them."

In short order, the High Constable himself arrived at Derwent House as a summons from Sir James Darcy was not to be taken lightly. The Darcys explained the situation to Mr. Minton until a footman arrived with a message that Miss Bennet's wounds had been cared for and the ladies awaited them in Miss Darcy's sitting room.

In response to the questioning, Elizabeth was able to give very precise directions to the place where she had interrupted the ruffians. Darcy was able to estimate the height and weight of the two he had fought off and Lizzy had noted a tattoo on one man's hand and a scar on the other's cheek. They were attempting to describe their features when Georgiana quietly picked up her sketch pad and drew two faces from her own memory, aided by Elizabeth and Fitzwilliam's suggestions.

Mr. Minton was extremely pleased. When the three men excused themselves from the ladies and descended to the front door, he explained that the descriptions were good enough for him to recognize the two criminals. Both had been too clever to be caught thus far but Minton was already plotting to watch their hideaway and capture them with the stolen goods in hand.

The constable was just departing when the Gardiners' carriage pulled up at the Darcys' front steps. When he had first met Mr. Gardiner in the park, Fitzwilliam's focus had been on Elizabeth. Now faced with a fashionable, polite couple whose only resemblance to Mrs. Bennet was in Mr. Gardiner's physiognomy, Darcy was thoroughly ashamed by his former condemnation of Elizabeth's relations.

Although dressed in play clothes appropriate for an afternoon at the park, the children were as well-behaved as any he had seen, standing quietly and responding perfectly to the introductions. The eldest boy was about twelve and he and his sister stood by the younger ones, making sure that curious hands didn't upset any valuable curios. It struck Darcy that this was where the two eldest Miss Bennets had learned their poise and manners. Once again, he mentally kicked himself for his previous prejudice against tradesmen.

After the couple had greeted Mr. Darcy, he turned to make introductions to his uncle. Before he could do so, the gentleman himself stepped forward with a smile.

"Mrs. Gardiner, how excellent to see you and your husband again. It has been too long since we dined together."

Darcy was surprised. "Uncle, I had not realized that you were acquainted with the Gardiners."

Sir James turned to his nephew; "Indeed, 'tis an acquaintance I treasure! This pair hosts some of the most entertaining dinner parties that I have ever had the good fortune of attending." Seeing his nephew was still uncertain, the judge expanded; "Mrs. Gardiner is the daughter of Sir Edmund Churchill— an excellent man, even if he is a *barrister*." He grumbled the last as if it was highly shameful but the twinkle in his eye belayed the condemnation.

Mrs. Gardiner responded with a smile of her own. "And Sir Edmund would say much the same of you, sir, though you are a *judge*." After some moments of shared laughter, she continued, "But I must correct you, Sir James. Sir Edmund is my uncle; my mother's brother. The Churchills took me in when my own parents passed away."

At that moment, Darcy's housekeeper entered and the Gardiners' attention was reclaimed by their niece's well-being. Mrs. Wilkins assured everyone that, aside from a few cuts and bruises, the young lady was well and would join the party soon, just as quickly as a tear in her skirt was mended.

Mrs. Gardiner insisted on being taken to her favorite niece so that she might inspect her with her own eyes. It was quickly arranged that the Gardiners' nurse and manservant would take their children home and then return the carriage to retrieve the remaining three. Mr. Gardiner waved off Mr. Darcy's offer of his own carriage.

"Thank you for the offer, sir, but my own driver is quite accustomed to running all over town, fetching and carrying various members of my family. Indeed, John often jokes that he knows London well enough to open a hackney service."

Thus it was arranged for Mrs. Gardiner to see her niece directly while Darcy and his uncle settled in the drawing room with Mr. Gardiner to discuss what was being done to bring Elizabeth's attackers to justice. Sir James did much of the talking, easily answering Mr. Gardiner's questions while the younger gentleman sat back and studied his two guests. It was immediately obvious to him that Edward Gardiner was an intelligent, well-educated man with a deep sense of responsibility to his family. The conversation turned to a more general discussion of the relatively recent establishment of a professional police force and Darcy found himself agreeing with many of Mr. Gardiner's opinions.

The three were still discussing the ongoing reformation of England's justice system when Miss Darcy and her two guests joined them. After all were reassured that Elizabeth had been examined by the doctor and pronounced "fit as a fiddle," Darcy directed a maid to fetch tea and refreshments for the group. Standing by the door for a moment, he observed the room.

Elizabeth had seated herself by the window while Georgiana was showing Mrs. Gardiner her harp. Darcy's stomach turned to ice when he heard Elizabeth's aunt speak to his sister. "Of course, I recently met your friend, Miss Bingley. She spoke very highly of your musical accomplishments."

By introducing the topic of music, Elizabeth's aunt was able to draw the shy girl into conversation. Mr. Gardiner was deep in discussion with Sir James, allowing Darcy a moment of privacy with Miss Bennet if he could only muster the courage to speak to her. If he had any hope of changing her opinion of him, he knew there would never be a better setting in which to begin. Taking a deep breath, he moved to sit beside the lady who had refused his offer of marriage not two months prior.

"I overheard Mrs. Gardiner mention Miss Bingley. I am glad to hear that she called, though I fear to ask if she was pleasant... or even polite." Although Mr. Darcy's voice was tense, Elizabeth had finally come to realize that the serious look in his eyes was not condemnation but rather a symptom of intense but repressed emotions.

She grimaced slightly but attempted to be delicate. "Miss Bingley was unable to return Jane's call for over a fortnight. I was not present but my sister's letter indicated that she was only able to stop at Gracechurch Street for a brief visit. No doubt she had many other engagements."

Elizabeth had turned slightly away from him and Darcy could tell from the set of her shoulders that she was thinking about the last time that they had discussed Bingley. Desperate, he forced himself to speak again although it felt as if his throat would close up at any moment.

"Please, Miss Bennet— allow me to explain. Miss Bingley does not speak for myself or my friend. She may regard Georgiana as a close acquaintance but, like me, my sister can barely tolerate her."

Fitzwilliam paused and was pleased to see Elizabeth turn back to him. Her eyes were still serious but at least they were considering his words. "Bingley has been visiting family in Yorkshire; he left before I returned from Kent. I... I did not want to tell him of my errors in a letter. I had hoped that he would return last week, allowing me to explain and apologize in person..." Darcy trailed off, not certain if she would approve or even understand his convoluted explanation. His pain was brief, however.

Elizabeth studied his face before nodding. "I can understand not wanting to entrust such a communication to the post." She paused, thinking carefully before speaking. "Your letter gave me much to ponder. Upon reflection, I found that I could well understand some of your actions. Jane guards her feelings very closely and our mother... does not."

Darcy was about to argue but stopped when Elizabeth made a motion with her hand. "I have not spoken to Jane about what you said regarding your friend, but I hope that you will still speak with Mr. Bingley when he returns. She tries to hide it but I can tell that my sister remains melancholic... and if he feels the same way..."

Fitzwilliam could not help but interrupt. "Then they must be reunited. I cannot apologize enough for my officious interference. It was the height of arrogance and I will confess it all to Bingley when he returns next week, although I would not blame him if he never speaks to me again."

Elizabeth managed a small smile at his heart-felt words. "I was recently reminded that I myself have had no qualms with turning Jane's head away from admirers that I deemed unworthy of her. She is very trusting..."

The two shared an understanding look before Elizabeth's eyes became worried again. "Is he always so easily led? Should I be concerned for my sister?"

Darcy understood her apprehension immediately. "Bingley is a man of great goodness and sense but with a profound personal modesty. He was not deterred from his pursuit of your sister by any of Miss Bingley's comments about your family's lack of wealth or consequence. He was only affected by my unfortunate observation that I was unsure of Miss Bennet's affections and feared she might accept his proposal to please her mother."

Seeing Elizabeth wince, he began to apologize again but she interrupted him. "No, I am well aware that my mother is all too public with her hopes and fears over her daughters' marriage prospects." Elizabeth had been studying her hands and Fitzwilliam barely quelled his desire to take them in his own and reassure her. He was startled when she lifted her chin and looked him straight in the eye.

"You must understand, however, that Mama loves us all dearly. She does not express it properly, but her fundamental desire is that we all have comfortable homes after my father's death. She knows something of old Mr. Collins' greed and has come to fear for reprisals from his son when it comes to the entail on Longbourn."

If they had been alone in the room or even in a private corner, Fitzwilliam would have dropped to his knees before her and begged forgiveness for causing the pain he saw in her eyes. As it was, he could no longer resist pressing her hand in remorse.

"Please forget those words I spoke. I cannot believe that I actually thought such things, much less spoke them aloud to you. Your mother acts no differently than many others, regardless of station, concerned for the welfare of their daughters. Even in the highest circles there are many parents who view their children's marriages solely as avenues to extend their own wealth, connections, and power."

His speech ran down as he noticed that Elizabeth was watching him very intently. After a few minutes of silence during which they each searched for answers in the other's eyes, she spoke with a slight smile. "I have always had a great deal of difficulty sketching your character, Mr. Darcy. You have puzzled me exceedingly, but I believe that I am beginning to get a glimmer through the fog of our previous misunderstandings."

Understanding that she was extending an invitation to begin again, Fitzwilliam could not help but break into a great smile, leaving Elizabeth blinking at dimples that she had never seen before. "I would by no means suspend any pleasure of yours, and I hope..." He forced himself to breath. "I sincerely hope that we may soon meet again so that you may..." He trailed off. He wanted to say that he wished for her to get to know him better, to like him, even to love him, but certainly that was much too forward.

For better or worse, the entrance of a maid with the tea tray gave Darcy an excuse to leave the sentence unfinished. Elizabeth gave him a soft, understanding smile before turning her attention to their hostess.

After the servant arranged a plate of ginger biscuits on the table and departed, Georgiana offered them around. "Please, do try one. Our housekeeper at Pemberley sent along a box with some other things that had to be brought down from Derbyshire. Mrs. Reynolds won't part with the recipe, no matter how we beg."

"And we do beg," added Mr. Darcy. "She claims that it is her best lure to bring us back home to Pemberley where we belong." The Darcy siblings smiled at each other and Elizabeth was warmed to see their mutual affection.

"Mrs. Reynolds... you can't mean that Susie Moore is housekeeper at Pemberley now!"

All eyes turned to Mrs. Gardiner and Elizabeth's aunt smiled with embarrassment. "Oh heavens, please forgive my manners—you just caught me by surprise... I should explain. I doubt you will remember, but my father had the living at the Lambton church until 1800. I was in London visiting my mother's family when the pox took my parents and siblings, and I've never returned."

There were some moments of silence as Darcy was reeling with astonishment. "But that would have been... Reverend Jonathan! And your mother would have been Mrs. Rebecca— we generally attended services at the Pemberley chapel, but I remember the vicar's wife would often visit and spend hours in the music room with Mother." He squinted and a younger version of Mrs. Gardiner shimmered into his mind. "You are Miss Maddy!" he blurted out.

Mr. Gardiner grinned while Elizabeth and Georgiana were wide-eyed and open-mouthed with astonishment, even more so when Fitzwilliam Darcy spontaneously embraced Madeleine Gardiner in the middle of the drawing room. When they drew back, both were laughing, although Mrs. Gardiner had tears in her eyes and Mr. Darcy's were suspiciously shiny.

"Very impressive, Master Wills. You can't have been more than ten when last I saw you. And Miss Darcy, so very grown up. I held you in my arms when you were but a few days old, all big blue eyes and wisps of flaxen hair. Your mother was so very happy to have a baby girl."

Just as Georgiana was thinking of a thousand questions to ask about her mother, Mrs. Gardiner's face was darkening with grief. "Oh, but I am so sorry. I sent a letter of condolence to your father after he wrote about what had happened, but it was so difficult to get any news out of Derbyshire."

Seeing the questions on her niece's face, Mrs. Gardiner explained. "When I was eighteen, my parents arranged for me to spend a few months with my aunt and uncle for a London Season." At Mr. Darcy's curious look, she expanded. "My mother's brother—Sir Edmund Churchill and his wife Agnes. I've felt guilty about it for years. There I was, shopping on Bond Street and enjoying all that London had to offer. And then I get a letter from old Mr. Darcy informing me that my parents were dead, along with my little sister and both brothers... and everyone else I knew, it seemed ..."

Madeleine Gardiner sniffed into the handkerchief offered by her husband as he wrapped his arm around her shoulders in comfort. Reassured, she continued, "The Churchills took me in until Edward and I married. I shall always be grateful to my aunt and uncle, and my cousins. I don't know what I would have done without them—they made me part of their family."

She looked up to Mr. Darcy who was still trying to take in their connection. "I tried to get news from Derbyshire, but it seemed as though everyone I knew to write to had either passed away or was frantically trying to rebuild their life."

Mrs. Gardiner looked at Mr. Darcy where he had settled in a chair just by his sister. She suddenly realized that these two siblings would understand her heartache as not even her husband could, because they had lived through it as well.

The Gardiners and their niece left soon after, but not before extending an invitation to all three Darcys for dinner the following week.

11 DINNER AND A SHOW

"Sir!"

Fitzwilliam Darcy was brought back to the present by his valet's utterance, only to realize that in the moments that Hawkins had turned his back to brush his master's coat, the gentleman himself had managed to completely mangle the intricate knot in his cravat. Will sighed. "I apologize, Hawkins. My mind wandered."

The servant nodded but couldn't quite control a sniff. After removing the ruined neck cloth, he moved deeper into the dressing room to retrieve a fresh one and then set about repairing his master's costume.

Darcy forced himself to keep his mind on the present (and hands at his sides) but feeling the cloth tighten around his throat once again, he objected, "A little looser, Hawkins. The theatre is likely to be overheated and I would prefer not to make a spectacle of myself by fainting from lack of air."

Hawkins said only, "Of course, sir," although his mouth twitched slightly at the image. He kept to himself the observation that he had never seen the young master so fidgety.

The valet had arrived in the dressing room at his regular time to prepare Mr. Darcy for an evening out, only to be struck dumb at the sight of his normally imperturbable gentleman standing before the mirror, attempting to button a waistcoat he had not worn since... Hawkins clicked his tongue, an old habit that he had never been able to break.

To the man who cared for his clothes, Fitzwilliam Darcy had never truly come out of mourning for his father's death; even after the official year had ended, the young man had persisted in his wardrobe of black coats and charcoal waistcoats. He had recently approved two new coats, one of a fine dark blue and another of forest green wool (the latter to be accompanied by a canary yellow waist coat), but the valet had not dared take it as any particular sign that his master's spirits might finally be rising.

Young Mr. Darcy had never been a flashy dresser, preferring understated styles unlikely to gain comment—he was no follower of Beau Brummell and had no desire to be classified as a dandy. The one area in which Fitzwilliam had allowed his valet to explore a bit of individuality had been in his waistcoats. Though never gaudy, he had enjoyed fabrics with subtle patterns of texture or embroidery. However, these had all been put away after his father's death.

To himself, Hawkins had suspected that the young man had seen them as evidence of youthful fancy and put them aside for the black that might make him seem older, wiser. Perhaps better than anyone, the valet understood the pressures and responsibilities that had descended upon young Mr. Darcy with his father's unexpected demise.

The waistcoat that Darcy was, even then, straining to fasten, had been ordered only weeks before his father's death and had never been worn. A deep wine-colored silk with a subtle embroidery picked out with silver threadwork, Hawkins observed and couldn't suppress a small smile. Mr. Darcy looked like a man readying himself to go courting. The valet stilled his face into its usual mask when he heard his master curse and observed that the gentleman was about to burst a button.

"Allow me, sir."

To say that Darcy started was an understatement. Armed with intelligence from his sister that Elizabeth would be wearing a rose-colored gown that evening, he had explored the depths of his own closets, too embarrassed to ask his valet if clothes tailored for him at twenty-one would still fit his twenty-eight year old frame. He had discovered that the waistcoat could be buttoned if he sucked in his breath and had been contemplating the result in the mirror when his valet interrupted.

Instantly realizing how embarrassed his master was to be discovered thus, Hawkins spoke quickly to smooth over the awkwardness. "If I may, sir. With a very slight alteration, you would be able to wear that this evening, if you wish."

Mr. Darcy had managed a nod, aware he was blushing, and Hawkins had assisted him in removing the garment. In minutes, Fitzwilliam was in his bath and the valet was moving the buttons.

Darcy had shut his eyes and leaned back in his tub for a moment, unable to banish the sight of straining buttons from his mind. Had he grown… heavy? Certainly he was not as active as he had been in his university days, particularly during the winter when most outdoor sport were all but impossible in Derbyshire. He could not abide by the corsets that some gentlemen had taken to wearing in order to fit the closely tailored clothes currently in style, but might Elizabeth prefer a younger, more svelte figure of a man?

It was probably lucky that Hawkins had entered at that moment and interrupted Darcy who was working himself into a most unaccustomed dither over his physique. As his valet moved him efficiently through shaving and dressing, Fitzwilliam had settled into the routine and told himself firmly that there was nothing he could do to improve his appearance before seeing Miss Bennet again.

When Hawkins was satisfied, Darcy retreated to his private sitting room, hoping to have a few minutes to himself. He walked directly to the window and stood with both arms braced against the casement, unable to control a groan when he considered all the things he must remember to do (and not do) that evening. At that moment, a soft giggle alerted him that he was not alone.

He turned quickly and caught sight of his sister curled comfortably in one of the armchairs by the fireplace. "Georgiana."

She giggled again and put aside the book she had been reading while waiting for him. "Oh Wills, I am sorry… I didn't mean to intrude; I only wished to see you before you left for the opera."

Darcy pulled the tips of his waistcoat down and fiddled with his cufflinks. "Shall I embarrass you, do you think?"

Detecting the note of nervousness lacing his jest, Georgiana studied her brother for a moment. "You look very handsome. I almost wish I could attend with you; Rossini may have a reputation for writing too quickly to produce a polished score, but I do enjoy his operas."

Darcy smiled crookedly and sat on the arm of Georgie's chair. "I wish you could come as well. I don't know what I was thinking."

"You heard Elizabeth and her uncle discussing their love of opera and invited them to share your box for the opening of *La Donna del Lago*. It was a wonderful gesture and they were delighted by the invitation."

"But you know how I despise opening nights. Everyone will be flouncing about, seeing and being seen. Opening nights are for Society's puffery, not for the music."

Georgiana thought for a moment, studying her brother. "Are you embarrassed to be seen with the Gardiners and Miss Bennet?"

"No!" he responded forcefully. "Not at all. It is only… I am not comfortable…"

Georgie took her brother's hand and squeezed. "Will, I of all people know what it is like to be uncomfortable at such a gathering, but you *must* try. If you turn into a grim statue, your guests will think that you do not want to be there… with them."

Darcy shut his eyes tightly and groaned. "And it will be the Meryton assembly all over again," he muttered to himself. "Perhaps you might send them a note that I'm ill? They could use the box without me." He was only partially joking.

Miss Darcy stood and crossed her arms. "Fitzwilliam Darcy, if you even consider such a thing I will never speak to you again! If you cannot find the strength in yourself… in your affection for Elizabeth, then do it for me, for I should dearly love to have her as a sister!"

Her brother sighed before standing and making a deep, formal bow to her. "I shall do my best, poppet."

The two embraced for a moment but pulled apart when the mantel clock began to toll. "I must go if I am to pick up the Gardiners on time."

"And Miss Bennet." Georgiana took his arm and they descended toward the front door.

"And Miss Bennet," agreed Fitzwilliam with slightly more force than necessary.

"Just remember, there are at least three other people in the audience who also wish to listen to the music, and conveniently, they will be in your own box." She smiled at him, willing all of her own strength to her brother for the evening ahead.

In minutes, Darcy was in his carriage on the way to Gracechurch Street. He appreciated his sister's support but it was good to have a few moments alone to gather his thoughts.

His first meeting with Elizabeth in Hyde Park had been such a surprise that he had not had time to be nervous. He had not been comfortable (nor had she), but even so they had been able to speak about Bingley and her sister. He had spent the rest of the evening reviewing her every look and word, over and over in his mind's eye. Georgiana had insisted that Miss Bennet could not help but think of him as a knight in shining armor from now on. He would settle for her no longer believing that he was the villain of the story.

Mr. Darcy and his sister had called on the Gardiners the very next day. They had spent an extremely pleasant hour with Mrs. Gardiner, exchanging stories about Pemberley and Lambton, but Miss Bennet had not appeared until just as the Darcys were preparing to depart. Fitzwilliam had turned around at the sound of children's voices in the hall and been struck dumb at the sight of Elizabeth, fresh from the outdoors.

With bright eyes and windblown curls, Elizabeth had swept in like a spring breeze. There had been no concealment in her eyes, only genuine pleasure. "Mr. Darcy… and Miss Darcy! I had not realized you were visiting or we should have returned from the park sooner!"

The Gardiners' younger daughter—Amelia, Darcy reminded himself—had remained close by her cousin's skirts. "But Lizzy… you said that you would like to stay in the park forever and live in a tree house!"

Fitzwilliam had recognized the mischievous glint in Elizabeth's eye as she bent down by the little girl. "I did indeed, Amelia, but I suppose we might still return home for tea and biscuits when there is pleasant company, don't you think?"

There had followed a brief conversation about a particularly fine old oak at Pemberley well-formed for climbing. Darcy had promised Amelia that she might play there whenever she was in Derbyshire and had received a brilliant smile from Elizabeth that he would treasure for the rest of his life.

They had returned two nights later for a dinner. Although Georgiana was not yet out, he had allowed her to attend after being assured that it would be a small party, mostly family. In hindsight, he was glad that he had, not only for his own selfish need of his sister's support but also to see her shyness melt away under the warm welcome of the Gardiners and Miss Bennet.

Several of Mrs. Gardiner's Churchill cousins had attended, as well as a niece who was Georgiana's age. Darcy had been stunned when, after dinner, the two girls had performed an impromptu duet of pianoforte and violin. Usually his sister was too shy to play for anyone beyond himself and Richard, but here she was performing to a roomful of strangers and laughing at a missed note!

Almost immediately upon his arrival, Mrs. Gardiner's uncle, Sir Edmund Churchill, had entered into a lively discussion with Darcy's own Uncle James on the political implications of Europe's trade with the Americas. When the party was seated for dinner, the discussion expanded to include the entire table and Darcy was struck by how effortlessly Mrs. Gardiner and Elizabeth guided the conversation and involved everyone. It was easily the most interesting dinner party he could remember in years; there was no discussion of fashions or gossip among the ladies and the men did not resort to talk of horse racing or sport. Instead, Fitzwilliam found himself stretching his intellect as he had not done since university; he felt like an old clock that had sat unused on the mantle for years but was finally wound up again and ticking, its works a bit gritty but running smoother every minute.

As they were farewelling their hosts, Darcy had spontaneously reached out to shake Mrs. Gardiner's hand. "Thank you—I do not know when I have spent a more enjoyable evening." He had meant every word and the bright, happy smile that he had received from Elizabeth was an additional prize, making him realize how much his manners had improved in addition to his openness to making new acquaintants from different walks of life. Fitzwilliam had not had the opportunity for any private discourse with her but her ease in helping her aunt host the evening had reinforced his belief that Miss Elizabeth Bennet was in every way suited to be the next Darcy family matriarch.

Fitzwilliam desperately hoped that he was not about to destroy any good opinion Elizabeth might have developed over their last few meetings with a single burst of poor behavior. When he attended the theatre alone or with Georgiana, he timed his arrival so that he could slip into his box just as the curtain was rising. His sister was perfectly happy to remain in their box during intermissions so they would talk quietly, sometimes approached by relatives or a close friend but generally safe from the social maelstrom outside.

Tonight, however, he would be arriving well before the curtain went up and, moreover, with a young lady who was most definitely not his sister. He could only hope that Lady Caroline Lamb and Lord Byron might have one of their increasingly public lovers' spats, thereby distracting the gossips from the Derbyshire bachelor and his guests.

"Are you embarrassed to be seen with the Gardiners and Miss Bennet?" Georgiana's question returned to him and Fitzwilliam was struck by the simple truth her words prompted. He was not ashamed of the acquaintance in any way, but he was so accustomed to guarding his privacy that it might appear so to others.

The carriage rolled to a halt just as Darcy was making a resolution. Stepping down to the street, he took a deep breath and squared his shoulders. Tonight, he would escort Elizabeth to the opera and he would make it clear to her and anyone who cared to look just how much he admired her. He was done with disguise.

Even as the maid was opening the front door, Fitzwilliam was greeted by the sight of a smiling Edward Gardiner. "Mr. Darcy! Excellent, I do appreciate a man who is punctual. The ladies shall join us in just a minute. A clasp on Lizzy's necklace broke and they are just repairing it. Would you care for a drink while we wait?"

Mr. Gardiner's offer went unanswered as Darcy turned, hearing footsteps on the stairs, and was instantly rendered speechless. Only distantly did he hear his host welcoming the ladies back and Mrs. Gardiner responding. All of his senses were focused on Elizabeth, such that he heard the tiniest squeak of a floorboard under her slippers when she came to a halt at the base of the stairs.

Elizabeth had admitted earlier to her aunt that she felt beautiful in her new dress and the appreciative look in Mr. Darcy's eyes as they swept over her brought a blush to her face. To Fitzwilliam, her pink cheeks and sparkling eyes made her even more beautiful; the rose-colored silk set off her complexion to perfection and the simple pearl pendant hanging around her neck emphasized the creamy luster of her skin. He couldn't help himself.

Darcy stepped forward and took Elizabeth's hand, kissing it as he bowed deeply. "Miss Bennet, you are exceptionally beautiful tonight."

It was a simple compliment but the intensity of his voice made Elizabeth shiver. "I thank you, kind sir." Their eyes met and for an instant, Darcy forgot his manners and continued to hold her hand.

The spell was broken when a maid approached with the ladies' wraps and soon they were all stepping out into the night. Darcy helped his guests into the carriage and was rewarded with another warm look from Elizabeth. Conversation in the coach was genial as Mrs. Gardiner immediately inquired if their host had heard anything about the opera's premiere in Naples the previous autumn. This led to a discussion of other performances they had seen in London and Darcy even found himself admitting that he usually avoided opening nights.

Elizabeth grimaced as the two Gardiners laughed at her. Her uncle explained, "We took Elizabeth to the premiere of Mozart's Magic Flute for her sixteenth birthday. The music was magnificent, but..."

Elizabeth couldn't help but interrupt, her voice laced with the irritation she had felt years before. "But the audience! Clapping at the wrong times, peering out of their balconies to goggle at each other instead of attending to the performance! And not a single original opinion to be heard during the intermission!" she ended with a humph, providing Fitzwilliam with an amusing vision of Elizabeth at sixteen.

"Lizzy," admonished her aunt with a smile. "That young man was only attempting to impress you."

"By insisting that there were no allegories to enlightenment philosophy in Mozart's story?"

"I don't believe that the gentleman quite understood you were referring to Kant. Rather, he thought that you were speaking more literally about the new lighting fixtures in the theatre itself."

"Oh," said Elizabeth, clearly embarrassed that she could have so misinterpreted the conversation. However she was soon laughing along with her relatives at the memory and they were joined by Darcy's own deep chuckle. She was still blinking at the handsome sight of his smile when the carriage slowed to a halt.

As the door to the carriage was opened on his side, Mr. Gardiner turned to grin at the others. "Well then, ready to run the gauntlet?" he quipped before stepping out and turning to assist his wife.

Darcy took the moment to shut his eyes and gather his strength, willing himself to be calm. When he opened them, he was faced with the lovely sight of Elizabeth looking at him sympathetically from the opposite bench. Stepping down from the carriage, he turned and offered his hand. She accepted his assistance as if it were the most natural thing in the world to rest her gloved hand on his. Speaking so softly that he had to bend down to hear her, she teased, "Shall we be quite safe here, Mr. Darcy? The crowd is looking somewhat ravenous."

Fitzwilliam couldn't help himself. He tucked her hand securely around his arm and squared his shoulders proudly. "Well, shall we give them something to chew on?" And then, London Society was gifted with the previously unknown pleasure of Fitzwilliam Darcy's full, dimpled smile.

Many *were* watching. The wealthy Derbyshire bachelor's tall, handsome form was rarely sighted but much looked for. To see him accompanying a fashionable couple (definitely not his family!) and escorting a lovely but unknown brunette (definitely not his sister!) was more than enough to set tongues wagging.

Luckily for Darcy, the light pressure of Miss Bennet's hand on his arm was enough for him to feel as if he were walking on clouds. The Gardiners greeted some acquaintances and he found himself listening attentively while Mrs. Gardiner made plans for a charity committee meeting with a countess who had approached her immediately. When they finished, the elderly lady turned and, after exchanging cheek kisses with Elizabeth, greeted him with a warm smile.

"Fitzwilliam Darcy; I am very glad to see you. You won't remember me but I counted your grandmother as one of my closest friends—a mentor, really. We were not often able to visit in her later years but I still go back and reread her letters when I am feeling low." The elderly woman turned back to Mrs. Gardiner. "Lady Edna Darcy was one of the reasons I became so involved in trying to reform the charity hospitals. I've never met anyone with so much energy and vision. Except perhaps this one…" She nodded at Elizabeth who blushed and studied the toes of her slippers.

Just then the bell was rung, signaling the audience to take their seats. Fitzwilliam offered his arm to Elizabeth and they shared a small smile. He was amused to see that she was still blushing from the countess' praise. Neither were aware that behind them, Mrs. Gardiner had paused for a moment when the countess tapped her arm. Gesturing with her fan at the young couple, she whispered, "*They* would be a superb match— Lady Edna would have approved, God rest her soul."

Madeleine Gardiner blinked and farewelled her friend rather automatically. As she took her husband's arm and they followed their host to the stairs, she studied the couple more carefully. Previously, she had assumed that Mr. Darcy had pursued their acquaintance because of her own connection to Lambton and Pemberley. Certainly Miss Darcy and her brother had enjoyed sharing stories of their childhoods and particularly her reminiscences of Lady Anne. However, now that Lady Alexandra had pointed it out to her, she easily recognized the admiration young Mr. Darcy held for her niece. And Elizabeth appeared to have overthrown her previous dislike of him.

Knitting her brows, Mrs. Gardiner stepped quickly to catch up. Mr. Gardiner steadied her arm. "What's the rush, my dear? I assume Mr. Darcy shall have enough seats in his box that we do not need to race."

He was intrigued when his wife turned mischievous eyes to him. "Oh, I simply did not wish to miss any of the performance."

With the ease of a happily married man, Edward guessed that his wife was not referring to the opera but was not quite certain what exactly she was about. He raised his eyebrows inquiringly but she shook her head. "Perhaps later, if you have not yet guessed yourself," she answered smugly.

When the foursome arrived at Mr. Darcy's box, Mrs. Gardiner managed it so that the ladies were seated together, with her husband at her right and Mr. Darcy beside her niece. After retrieving her own opera glasses, she was pleased to see the young gentleman offering a pair to Elizabeth.

"Miss Bennet, my sister thought that you might enjoy using these for the evening." He held out a pair of elegant silver binoculars.

Elizabeth took them carefully from his hand, marveling at the intricate engraving. "They are lovely; almost too beautiful to use. Are they Miss Darcy's?"

"They are now, yes. My father gave them to my mother as an anniversary present early in their marriage," he said softly.

Immediately understanding the personal nature of the gesture, Elizabeth traced a tiny vine that had been engraved along the lorgnette handle and inlaid with mother-of-pearl flowers. She was unable to manage more than a soft "thank you" before the conductor called for the audience's attention, but a quick glance at Mr. Darcy's face suggested that it was enough.

Elizabeth clicked open the glasses and held them to her eyes, though she saw little of the stage. Instead, all her being was aware of the gentleman sitting next to her. She could no longer pretend to be indifferent to Mr. Darcy. She was not certain if she was falling in love with him but she was keenly aware of the slightest movement of his leg, his appealing scent of sandalwood and soap, and the fact that she knew his eyes were resting upon her even before she glanced toward him.

Although Elizabeth was beginning to recognize that he attracted her, she was still bothered by the feeling that she did not know him very well. Resting Mrs. Darcy's opera glasses on her lap, Elizabeth rubbed a finger across an engraved rose and sighed very softly. The opportunity was there (or rather, sitting beside her) if she was willing to swallow the embarrassment of her previous misconceptions of the man.

Fortunately, Elizabeth was never one to let a little discomfort deter her and soon she straightened her shoulders, making a decision. She *did* want to understand Fitzwilliam Darcy, even if it required teasing him into a conversation. The intermission would be a perfect time to begin.

Meanwhile, Darcy was having difficulty keeping himself under good regulation. Upon entering the box, he had eased his chair back slightly so that he was hidden in shadow from most of the audience. This position also made it easier to study Elizabeth's profile without notice and he could not resist the temptation until she turned her head to glance at him. Embarrassed, Fitzwilliam sternly took himself to task and focused his eyes on the stage.

It was not easy—her lavender scent tickled his nose with every breath—but Darcy reminded himself sternly that attention paid to the performance now would give him material for conversation later. With that thought, he turned his focus to the singers and found himself drawn into the story with little effort, although he was never unaware of the lady at his side.

The four occupants in Mr. Darcy's box joined in the applause as the Highland warriors departed the stage to prepare for battle. While the Gardiners were speaking to each other, Fitzwilliam finally allowed himself to turn and look directly at Elizabeth. He was rewarded with a happy smile that clearly spoke of her enjoyment.

Will reminded himself of his resolution to speak with her, not just stare. "Are you enjoying the performance?" he asked before mentally kicking himself for such an inane question.

"Oh yes, thank you. I feel as though I have travelled to Scotland!" Elizabeth responded, clapping her hands together with a brilliant smile.

Buoyed by her obvious pleasure, Darcy surprised even himself with a tease. "Where they all speak in Italian?"

Elizabeth laughed out loud. "And break into song during every conversation!"

The pair stood and turned to the Gardiners, still smiling. "Lizzy?" spoke her aunt. "Your uncle has offered to fight the barbarian hordes and bring us back a cup of punch. Shall you come with me? I saw Mrs. Watson earlier and would like to speak with her, if I can."

Even as Elizabeth was nodding in agreement, Mr. Darcy bowed to Mr. Gardiner. "If you would allow me, sir, I would gladly join you in the attempt."

Edward Gardiner laughingly allowed that he could use such a strong young man as a second in the battle to come.

The crush in the foyer was just as horrific as Darcy had expected, but warmed by Elizabeth's smile and buoyed by Mr. Gardiner's running commentary, he was not as bothered by the multitude as he would have been usually. It took some time to navigate through the crowd but the older man's amusing anecdotes of other crowded performances made the wait fairly easy. Eventually, they arrived at the punch table and each gathered cups for themselves and the ladies.

Darcy lost track of what Mr. Gardiner said next when, upon turning, he caught sight of a laughing Elizabeth being attended by several gentlemen. He stopped so suddenly that Mr. Gardiner had to do some fancy footwork in order to avoid spilling wine on his host.

When Elizabeth's uncle had regained control of his stemware, he looked around to see what had caught the younger man's attention.

Darcy started when he heard Mr. Gardiner chuckle. "Like hummingbirds to a particularly lovely flower. Luckily she is quite adept at brushing them off without giving offence. You should see the flutter when we attend with both Elizabeth *and* Jane. Dark and light, wit and serenity, and neither with a clue as to how beautiful they truly are."

While his host seemed frozen in place, Mr. Gardiner caught a pointed glance from his wife. Smiling, he shouldered forward through the crowd to assume his role as chaperone. However, even as he deflected the overeager attention of a young earl from his unimpressed niece, he cogitated on Mr. Darcy's recent actions.

Mrs. Gardiner had assured him that the Darcy's eagerness to further their association had been due to their Derbyshire connection and Madeleine's ability to tell stories of Lady Anne in particular. However, Edward had noticed that young Mr. Darcy looked at Lizzy a great deal and his reaction to the crowd of admirers currently surrounding her was not that of an indifferent acquaintance.

At her uncle's remark, Fitzwilliam felt as though a last blinder had been ripped from his eyes. Miss Elizabeth Bennet was not just a pretty country miss but a truly beautiful woman, admired wherever she went. It was no wonder that Caroline Bingley had been so instantly and insistently disparaging of the Bennets. Charles had seen what he had not; Jane and Elizabeth had the manners, intelligence, and poise to hold their own in any circle, be it a small country village or London High Society.

As though fate wished to flog him for his previous stupidity, a new voice appeared at his shoulder. "Darcy! It's been too long, old chap. Have you been hiding away in the country again?"

Darcy turned to face the Viscount Hampden. "Trevor, it is good to see you, too." The two shook hands in the manner of old friends who had been close in school but drifted apart in the passing years. "How have you been? I had heard that your mother was ill— I hope that your appearance here tonight indicates she is recovering?"

"Indeed. We have been in Bath for several months and her strength is gradually coming back to her. I am just in London for a week to attend to some business before returning."

Michael Trevor and Fitzwilliam Darcy were the same age and had attended Eton and Cambridge together. Of equal intelligence but different scholarly interests, both had a deep respect and understanding of the other born of similarity in character and position. While Trevor held a higher rank (and all the duties and obligations that came with membership in the peerage), Darcy had inherited the greater fortune, larger estate, and all the responsibilities that his name entailed.

Trevor was intrigued by the way Darcy kept glancing back to his party. Normally a man who kept his emotions under excellent regulation, it was no great leap for the viscount to guess what had his old friend so distracted.

"So, Darcy... Who is that exquisite creature that accompanied you tonight? If you are so stupid as to not yet have secured her, I would be much obliged for an introduction…" The frozen look on Darcy's face was enough to make the other man laugh out loud.

"Easy there, old friend. I shall not poach on your territory… but if you wish a bit of help in defending it from those fools, you might introduce me anyway." He nodded at the cluster of gentlemen who were still maneuvering for Elizabeth's attention.

Darcy's stony face eased a bit and he managed a half smile. Looking down at his shoes, he spoke so quietly that Trevor had to lean in to understand him. "I could use all the help I can get. I have done little enough to please her, and she is no bumblebee."

His friend chuckled at Fitzwilliam's use of their old code. Once, after an evening of fending off society ladies, the two friends had retired with a bottle of brandy to commiserate over the woes of being a desirable 'catch,' surrounded by women who saw only wealth and connections but had no interest in the man within. Darcy had likened them to brightly colored bumblebees, constantly buzzing around, trying to suck him dry. Trevor had rejoined that bumblebees had to be brushed aside carefully or they would sting. The nickname had stuck.

With a quick pat on the back, the viscount nudged his old friend forward. "Well then, introduce me, I beg you. If you have managed to find one lady not assignable to the genus *Bombus*, then it gives me hope that I might yet discover another for myself!"

The two men shared a grin of understanding and then maneuvered their way through the crowd. They arrived at Elizabeth's side just in time to hear a pompous young earl speak. "Oh no, Miss Bennet, I assure you. All of Senior Rossini's operas are original stories—he would never steal a plot from this Scott fellow you speak of… That would be plagiarism, after all!"

Darcy fought the urge to laugh aloud at the plump gentleman's error-ridden little speech. Instead, he gained a position for himself in the circle beside Elizabeth by offering her the glass in his hand. "Miss Bennet, your punch."

Elizabeth had never been so glad to see Mr. Darcy as she was at that minute. She only barely suppressed the urge to roll her eyes at him. "Thank you, Mr. Darcy," she said simply but then nearly dropped her glass when that perennially serious gentleman winked at her before turning to greet the others.

"Lord Cowen, I could not help but overhear your statement on *Signore* Rossini. I believe that if you take the time to read Sir Walter Scott's poem, the Lady of the Lake, you will recognize the plot from what we have seen staged tonight. It is quite a common practice for operas; I do not believe that Miss Bennet was accusing the composer of plagiarism but simply commenting on the history of the myth."

The young earl was instantly reminded of why he had never particularly liked Darcy and, after a few comments meant to cover his retreat, was soon off to find a young lady who would be properly awed by his charms.

When the others had moved on, Darcy turned to Elizabeth with a more serious look although amusement still danced in his eyes. "Miss Bennet, may I introduce someone far more worthy of your attention?" At her nod, he continued, "My friend, Lord Michael Trevor, Viscount Hampden. Trevor, it is my honor to present Miss Elizabeth Bennet."

The young lady turned toward Mr. Darcy's companion and he blinked at the intelligence sparkling in her eyes. "And what makes you more deserving of my attention, Lord Hampden? Are you truly *worth* more?"

Trevor blinked again and, tossing a pleased look to Darcy, scrambled to keep up with her word play. "Perhaps not worth more intrinsically, Madam, but I believe I have *spent* more on that which truly matters."

Elizabeth nodded with mock solemnity. "Ah yes. What a man spends in consideration of his worth can only raise his value."

"Except when he concludes himself worth *more* consideration and abandons his values, perhaps."

"Of course, but one hopes that such *revaluation* will lead to *revelation*, not devaluation." With this final sally, Elizabeth was distracted by her aunt and turned away.

"Errr… yes, indeed." Relieved that he had been let off just when he was coming up dry for a witty rejoinder, Trevor turned to his friend and noticed that Darcy looked like a cat replete from a bowl of cream. With a slight bow, the young lord gestured his capitulation. "Brilliant," he said softly. "But do try not to burst your buttons over your pride in her."

Although he knew that Trevor was not speaking literally, Darcy couldn't stop himself from sucking in his stomach and checking Hawkins' re-sewn buttons, although he need not have worried.

Before he could respond, Elizabeth turned back and gracefully introduced the Gardiners and Mrs. Emma Watson who nodded approvingly at the two young men. The six entered into a lively and insightful discussion of the first half of the opera and even Darcy was surprised when the bell was rung, indicating that the intermission was coming to an end.

Trevor excused himself and returned to his own group, though not before admitting quite honestly that he would have preferred to remain with Darcy's party. Fitzwilliam found himself beside Mr. Gardiner mounting the stairs, trailing behind the ladies as they continued discussing one of Mrs. Watson's charity ideas. He was pleased when they all settled into his box in their original seats. Although it was an effort to keep himself under good regulation, every moment spent at Elizabeth's side seemed a blessing.

Darcy had just drifted into a daydream in which he and Elizabeth were attending the opera as husband and wife when his ankle was tapped by a slipper-covered foot.

"What do you think, Mr. Darcy?" Suddenly Fitzwilliam was keenly aware that Mrs. Gardiner was looking at him expectantly, even as Elizabeth's eyes were laughing with mirth.

Swiftly deciding that honesty was the better part of valor, he admitted his inattention. "I apologize, Mrs. Gardiner; I fear I was woolgathering. What was your question?"

Unlike many of Darcy's acquaintances (and relatives) who would have used his poor manners as either an excuse to take offence, or an opportunity to remonstrate him as if he were still a schoolboy, the Gardiners merely laughed jovially. "It is no great matter, sir. You are quite as bad as Mr. Bennet for loosing track of conversations!"

Unaccustomed to such easy manners, Darcy was readying himself to apologize more profusely when the curtains began to rise and the orchestra signaled the second act to begin. Elizabeth must have caught sight of the disturbance in his emotions because she leaned over and patted his arm.

"Do not concern yourself, sir. We were merely discussing the difficulties of wounded soldiers and sailors returning from the wars; not only in recovering from their injuries, but finding work for which they are fit. My Aunt wondered if your cousin, Colonel Fitzwilliam, had mentioned anything about it."

Fitzwilliam snuck a peek at Mrs. Gardiner and it appeared to him that the lady seemed perfectly unconcerned. Still, he was anxious. "I must apologize again. It was impolite of me not to attend to her conversation."

"Mr. Darcy," said Elizabeth firmly. One glance told him that, were they not in a quiet theatre, her laughter would be ringing like silver bells. "Truly, you have met my family. Not attending to a conversation is a necessary survival skill in the Bennet household. If one carefully attended to each and every word, any sensible person would go quite insane… or perhaps just become very, very silly."

Partially convinced, Fitzwilliam nodded his head slightly. "Still, your aunt and uncle are intelligent, interesting people and I did not mean to be disrespectful."

Elizabeth rolled her eyes and, wishing to put an end to Mr. Darcy's guilt and turn her full attention to the performance, spoke softly but with absolute certainty. "Mr. Darcy, as you have just noted, my aunt is an intelligent, sensible person. Respect her ability to discern between an intentional slight and an unintentional lapse in manners. They are very different things, as you well know. Now, if we do not turn our full attention to the players, we ourselves will be guilty of the very offence which you seem intent on blaming yourself."

With that, the lady turned to the stage and raised Mrs. Darcy's opera glasses to her eyes. Fitzwilliam watched her for some moments before remembering to turn his own forward although it was some time before he began to regard the performance again.

How was it that this young lady, grown in a small country hamlet with no formal education, could present him with such simple truths that struck him with all the éclat of a proverb? She cut through the superficial and got at the fundamental issues. It was not the flowery words and fine gestures that the ton was so enamored with that were important but the underlying intentions, the heart of the matter. Poor manners could be disregarded if the intentions were honest but pretty words should not be allowed to cover malicious intent. His mind automatically turned to Wickham, but he readily admitted that others of his acquaintance were equally guilty; Lady Catherine, Miss Bingley, even his own Uncle Fitzwilliam would often work to manipulate his sons and nephew with his offers of "advice."

Darcy was startled when the audience began to applaud at the end of the scene. Sternly, he reminded himself that he could ponder Elizabeth's words at his leisure, when she was not seated beside him and expecting some informed conversation on the opera he was supposed to be watching. Turning to the lady herself, Fitzwilliam caught her studying him with an curious look on her face. Not quite certain what to say, he merely raised his eyebrows in question. Elizabeth laughed softly and colored, dropping her eyes to her hands.

He dared to lean closer and whisper, "Do I have something on my face that amuses you? Perhaps a bit of spinach between my teeth?"

Elizabeth giggled again and risked a glance up at him. Waving her hand negligently, she took note that the next scene was about to begin so leaned toward him and spoke softly, "Not at all… I was just thinking that a few months ago I would never have believed that I would be here, in such company, let alone enjoying it so."

She straightened and turned her attention to the play. After staring at her for a few moments longer, Darcy also turned his eyes forward, although he could not restrain a contented sigh. He felt rather than heard another giggle at his side.

For the remainder of the evening, Darcy felt a warmth in his breast that was perhaps not entirely in keeping with the angst and tragedy of the plot being played out on the stage. When the performance ended and the audience stood to clap, it was almost a surprise to Fitzwilliam that the evening had passed so quickly. As he joined the applause, he couldn't help leaning closer to Miss Bennet and asking, "Did you enjoy it?"

Her shining eyes told him more in a glance than a thousand words. "The music was superb and the soprano playing Elena has a magnificent voice."

He nodded. "I must see if I can find sheet music for my sister; I believe she would enjoy it."

"And thus *you* shall be given the very great pleasure of hearing her play it."

He actually grinned at that. "Ah, you have discovered my very selfish interest in encouraging Georgiana to practice so constantly."

Darcy could tell that Elizabeth was getting ready to tease him when she was distracted by her aunt. Soon the foursome was collecting their coats and preparing to brave the crowd exiting the theatre. Fitzwilliam was more than happy to offer Elizabeth his arm as they followed Mr. and Mrs. Gardiner down the steps.

After fighting their way through the throng, they stepped out into the cool night air. Mr. Darcy was pleased to see that his carriage had been maneuvered close to the door of the opera house, his staff familiar with their master's dislike of lingering after a performance. Fitzwilliam was just about to follow the ladies and Mr. Gardiner into the coach when a high-pitched voice cut across the crowd's murmur with such volume that he could not pretend to have missed it.

"Oh Mr. Darcy! Yoo-hoo! Mr. Darcy!"

Barely stifling a groan, Fitzwilliam cast a last longing look at the dark privacy in his coach before squaring his shoulders and turning back toward the throng. Bustling toward him was an overweight matron in emerald green, eligible daughter trailing in her wake. He stilled his face and gave a very correct bow.

"Mrs. Rockwell."

"Oh, Mr. Darcy... Forgive me for not greeting you earlier; my dear nephew only just mentioned that he had seen you at the intermission!"

Fitzwilliam caught a glimpse of Trevor's embarrassed face approaching them.

"Oh, but where are my manners?" The matron's hands were constantly fluttering, patting her hair, brushing her skirts, waving a handkerchief at her face. Darcy had half a mind to grab them and force her to be still for a moment.

"I knew you would wish to meet my daughter..." Like a curtain, feathers and green silk moved aside to display the prize. "Miss Clarissa Rockwell. Clarissa, greet Mr. Darcy, dear."

Like a doll pulled forth by a puppeteer's strings, the young lady stepped forward and curtsied perfectly, though with absolutely no emotion showing on her doll-like face.

For once feeling more sympathy for the girl than for himself, Darcy bowed correctly to her. "Miss Rockwell." Before either were forced to speak further, Trevor finally broke through the crowd and stepped up to his cousin's elbow.

"Hello again, Darcy. So glad you've had the chance to meet my aunt and cousin."

The two men greeted each other with handshakes, Trevor managing a slight eye roll that Darcy took correctly as an apology for the manners of his relation.

"Michael! You must invite Mr. Darcy to dine with us tomorrow! Surely sir, you will honor us with your presence?"

For once, Fitzwilliam was more amused than disgusted. "My God!" he thought to himself. "She is even more forward than Mrs. Bennet!" Luckily, Trevor intervened before Darcy was forced to begin evasive maneuvers.

"Aunt, have you forgotten that I depart for Bath tomorrow morning?"

"Oh, my dear boy. Surely you can stay another day? To do your cousinly duty?" Her arguments took some minutes but the gentleman was not to be convinced. Darcy recalled that Mrs. Rockwell was several years widowed so it made sense that she would use her nephew's presence in her home to encourage potential suitors to visit and show off her unmarried daughter.

In short order, Trevor brought the argument to a close. "Aunt, Mother expects my return tomorrow and I do not wish to distress her by being tardy just as her health is beginning to return." Mrs. Rockwell was unable to argue with that and he turned to his cousin. "Clarissa, you are looking chilled. It is not good for you to be standing here in the night air without your wrap—we would not want you to catch cold."

The thought of her pretty daughter with a red nose and sniffles in the middle of the Season was enough to propel the matron into action. "Oh no, my dearest girl. How silly to have forgotten our wraps! Come along, Clarissa, come along. Farewell, Mr. Darcy! Please do call on us soon!"

The daughter's farewell was all that was polite, but Darcy caught a flash of relief in her eyes as she turned to follow her mother.

The two gentlemen shared an understanding grin. "Sorry, old chap. She was off like a Derby winner when she caught sight of you."

"Not to worry. Just keep it in mind if my own relations ever descend upon you thus." Although Trevor assumed Will was speaking of his Fitzwilliam kin, Darcy was actually thinking of Mrs. Bennet, fluttering after the viscount with her unmarried daughters in tow. The vision made him smirk.

The two men shared a handshake. "Let us not become strangers again, Darce. I shall write you from Bath and I expect a detailed response!" Trevor glanced at the carriage and managed to shut his mouth before any indiscretions popped out. After a few more words, he departed and Fitzwilliam climbed into the carriage, breathing a sigh of relief when the door was shut and fastened.

Mr. Gardiner could not resist teasing the younger man. "Ah, such a trial to be a single man of large fortune." Darcy rolled his eyes and slumped back into the squabs, prompting the others to laugh as the carriage jerked forward. By the time the horses reached the corner, he had snuck a glance at Elizabeth and, seeing her dancing eyes, joined the laughter with his own deep chuckle.

When Darcy finally climbed the front steps of Derwent House, it was well past midnight but he was unsurprised to be met by his sister, looking sleepy but determined.

"Well?"

Fitzwilliam smiled, handing his coat and hat to the butler and divesting himself of his gloves before turning back to her. "It was a most enjoyable evening."

With a squeak of pleasure, Georgiana gave her brother a hug before drawing him along toward the family sitting room. "Come and tell me all about it! And I've had the most wonderful idea! Why don't we invite Miss Bennet and the Gardiners for a day trip to the gardens at Kew? It is beautiful this time of year and we could have a picnic lunch... and perhaps Uncle James might come to point out all the best plants?"

Will laughed with pleasure to see his formerly melancholic sister bubbling over with ideas and happily resigned himself to not retiring for another hour or so. He had to admit that the idea of exploring the Royal Botanic Gardens with Elizabeth on his arm was vastly appealing.

12 DRUNK AND DISORDERLY

The morning after the opera, Darcy woke with the dawn despite his late night. He lay in bed for a few minutes, running his mind over the previous evening's highlights and allowing hope to blossom in his heart. He was fairly certain that Elizabeth had forgiven him and indeed, the warm look that she had gifted him upon his departure the previous night left him with some optimism that she might come to love him in time.

Will's hope made him restless and he soon left his bed and began his morning ablutions. He was desperate to talk to Elizabeth privately; not to propose again (he knew it was too soon for that), but simply to speak with her... to get some sense of where he stood. Fitzwilliam was well pleased with Georgiana's suggestion of inviting the Gardiners and their niece for a day trip to Kew Gardens; he decided that such an invitation was a reasonable excuse to visit them again so soon.

Darcy's late night discussion with his sister had also given him the glimmer of another idea—one which his sister had immediately agreed was brilliant in its conception. He knew that the Gardiners were planning to depart within a fortnight for an abbreviated tour of the northern counties. With his new knowledge of Mrs. Gardiner's connections to Lambton, he planned to invite them to stay at his estate. Mrs. Gardiner could reacquaint herself with Lambton and they might be able to recover any artifacts that remained from her family. And Fitzwilliam would be able to show Pemberley to Elizabeth, the one place in the world where he felt completely comfortable.

Darcy arrived at Gracechurch Street much too early for a proper call. He was informed by the Gardiners' manservant that the family was in the park across the street but was expected to return within the hour. Darcy declined an invitation to wait for them in the parlor and crossed the street to the park. Suddenly bashful over his eagerness to see Elizabeth again,

Fitzwilliam found a bench protected from other walkers by a tall hedge and prepared to wait.

Unfortunately, although the dense yews kept him from being seen, it did not shield him from overhearing conversations. Not long after sitting, Darcy recognized Mr. and Mrs. Gardiner's voices coming from the other side of the hedge. He was about to move on but could not help but overhear part of their discussion, and what he heard felt like a knife to his heart.

"It is very good to have Lizzy here with us. Her spirits seem to have risen since she first arrived," spoke Mr. Gardiner's deeper voice.

Mrs. Gardiner replied, "Well, I cannot imagine that being in Kent was very pleasant after enduring that man's proposal. And Longbourn must have been completely intolerable. Her mother would never allow her to forget that she turned down such an *eligible* offer."

Edward sighed heavily. "In my heart, I know that my sister loves her girls, but I do wish she would not look at her daughters' marriages with such an eye to her own comfort."

"Jane and Lizzy have too much sense to accept a proposal that is not founded on respect and affection. I do worry about the other girls, though."

"Yes, I wish Thomas would exert himself to check Lydia and Kitty's manners instead of amusing himself over their performances, as he calls it."

"He seemed different on this last visit. He actually told me that I should appreciate my children while they were still young— that they would grow up far too quickly, particularly the girls."

Darcy forced himself to stand and walk away. He could not bear to hear any more; his heart was already shattered. To think that he had been considering asking Elizabeth for permission to court her! Clearly she had been only tolerating him, just as she ever had. And now she probably had some misbegotten sense of gratitude for him having come across her at the right time to rescue her in the park. Once again he had entirely misread her.

When would he learn? Even if she *had* absolved him of his actions toward Wickham and Bingley, her basic dislike remained. Had she not made that abundantly clear on that hideous evening at Hunsford? Was he such a masochist that he desired her to repeat that litany of faults?

It made Fitzwilliam physically ill to think that Mrs. Bennet knew all about his proposal and Elizabeth's rejection, for certainly it meant that all of Hertfordshire knew as well. He could not bear to imagine the attention he would have received at Longbourn, had he arrived to ask permission to court the second daughter of the house.

Mr. Darcy was forced to drag his attention to the present when the Gardiners' stable boy appeared before him. After the gentleman made known his desire, the lad was quick about retrieving his horse. Fearing who he might meet if he returned to the front of the house, Fitzwilliam rode out through the mews. It was probably lucky that he had ridden an older, well-trained mount that day for he gave little attention to his direction. When he arrived at his own home on Grosvenor Square, he was surprised, having no memory of the return trip. He dismounted with little of the grace he normally possessed and handed the reins over with barely a word.

Upon entering the house, Darcy stood for a moment in the foyer, removing his hat and coat. He knew he should go to his study and work but he could not face it. He spoke curtly to the butler; "Holmes, I shall be unavailable for the rest of the day. Please inform my sister that I shall not be able to dine with her this evening."

And with that, Darcy climbed the stairs to his private chambers, making a brief detour to the billiards room to collect the decanter of brandy that was kept there. After instructing his valet that the master was not to be disturbed for the remainder of the day, Will proceeded to drink himself into oblivion.

Fitzwilliam Darcy was not a man given to excessive consumption of spirits; he valued his self-control too much for that. He enjoyed a glass of wine with dinner and the cellars at both Pemberley and Derwent House were well-stocked with an array of fine vintages. Although he disliked cigars and snuff, he would not turn down a good brandy or port after dinner. Though his staid reputation did not include that of teetotaler, even at university he was more likely to be the one who saw his mates home safely after a night spent indulging.

In truth, Darcy had only been truly drunk once, when he had graduated from university and come of age, and it was an experience that he tried assiduously to forget for more reasons than one. Today, however, he locked the door to his rooms and poured himself a brandy before even loosening his cravat. By the time he had removed it along with his coat and boots, he had emptied the glass.

Grabbing the decanter, Darcy settled into one of the comfortable settees that were arranged before the fire in his private sitting room. Slumping back and stretching his legs out before him, Will took a long sip and welcomed the fuzziness creeping into his mind.

"Foolish idiot," he said to himself.

Raising his eyes, he studied the painting above the mantle. These rooms were wholly his own; he had not seen the need to move into his father's chambers upon the late Mr. Darcy's death as his own apartment was already arranged to his liking. That he had recently been thinking of redecorating the Master's rooms (and the Mistress' chambers that were connected to it) was a painful notion that he crushed as quickly as he could.

The painting was a landscape done in oils. It had been the first piece of art Will had bought himself and though he could not explain why, it had always reassured him. The artist had been traveling through Derbyshire on the way to the Lake District during the summer after Fitzwilliam's father had passed away. The young man had presented himself at Pemberley and requested permission to wander the park for a few weeks to sketch and paint where he found inspiration. Mired in his own mourning and overwhelmed by estate business and a distraught twelve-year-old sister, Darcy had given permission without a thought.

On his last day before departing Derbyshire, Mr. John Constable had presented himself at Pemberley House again, this time with a beautiful landscape for the master to thank him for his hospitality. Darcy could spend hours studying the painting; its clouds recalling a summer day in Derbyshire and the trees and grass so realistic that he could almost feel the wind blowing through them with the smell of home. He had brought the painting to London so that he might have it to comfort him while he did his duty to maintain the Darcy place in Society.

Fitzwilliam had been considering commissioning Constable to paint a landscape of the countryside around Longbourn—perhaps from Oakham Mount— for Elizabeth, thinking that it might help heal any homesickness she might have for Hertfordshire. When they were married. *Something that would never happen.* All the pain came crashing down on Fitzwilliam again and he covered his eyes with his arm.

Although curious, Georgiana did not worry excessively about her brother until the following morning. She had assumed that he was out for dinner the previous day but when he did not join her for breakfast she questioned the butler more closely. Upon hearing that the Master had in fact been closeted in his rooms for most of the previous day and had not yet risen, she pondered the situation but did not have the courage to confront him.

When it came time for dinner, Miss Darcy sent a message up to her brother's room, asking if he would be joining her. She was dismayed when the butler himself came to her.

"Miss Darcy, Mr. Darcy has indicated that he will not be dining with you."

Georgiana's increasing anxiety overrode her innate shyness. Even with the new closeness which the Darcy siblings had shared over these past weeks, she had never probed into her brother's private affairs without his express encouragement.

"Is he going out?" she asked timidly.

"No, Miss." Holmes cleared his throat but decided that the situation was dire enough to convey a few details to the Master's sister. "Mr. Darcy has not left his rooms since he returned from a ride yesterday morning."

The young lady wrapped her arms around herself. "Is he ill? Should we have the doctor fetched?"

The butler prevaricated. "The Master does not appear to be in need of a physician."

"Has he eaten?"

Holmes looked decidedly uncomfortable. "His valet sent for a plate of cold meats, cheese, and bread around noon, but it was returned largely untouched." He sighed and could not meet the young lady's eyes. "In truth, Miss Darcy, the only request that the Master himself has made was for another decanter of brandy."

Georgiana could not help stare at the servant for several minutes. "Brandy!? Wait, did you say *another* decanter?"

"Yes, Miss. He took one from the billiards room when he arrived home yesterday."

"And it is empty? And he desired another?" Georgie had never seen her brother drink to excess (unlike some of her other relatives).

"Yes, Miss." For a moment, servant and mistress looked each other in the eye, their concern mirrored.

Georgiana's mind spun. Her first impulse was to send for her Cousin Richard, but Colonel Fitzwilliam's duties currently had him in Newcastle. She shied away from seeking help of any of their other relations; her brother would be mortified if they were to know of his behavior and her Uncle Henry might even try to force him to turn over Georgiana's guardianship. For a moment she considered sending for Miss Bennet, but surely her brother's attempt to gain that lady's good opinion would not be aided by her seeing him in such a state.

Miss Darcy squared her thin shoulders and stood. "Well, I suppose I shall have to see him myself," she said softly.

The walk to her brother's rooms had never seemed so long. For the first time, Georgiana noticed that the servants were being exceptionally quiet as they went about their usual duties. When she reached the door to her brother's private sitting room, she paused to gather her courage before tapping her knuckles lightly on the wood. She waited nearly a minute but there was no response. Steadying herself, Georgie knocked harder.

The wood was very thick but she could hear a faint response that sounded like her brother's voice in pitch but not in tone. "Go away! I gave explicit orders that I am to be left alone."

"Fitzwilliam? It is I, Georgiana. Please let me in. I am worried about you." She wasn't sure if her voice could be heard through the solid oak door, so she knocked again.

She couldn't hear anything from the inside, but suddenly a door down the hall opened and she recognized her brother's valet.

Hawkins looked as if he were about to say something, but upon recognizing Miss Darcy he shut his jaw with a snap and retreated back into her brother's dressing room.

After some minutes Hawkins reemerged, looking awkward. "Miss

Darcy, Mr. Darcy has asked me to inform you that he will be unable to dine with you."

"But I just want to see him for a moment!"

The servant looked even more uncomfortable. "I am sorry, Miss, but Mr. Darcy has made it clear that he desires solitude."

Georgiana turned away and walked quickly to her own rooms, barely closing the door behind her before bursting into tears. An hour later, her maid found her curled up in the window seat of her own private sitting room, hugging an old doll and still crying.

An older woman who had served the Darcy family all her life, Penny did her best to comfort the girl. "There, there, Miss. I've sent for some broth and a bit of pudding. Should you like to wash your face? There's fresh, cool water in the basin."

For the most part, Georgiana let her maid mother her without complaint. Soon she found herself in her robe with a clean face, eating Mrs. Davies' delicious chicken soup and eyeing a large wedge of apple tart.

"Oh, Penny! What am I to do? I've never seen Wills like this," she wailed, her bewilderment clear in her expression.

"There, there, Miss. You put it all out of your mind and get some sleep. Solving problems is always easier after a good night's rest." Penny settled into the chair beside Georgiana's bed and hummed quietly. Though Georgie had expected to be up all night with worry, the humming and the familiar clicking of Penny's knitting needles soothed her and she slept deeply.

It was almost a surprise to be awakened by morning sun streaming through the windows. For a moment, Georgiana remembered nothing of her worries and simply enjoyed the dawn of what looked to be a lovely spring day.

Penny's appearance brought back the bad memories but she refused to let Fitzwilliam's behavior overwhelm her again. Choosing a pretty pink gown that never failed to comfort her, Georgiana dressed carefully before going down to the breakfast room. She was disappointed but not surprised when her brother did not join her. Sipping her tea, she considered her day.

When the butler appeared, she forced herself to speak with authority. "Holmes, I will be busy with my music lesson this morning—I believe that Mr. Alexander will be arriving at half past ten. I would like to have luncheon at one, and then I may be making a call in the afternoon, if you could have the carriage ready for me at three."

Holmes was nodding attentively but Miss Darcy still had to gather her courage to add her last request.

"If my brother emerges from his rooms, please tell me immediately, regardless of what I am doing."

She was somewhat reassured when the butler gave her a brief smile. "Of course, Miss."

Miss Darcy was a dedicated musician but that morning she was disappointed when her lesson was not interrupted despite the excellent instruction and interesting new piece she was working through. After Mr. Alexander departed, she continued to play, attempting to focus her angst into a grueling new piece by Mr. Beethoven. She was only partially successful.

That afternoon, after again dining alone, Georgiana decided to mount an offensive. Settling in her own sitting room, she directed her maid to speak to Fitzwilliam's valet.

"Tell him that I am hurt, and you will send for my Aunt and Uncle Fitzwilliam if Mr. Darcy is not able to come to me. You do not need to tell him how I am hurt and belay any order he sends to fetch the doctor."

In short order, Fitzwilliam appeared at the door to her sitting room, clearly concerned. However, his appearance quelled any guilt she felt over her misdirection. Georgiana had never seen her brother look so disreputable, wearing crumpled clothes and sporting two days' growth of beard.

"Georgie—what has happened? Hawkins said that you were hurt!" He came and sat beside her and Georgiana wrinkled her nose at his odor.

"I *am* hurt; my heart hurts! You have been shut up in your room for days without a word to me or anyone! What has happened, Fitzwilliam? What is wrong?"

Her brother directed a furious look at her unlike she had ever received from him before. She only kept going because she also saw a great deal of pain in his eyes. Rising, she stood to take her brother's hand, holding tightly when he tried to pull away.

"Please, Brother! Is it me? Have I done something wrong?"

Instantly, Darcy's face changed to contrition. "No, Georgie. You have done nothing wrong. You must not worry; it has nothing to do with you."

A bit of frustration edged Miss Darcy's voice. "Then *what?* Have you lost all our fortune? Shall we be thrown out into the hedgerows without a farthing to our name?"

A tiny smile touched Fitzwilliam's face for a moment. "No, dearest. Every sovereign is accounted for." Suddenly he looked exhausted.

Georgie tried for a bit of levity. "Well, that is a relief. I might make a living from my music, but I very much doubt you would ever make a good servant."

Darcy merely blinked at her, his residual intoxication making it difficult to comprehend even a mild tease. Georgie searched her mind for any clue as to what had so devastated her brother. Perhaps...

"I had thought to call on the Gardiners this afternoon. Will you join me? It has been some days since we saw them or Miss Bennet." Her unasked question was answered by the black look that settled on her brother's face.

"*NO!* No, I shall not be joining you." And with that, he strode from the room without another word to his sister.

It was some time before Penny was able to calm the distraught girl enough that she could sleep, tucked in with a doll she had not slept with for months. The former nurse turned lady's maid descended to the kitchens, clucking her tongue with displeasure.

"I've gotten her to nap for a bit, poor mite." Penny spoke quietly to the cook and housekeeper. "A bit of chicken broth and some new bread when she wakes, Mrs. Davies, if you please. I'm not sure what has so upset the master but someone needs to get him straightened out before the young miss worries herself to death." The older servants spoke a few words in commiseration before turning back to their duties. They were all deeply loyal to the Darcys and such turmoil in the family disturbed the staff greatly.

The next morning, Georgiana rose late from her rumpled bed with grim determination. After a lonely breakfast in her room (she could not face the family breakfast room alone again), she sat down at her writing desk and penned two notes in her clearest script. The first was soon on its way to Gracechurch Street, inviting Miss Elizabeth Bennet to spend the afternoon with her.

The second note was given over to the butler to deliver to her brother immediately upon Elizabeth's arrival at Derwent House. Miss Darcy gave careful instructions that, should her brother refuse to open it, Holmes or Hawkins was to read it aloud to him.

> *My dear Brother,*
> *Miss Elizabeth Bennet will be spending the afternoon with me and I hope to take her on a tour of our home. I would be very happy if you joined us for tea.*
> *Georgiana*

Miss Darcy was not certain what response she was hoping to garner from her note. Ideally, Fitzwilliam would clean himself up and join them. She had a brief flight of fancy in which she would include her brother's rooms on Elizabeth's tour of the house and that lady would tease Will out of his funk. Georgie was certain that Miss Bennet was fully capable of it but unsure if Darcy would ever forgive his sister for allowing his beloved to see him in such a state.

The messenger soon returned with a note from Gracechurch Street accepting her "kind invitation" and Georgiana was left with several hours to pass before her visitor arrived. She attempted a book on the history of the

Roman Empire but soon abandoned it in favor of a lighter book of verse; however neither held her attention for long. She turned to a piece of embroidery that was half finished but succeeded only in stabbing her finger several times.

Throwing the offending needlework into her basket, Georgiana slumped back in her chair with a most unladylike grumble. Looking around her room, she was struck with a sudden desire that the Derwent House servants would not be quite so efficient—she had a great craving to straighten, sort, or clean something. For a moment she considered finding the linen closet and refolding the sheets.

It was probably lucky for the housekeeper's nerves that Miss Darcy's eyes fell upon her own desk and bookshelves at that moment. Instead of joining the scullery maid in the kitchens washing dishes, Georgie spent the remainder of the morning organizing her correspondence and alphabetizing her books. As for many, a tidy house begat a tidy mind and before she knew it was time to ready herself for her visitor.

Elizabeth arrived promptly, descending from the Gardiner carriage and blowing into the foyer of Derwent House with a gust of May wind. Miss Darcy did her best to focus on her guest and hide her emotional distress as they greeted each other. Even so, Elizabeth caught a glance between the young mistress and the butler that led her to intuit that something was not quite right.

The two ladies were just sitting down to tea in the music room when the butler announced Mr. Bingley. Elizabeth easily recognized that her new friend was just as surprised as she was. She watched carefully, but there was no sign that Mr. Bingley viewed Miss Darcy as anything other than the young sister of his good friend.

She did notice that the gentleman appeared a little thinner than he had been in Hertfordshire and had shadows on his face suggesting a lack of sleep. His eyes seemed to search her face with a desperate intensity that she had never seen in him before, and in a flash of intuition she understood that he was looking for similarities to her sister.

As her two guests were greeting each other, Georgiana was thinking furiously. Her ploy to lure Fitzwilliam from his rooms with a visit from Miss Elizabeth had not worked and she could not take a single lady into his apartment, however good her intentions. But Mr. Bingley... even in his worst moments, her brother had stressed his intention to confess everything to his friend and surely Mr. Bingley could cheer up anyone short of a corpse.

Mind made up, Georgiana waited for a natural break in the conversation. "Mr. Bingley, I know that my brother wished to see you immediately upon your return from Yorkshire. However, he is unwell and is forced to remain in his rooms today. It is nothing contagious, I assure you, but would you mind visiting him in his chambers? I know he very much wished to speak with you." Georgie finished in a rush, slightly embarrassed by her prevarication to such a gentle, friendly man.

As she expected, Mr. Bingley was all concern and friendliness. "Of course! I admit that my purpose in calling was to see your brother. Darcy's note left me very curious—hence my appearance on your doorstep just an hour after my return to London. But is he well enough to receive a visitor? I can't imagine Darcy being ill—he always seems immune to whatever befalls us lesser mortals."

Georgiana was already leading him to the door where a footman would guide him to her brother's private sitting room. "Oh, your visit will do him a great deal of good. He can tell you all about it." And with that, Charles Bingley was bustled off to visit his friend. It was only after he had departed up the stairs that Georgie realized that Holmes himself was doing the honors. She smiled slightly; her Aunt Eleanor had once told her that the best servants knew what their master or mistress wanted before they knew it themselves.

Georgiana's smile vanished when she turned back to the room and saw the concerned look on Miss Bennet's face. "Mr. Darcy is ill?" Unable to conceal her worry in the face of such genuine solicitude, the younger girl burst into tears and was soon guided to a settee and wrapped in Elizabeth's arms, taking comfort as her back was rubbed and soothing noises made.

"Is this what it would be like to have a sister?" she wondered to herself inconsequently.

Meanwhile, Charles Bingley was having a very odd afternoon. Guided upstairs by the butler, he gave it little thought when the servant tapped on a door that was opened by Hawkins, Mr. Darcy's valet. It was a little strange that the two led him through the master's dressing room but if Darcy was indeed ill, then perhaps the rooms had been rearranged to suit whatever his needs were.

It was not until Mr. Bingley stepped into his friend's private sitting room that he realized that something was definitely wrong. Fitzwilliam Darcy, Master of Pemberley, owner of half of Derbyshire, nephew of the Earl of Matlock and head of the illustrious Darcy family was seated on the floor by a large chest that he appeared to have been pushing to block the hall door. He was dressed only in a shirt and breeches and appeared to be growing an impressive set of whiskers.

"Charles?" asked a slurred voice. At that moment, Mr. Bingley noticed the half-empty whiskey bottle in his friend's hand. He was too stunned to reply.

"Charles? Is that you? Or perraps I'm to be visited by visions of all the people I've wronged... serves me right... half of England will be here..."

Bingley shook himself. He might never have seen Darcy soused to the eyeballs before but he certainly had experience with friends drowning themselves in a bottle and could recognize a maudlin drunk at fifty paces.

"Hullo, Darce. I'm just back from Yorkshire and dropped by. Miss Darcy sent me up. How are you?" He adopted a light tone even as he studied the other man carefully.

"Oh... course she sent you up... I's afraid she'd send *HER*." Suddenly Darcy looked up from the patch of carpet he had been studying. "But how'd you get in? Thought I'd battened down the hatches so's any raiding parties couldn't... couldn't... get in." After waving the whiskey bottle around the room, Darcy peered up at the other man. "Can't let 'em in, you know. Hurts too much."

Charles didn't know, exactly, but he had enough information to be of service to his friend. The first step was to separate the man from the immediate source of his downfall. Keeping his tone friendly and conversational, he bent down on his knees. "Hmmm... Well, I've pulled up the gangplank behind me and Hawkins is guarding it, so I'd say we're safe for the present."

When Darcy grunted and seemed somewhat mollified, Charles continued. "Mind if I have a taste of that? I've just spent an hour being henpecked by Caroline; apparently I've wrecked her Season because I wasn't in town to provide an escort." He was pleased when the other man grunted and handed over the bottle.

"Must tell her I'm not going to marry her. Not going to marry anyone, but 'specially not her. Too much orange... feathers... can't be natural." Bingley hid his smirk at his friend's slurred words by rising and carrying the bottle to the side door where he had entered. He was not surprised to find both Hawkins and Holmes standing on the other side. Handing them the bottle, he spoke quietly and then turned back to his unlikely charge.

"Hope you don't mind, Darce; I've asked Hawkins to bring us some food. I'm a tad peckish after the carriage ride this morning. We came straight on from Biggleswade without a stop."

It was odd to find himself in the role of caretaker but Bingley assumed the mantle without much thought. He seated himself on the floor by Darcy and listened to the man's drunken ramblings with only minor contributions until the food arrived. Then he helped his friend to a pair of armchairs by the window and encouraged him to eat some sandwiches and drink a large mug of strong tea.

Both men ate quietly. Bingley had been honest in his admission of hunger and Darcy had eaten little in days and found food surprisingly appealing. When Fitzwilliam finally finished his sandwich, he leaned back into the armchair, cradling the mug to his chest. His eyes looked a bit clearer and his friend watched him curiously out of the corner of his eye.

When Darcy spoke, his diction was improved but the tone was no less morose. "Charles, you shouldn't be so kind to me. I've ruined your life."

Bingley finished chewing his last bite and swallowed, not quite sure where to start on such a sweeping statement. "Well, that's rather extreme, don't you think? I'm not out on the street or shut up in Newgate prison yet, am I?"

"But Miss Bennet... if you love her as I do, you would not care what your life is like if she is not in it."

Bingley was startled. He had put Miss Elizabeth's presence in Derwent House out of his mind when faced with the ragged state of his friend. He had dallied in Yorkshire, free from sisters and friends, to sort through his feelings for Jane and had returned with a determination to seek her out again. Now here was his closest friend, seemingly declaring that he himself loved Miss Bennet.

"You love Miss Bennet?" was all he could think to utter.

Fitzwilliam pressed himself back further into the cushions and covered his eyes with one arm, completely unaware of the confusion he was causing in his friend. "Yes, may God help me, yes. I think I've loved her since we were all at Netherfield. But what *I* enjoyed as friendly banter, she took as arguments. She hates me. She *hates* me, and I cannot help but still love her."

Something was off, but Bingley could not quite put his finger on it. Darcy had argued often enough with Miss Elizabeth, but Miss Jane Bennet tended to watch her younger sister with amusement rather than actively participate in the debate.

"Darcy, are you telling me that you warned me off of Jane so that you could pursue her?" Bingley did not bother to keep the boiling anger out of his tone.

The other gentlemen moved his arm enough to look at Charles, his face wreathed with confusion. "Jane? Jane loves you. Even though she hates me, Elizabeth assured me that *you* were held in affection."

Bingley was still confused but Darcy's words were giving him a glimmer of hope that he had not felt in months. "Jane loves me? But why would you be discussing it with Miss Elizabeth? And why does Jane hate you?"

"I don't know if Jane hates me, though I suppose she will when she learns I am to blame for her months of heartache..." Will trailed off morosely, unaware of how his sloppy use of pronouns had confused his companion.

Charles had a flash of intuition. "You are in love with Miss Elizabeth!" When his friend groaned in agreement, he continued; "And she hates you? It was obvious that she did not *like* you much when we were all together in Hertfordshire, but why on Earth would you think she hates you? Why, she is downstairs visiting with your sister at this very instant!"

It was a long, enlightening hour later that Charles Bingley let himself out of Darcy's rooms, leaving the master to be tucked into bed by his faithful valet. For a moment, the young man leaned back against the door and closed his eyes. In Hertfordshire, he had guessed that his friend had admired Elizabeth Bennet's sparkling wit and slim figure but had said nothing, having been consumed by his own infatuation with another Bennet sister.

In truth, Charles Bingley had never given matrimony much thought before meeting Miss Jane Bennet. Although Darcy was several years older, Charles had never considered that his friend might be seriously considering taking a wife. The depth of Darcy's emotions for Miss Elizabeth and his subsequent wretchedness after her refusal left Charles stunned. He was determined to aid his friend, even as he was determined to help himself now that the truth of Jane's feelings had been revealed.

But how to go about it? His final words to Darcy, voicing a hope that all might yet be set to rights, had been met with total condemnation for his own situation, even as he hoped Bingley and Jane might recover their affection. Charles had chosen to delay that discussion for another day when his friend had had time to rest and recover. To himself, Charles recognized that Darcy had advised him but he himself had made the decision to drop his pursuit of Jane. Or rather, he had made no decision at all and just allowed himself be drawn along by his sisters and friends.

Charles Bingley's brows knit together in an uncommon expression of thoughtfulness. Darcy had given him advice based on his honest perception of the lady and his desire to protect his friend. Now that he realized that he was in the wrong, he had acted immediately to rectify the matter and was obviously experiencing no little guilt over his error. Charles could not condemn that. His sister (possibly *both* sisters) was a different matter altogether.

Although Charles might be generally absentminded, he had a very clear, precise memory of anything that concerned Jane Bennet. He was absolutely certain that, on multiple occasions over the last few months, he had asked Caroline if she had received any correspondence from their Hertfordshire acquaintances in general and from Miss Bennet in particular. Caroline had denied it unequivocally and had used this supposed termination of the ladies' friendship as further evidence that Jane held little affection for him.

Now he had learned from Darcy that Jane had not only written to Caroline repeatedly but had exchanged visits with her in London, right under his nose. In that instant, Charles Bingley experienced a rare moment of fury and, if it all turned out as he expected, disgust, with his sister. He would give her a chance to explain herself but her manipulation of him as part of her own desperate social climbing was at an end.

Deep in thought, Charles did not realize that he had been standing alone in the hall for some minutes until he heard another door click shut further along in the family wing. Opening his eyes and turning his head, it was somehow completely appropriate to offer a companionable if tired grin to Miss Elizabeth Bennet.

She returned his greeting with a similar expression and took his proffered arm as they turned to descend the stairs.

"I have just left Miss Darcy to rest. She has been very concerned…" Elizabeth paused, not sure how much to say. Her head was filled after providing a willing shoulder for the younger girl to cry on. The confusing emotional flood that had resulted from just a little compassion had left Elizabeth spent, as well as more appreciative of her own sisters than ever.

"And I have just left Mr. Darcy to sleep off his… indisposition." Charles wasn't certain how much Miss Darcy might have told Miss Elizabeth and he wasn't about to reduce his friend's chances of gaining her good opinion by revealing that the man had gotten sloppy drunk after overhearing a few words in the shrubbery.

Reaching the bottom of the stairs, the pair paused uncertainly for a moment; two guests alone, having just put their host and hostess to bed after sharing the most intimate of confidences. Bingley caught her eye and his chuckle was met with a corresponding grin over their situation.

In that instant, having so recently been disillusioned over the actions of his own siblings, Charles Bingley was struck by how much he would enjoy having the woman standing before him as a sister. He rapidly made a decision.

"Miss Elizabeth, I should very much like to speak with you for a few minutes. Though we appear to have lost our hosts, Darcy has often urged me to treat Derwent House as my own. Would you consider it very improper if I suggested we share some refreshment before departing to our respective homes?"

Elizabeth smiled, finding that her esteem for Jane's admirer had not dimmed in the months of his absence. "Yes, Mr. Bingley. I would like that very much, although I shall have to rely on you to direct me; I am afraid that I am quite lost."

"Of course." And with a grin and a flourish, Bingley offered his arm again and guided them to a small sitting room, leaving Elizabeth alone for a moment as he consulted with Mr. Holmes. The tray of cakes that appeared within minutes was testament to both the staff's efficiency and the butler's belief that these visitors had brought much needed relief to whatever had been ailing the master over these last days.

After devouring several biscuits along with a cup of tea, Bingley looked up to see Elizabeth's sparkling eyes laughing at him. He smiled guiltily. "Forgive my manners, Miss Elizabeth. I find that playing Father Confessor is hungry work."

With an ostentatious flourish, Elizabeth filled her own plate equally full before nudging the tray back toward Mr. Bingley. "I quite understand, sir.

Having four sisters, I am well aware of the curative powers of a bit of pudding!" After sharing conspiratorial grins, she added, "Have you ever noticed that many of the good clergy portrayed on the stage are given toward plumpness? I have often wondered if shouldering the concerns of so many must require greater sustenance than the average mortal."

The two shared a chuckle and Bingley helped himself to another biscuit before steering his mind to the discussion he wished to have. After giving up on several possible openings, he put his cup on the table and slouched back in the settee.

"Miss Elizabeth, I have had a great deal revealed to me today, much of it exceedingly personal in nature. I am no good at subtlety and I rather think that I've seen quite enough of what happens when someone bottles up all their feelings behind a mask."

Elizabeth's features had immediately assumed a more serious cast and she nodded for him to continue.

Bingley sighed and ran one hand through his hair. "Darcy has told me what occurred between the two of you in Kent, as well as confessing the errors in judgment that led to his advice that I... that Miss Bennet..." He could not quite work out how to phrase it, but looked up when he felt a hand on his arm and was reassured by the strained but compassionate smile on Elizabeth's face, so like that of her sister.

Encouraged, he continued in a rush. "I want you to understand that I have felt a force of attraction for your sister that is beyond anything I have ever experienced, from the first moment I saw her. I'd never considered marriage before, you see."

Hearing a sharp intake of breath, Charles looked up and saw that Miss Elizabeth's visage had moved from strained to discomposed. "Forgive me for such honesty; I do realize it is totally improper to discuss such things but I beg you... I know I must confess all of my feelings to Miss Bennet and earn her forgiveness, indeed I had come to that conclusion even before I returned from Yorkshire, but... perhaps if you would just hear me out?"

He had such the appearance of a little boy desperate for approval that Elizabeth couldn't help but pat his arm again and laugh slightly. An odd feeling of euphoria enveloped her; a sense that all was soon to be set right.

"Mr. Bingley, I admit that I have always valued honesty over protocol and, having listened to Miss Darcy's worries for the last hour..." She sighed and leaned forward to cup her chin in her hand. "I will not betray any confidences that my sister has shared with me, but everything else... it would be a relief, to be truthful."

The two shared an understanding look and Bingley took a moment to organize his thoughts. "Let me start, then. I care for your sister a great deal... I knew that in Hertfordshire, although I suppose I did not realize just how much I *loved* her until we were separated. Last fall, I came to

London with every intention of returning to Netherfield within the week. I… I suppose I let my insecurities get the better of me." Seeing that Elizabeth was about to speak, he waved her off.

"Darcy said his piece and that was the end of it, but Caroline had some catty comment every time Hertfordshire or country society was mentioned." He grimaced down at his hands. "I visit my family in Yorkshire every spring, but I freely admit to being relieved that my sisters chose not to accompany me this year. The time alone… it gave me time to think. To consider what *I* wanted… What is important to *me*. And it is certainly not the social climbing that Caro has been using me for."

Charles took a sip of tea, appreciating Elizabeth's ability to listen quietly. "By the time I returned from Yorkshire, I had decided that the only reason to avoid Miss Bennet's company that carried any weight with me was Darcy's concern that she did not show any particular regard for me… but might be convinced to accept an offer of marriage because of… familial… obligations." He looked apologetically at his companion.

This time Elizabeth could not remain silent. "Mr. Bingley, I assure you, Jane and I have long sworn to each other that neither of us will ever marry without first being assured of the respect and affection of and for our partners. Regardless of what my mother may say, our father will support us."

Charles nodded vigorously. "That is exactly what I would have thought of you… of both of you. Jane is so gentle and serene, but there is a strength about her…" He trailed off, his eyes looking off into the distance. When he recalled himself to the present, Elizabeth was smiling warmly at him.

"Mr. Bingley, as I said, I will not betray anyone else's confidences. However, I am comfortable telling you of my own observations. My sister hides her emotions but she feels very deeply. I can tell you that I have never seen her happier than she was last autumn, and I have never seen her lower than after your party departed Netherfield. She took your sister's note commenting on your increasing intimacy with Miss Darcy as a friendly warning."

Mr. Bingley sat up straight, eyes blazing. Elizabeth grimaced apologetically. "I am sorry, but I suggested that Miss Bingley might have an ulterior motive. However, Jane is far more trusting than I and could not believe that her new friend would tell her anything but the absolute truth." Elizabeth took a deep breath and let it out slowly.

"Jane came to London to stay with our uncle and aunt after Christmas. After several notes to Miss Bingley went unanswered, Jane called at Mrs. Hurst's home. Your sisters expressed surprise at her appearance and indicated that none of her letters had been received. They were unable to visit with her for long as Miss Bingley indicated that she had an appointment that could not be delayed. My sister departed under the impression that her friends would return the call, but it was three weeks before Miss Bingley appeared at Gracechurch Street. From what my aunt has said, it was a very brief, very uncomfortable visit."

Elizabeth stopped herself for a moment, reminded that she was speaking to the lady's brother. However, a look at Charles Bingley's face reassured her. His eyes were focused on her and his face held a grim determination that she had never seen there before. "Please continue, Miss Elizabeth. I would very much appreciate hearing the truth."

Thinking carefully about what she could and could not say, Elizabeth spoke carefully. "My sister wrote to me in Kent after Miss Bingley's call and indicated that she considered the connection severed. Since then, she avoids speaking of anything related to the Netherfield party." She stopped. Anything further would have to come from Jane.

"Is your sister still here in London?"

"No, sir. She returned to Hertfordshire in April."

Charles couldn't resist one last question. "And is she receiving any suitors?"

Elizabeth smiled softly at the eager gentleman. "No, sir."

Although Charles would have preferred to spend the next hour quizzing Miss Elizabeth on anything and everything to do with Jane, her mention of Kent had reminded him of his friend's heartbreak. After allowing himself one last vision of Jane smiling at him during their dance at the Netherfield ball, he forced his mind away.

Considering his words for a moment, Charles spoke carefully. "Miss Elizabeth, as I said earlier, Darcy told me a great deal about what occurred between the two of you in Kent."

Seeing his companion's cheeks flush and her eyes drop to her hands, it was Charles' turn to pat her arm reassuringly. "Please understand, my friend is not in the habit of exposing his personal problems, particularly when they involve someone else, and I shall never speak of it to anyone. He was not... not well... and desperately needed a confidant."

Charles paused for a moment and found that Elizabeth's eyes were focused intently on him. "Sir, you mentioned that Mr. Darcy is unwell but I still do not understand. Is he ill? I saw him earlier this week when he accompanied my uncle's family to the opera and he appeared to be in fine health."

Bingley was uncertain how to proceed, but the concern in Elizabeth's eyes made him believe that Jane's sister might be well on her way to returning his friend's feelings. "Miss Elizabeth, I will be blunt. My friend has drunk an excessive amount of sprits these last two days, which is something I have never seen him do in the many years of our long friendship. Darcy is always the responsible one; he would nurse a glass though the evening and then shepherd the rest of us home safely."

Elizabeth covered her mouth with her hands but when Bingley looked into her eyes he saw concern mixed with embarrassment, not condemnation. This encouraged him enough to continue. "As best as I can tell, Darce was feeling hopeful that he might be able to improve your opinion of him. Your words in Kent shook him to the core, but also opened his eyes."

"But I was wrong about so many things, so angry." Elizabeth was clearly anguished and Bingley couldn't help but pat her arm again.

"As I understand it, you were misguided in some of your accusations, but not all. I, for one, am deeply grateful that you enlightened him with regard to your sister's feelings!" Pleased to see his companion manage a small smile, Charles continued, "You should know that I have forgiven him for his interference; it was kindly meant, if poorly conceived."

Elizabeth nodded slowly. "I had to consider it for some time after reading his letter but I arrived at the same conclusion." She looked up. "But I had thought he knew that? He informed me that he planned to speak to you the instant you returned from Yorkshire and I agreed that such a communication was best not entrusted to the post..."

Bingley was already nodding. "Yes, yes. He still feels an inordinate amount of guilt but I suspect *that* is the result of having believed he was absolutely correct. He was left with a great many responsibilities when his father died and he takes them very seriously. To find that he was so wrong in his thinking on this matter has left him questioning everything he has ever believed."

Elizabeth shook her head sadly. "I had no idea that my words would be taken so seriously. Oh... that I had never opened my mouth!"

"Don't be; Darce needed to hear the plain, unvarnished truth from someone he respects. I've been covering for his social gaffes for years because I knew his reserve made it difficult for him to act otherwise... just as I rely on his decisiveness to cover my aversion to conflict. But *that* is another matter... What is important is that *you* finally made him understand how he is seen by those who don't know him so well. Until now, he only thought of his own discomfort, never that his manners might pain others. Darcy is a good man—I do not know a better one—but he has few close family or friends who will speak the truth to him— that and his position in Society quite cuts him off from anyone who will take him to task for his faults."

Unaccustomed to such long, heartfelt speeches, Bingley took a few deep breaths. Seeing that Miss Bennet had flushed a deep crimson, he chuckled. "Truly, Darcy has been making an effort to... how did he put it? To practice, I believe."

Elizabeth smiled slightly at hearing her admonishment from Rosings repeated, but her emotions were still in turmoil. "I believe that he has. The gentleman that has befriended my aunt and uncle here in London is very different from the one I perceived in Hertfordshire and Kent." She looked up at the man sitting across from her. "I was shocked by how wrong I was about him."

Charles was beginning to comprehend the odd courtship that had progressed between his friend and the lady before him. There was one last riddle to solve, however. "Darcy seems to have seen your meeting in London as a second chance; an opportunity to redeem himself."

Elizabeth nodded. "I was surprised he would even acknowledge me after the things I said to him in Kent, but he spoke to me and even allowed an introduction to my relations. His manners were so altered."

"You were agreeable to continuing the acquaintance?" Charles asked carefully.

The lady smiled. "I feel as if I am just *beginning* the acquaintance. I had formed such a false impression of Mr. Darcy so soon after meeting him in Meryton that I had never bothered to get to know his real character. After Kent, I understood how wrong I had been but had no hope that I would ever have another chance."

"He is not an easy man to know, but when he does open up to you there is no truer friend."

"I am beginning to see that." Suddenly, Elizabeth's smile vanished. "And that is why I don't understand his current unrest; we have met four times in London and I had thought we parted amicably after each."

Bingley kept himself from breaking into a sunny grin but his eyes were warm. The lady might not be ready to admit to loving his friend but her concern for his well-being was very real. Charles sensed that all the couple needed to cement their mutual affection was more time in each other's company.

But first, an obstacle must be removed. He wrinkled his brows in thought. "As best as I can understand, Darcy was equally pleased with your renewed association. And he has enjoyed getting to know the Gardiners— he said repeatedly that they were excellent people."

"Then what... Why..."

"From what Darcy said earlier, he returned to Gracechurch Street the morning after you all attended the theatre; he hoped to invite you all for a walking tour and picnic at Kew Gardens. When he arrived, you and your family were out so rather than wait in the parlor he walked to a park nearby. As I understand it, he overheard part of a conversation between your aunt and uncle... and what they said left him under the impression that his proposal and your refusal was known to a much wider audience than he had previously supposed."

Elizabeth's eyes were wide and her blush was obvious even as her hands covered her mouth. "No! I have only spoken of it with Jane and my father, and neither would ever betray my confidence."

Although Bingley had suspected some sort of misunderstanding, he *was* relieved to hear her confirm it. Darcy had sounded as though half of London and all of Hertfordshire were snickering at him from behind their hands. "Darce seems to think that your mother is upset that you turned down an eligible offer."

After blinking owlishly at him for some minutes, clearly confused, Elizabeth slapped her forehead and slumped back in a most unladylike manner. "Oh for heaven's sake! Mama knows nothing of my acquaintance with Mr. Darcy beyond Hertfordshire... but she *does* speak often of her disappointment that I did not oblige her by becoming... Mrs. Collins." She shut her eyes tightly and only opened them again at the sound of Mr. Bingley's chuckle.

"Forgive me, Miss Elizabeth. I could not resist imagining Darcy's reaction when he learns that his position is shared with your cousin."

Lizzy rolled her eyes.

Charles attempted a more serious tone. "Anyway, that explains a great deal. Perhaps the Gardiners said something about how uncomfortable you were in Kent after Collins' proposal. Am I correct in understanding that you were visiting your cousin and his new wife while Darcy was at Rosings?"

Despite her embarrassment, Elizabeth could still appreciate the humor in the situation. "Yes; Mr. Collins married my good friend, Charlotte Lucas, in December. I am not certain that it was the wisest decision she made in accepting him, but she is pleased with her new situation. She pressed me to accompany Sir William and her younger sister on their visit to Hunsford in March."

The pair sat quietly for some minutes, considering their conversation. Both were slightly startled when Holmes entered the room. "Miss Bennet, your carriage has arrived. Should I tell them to return at a later time?"

Checking her watch, Elizabeth was surprised to see she had been in Derwent House for nearly three hours. She stood and began collecting her things. "Thank you, Holmes. Please tell the driver that I shall be out in a few minutes." When she turned to Mr. Bingley, both smiled.

"I must return to my uncle's house or they will worry."

Bingley was already moving to accompany her to the door. "Of course. Thank you for staying, Miss Elizabeth; I think I know enough now to clear up the most fundamental aspects of Darcy's misapprehensions. For the rest, he will need to speak with you directly."

The pair made their way companionably to the entry hall where Elizabeth donned her coat and gloves. When she was ready, she turned to her sister's admirer with a great deal of affection. "Well, Mr. Bingley, it has been a most interesting afternoon. I hope to see you again very soon."

They shook hands and Elizabeth departed in the Gardiner carriage, leaving Mr. Bingley standing at the front door of Derwent House with the Darcys' venerable butler. Charles was struck with a most pleasant vision of the future when visits between two couples, sisters and the best of friends, would be a regular occurrence.

Squaring his shoulders, Bingley turned to the butler. "Holmes, this is a bit irregular, but I should like to make use of one of the guest chambers tonight. I have a great deal to relay to Mr. Darcy that should improve his disposition, but I believe it would be better to let him sleep as long as he can, for now."

The servant agreed immediately. Mr. Bingley was an intimate friend of the master and regularly stayed at Derwent House when both were in town. "Of course, sir. I shall have your usual rooms readied immediately."

Bingley grinned. "Thank you, Holmes! I shall send a note along to my valet and have him pack a few things." With a sense of mutual understanding, the two men parted, Bingley to the library to pen his note and Holmes to set the necessary wheels in motion for an overnight guest. The master might be asleep, but Derwent House was reviving after days of worry.

13 CLEARING THE AIR

The morning after his sister's intervention, Fitzwilliam Darcy woke from a sleep lasting nearly twenty hours. A powder prepared by his valet relieved the last traces of his headache and by the time he left his rooms he felt very nearly like his usual self. That feeling came to an abrupt end when, upon entering the breakfast room, he spied Charles Bingley chatting merrily with Georgiana.

Not being a drinking man, Darcy was not practiced in the art of differentiating truth from fiction in the alcohol-induced haze of his memories. Had he indeed bared his soul to his friend or was it all a nightmare? Fitzwilliam chose to prevaricate. "Good morning, Georgiana. Bingley, it is good to see you again."

He was not pleased when the pair were barely able to control their laughter while responding to his sober greeting. Gritting his teeth, he poured himself a cup of coffee and filled a plate at the sideboard before sitting.

After taking a long sip, he glanced up to see two pairs of amused eyes watching him. Finally accepting that he would not be able to bluff his way out, Fitzwilliam hunched his shoulders and stared down into his cup. "Was I so very ridiculous?"

"More pitiful than ridiculous, old man," responded Bingley with a chuckle.

Darcy looked up and saw that both were looking at him with a combination of amusement and compassion. He heaved a great sigh. "I owe you both an apology for my behavior."

Bingley cut his host off with a chuckle before the man could continue. "I was only here for the final performance yesterday afternoon and you owe me no apology for that. Or rather, your apologies at the time were quite sufficient." His expression became more serious when he glanced toward

Miss Darcy. "Your sister, however, deserves a great many pretty trinkets, dresses, ponies, or whatever you bribe her with to put up with you."

Georgiana was amazed to see a blush color her brother's face as he turned to her, barely able to meet her eyes. "Georgie, I can't tell you how sorry I am." He paused and she saw him swallow. "If you wish to go stay with our aunt and uncle, I will quite understand…"

"Oh Wills, don't be silly!" She flew to his side and hugged him tightly. "You're my brother— I could never leave you!" After a moment, she leaned back so that she could look him in the face. "You stood by me last summer… surely I can manage when you need a day or two to sulk in your room." Darcy might have raised one eyebrow slightly at her impertinence but it was accompanied by a slightly watery smile.

After a few more minutes of reassurances, Georgiana noted dolefully that her music master was expected within the hour. "I must go apply myself to my lesson before Mr. Alexander returns to point out all of my mistakes. Besides," she smirked, "I believe the two of you have a great deal to talk about." Squeezing her brother's hand, Georgiana gave Mr. Bingley an encouraging smile before leaving the room, taking care to shut the door behind her.

Darcy heaved a great sigh of relief, although some of his anxiety returned when he faced his friend again. "Charles?"

The younger man couldn't stop a bark of laughter. "Oh Darce! You should see your face— you look like a man being forced to walk the plank over a sea of man-eating sharks!"

Will managed a faint smile. "I shall not say how close you are to sketching my thoughts; you think it a faithful portrait undoubtedly."

It was some minutes before Bingley's chuckles calmed enough that he could speak coherently. Seeing that his friend had barely touched his plate, Charles waved at it. "Eat up— I'm in no rush. We can talk when you're done." He kept up a cheerful commentary about his trip to Yorkshire until it became obvious that Darcy had eaten his fill and was merely moving crumbs of egg around on his plate.

Still reveling in this new feeling of playing counselor to his older and usually wiser friend, Charles chuckled again before jumping to his feet. "I say, shall we go to your library? Nice and private, there." Without waiting for an answer, he dropped his napkin on the table and practically skipped out the door.

Darcy sat silently for a moment before heaving a heavy sigh and following grimly.

When both men were seated comfortably by the fire, Charles broke the silence. "So, exactly how much do you remember of yesterday?"

After catching the twinkle of amusement in his friend's eyes, Darcy focused on the rug. "Charles, just tell me what happened. It will be easier for both of us."

Bingley snorted. "Easier for you, I suppose. Been having some extraordinary nightmares and not sure if they are true or not?" Though he had determined to forgive the man, Charles was not above enjoying the pained look that flashed across his friend's face.

"Well, you may rest easy in one fact: although Miss Elizabeth Bennet did visit the house yesterday, she did not enter nor make any attempt to enter your chambers; your efforts to block the doors were quite unnecessary." Such a range of emotions flew across Darcy's face— dismay, embarrassment, relief—that Bingley began chuckling again.

Will looked up at him with such a lost look that the younger man sobered quickly and explained, "I arrived home from Yorkshire yesterday around noon and, as your note sounded rather urgent, came straight over."

Darcy opened his mouth but then closed it without speaking. Charles paused until it was clear that his host was not going to respond. "I was certainly surprised to find Miss Elizabeth here, taking tea with your sister! We didn't visit for long; Miss Darcy indicated that you wished to speak with me but were 'unwell'—I believe that is how she phrased it—and suggested that I visit you in your rooms. When I was let in, you were half-dressed, sloppy drunk, and attempting to barricade the doors against invaders... whom I eventually came to understand meant Miss Elizabeth Bennet. Hawkins and Holmes both deserve exorbitant raises, by the way."

Darcy had turned sideways in on the settee and covered his eyes with his arm. "Charles.... I apologize... I don't even know how to express how sorry I am..."

Bingley crossed his legs at the ankles and waved a hand at his friend casually. "Yes, yes. You apologized yesterday. Repeatedly. Groveled, really. A simple, sober expression of regret is all that is necessary now."

Upon seeing his friend's look of disbelief, Charles shrugged but his tone became more serious. "I spent a good deal of time in Yorkshire thinking about what I want in my life and it comes down to something very simple; I want to be happy. I am not ambitious, socially or politically. I have been blessed with enough money to do as I please, and Jane Bennet is what pleases me. She makes me happy." His eyes took on a faraway, dreamy look and he was quiet for a moment before focusing on Darcy again.

Fitzwilliam took that moment to express his regrets. "Charles, again, I can't apologize enough. I never should have interfered..." He stopped when his friend raised his hand and asked a simple question.

"Why did you do it?"

Darcy rubbed his face with both hands. "The neighborhood was buzzing with gossip—Mrs. Bennet was telling everyone of her expectation that an engagement was imminent. Your affection was obvious, but..." His discomfort was clear. "I watched Miss Bennet but I didn't see any difference between her manner towards you and any other gentleman. I am so sorry, Charles. I was an arrogant fool. I never should have said anything." He finally glanced up to see his friend regarding him calmly.

"You knew that Jane was in London?"

Darcy's tone was deeply apologetic. "Your sister told me that she had called at the Hursts' home in January."

"Caroline?"

Fitzwilliam nodded. "Miss Bingley tried to ask me for advice on how best to discourage her. I should have recognized it as a sign of Miss Bennet's continuing regard, but I was so wrapped up in..." He trailed off and covered his eyes with his hands.

Charles prodded him. "You were so wrapped up in...?"

Will sighed before speaking softly. "I fell in love with Miss Elizabeth from almost the first moment I saw her but I was determined to convince myself that she was not *good* enough to be Mrs. Darcy."

Bingley snorted and Fitzwilliam could only grimace in agreement. "I know; I was utterly ridiculous. It all seems so strange now... as if I was a different man." He paused before continuing. "In hindsight, my assessment of Miss Bennet's emotions were most certainly tainted by my own illogical desire to avoid my feelings for Elizabeth.

The two men sat for a few minutes in silence, both considering the far-reaching effects of their visit to Hertfordshire. "Charles, if you can ever forgive me..."

Bingley waved him off and spoke before his friend could begin another lengthy exposition of his regrets. "Will, you don't apologize very often but when you do, you are exceedingly thorough. I forgive you. Your advice was given in good faith and you never lied to me. Unlike *Caroline*." His face darkened for a moment before returning to his point. "You are neither my father nor my keeper; you are my friend. You advised me to the best of your ability—we all have our judgment skewed by emotions now and then. When you discovered that you were wrong, you told me so immediately.

"I take responsibility for my own decisions, which is why I can forgive you more easily than I can forgive myself. In this instance, as with many others, I found it easier to be guided than to argue for what I wanted. I knew how Jane felt about me; I was the recipient of her looks and smiles, not you or Caroline. Yet, when you all followed me to London after the ball, it was easier to settle here for Christmas and then remain for the Season than to fight for what I desired."

Bingley looked over at Darcy who was watching him intently. "I am uncomfortable with disagreements, as you know. But I must not continue to allow my dislike of conflict to direct my life... and perhaps ruin my happiness."

The two men sat in silent reflection for some time before Fitzwilliam cleared his throat and spoke quietly; "The evening that we attended the Meryton assembly, I wanted to sprint from the room and hide. Everyone was staring, gossiping about how much I was worth and who my uncles and aunts were."

Charles opened his mouth but found he could not laugh at his friend's honest confession. "I hadn't realized just how uncomfortable you were. Is that why you're always stalking around, stone-faced, hiding in corners?"

Fitzwilliam nodded slightly, studying his signet ring intently. "I would have been hard pressed to remember a single name or face to whom we were introduced."

The younger man grunted. "One of them was Miss Elizabeth."

Darcy groaned and slumped back into the chair, closing his eyes again. "Oh Lord, yes. You tried to convince me to dance and she heard every word of my conceited, self-important refusal."

Charles blinked, barely remembering the conversation. "What happened?"

"You had just danced with Miss Bennet and were encouraging me to dance with her sister. I assumed that you were pointing out Miss Mary who, shall we agree, is not quite of the standard set by her elder sisters."

Bingley nodded; any man with eyes would acknowledge that the middle Bennet daughter was not a great beauty.

Fitzwilliam continued, his tone self-mocking. "I was... excessively forthright in my opinion, shall we say. Unfortunately, Elizabeth overheard our conversation and correctly understood that you had been recommending herself as a dance partner. Quite logically, she also took my words to be referring to herself, however wide of the mark. Thus was born Miss Elizabeth Bennet's opinion of my arrogance, my conceit, and my selfish disdain for the feelings of others."

Despite his prior knowledge, Charles was stunned. He had understood that Miss Elizabeth disliked Darcy and enjoyed tweaking his nose in debates; that much had been obvious to all but his friend. That she had formed such a strong prejudice and so early in their acquaintance was a shock.

"I'm sorry, Darce. I can't even imagine. Did you really suspect nothing of her feelings before you proposed?"

Darcy flushed and looked at him sharply. Charles shrugged and explained, "We spoke a great deal yesterday. Or rather, you talked and I listened." He looked at his friend with a hint of challenge in his eye. "Is it such a bad thing, to share your problems with me?"

Fitzwilliam slumped back again. "No, of course not... I should appreciate it, I am just not accustomed to... to..."

"Sharing your troubles?" Charles laughed. "No, I should say not. But it would do you good to practice, for I do not believe that Miss Elizabeth

Bennet will stand for having you shut her out!"

Darcy's eyes popped open. "I must disgust her... she shall never wish to see my face again! Good God! What was I thinking? Getting myself blind drunk, and with my baby sister in the house of all things! Elizabeth must despise me..."

Charles cut his friend off before he could progress any farther in his self-condemnation. "Relax, Will. She does not despise you—she was... concerned."

Darcy's mouth remained hanging open for a moment before he snapped his jaw shut. "Concerned?" he finally ventured.

Bingley rolled his eyes. "After I left you to be tucked into bed by your excellent valet, Miss Elizabeth and I had a bit of a chat." He couldn't help but chuckle when Fitzwilliam blanched.

"I laid out the facts as best I understood them and we straightened out a few misunderstandings."

Suddenly the original reason that had driven him to hide in his rooms for days crashed down on Darcy like a pile of bricks. Before he could say anything, Charles was waving his hand in front of his face.

"Darce? Ho there, Will? Try to focus while I valiantly work to fix your love life."

When he was sure that at least some of his friend's attention was back on him, Bingley continued. "First off, your letter seems to have corrected many of her misconceptions. She has even forgiven you for your actions separating me from her sister, as have I. In fact, she thought that you were aware of that."

Bingley looked inquiringly at Darcy who nodded slightly, although he continued to look morose.

Charles continued, "In short, she does not hate you but she does not feel that she knows you very well. I believe her exact words were something like 'the man I thought I knew turns out to have been a figment of my imagination.' However, she is not at all averse to expanding your acquaintance; quite the opposite, in fact. It is my opinion that you have an excellent shot at making her fall in love with you... if you can avoid insulting her and her family for an hour or so, that is."

Not even this last bit of teasing could quench the happiness spreading through Fitzwilliam. There was one last thorn still worrying him, however. "But, I heard her aunt and uncle speaking... speaking of..." He trailed off.

Bingley chuckled, exceedingly pleased to be of use to his friend for once. "Ah yes, your latest bit of ill-placed eavesdropping. You and Miss Elizabeth both seem to have quite a talent for that." He grinned. "I explained what you had heard to Miss Elizabeth as best I could. You were rather expansive in your story yesterday; I took the liberty of presenting her with a summarized version only."

Charles was amused to see his usually stoic friend positively cringe. "I explained that you had overheard her relations saying that she had been uncomfortable in Kent after refusing a proposal and that Mrs. Bennet was quite upset about it."

Darcy groaned and Bingley couldn't help but be amused by the normally imperturbable man's discomfort. "At first, Miss Elizabeth was confused; apparently only her sister and father were aware of your proposal." Darcy's eyes popped open; relieved but also discomfited by the new thought that *Mr. Bennet* knew of his unfortunate addresses to that gentleman's favorite daughter.

"But after further discussion, she realized that it was not *your* proposal to which the Gardiners were referring."

Darcy shook his head, trying to understand. "But they said that she must have been very uncomfortable staying at Hunsford. And that her mother was upset that she had turned down an eligible offer."

Bingley smirked. "They were referring to Mr. Collins." He sat back and watched the impact of his words.

Fitzwilliam still didn't quite understand. "My aunt's curate?"

Charles bounced slightly in his chair. "Mr. William Collins, Miss Elizabeth's cousin and Mr. Bennet's heir." He paused but added another bit of explanation when Darcy remained silent. "The inheritor of their father's estate would have been a most eligible match for any of the Miss Bennets."

Will gaped with astonishment and Charles couldn't help bouncing in his seat again, his face wreathed in smiles. "Apparently your aunt sent her parson into Hertfordshire with the explicit goal of choosing a wife from among his cousins. When Miss Elizabeth declined his *kind* offer, Mr. Collins promptly turned his attentions toward her good friend and neighbor, Miss Lucas, who accepted him in short order."

Darcy burst to his feet and strode about the room. "That... that... toad! That groveling, sniveling, ridiculous creature dared ask for Elizabeth's hand in marriage?!?"

Charles was having a most amusing day. "Oh yes, indeed; he most certainly did. And from what I gathered, Mrs. Bennet was all for the match—it would have secured her own future, after all."

When Fitzwilliam glared at him, Bingley shrugged. "With five unmarried daughters and the estate entailed away, she is in a precarious position. I discussed it with Mr. Bennet one evening after supper. Apparently there's some bad blood between the families and Mrs. Bennet knew better than to trust Collins for any benevolence toward her and her daughters, should her husband pass."

His friend's words floated across Fitzwilliam's consciousness but most of his mind was focused on sorting out his previous misunderstandings. "So Mr. and Mrs. Gardiner were discussing how uncomfortable Elizabeth had been, living in the parsonage with her rejected suitor-*cum*-cousin and that man's new wife, her childhood friend."

"As I said."

Darcy's voice gained force as his understanding grew. "And her mother's fretting over Mr. Collins made it insufferable for Elizabeth to remain at Longbourn. By God, I still can't believe that she was forced to endure a proposal from that… that imbecile! It must have been completely intolerable!"

Fitzwilliam caught sight of his friend's amused face and suddenly all his fury dissolved and he flopped back into his chair. "And yet, *I* was the last man in the world whom she could ever have been prevailed on to marry."

Charles' face grew compassionate. "She actually said that? You mentioned it yesterday but I'd hoped it was just a drunken exaggeration."

Darcy tilted his head back and stared at the ceiling. "Oh, she said it, all right. My pretty little speech made her so angry that she was well beyond polite prevarication when I demanded an explanation for her rejection. My mind has been repeating her words for a month now, day and night it seems."

Not wanting his friend to slide back into melancholy, Bingley spoke up brightly. "Well! The number of misunderstanding that has arisen between the two of you is astonishing, but let us focus on how best to heal the breach. It should take very little, I believe."

Fitzwilliam shook his head and focused sober eyes on his friend. "Why are you doing this for me, Charles? I don't deserve your friendship, much less your help."

Bingley was about to shrug off the question with a quip and a laugh, but saw that his friend was serious. He sighed. "Will, you are my friend, and I hope that I am yours. Friendship does not mean that one is always taking and the other always giving, you know? I have relied on you for years; you helped me fit in at school when I was the unpolished son of a Scarborough carriage-maker, reeking of new money. And when my parents and brother died, I can't imagine what I would have done without your guidance. I'd never expected to have to take over Father's business; we all knew that Arthur was being groomed for his place since birth. When they both died, I have no idea what I would have done if you hadn't been there to guide me through all the legal details and business meetings."

Charles paused, momentarily overwhelmed by the emotional memories. Finally he turned to Darcy who had remained silent for many minutes. "Now, you must allow me to be of some help to you. Please." He grinned. "If for no other reason than for my ego; helping you with your problems makes me feel like a man instead of a little brother always scampering along behind you!"

If anything, Will's face became more solemn. "Charles, I never meant to make you feel that you were the lesser partner in our friendship."

He was about to speak again when Bingley waved him off. "Darce, as I said, I've spent a great deal of time thinking, lately. You've always had a great deal of responsibility placed upon you. Certainly more so since your father's death, but really you were raised to know your duties from the moment you took your first steps. I could have been anything—clergyman, soldier, barrister, doctor, politician, tradesman. Father gave me a good education and would have given me a financial start in whatever profession I chose.

"I never got around to making that decision because he and my brother died, thrusting me into a position I'd never expected. I've been drifting—making the decisions that were thrust upon me but more often allowing others to do so for me.

"That is why it is so easy for me to forgive you your interference in my relationship with Jane. It came easily to me to depend on you to make decisions for me; you are good at it."

Seeing that Darcy was about to argue, Charles spoke over him, attempting to explain. "Will, you are one of the most intelligent, honest, and above all, responsible men that I know. You take your duties very seriously and you kindly made my well-being one of those responsibilities. However, it is high time for me to take control of my own life."

Bingley looked his friend straight in the eye, desiring him to understand. "I appreciate your aid and advice and always will, but the best help you can give me now is to be a friend. Tell me if I am being too easily swayed—by my sister, for example—give me advice, but step back and make *me* take responsibility, even if it makes me miserable by forcing me into conflict."

Fitzwilliam spent several minutes pondering Bingley's words before realizing that his friend was watching him intently, awaiting a response. Will shook himself and spoke carefully. "I hadn't thought of it that way, but you are correct. I've gotten into the habit of believing that it is my responsibility to solve everyone's problems."

At Bingley's raised eyebrows, he shrugged. "I've been talking to Georgiana as well. It is not easy for her to grow up into a young lady when I still treat her as my baby sister and try to shield her from everything bad or uncomfortable in the world."

The gentlemen were quiet for some time before Charles finally laughed out loud. When Will looked at him questioningly, he shrugged. "I was just thinking that we should submit your name for the next election; surely a stint as prime minister would provide you with enough problems to solve... I can't even imagine what you will be like when the suitors begin to flock after Miss Darcy's debut!"

Fitzwilliam slumping back in his chair and groaned theatrically. "I don't want to think about it! Do you know of are convents in Yorkshire where I might lock her up? She would make a lovely nun, don't you think?"

The two men laughed and spent some minutes jesting over their sisters' differing personalities and prospects for matrimony. For the first time in many years, Fitzwilliam Darcy felt the relief of a friendship based on camaraderie rather than responsibility.

Georgiana found them some time later, still in the library and with such a sense of fellowship between them that she could not help but smile. "Shall you and Mr. Bingley be joining me for luncheon, Wills?"

The two friends agreed and the trio enjoyed an amiable meal. By the end, they had agreed to call on the Gardiners and Miss Bennet that very afternoon and invite the family on a day trip to the Kew Gardens. Darcy was uncomfortable with the idea of facing Elizabeth so soon after his recent behavior but was reassured by Charles and Georgiana. Regardless, he took the first opportunity to change the subject.

"Charles, now that I think on it, you will enjoy meeting Mr. Gardiner; his life has many parallels with your own. His own father died just as he was finishing university so he was thrust into managing the family business at a young age."

Bingley was intrigued (particularly as he wished to make a good impression on Jane's favorite uncle and aunt) and asked for more details. He and Darcy also discussed the best way for him to approach Miss Bennet and gain her forgiveness. With suggestions from Georgiana, Charles decided that he would send notice immediately to his housekeeper to begin opening up Netherfield for a long visit. While that was being accomplished, he would remain at Derwent House and visit with the Gardiners and Miss Elizabeth, hoping to gain a positive recommendation from them to the family at Longbourn.

As Georgiana prepared to find the housekeeper and inform her of their plans, Charles was thinking. "As distasteful the task, I must also deal with my own sisters before I depart for Hertfordshire."

Both Darcys looked over at his solemn tone.

Fitzwilliam asked softly, "Shall you confront them?"

Charles sighed but then sat up and straightened his shoulders. "Yes," he responded decisively, brows knit. "But first I need to determine a few facts. To be quite honest, I've been in a bit of a fog for the last few months. I need to know just how far Caroline has gone in her deception and, if I can, why." Charles nodded at Fitzwilliam. "Darce, you had good intentions. I am not so sure of Caroline. She is obsessed with clawing her way up the social ladder regardless of who it hurts; I need to see how she acts before I decide what to do about her."

The three sat quietly for a few minutes until Charles spoke again in a slightly lighter tone. "And Miss Darcy, I would be greatly obliged if you do *not* invite my sisters on our little walking tour of the gardens... I am fairly certain that Caroline would do all she can to make it unpleasant for some others in our party even more than myself." He grinned at Darcy who rolled his eyes good-naturedly.

In short order, the Darcy carriage was stopping in Gracechurch Street and the Gardiners' butler announced the visitors. "Mr. Darcy, Miss Darcy, and Mr. Bingley to see you, ma'am."

The visit was short and Darcy could recall little of the conversation after Mrs. Gardiner accepted the invitation and it was arranged that the group would venture out to Kew in two days. He ventured several glances toward Elizabeth; her countenance seemed more strained than usual but Mrs. Gardiner's friendly conversation made up for any lack in her niece's.

Fitzwilliam caught her studying him several times with a concerned look in her eye but there seemed to be no chance of any privacy for them to speak. This was reinforced when several ladies were shown into the parlor, obviously come to visit with Mrs. Gardiner and discuss some charity work.

Mr. Darcy and his party politely made their farewells. Just as Fitzwilliam was about to follow his friend and sister out the front door, he heard light footsteps tripping down the hall. He turned and found that Elizabeth had followed him.

Unconsciously, she stretched her hand out and touched his arm, looking up at him with worry clear in her eyes. "Mr. Darcy, I wanted to see... to make sure that you were quite well, sir. Yesterday, your sister mentioned that you were unwell..." Elizabeth trailed off and colored slightly, dropping her eyes.

Darcy's heart was ready to burst. She might not love him yet, but it was unmistakable that she cared. He covered her slender hand with his own and spoke gruffly. "I am perfectly well; the affliction was a result of my own stupidity and was quite cleared up this morning."

She looked up at him, eyes serious. "I am glad."

Feeling as though his heart might pound out of his chest, Fitzwilliam pressed her hand slightly. "I look forward to our outing the day after tomorrow. Have you visited the gardens before? They are exquisite at this time of year."

Elizabeth colored slightly at the feeling of his hand upon her own but did not remove it. "I have been there but it was some years ago. I shall look forward to it a great deal." She smiled and attempted a jest to lighten the mood. "For I do love to walk, as you know."

She was left blinking at the sight of Fitzwilliam Darcy's full, dimpled smile. "I do know. I..."

At that moment, a maid entered the hall, carrying a fresh tea tray toward the parlor and Elizabeth jumped slightly and withdrew her hand.

Understanding that further conversation would have to wait, Fitzwilliam bowed deeply and took a last look at her dear face before departing. "Good day, Miss Elizabeth. Until Saturday."

That evening, the Darcy siblings enjoyed a quiet yet amiable meal together while Mr. Bingley dined with his own family. He was more restrained than usual but it went unnoticed as Caroline chattered on about parties and gossip. At one point during the fish course, she paused to remonstrate one of the Hursts' servants and Louisa slipped in an inquiry about their relations in Yorkshire. Charles managed only a few words before their younger sister demanded the attention of the table again.

"Really, Charles! I can't imagine why you had to stay there so long! You should have returned to London weeks ago. Surely a letter would have been sufficient—there is no reason to waste your time on such long visits when you had much better be in London." She smiled cunningly toward Mrs. Hurst. "Miss Darcy has been asking after you, you know."

Having just spent some hours in Miss Darcy's company and knowing precisely what she and her brother thought of Caroline, Charles could barely restrain himself from rolling his eyes. "They are our closest relations, Caroline. Besides, I needed to sit in on several meetings. The Luddite problem seems to be settling down, but our cousins still wished to discuss issues of working conditions and security for the machinery. It was quite interesting, actually."

Bingley looked up and noted the variety of expressions on his family's faces. Mr. Hurst seemed to be trying to process his comment but was hindered by the excessive amount of wine he had imbibed. Louisa was staring at her younger brother as if she had never seen him before. And Caroline.... his younger sister was glaring at him with a mixture of disgust and horror that she made no attempt to hide.

"Charles—what can you be thinking, to involve yourself so!?!"

Bingley sighed and signaled the servants to clear his plate. "I was thinking that I have a responsibility to our father's business, even if I do not take as active a role in its management as Arthur would have."

Louisa's face tightened with grief at the mention of their elder brother.

There was no hint of sadness in Caroline's voice, however; only disdain. "Don't be ridiculous, Charles. You are a gentleman and all of our efforts will be ruined if it becomes known that you are involving yourself in trade."

Bingley eyed his sister carefully. Had she no pride in their family? "Caroline, our father (and his father before him) worked very hard to provide us with a better chance in life than they had. I, for one, am proud to be known as his son and plan to fulfill the responsibilities left to me to the best of my ability. If that means attending a few business meetings or even visiting a factory or warehouse, then so be it."

Caroline was aghast. "Are you insane? Our acquaintances will shun us! It is bad enough that our grandfather worked with his hands; at least Father planned to buy an estate. Louisa—tell him!"

Charles shrugged casually although he was listening closely to Caroline's diatribe. Her words were more revealing than she realized. "Darcy and I were talking about families and duty this morning; it reinforced my determination to be more attentive to my responsibilities."

Miss Bingley blanched. "You discussed our family business with Mr. Darcy?!? How *could* you, Charles?!? We shall be lucky if he doesn't rescind our invitation to Pemberley this summer!"

This time Charles *did* roll his eyes. Did Caroline really understand so little of the man she plotted to marry? "Darcy has a great deal of respect for our family; his own father invested in our father's business." When Caroline looked dismayed, he shook his head. "Really, Caro; he has been my friend since school. He knows everything there is to know about me."

While his sister was sputtering in consternation, he waved his fork at her dismissively. "Besides, I will not have time to travel to Derbyshire this summer."

There was a moment of stunned silence before Caroline began to shriek. "Whatever are you speaking of? Of course you are going to Pemberley! We are all going to Pemberley! I must... You must..." In her anguish she tipped over a wine goblet.

Charles sighed and righted his sister's glass; luckily it had been nearly empty. When she finally paused to take a breath, he spoke firmly, "As you said, our father wished me to purchase an estate. I spent some time today with Darcy, discussing the responsibilities of an estate owner. I shall not be going to Pemberley because I must be in Hertfordshire."

Caroline gaped like a fish. "But Charles—we decided that you were to give up the lease on Netherfield. It was completely inappropriate. Certainly Mr. Darcy told you the same; you would do much better to spend the summer at Pemberley, learning from him." She brightened, certain of her ability to manage her brother. "And of course I shall come to look after dear Georgiana; Mr. Darcy shall need an experienced hostess as she is not yet out and I expect we shall be doing a great deal of entertaining."

Bingley was becoming increasingly disgusted by his sister. He took a sip of wine before speaking with a great deal more determination than his family was accustomed to hearing from him. "No, Caroline. I shall be returning to Netherfield in about a week; time enough for me to tie up my affairs here in London and to allow Nichols to open up the house."

Seeing that his sister was about to begin protesting again, he spoke over her. "I have not decided whether or not to purchase Netherfield, but I will be continuing the lease for at least another year. Darcy and I agreed that it is an excellent situation for me to learn the duties of a gentleman farmer."

Charles decided that his pudding was quite unappetizing and put his fork down carefully before looking up at his sister again. A flicker of cunning flashed across her face before she donned a conciliatory mask.

"Of course, Charles. If Mr. Darcy has recommended it, then it must be so. But are you certain that you are quite ready to take on the management by yourself? Wouldn't it be better to have Mr. Darcy come with us to Netherfield so that he may assist you? And dear Georgiana must come as well—she will be such a source of good breeding and refinement in that dreadful backwater."

Caroline's calculating smile became even brighter. "Of course; we could spend a few weeks at Netherfield and then all travel to Derbyshire together! What a wonderful way for our families to become even closer..."

Watching his sister's machinations was making Charles feel slightly ill, but he still had a few facts to determine before he could remove himself from her presence.

"No, Caroline. Darcy and his sister will be leaving for Derbyshire about the same time I depart." Before Caroline could concoct any more schemes, Charles turned the conversation. "I meant to ask; what correspondence have you had with our Hertfordshire acquaintances? We left rather abruptly last November and I am afraid I shall have to make my apologies to our neighbors for not taking my leave in person."

Miss Bingley's eyes were wide and it was obvious to her brother that she was scrambling to cover her lies. "Oh, really Charles. You need not bother with any of them; there was no one of any significance in that miserable place."

Charles kept his face neutral but watched her very carefully. "Surely you understand that, as the master of Netherfield Park, even the most minimal politeness requires me to call on my immediate neighbors, at the very least. Besides, I had thought that you were corresponding with Miss Bennet?"

Caroline attempted to look compassionate without much success. "Oh, Charles... I'm so sorry. I know that you liked her but you will only bring yourself pain if you put yourself in Jane's company again."

"You have not heard from her at all?"

His sister shot a worried look at Mrs. Hurst but lied without hesitation. "No, Charles, just as I told you before. I wrote as you requested but she never replied. Miss Bennet was a very sweet girl but she made it clear that she was quite indifferent to you. If you insist on venturing into Hertfordshire, I would recommend that you avoid those artful Bennets altogether." This last was said with a sneer.

Bingley sat quietly for some minutes, thinking on what his sister had told him and comparing it to what he now knew to be the truth. Suddenly he felt very, very tired and wished only to be relieved of her company. Bringing his attention back to the present, he realized that Caroline had been talking the entire time and had argued her way back to the idea that the Bingleys and Hursts would accompany the Darcys to Derbyshire for the summer, bypassing Hertfordshire altogether.

Sighing, Charles pushed his chair back and stood, fixing his sister with a stern look. "Caroline! You are *not* going to Pemberley. I have attempted to spare your feelings, but the fact is that Darcy invited me; you were only welcome as part of my party. As *I* am not going, *you* are no longer invited."

Thinking of all the pain his sister had caused, Bingley couldn't resist a final dig. "Besides, I have it on good authority that Darcy will soon be engaged and hopes to have the lady's family visit Pemberley this summer. You would only be in the way."

With that, Bingley pushed his chair against the table and headed for the door. He made it halfway before Caroline began shrieking.

"Of what are you speaking!?! I demand to know, Charles! I have heard nothing of Mr. Darcy courting anyone! Surely you don't mean that sickly cousin of his?"

Bingley stood with his hand on the door and looked back at his family. Mr. Hurst seemed amused at his sister-in-law's histrionics. Louisa was watching her brother questioningly but without any apparent malice. And Caroline... Caroline was clawing her way out of her chair, nearly taking the tablecloth with her as she stood.

"Charles—tell me immediately! What do you know?" she ordered, her voice rising with desperation.

If there had been any hint of sadness over a lost love or even affection, he would have been inclined to forgive her. As it was, he had no qualms with dismissing his sister's hopes with a seemingly offhanded remark designed to cut deeply.

"No one in our circle, I'm sure. Someone in Darcy's position would only consider a gentleman's daughter worthy of becoming the next Mistress of Pemberley."

Caroline fell back into her chair, devastated. Feeling rather ashamed of himself, Charles decided to gift her with a bit of truth. "Sorry, Caro—I'm teasing a bit. Darcy doesn't care as much about the social standing of his future wife as much as he does about her intelligence and character. He believes that he has found someone with whom he can build a marriage based on mutual affection and respect. I, for one, plan to support him in every possible way in his quest for happiness, just as he has done for me."

With those words, Charles Bingley left, shutting the door firmly behind him so that he would not hear any of his sister's further outbursts. Quietly accepting his coat and hat from the butler, he declined the offer of a carriage and departed his brother-in-law's house on foot. It was a lovely night for a walk and, although he was exhausted, he also had a sense of lightness that he had not felt in years.

14 A WALK IN THE PARK

Thanks to a slightly sheepish warning from Mr. Bingley, the Darcys made certain that their butler knew to turn away all but a select few callers. When Miss Bingley was not admitted to Derwent House the next day, her panic-fueled fury exploded to such a degree that her own sister all but leapt from the carriage when they arrived back at the Hursts' home. Weary of Caroline's ranting, Mrs. Hurst took refuge in her husband's private sitting room—a space that she had not ventured into in many months.

When the housekeeper came to speak to Mrs. Hurst, she was surprised to find the Mistress chatting amiably with her husband. The couple exchanged a decidedly unhappy look when the long-suffering servant informed them that Miss Bingley was currently in the drawing room throwing old Mrs. Hurst's collection of porcelain ornaments at the portraits and that the parlor maid was bleeding from a particularly well-aimed shepherdess. Mrs. Donald decided to delay tendering her resignation only when Mr. and Mrs. Hurst rose and prepared to deal with the bitter young woman together.

In truth, Miss Bingley had been met with no deception when she was turned away from Derwent House. Her brother had departed earlier to meet with his solicitor and Miss Darcy was practicing the pianoforte under the exacting tutelage of her music master. The gentleman foremost in Caroline's thoughts was not even in the house, although her nightmare of Mr. Darcy spending the day with a fiancée was incorrect in more ways than one.

Fitzwilliam had devoted the morning to organizing details of the excursion to the Royal Botanic Gardens at Kew, determined that it would be an unqualified success. A cart with food, blankets, and picnic supplies was to be sent ahead while Darcy and his guests would travel by water on one of the new paddle steamers that plied the Thames.

The servants soon caught on that their fidgety master desired to please Miss Bennet and her party. It was only when he began questioning the cook on her recipes that the housekeeper finally propelled him out of the kitchens.

"It shall all be just as you wish, sir. Perhaps you should check on Miss Darcy now? Luncheon shall be served in a half hour."

Fitzwilliam could not help but chuckle when he found himself standing alone in the hallway, the green baize door shut firmly behind him. However, he was clever enough to take Mrs. Wilkins' advice and head toward the sounds coming from the music room.

Determined not to spend the afternoon worrying over Elizabeth, Darcy filled it running various errands about town. After stopping at his tailor's and choosing fabrics for several new waistcoats, he was disappointed to find that the sheet music for Rossini's latest opera had not yet been published; Fitzwilliam had hoped to purchase it for his sister as a gesture apologizing for his recent behavior. He left the music shop with instructions to send the piano reduction on to Pemberley when it arrived and stepped out onto the sidewalk.

The air was remarkably clear for London, a brief morning rainstorm having washed everything clean. With a spring in his step, Darcy headed toward Hatchard's bookshop, tossing a copper to the urchin sweeping the street where he crossed.

Fitzwilliam paused in front of a Bond Street jeweler, eyeing several lockets in the window and considering Bingley's suggestion that Georgiana might like a trinket of that sort. However, he was quite certain that if he entered he would be unable to resist buying something more substantial for Elizabeth, even though he knew it was unlikely that he could present her with the gift for months, if ever. Somehow, such a purchase seemed too much like tempting the Fates, so Will gave a particularly lovely amethyst set a longing look but turned his steps back toward his favorite bookstore.

Mr. Hatchard himself was manning the counter and the venerable book dealer was familiar enough with Mr. Darcy to show his amusement over the variety of that gentleman's selections once he was finished browsing. Indeed, Fitzwilliam himself was forced to chuckle when he looked over the odd array of titles.

Between a manual on crop rotation that Darcy often used as a reference (a gift for Bingley) and John Farley's recently published report on the agriculture and minerals of Derbyshire (he tried to keep up with new scientific advances particularly in colliery) was a three-volume novel by "a Lady" (a gift for Georgiana) and a copy of Mary Wollstonecraft's *Vindication of the Rights of Women*.

Mr. Hatchard's eyebrows rose at the last and he glanced up at Darcy. The gentleman shrugged. "I am responsible for the education of my younger sister and someone I respect a great deal recommended that we read it."

The older man nodded decidedly. "Excellent advice, if I might say so, sir. Society has fairly pilloried her, especially after that husband of hers exposed all of the... err... unconventional aspects of her life in his *Memoir*. But she was no anarchist, whatever they say. I have a daughter myself and that book made me think differently about how to raise her. Sometimes Wollstonecraft's prose gets a bit overly dramatic, but I believe the logic and fundamentals to be sound."

Tucking away his money clip and watching as a clerk wrapped up the books, Darcy answered thoughtfully, "I must admit that I have long taken the gossip as fact and never bothered to actually read any of her essays, believing the publicity that they were little more than radical filth."

Mr. Hatchard smiled. "Ah, well. You're not alone. I wouldn't be surprised if the next generation discovers her work as if it were completely new, the stench of society's condemnation washed away by time. Happens again and again with literature through the ages. After all, isn't Plato supposed to have buggered young Aristotle when the lad was one of his pupils?"

Seeing that he had thoroughly embarrassed his customer with his explicit talk, the elderly book dealer waved a hand as though dispelling a foul odor from the air. "Never mind, young man, never mind. I'm getting old and forget whether I'm addressing a respectable gentleman such as yourself or one of those radical philosophers that come by to rant now and then on their way to the Speaker's Corner." He winked and Darcy left the store with his books, unsure if Hatchard might not be one of those liberal-leaning philosophers himself.

That evening after supper, Darcy distributed his gifts and the three residents of Derwent House spent an amiable evening reading before the fire. Bingley found the farming manual and even Darcy's geological report surprisingly fascinating and was soon making notes for himself. Fitzwilliam was quietly pleased when Georgiana chose to begin her new novel, leaving him with Mrs. Wollstonecraft.

The further he read, the more interested he became. Darcy had always considered himself a broad-minded man, but he was forced to admit that many of society's mores which he himself had always accepted were wholly illogical when considered more impartially.

Fitzwilliam was so engrossed that it came as a surprise when the clock struck eleven. Charles smiled at the two Darcys and stood, gathering his books and papers together in a lopsided pile.

"This has been an excellent evening!" announced the younger man enthusiastically. "I have quite a list of questions to discuss with the Netherfield steward when I return to Hertfordshire; I begin to understand why you so value your library, Darce. I'm sorry to break up our little reading party, but I believe I shall need a good night's sleep for our expedition tomorrow." He winked.

After bidding their guest a good night, brother and sister turned back to each other. Fitzwilliam nodded at the volume in her hand. "Are you enjoying your new novel, Georgie?" He was pleased with the sunny smile that bloomed in her face.

"Oh Wills, it is wonderful! The characters feel like people I might know."

"Nothing like Mrs. Radcliffe, then?"

Georgiana rolled her eyes and they both laughed. Darcy tried to read all of the books his sister did so that they might discuss them. They had agreed that, although the gothic romances could be quite amusing on occasion, the plots were often ridiculous and the characters quite unlikely outside of fiction.

When their laughter quieted, Georgiana dared her own question. "What do you think of Mrs. Wollstonecraft's book? I had never heard of it before Miss Bennet mentioned that she was rereading it last week."

Darcy colored slightly and looked at the book in his hands. It was still difficult for him to admit that even such an indirect recommendation from Elizabeth had him running out to purchase the volume.

"You have not heard about it because Mrs. Wollstonecraft's writing is considered quite unsuitable these days; her personal life was... unconventional, shall we say." Darcy adopted Hatchard's euphemism and hoped his little sister would not ask any further explanation for a decade or two.

"However, her writing is thought-provoking, to say the least." Fitzwilliam turned the book and rubbed a thumb up the spine contemplatively. "I had never truly considered how biased our legal system is against women; I am ashamed to admit that I believed it necessary to protect females in our society."

Miss Darcy's eyebrows had risen to her hairline; she was still amazed at how much the acquaintance of Miss Bennet had changed her brother. "Will you allow me to read it?"

Fitzwilliam turned the book over in his hands again so that he might read the title. Sheepish over his pause, he looked up at his sister and quirked an eyebrow. "Yes, although as your guardians, Richard and I shall probably live to regret it." He smirked at her. "And for Heaven's sake, don't ever speak of it to your Uncle Henry!"

Georgiana giggled and in short order, the siblings retired for the night with a warm feeling of camaraderie between them.

Darcy fell asleep quickly but woke well before dawn, his mind stewing with anxieties over the coming day. Unable to remain in bed, he pulled on a robe over his nightshirt and wandered into his private sitting room. He picked up and set down several books before finally slumping back in a comfortable armchair where he could look out of the window at the blue-black pre-dawn sky.

Even with Charles and Georgiana's assurances added to his own observations, Will was still wholly uncertain of Elizabeth's opinion of him. Certainly she had smiled at him more in the last week than she ever had in their entire previous acquaintance, but his experience in Kent had left him thoroughly uncertain of his ability to guess at her thoughts or feelings.

Darcy groaned and rubbed his eyes but before he could come to any resolution, there was a soft tapping at his dressing room door. He called to come, guessing correctly that it was his valet. "Hawkins, I am sorry to have disturbed you. I woke early and couldn't fall asleep again."

His man knit his brows for a moment. Few gentlemen would make such an apology; most would consider it the servant's duty to know his master's needs before he did himself. Mr. Darcy had always been a generous employer, but in the last month he had become a more liberal one as well.

"Not at all, sir. Shall I fetch you some coffee?"

"That would be excellent, thank you." Mr. Darcy pursed his lips and then gave his valet a look like a mischievous schoolboy. "Would you also check on the preparations for our outing today? Without making Wilkins or Davies think that I'm peeping over their shoulders again?"

Hawkins couldn't quite quell his own answering grin. The cook had grumbled excessively the previous evening over the Master's 'nerves' nearly ruining her meal. "Of course, sir."

In short order, Darcy was drinking his coffee and nibbling on a pastry. He cracked the window and was relieved to see no hint of rain clouds in the dawn sky. Listening to the sounds of London coming awake, Fitzwilliam returned to his earlier quandary.

He had no doubts that he loved Elizabeth with all his heart and soul. However, he had to admit that he had seen new dimensions of her to appreciate during their recent meetings in London.

Bingley's explanation came back to him. "I think her words were 'the man I thought I knew turns out to have been a figment of my imagination…'" And with that memory came Fitzwilliam's solution. If he wished to further his relationship with Elizabeth, then he must allow her to know him. He had to trust her; to drop his mask and allow her past his defenses. And that meant talking with her; he must not again make the mistake of assuming she could intuit his thoughts and character from the blank face he habitually presented to society.

Even as he was forming his new resolution, there came a new tapping from the hall door. With a smile, Darcy invited his sister in to his sitting room and sent for a fresh pot of tea. He had a favor to ask.

Oddly enough, a similar conversation had taken place the previous evening at the Gardiners' residence. Sitting with her aunt and uncle after the children had been put to bed, Elizabeth did her best to summarize her history with Mr. Darcy as delicately as possible. Though she left out the actuality of a proposal, the Gardiners were given to know that the gentleman had professed an admiration with honorable intentions but the lady had refused him based on misconceptions. She also told them of how her father was in possession of all the details and had encouraged her to reassess the man, should the opportunity arise.

The Gardiners were not tremendously surprised by the story; Mr. Darcy obviously knew what it was to love and their niece seemed open to knowing the gentleman better.

In short order it was agreed that, as long as the young couple did not venture out of sight or do anything excessively improper, the Gardiners would allow them a certain amount of privacy to talk while the party explored the gardens.

Elizabeth settled into her bed with a great feeling of satisfaction. Tomorrow, she would have the opportunity to work on the puzzle that was Fitzwilliam Darcy and she was determined to make sense of him, however much questioning, teasing, or arguing it took. She fell asleep thinking that, if all else failed, she might bribe the Gardiner children to push Darcy into the duck pond. Surely no man could maintain his stoic demeanor while dripping wet and covered with slimy green pond scum.

Miss Bennet need not have worried. The next morning, Mr. Darcy arrived determined to please and be pleased. By the time they had all boarded the paddle steamer, Elizabeth was certain that she had never seen the gentleman more eager to interact with his companions.

Darcy himself was impressed with the prompt service that his party received on the small vessel. It was not until they had pushed off and were chugging steadily up the Thames that he heard one of the ship's officers addressing Mr. Gardiner by name. He soon came to understand that Elizabeth's uncle owned a share in one of the companies that ran steam ship excursion trips up and down the river.

Mr. Gardiner grinned and bowed slightly with a twinkle in his eye. "You have excellent taste in transportation, sir."

Darcy admitted that he had asked around and chosen the line with the best safety record and soon the pair were involved in a good-natured discussion on the potential of steam-powered ships and the need to regulate traffic along the river. They became so engrossed in the subject that neither noticed the passage of time until Mrs. Gardiner and Miss Darcy joined them.

Suddenly recalling himself, Fitzwilliam looked about to check on the whereabouts of his party. "I apologize, Mrs. Gardiner, Georgie. I have been so involved in our conversation that I forgot to check on your comfort."

He was pleased to see Georgiana share a warm smile with Elizabeth's aunt even as Madeleine spoke gently, "It is no matter, Mr. Darcy. Your uncle has been entertaining us all."

Darcy turned and was amused to observe his Uncle James, attired in his informal 'rambling suit,' energetically pointing out various species of birds to the children, Elizabeth and Mr. Bingley at his side.

Mr. Gardiner chuckled. "Between Lizzy's knowledge of botany and Sir James' mastery of ornithology, we shall not need a guide!"

His wife laughingly disagreed. "Oh no, Edward, Elizabeth was telling me just this morning that she heard that the curator at Kew Gardens may be setting up a seed exchange just as the Chelsea Physic Garden does. She has every hope of procuring some mysterious new plants for Longbourn's gardens."

Seeing that the Darcys were intrigued but slightly confused, Madeleine explained; "Mrs. Bennet and her daughters have always been very involved in planning the estate's gardens."

The Gardiners told the history together, with the ease of a happily married couple. "When Fanny and Thomas married, Longbourn had been without a real mistress for nearly twenty years. Elizabeth's grandfather made sure the yard was kept trimmed, but it was nothing very… attractive."

"Fanny spent her first year as a married woman redecorating the house. When she was finished with that, she needed a new outlet for all that energy so she turned her focus on the gardens."

Madeleine smiled fondly. "She spent her first confinement reading gardening magazines and planning. Fanny once told me that, with the maiden name of Gardiner, it would have been a great embarrassment if Longbourn's park was wasn't beautiful!"

"Are you speaking of Mama and her gardens?" Darcy turned and was delighted to see that a smiling Elizabeth had come to stand at his elbow. "One of my earliest memories of my mother is of her trying to teach me to recognize the difference between spring clover and sweet pea seedlings."

Mr. Gardiner grinned. "I believe Jane was barely six and you were four when Fanny decided that each child should have your own bit of soil to plant."

His niece rolled her eyes impishly. "Yes, I'm afraid that was just after I had pulled up all of her lupines, thinking that they were weeds…" The group laughed with her.

Determined to follow his resolution to speak more, Darcy inquired. "I don't believe I saw more than the front yard at Longbourn. Are each of the gardens as unique as each of the Bennet sisters?"

Elizabeth smiled with obvious pleasure in the topic. "You visited Hertfordshire so late in the autumn that there was not much left to see, I'm afraid." She sighed, her eyes looking out across the water. "And April was so wet this spring that we weren't able to do much more than plan."

Edward Gardiner put one arm around his niece, hugging her shoulders to him. "Ah, my poor, dear girl. We do appreciate you giving up your 'planting season' to stay with us in the big, ugly city." Everyone laughed at his turn of phrase.

Elizabeth grinned up at her uncle. "Well, it shan't be a complete loss, thanks to Mr. Darcy's invitation!"

At that moment, Mr. and Mrs. Gardiner were distracted by the approach of their children with Sir James Darcy. When the others turned away, Darcy was pleased to see Elizabeth remain at his side.

He spoke softly. "You did not answer my question about the differences among your sisters' gardens."

She glanced up at him and then turned to lean against the railing, looking out across the water. "I had not thought about it in quite that way before, but you are right. Jane's garden has several very proper rose bushes, lilies, delphinium, and such... all very neat and well-behaved. Mary tends to be a bit more practical; she began working on a knot garden of herbs several years ago.

"You might be surprised, but Kitty actually has a lovely sense of landscaping... what to plant where so that the colors and bloom times create beautiful combinations from season to season. Unfortunately, these last years she has been spending far more time with Lydia than in the garden." She sighed. "My youngest sister spends a day or two in the spring rushing around fussing, planting, and transplanting, but she never bothers to care for it. Her border would be nothing but a weed patch if Jane and I did not look after it."

Elizabeth's thoughts flickered back to Longbourn and she wondered briefly if their father had continued his efforts to improve his daughters' behavior.

Although he very much wished to ask her about her own garden and tell her of Pemberley's, Will saw that her mind had drifted to something more serious. Guessing, he asked, "Have you heard from Longbourn recently? Is everyone well?"

"I received a letter from Jane yesterday." Elizabeth shot a smile at him. "I would not say that they are all perfectly well, but they are certainly all healthy." Remembering that she wanted to speak to Mr. Darcy about his letter and her father's awareness of it, she sighed and turned to him.

"Mr. Darcy, I wished to speak to you about..."

Elizabeth was interrupted by the shriek of the ship's steam whistle. Both turned to look toward the bow and were surprised to see that the crew was already readying the lines as they maneuvered into the dock at Kew.

Fitzwilliam dearly wished to know what she wanted to say to him, but clearly there was no time. "Miss Bennet, I should very much like to continue this conversation but I fear we must prepare to disembark. Perhaps later?" He caught her eye, hoping that she would understand.

With a pleased smile, Elizabeth agreed and they both turned to check on their party.

Mr. Gardiner had lifted young Tommy to his shoulders and was trying to convince the boy to stop grabbing his father's ears as handles, much to his mother and Miss Darcy's amusement. Jonathan and Rebecca were following Sir James like a pair of ducklings, obviously enthralled by the older man's stories.

"Amelia?" Darcy was about to offer Miss Bennet his arm when he noticed that her attention had been distracted by a little girl with curly brown hair who had latched onto her cousin's skirt. He smiled when blue eyes peeked around at him.

"Lizzy, he is very tall," whispered Amelia.

Elizabeth's eyes sparkled mischievously. "Amelia, you have met Mr. Darcy, have you not?"

The little girl nodded but remained silent, still peering up at the gentleman.

Darcy grinned and knelt down on one knee. London Society's ladies might terrorize him but he was entirely comfortable with six-year-old females. "Should you like to ride on my shoulders like your brother, Miss Amelia?"

The offer garnered him a brilliant smile. "I would be taller than Jonathan!" She darted out from behind Lizzy's skirts and had just taken Darcy's hand when the deck shuddered beneath their feet.

Holding tightly to the little girl and reaching out a hand to steady Miss Bennet, Fitzwilliam looked around to see what had happened.

Noting her new friend's anxiety, Amelia patted his arm. "It's alright, Mr. Darcy. We've just pulled into the dock. It goes bump."

Fitzwilliam stood and noted that she was quite correct. Turning his attention back to the little girl, he smiled. "Quite right, Miss Amelia. It is a great comfort to have an experienced sailor such as yourself to sooth my fears."

She nodded calmly. "I was scared the first time Papa took me on a boat." Seeing that the others were heading toward the ramp, she reached up to take her cousin's hand while still holding on to Mr. Darcy's. "Let's just walk now. You may carry me when we're on the ground... it's not tippy there."

Fitzwilliam and Elizabeth shared a smile and then obediently followed the rest of their party.

Will's sister caught sight of the trio descending the gangplank, the two adults swinging Amelia forward between them. Georgiana smiled wistfully, easily imaging what the couple would be like as husband and wife with children of their own.

This pleasant exchange set the tone for the day. The weather could not have been lovelier; a warm, sunny, spring day with a clear blue sky and a hint of breeze. The open carriages that Darcy had arranged were waiting at the docks for them and in short order the party was descending to meet their guide at the front gate of the Royal Botanic Gardens.

Darcy's servants served coffee and buns and soon the group was ready to begin their walking tour. The guide was a rather odd young man named John Smith whose innocuous name and quiet manners belied a vast knowledge of plants from around the world and the history of those planted at the Kew Gardens in particular.

Mr. Smith and Sir James were rapidly assured of their mutual passion for natural history and soon the party was being led about by the two men, closely trailed by young Jonathan Gardiner who appeared to have been infected by their enthusiasm for botanizing.

Darcy was pleased to see Bingley deep in conversation with Mr. Gardiner, the pair paying little attention to their surroundings. Knowing something of the similarities in their backgrounds, he had every hope that Elizabeth's uncle might serve as a superb advisor for the younger man.

Finding Elizabeth trailing behind the group, he offered his arm and nodded genially toward his sister. The normally shy Miss Darcy was chattering away with Mrs. Gardiner, surrounded by the younger Gardiner children who appeared to have cheerfully adopted her as a playmate. "I have not seen her so happy since our father died, and perhaps not even then."

Elizabeth smiled easily. "My aunt and uncle have that effect on people."

"I am very pleased to have made their acquaintance. They are truly excellent people."

Elizabeth glanced up at him and he caught her eye. She nodded, accepting the implicit apology for his past words. "Jane and I have always treasured our time with them. I miss Longbourn, of course, but the house on Gracechurch Street is so much more..." She paused, searching for the right word. "Sensible? That does not quite encompass it."

Darcy was already nodding. "They understand you; they share your intellect and character. And it is easy to see that they have an excellent relationship."

Elizabeth smiled sadly. "After seeing the contrast to our own parents, Jane and I promised each other that we would only marry for the deepest love." Suddenly remembering to whom she was speaking, Miss Bennet blushed a rosy pink and tucked her chin.

Feeling the tension but recognizing that it provided him with the opportunity he sought, Fitzwilliam cleared his throat. "I wish more of our society shared your resolution. It is what I hope for my own sister…" He hesitated before continuing more quietly, "and for myself."

There was a pregnant pause as both thought desperately of what to say. Even the sound of their steps on the gravel path sounded incredibly loud.

"Miss Bennet…"

"Mr. Darcy…"

Both spoke at once, but Will motioned for Elizabeth to go first.

"I only wished to apologize for how I spoke to you… in Kent. Your letter…"

"Please, Miss Bennet, do not make yourself uneasy…"

"But the things that I accused you of!"

"What did you say of me, that I did not deserve? For, though your accusations were ill-founded, formed on mistaken premises, my behavior at the time had merited the severest reproof. It was unpardonable. I cannot think of it without abhorrence."

Elizabeth had come to a halt and turned to him, looking into his eyes with absolute seriousness. "As was my own behavior."

Without thinking, Darcy took her hands in his own. "You have nothing to apologize for. I drove you to anger…"

Lizzy pursed her lips and paused before rolling her eyes and turning, taking the gentleman's arm and tugging on it so that they continued to walk together. "Mr. Darcy, we should not quarrel for the greater share of blame annexed to that evening. The conduct of neither, if strictly examined, will be irreproachable; but since then, we have both, I hope, improved in civility."

"I cannot be so easily reconciled to myself. The recollection of what I then said, of my conduct, my manners, my expressions during the whole of it, is now, and has been for the last month, inexpressibly painful to me. Your reproof, so well applied, I shall never forget: 'had you behaved in a more gentleman-like manner.' Those were your words. You know not, you can scarcely conceive, how they have tortured me."

"I was certainly very far from expecting them to make so strong an impression. I had not the smallest idea of their being ever felt in such a way."

"I can easily believe it. You thought me then devoid of every proper feeling. I am sure you did. The turn of your countenance I shall never forget, as you said that I could not have addressed you in any possible way, that would induce you to accept me."

"Oh! Do not repeat what I said then. These recollections will not do at all. I assure you that I have long been most heartily ashamed of it."

Darcy mentioned his letter. "Did it," said he, "did it soon make you think better of me? Did you, on reading it, give any credit to its contents?"

She explained what its effect on her had been, and how gradually her former prejudices had been removed. "I soon believed your account of Mr. Wickham, for I knew you to be a devoted brother and one who would never tell such a story if it were not of the utmost importance."

Darcy paused. "I hope that the truth did not hurt you too deeply."

Elizabeth smiled sardonically. "There was no great affection on either side, I think. He flattered my vanity; I thought myself very clever to have taken such an instant dislike of you, and then to have it proven so completely was... heartening."

She waved a hand as though brushing away an irritating insect. "Soon after your party left Hertfordshire, Mr. Wickham transferred his attentions to a young lady whose primary virtue seemed to be that she had recently inherited ten-thousand pounds."

Seeing that Darcy looked instantly wary, Elizabeth rushed to reassure him. "Miss King is quite safe from him; not long before I returned from Kent, her uncle removed her to Liverpool."

Darcy nodded but remained silent for a few minutes, his mind having returned to his resolution to make sure Wickham could no longer prey on any young ladies. Upon their return from Rosings, Colonel Fitzwilliam had agreed to quietly gather information on Lieutenant Wickham. However, Richard was currently on an errand for his general and Darcy had no idea what progress had been made.

As her companion meditated on his boyhood playmate, Elizabeth's thoughts had returned to his letter and she remembered another resolution that she needed to keep. "Mr. Darcy, there is another matter for which I must apologize. It concerns your letter, sir."

The mere mention of that epistle was quite enough to immediately engage Fitzwilliam's attention and he spent several minutes protesting again that she had nothing for which to apologize.

Finally Elizabeth stopped and turned to him. "Please, Mr. Darcy. This is not easy for me, but you must allow me to speak." Seeing that the gentleman looked somewhat startled, she smiled and lightened her tone. "Meryton society would be quite astonished to see us now; the ever-chatty Lizzy Bennet unable to get a word in edgewise with the silent, serious gentleman from Derbyshire."

Her smile diminished when she saw that her companion was embarrassed. "Please forgive me, Mr. Darcy. I forget that you are not accustomed to my teasing..."

However, Elizabeth's awkwardness dissolved when she caught a mischievous glint in the gentleman's eye. "So, am I to understand that you wish me to talk *more* while dancing, but *less* when walking? I confess I am unclear on the protocols, Miss Bennet. Perhaps I require lessons, or is there an instruction manual?"

Both laughed at the reference to her spirited reprimand during their dance at the Netherfield ball. The couple turned to continue their walk in a pleasant mood, although Elizabeth was determined that he would know of the effect his letter had had not only upon her, but on her father as well.

The information was relayed in segments, interrupted by a pause to admire a Chinese pagoda and various other sights. When Elizabeth was finished, she waited anxiously for Mr. Darcy's response and was relieved to see that he looked thoughtful rather than angry.

When Fitzwilliam realized that she was finished, he smiled wanly. "Please, do not make yourself uneasy, Miss Bennet. You have just solved two problems created by my previous behavior that I had recognized but not yet conceived of how to mend."

Elizabeth shot him a confused look and he shrugged helplessly. "First, I should not have left Hertfordshire without alerting the neighborhood of Wickham's true nature. I have been paying his debts and generally cleaning up after him for years; I knew what sort of damage he would leave in his wake and should have acted to prevent them."

"Mr. Darcy, he is not your responsibility…"

"I must beg to disagree, Miss Bennet. It is just the same as if I saw a group of people walking on ice that I knew to be too thin to hold their weight. It is my responsibility to warn them."

Elizabeth tilted her head to one side, forced to admit that his logic was sound. "Very well, I will agree to that. However, whatever your past acquaintance, Wickham's misdeeds are his alone; *you* are not responsible for *his* wickedness. Just as I may attempt to curb my youngest sister's behavior but in the end, her mistakes are her own."

Darcy conceded her point and they walked in silence for several minutes before he recalled the other item he wished to discuss.

"Though I fear it shall not improve his opinion of me, I am glad that Mr. Bennet has seen my letter and heard the details of our… interactions… from you. Not long after I placed that letter in your hands, I realized how hideously improper my actions had been. Had someone approached Georgiana in such a way, I would have been furious."

Oddly pleased by his admission, Elizabeth nodded somberly. "For once, I find myself appreciative of my father's permissiveness toward his daughters." She glanced up at the gentleman beside her and added quietly, "For I very much needed to hear what you wrote but I am afraid that, at the time, I was not in the mood to give credence to any speech of yours."

Darcy heaved a sigh, for the impropriety of his actions had been weighing on him.

The couple walked silently for some minutes. Elizabeth was secretly forming a desperate resolution and perhaps he might be doing the same.

However, before either of them could act upon their resolve, the sound of running feet and joyful cries alerted them to the approach of the

Gardiner children.

"Lizzy!"

"Come quickly!"

"There is such a wonderful luncheon set out for us but Mama won't let us begin until you and Mr. Darcy catch up!

"Please hurry—there are apple tarts and cake and ever so many good things!"

This last was said in a rush by Tommy who, though an otherwise serious, bookish little boy, was well-known in his family circle for his sweet tooth. Luckily, in this he was joined by his cousin.

Elizabeth smiled. "Apple tarts? Had I known that such delicacies awaited us, I would have been first in line!"

With happy laughter and a bit of playful teasing, the children led the wayward couple to the picnic site where Mr. Darcy's servants had set things out.

While most men of his station would have demanded a full complement of liveried footmen serving courses on a table with silver and china, not unlike what might be found in his own dining room (the only difference being the tented walls), Darcy preferred a much more informal version and had planned only a slightly enhanced form of the picnics he and his cousins had enjoyed in their boyhood.

For a moment, Will worried that the informality might have been a mistake but he was quickly reassured as all of his guests happily settled themselves on the blankets and were soon passing around the food prepared by his cook. Georgiana was more comfortable than he had ever seen her in company, easily recommending various dishes and directing the servants.

After eating his fill, Fitzwilliam leaned back on his elbows, legs crossed at the ankles, and allowed himself to relax and simply enjoy the moment. Their guide had been encouraged to join them and, once reassured of the genuine amiability of the group, Mr. Smith was found to be a superb story teller. As a lad, the young man had been employed as a stove boy and he had a wealth of tales from his time stoking the heaters that warmed the greenhouses in addition to the plant collecting trips he had assisted on.

Eventually Darcy's attention was caught by an exchange between Mrs. Gardiner and Mr. Smith. It seemed that John Smith had a particular love of ferns and was eagerly instructing Mrs. Gardiner and her niece for an upcoming holiday trip.

Fitzwilliam waited until a suitable pause in their conversation. "Mrs. Gardiner, do I understand correctly that you and your family shall be travelling to the northern counties soon?"

Madeleine Gardiner smiled at the young man. "Yes, indeed, Mr. Darcy. In fact, we had planned to depart a week ago, but a family matter delayed our departure."

Turning to his host, Mr. Gardiner added, "We had originally planned to visit the Lake District but I am afraid that my business requires me to return by the end of July so we shall have to cut our tour a bit short."

Darcy appeared thoughtful. "That is unfortunate; it has been some years since I have been there but the landscape is beautiful."

That lady smiled. "Yes, Lizzy is too polite to let us know how disappointed she truly is to miss it, I think."

Her comment drew Miss Bennet's attention away from young Amelia. "Not at all, Aunt! I shall not say that I do not hope to see them some day, but I shall be very happy to spend time exploring the Peaks." She could not help but glance shyly toward Darcy. "I have heard that the landscape there is quite spectacular, as well."

Darcy appeared as if he was about to speak, but after a long look at Elizabeth, he remained silent. The party continued to chat about the natural beauties of northern England and the differences between north and south until it became clear that all were finished with their meal. As the servants began to pack up the detritus from the picnic, Fitzwilliam offered his arm to Elizabeth and the pair strolled slowly in the direction of the rose gardens.

Elizabeth's curiosity had been fanned by Mr. Darcy's thoughtful silence during the latter part of the meal so she remained quiet at first. However, after some ten minutes with no word from the gentleman, she was reminded of her resolution to question, tease, or otherwise argue the man into talking with her.

With a sparkle of amusement in her eye, Miss Bennet made some slight observation on the roses. Will replied appropriately but his mind was obviously far away. After a pause of some minutes, she addressed him a second time.

"It is your turn to say something now, Mr. Darcy. I talked about the roses; now you ought to make some remark on the size of the gardens, or the number of plants."

He smiled immediately and she was pleased to see that he recalled the details of their conversation from the Netherfield ball as clearly as she. "Miss Bennet, I might ask if you talk by rule while you are walking, but I fear that should we continue the conversation, it might lead to words I would wish unsaid."

Elizabeth was suddenly reminded of the poorly conceived admonishment she had delivered on his treatment of Wickham at the end of their dance. She blushed and was about to apologize when Fitzwilliam took her hand and squeezed lightly.

"Please, I did not bring it up to make you uneasy. As you said earlier, we should not quarrel for the greater share of blame annexed to *that* evening, either."

Elizabeth looked carefully into his eyes and was reassured by what she saw there. After a pause, Darcy attempted a lighter tone. "As much as I would like to tempt you into a discussion of books, there is another matter…" He trailed off for a moment before gathering himself again to speak, this time in a voice roughened by strong emotions under tight control.

"Miss Bennet, we have spoken of the errors that we both made in our prior acquaintance, and most particularly on that evening when I addressed you in the parsonage. I… I value your forthrightness for, although your words were painful at the time, I hope that they have also taught be to be a better man.

"I wish to believe that your opinion of me has improved, but I no longer trust my ability to interpret your thoughts, so I shall be blunt; if your feelings are still what they were in April, please tell me so at once. My affections and wishes are unchanged, but one word from you will silence me on the subject forever.

"When Mrs. Gardiner mentioned that you would be traveling to the Peak District, I was instantly resolved to invite your party to stay as my guests at Pemberley. However, I… I realized that I do not know enough of your… feelings… to know if such an invitation would please you… or if it would place you in an… uncomfortable… position…"

It took Elizabeth several moments to gather her wits about her after such a speech and the pause left Fitzwilliam feeling even more exposed. He began talking again before she could frame a response. "I understand completely if you do not wish to extend our acquaintance… you have been very kind to tolerate me for the last fortnight and I am deeply grateful that my sister has had the honor to meet you…"

Vaguely amused to hear the normally stoic Mr. Darcy rattle on, Elizabeth stopped and turned to face him. Fitzwilliam fell silent when she took his larger hands in her own.

"Mr. Darcy, please." She paused and shut her eyes tightly for a moment, attempting to align her thoughts cogently. However, the only thing she could think of was how right it felt to have her hands held in his. She opened her eyes and looked up at him.

"Mr. Darcy, my feelings are quite different from what they were in the spring, and I should very much like to further our… acquaintance. I… I believe that my aunt and uncle would be honored by an invitation to visit Pemberley." She was rewarded by a look of heartfelt happiness on the gentleman's face.

Will quelled his first impulse to pick Elizabeth up and twirl her around before kissing her senseless; it was too soon for her, as would be any explicit discussion of love or marriage. He was not so timid, however, as to resist pressing his luck á bit further.

"Thank you. I shall speak with the Gardiners immediately." He took a deep breath and asked softly. "Would you allow me, or do I ask too much, the honor of courting you?" He caught sight of a deep blush flooding the lady's cheeks just before she tucked her chin and seemed to study their joined hands.

Just then, the sound of running feet alerted them to the approach of the three eldest Gardiner children. "Lizzy! Mama says that you must catch up!"

"You must come and see the prettiest pink rose; Mr. Smith says it's called a Fairy Rose!"

Elizabeth stepped back and freed one hand to ruffle Tommy's hair, but Darcy was keenly aware that she allowed him to retain the other in his grasp. Smiling, she spoke to them all.

"Yes, the answer to all of you is yes! Jonathan, please lead off—I must say I have become quite turned around and have no idea where we must go." She turned to Mr. Darcy and tugged at his hand to walk with her. Smiling brilliantly up at him, she repeated, "And yes to you as well, sir."

Fitzwilliam allowed her to pull him into walking but before he allowed his happiness to overcome him, he had to make certain he had understood her correctly. "Shall I speak with your uncle, then? And your father?"

Elizabeth's dear face was a mixture of happiness and embarrassment. "Yes, sir. Both, I suppose. Although I would prefer to keep the duty of speaking to my mother for myself."

"Whatever you wish." Darcy was not of a disposition in which happiness overflows into mirth, but it was immediately apparent to the Gardiners that the couple that joined them in the rose garden had reached some new understanding.

After a quiet word, Fitzwilliam broke away from Elizabeth to speak quietly with his sister. In short order, the siblings had proffered an invitation for the Gardiners' party to stay at Pemberley for an extended visit. Darcy was not above using the temptation of seeing her childhood haunts and possibly recovering some of her family's mementos to bring Mrs. Gardiner to his side.

In reality, Mr. and Mrs. Gardiner were very pleased by the invitation and any initial reservations were dispelled by their niece's obvious approval of Pemberley's master.

Before the party had reached the carriages, packed and readied to return to London, plans had been made. Only Mr. Bingley declined the invitation, insisting that he was needed at Netherfield and would be remaining there for much of the summer. A quick look to Jane's sister assured him that he was making the correct decision.

The next few days passed quickly. Darcy spoke with Mr. Gardiner and it was agreed that the young man could call upon Elizabeth at Gracechurch Street, although the courtship would not be considered official until he had secured Mr. Bennet's approval.

As soon as he had conceived of the idea of inviting the Gardiners and Miss Bennet to stay at Pemberley, Darcy had written to his housekeeper with instructions to prepare the house for very special visitors. He also hoped to have her check the attics for anything from the vicarage that had been packed away after the death of Mrs. Gardiner's family. He admitted to himself that he hoped such actions would aid in his quest to make Elizabeth think better of him, but he also understood how important such artifacts would be to her aunt.

Fitzwilliam had lost both father and mother, but at least he still had the house in which he had grown up and all of its contents to remind him of his parents, in addition to a sister who reminded him of his mother more each day. He could not imagine the sorrow of having no such mementos of one's family and was determined to discover them for Mrs. Gardiner, if any remained to be found.

Unfortunately, as much as Darcy cudgeled his brain, he was embarrassed to realize that he could only recall referring to the rector and his wife as "Reverend Jonathan" and "Mrs. Rebecca." He thought that their surname might have been something like "Burns" or "Bergram" but could not be certain. After several days, he finally admitted to himself that he would simply have to petition Mrs. Gardiner as to her maiden name before sending the request to Pemberley. He was not concerned that his ignorance would offend the kind woman, only that he was disappointed not to be able to surprise Elizabeth's aunt with a *fait accompli*.

Darcy was provided with an opportunity to question Mrs. Gardiner one evening when he and his sister dined at Gracechurch Street. Much of the dinner conversation revolved around the group's travel plans; the two Darcys would travel to Hertfordshire with Elizabeth and the Gardiners, where Fitzwilliam would talk to Mr. Bennet and request that gentleman's permission to court his daughter. While the Gardiners would remain at Longbourn for several days, Darcy would depart for Derbyshire as soon as his errand in Mr. Bennet's study was accomplished. He wished to complete as much business with his steward as possible before Elizabeth arrived so that he might spend as much time as possible showing her around Pemberley.

Georgiana was bubbling with excitement; her brother had agreed that she might remain at Longbourn after he departed and then travel north with the Gardiners and Miss Bennet. The Gardiners laughingly warned Miss Darcy that she would share in the responsibility for entertaining the Gardiner children during the trip but she acquiesced happily and began tallying the various puzzles and toys that she would bring. Over the years, her brother had given her any number of compact games to keep her entertained during the long coach ride from Derbyshire to London and she was determined that the Gardiner children would never be bored.

Darcy was reminded of the question he must ask Elizabeth's aunt and took the opportunity to speak. "Mrs. Gardiner; I wished to have our housekeeper at Pemberley check the attics for any of your family's belongings that might have been stored there."

Mrs. Gardiner nodded, her bright eyes clearly intrigued by the idea of reclaiming some physical mementos of her family.

Fitzwilliam's face showed his distress. "However, although I remember that your mother's maiden name was Churchill, I fear that I cannot recall your own."

Mrs. Gardiner nodded again but seemed slightly more reserved, as though dreading the question. Unsure what might cause such a reaction, Darcy continued in a more hesitant tone, "I always referred to your parents as 'Reverend Jonathan' and 'Mrs. Rebecca, you see.'"

Mrs. Gardiner smiled softly at the serious young man. "Mr. Darcy, you have no reason to be ashamed; you were but ten years old when my parents passed and I left to live in London."

The lady lapsed into silence, studying the wedding band on her left hand. Finally her husband chuckled and wrapped his arm around her shoulders, hugging her to him. "Come now, my dear Madeleine. Tell him, or I shall be forced to do so. I do not believe that Lizzy has heard the story either, for that matter."

Mrs. Gardiner gave her husband a long look before rolling her eyes and turning to the other occupants of the room. Miss Darcy sat with the Gardiner's calico nestled in her lap, purring loudly. Mr. Darcy and Lizzy were seated comfortably, side-by-side on the settee, and all three were clearly intrigued by her reluctance.

Madeleine Gardiner sighed. "Mr. Darcy, my parents avoided using my father's surname because they broke all relations with his family when I was a little girl, just before we moved to Derbyshire, in fact." She sighed again before continuing, "My father was born Jonathan de Bourgh, you see, the youngest son of Lord Maxwell de Bourgh and brother to your aunt's late husband."

15 BROKEN CONNECTIONS

Jonathan de Bourgh recognized early that his calling was the church. Although on the day of his birth in 1751, his father had decreed that this fourth son would enter into the military upon reaching his majority, Jonathan's status as youngest of six children combined with excellent marks at Oxford made it relatively easy to continue quietly upon his chosen course.

One evening at a family supper, during a pause in a spirited discussion over ranking marital prospects for his two elder sisters, he quietly offered up the news that he had been offered the position of curate at St. Mary-le-Bow near Cheapside.

His sisters stared at him oddly for a minute but then returned to their debate over the relative merits of title and income, and how much the more attractive visage of one particular suitor should outweigh his status as a younger son. Taught their values by a superficial mother determined to advance her own social status through the marriages of her children and having lived their lives in the same house as a father with little respect for females, their considerations of marriage did not bother with concepts such as affection or respect.

The men at the table paid more attention to Jonathan's statement. The family attended church as a matter of course and without question, if little devotion. Lord Maxwell went because the de Bourghs had always gone. Not making a regular appearance in the family pew in their fashionable London church would have made as little sense to him as not collecting the rents due him from the tenants who farmed his estates.

He accepted as his due the deference he received upon his appearance and he perceived no moral conflict when he spent much of the time during the sermon considering such weighty concerns as whether the demands of his current mistress for increasingly expensive baubles were worth her considerable favors, or if it was time to discard her in favor of a younger and more tractable girl.

His eldest sons attended with similar regularity, if even less attention. They typically returned to their father's house in the wee hours of the morning after a night of gambling, drinking, and whoring with just enough time for their valets to redress them in appropriate attire, apply cologne to mask inappropriate odors, and ply them with enough coffee to make it through the service without passing out. Their thoughts during the sermon, when they exerted themselves to have them, were primarily focused on totting up their wins and losses at the card tables from the night before.

"You've been offered *what?!?*" exclaimed Lord Maxwell. "You're going into the army like James. Or perhaps the navy… When are you going to be done at university, boy? We'll need to see about getting you a commission, I suppose. Damn fool things are getting more expensive by the year. Can't have a de Bourgh any lower than a lieutenant, though, so I'll have to see about freeing up some blunt."

Jonathan's eldest brothers glanced at each other—anything that might deplete their future inheritance was of great import. "Which church was that?" asked Lewis. As the second son, he was particularly interested in minimizing the funds his father spent on his younger brothers as it directly impacted his own future finances. He guessed correctly that the first solution that occurred to his father would be to sell off a living at Rosings Park, a family estate in Kent designated for the second son.

"St. Mary's," replied Jonathan. "Reverend Annesley has been raised to bishop. He asked my divinity professor if there were any promising students who could be prepared to take on the day-to-day affairs at his current parish by September. Professor Fenton suggested me and Reverend Somersby supported the recommendation."

"Somersby! What does Reverend Somersby know about it?!" queried his father in a mild roar. His only interaction with the personnel at the family's church was a nod as he departed each Sunday, or possibly a "Good day" if the service had been particularly brief. It had never occurred to him that any of his sons might purposely expand their relationship with a cleric beyond that necessary to maintain a good standing in Society.

"Annesley did you say?" asked Lady Harriet, her attention caught by the name. "Excellent family, if a little dull. The wife was a Pettigrew, you know." The de Bourgh sisters nodded sagely. Edna was twenty-three with a dowry of twenty-thousand pounds and an unfortunate nose. Edith was two years younger with a similar dowry, a more fortunate nose, and was currently enjoying the increasingly serious attentions of the elder son of the Earl of Parsley.

Their mother continued, "Juliette Pettigrew was quite popular when she was introduced to society. I remember how surprised we all were when she accepted Paul Annesley. The family was certainly good enough, but none of us could ever understand half of what he was saying. And he didn't like to dance, of all things." The sisters frowned in unison.

"*Humph.* I remember Annesley at Eton. Studious chap. Not interested in sport, or cards for that matter. Always had his nose in a book. Tutors loved him. *Humph.*" Lord Maxwell didn't resent those men with a more intellectual bent than himself, he simply couldn't comprehend them and thus they weren't worth bothering over. He himself had spent his time at school and later university with a mob of like-minded lordlings and wealthy gentlemen, playing cricket and boxing during the day and gambling and drinking in the local pubs at night.

As long as the tuition was paid and no great offences were caught, a gentleman's pass was awarded and friendships made for life. So it had been for his father and so had he expected of his own sons. The concept that one of them might wish to have more to do with the church caused him to squint oddly at Jonathan, rather as though the young man had sat down to supper wearing one of his sister's excessively lace-trimmed bonnets.

"Since end of term, I have been assisting Mr. Somersby with some parish matters." Jonathan knew better than to include the details that he had been in fact drafting sermons for the aging vicar and representing him at various meetings with other clerics to coordinate charities for the poor; his father's eyebrows had already drawn together to resemble a single, very prickly grey caterpillar moving across his brow. "Father, I would very much like to accept the position. It is respectable, and I would greatly prefer it to the navy."

In fact, Jonathan had spent enough time listening to the stories of the old soldiers and sailors at the free medical clinic where he ministered to know that he was not meant for the military. He saw no good in the deaths and maiming of hundreds of young men on the battlefields of America or the seas off France.

"*Humph.* A churchman, eh. Never really considered the idea. Respectable enough though, as you say. Cheaper than a commission, too." Jonathan's brothers shared another look as their father motioned to a footman to refill his wine glass, but said nothing themselves. "Well, if you'd rather a cleric's collar than a red coat, I suppose I can speak with Annesley and consider the matter."

Jonathan and his brothers understood this to mean that their father would discuss the matter with his friends at the club (many the same men with whom he had been at school) and then, if no significant financial or social concerns were raised, Jonathan's course of life would be approved, if not understood. The elder brothers let out their breath quietly and nodded in support of the decision. They were pleased, if not for the same reasons as Jonathan.

A fortnight later, it was done. Lord Maxwell was pleased to have disposed of his youngest son with no great financial expenditure or particular effort on his part. Lady Harriet spent a minute considering if Jonathan's position could be used to gain any social cachet, but promptly forgot the matter when perfume was dripped on the bodice of the gown Edith had chosen to wear for an afternoon garden party, rendering it unwearable and prompting a flurry of redressing.

Jonathan's eldest brother congratulated Lewis on the continued health of their inheritance before the two left to see a bare-knuckle boxing match organized in a particularly seedy section of Seven Dials. James, the third son, was in Brighton training with his regiment and didn't hear the news for several months. In all, the reassignment of Jonathan's life from war to God was accomplished with barely a ripple in the family dynamics. Jonathan was pleased.

Jonathan de Bourgh had inherited ten thousand pounds from a maiden aunt on his father's side. The lady had lived out her last years in her brother's house in London, though interacting with the family as little as possible. As a child, Jonathan had crept up to her apartments almost daily and spent hours, first being read to and later reading from her extensive collection of books. An oddity in the family, she had liked the quiet, intelligent boy and taught him chess and discussed books with him. His best memories of boyhood were of Sunday afternoons in Aunt Madeleine's sitting room, discussing the morning's sermon over tea and scones with two enormous, orange cats purring on the chaise beside him. When he left for school, he knew most of the scriptures by heart and could easily cite them in debate.

His father had assumed that Jonathan would supplement his inheritance, either through the accumulation of awards in his military career or by marrying a wealthy heiress. The young man had no interest in either. The curate's position came with a small cottage near the parsonage and a stipend that would support his meager expenses without forcing him to dip into his inheritance. He felt no great need to marry any time soon—the church called him and he hoped to do some good.

Jonathan de Bourgh spent ten years at St. Mary's. His sermons were considered to be well-formulated and theologically sound by his peers. If some of the young ladies blushed and giggled over his sonorous voice and blue eyes, it went relatively unnoticed except in that attendance grew during his tenure. He continued his work amongst the poor and soon had organized a home for crippled soldiers and sailors who had no money or family to support them. The parish tithed funds for the lease on a house; the ladies sewed various necessities and donated baskets of foodstuffs. Jonathan was even able to hire two nurses, knowledgeable women recently returned from the American wars, to tend to the men's injuries and assist in their recovery and rehabilitation.

Although Jonathan did not seek notice, his work came to the attention of many, including Sir Paul Churchill. A former navy commander before retiring to a desk job in the War Department, Churchill had cared deeply for his men and kept track of them in later years as best he could. After hearing praise for the young curate from several of his former sailors, he made an unannounced visit to the home for veterans, now called St. Elmo's House in honor of the patron saint of sailors.

Pleased with the clean conditions and the cheerful attitude of the men, he identified himself to the nurse and housekeeper, intimating that he might be willing to provide some financial support. He was further impressed with the businesslike manner with which the staff treated him—giving him a brief tour and summarizing the services, noting what they had and what was needed without any groveling.

Sir Paul sent his card around, applying to the young curate for a meeting. The two men were pleased with each other and the meeting was extended into a luncheon. Jonathan discussed oddities at St. Elmo's that had become innovations. The adoption of a miserable little dog with a gash on its leg that had been found huddling under a bush in the rear garden had provided the men with a mascot. One young ensign who had not spoken in the six months he had spent recovering from the amputation of both legs and bad burns over his face and torso, had finally begun talking while clutching the yellow mutt to his chest and hiding his tears in the dog's fur. Later, two bedraggled kittens were added to the menagerie after being rescued by a nurse on her walk to work.

The rear garden had been another unexpected innovation in recovery. Originally a rather dull patch of lawn ringed with unprepossessing yews, it was rapidly being converted into a rather spectacular garden. One area had been sectioned into patches for those men who wished a small plot of their own, and, as many of the sailors had been farmer's sons before escaping to the sea, the kitchen at St. Elmo's was soon serving fresher produce than many a Mayfair townhouse. A rainbow of annuals, perennials, and rose bushes were flourishing and the men had established a rota for "garden duties" as they had come to be called.

Sir Paul smiled at this, easily recognizing that these former military men were unconsciously defining a structure in which they were familiar—few of the invalids would be comfortable going outside to simply "take the air" with no goal. Now, even the amputees were involved, finding niches for themselves and comfort in their ability to work. A small library of gardening books was being built up and a day trip to the Chelsea Physic Gardens was being discussed.

Jonathan paused for a sip of wine and suddenly realized that, in his enthusiasm, his host had cleared his plate while Jonathan's was barely touched. Sir Paul chuckled at the younger man's embarrassment. "Not to worry, my boy. It warms my heart to hear of your progress and plans. I've seen too many good men fall into melancholy upon returning to Britain after serving abroad."

After some further conversation, Jonathan mentioned that a house across the square from St. Elmo's had been shut up for all the years he had known it and Sir Paul agreed to look into its ownership and see if it might be possible to lease or even purchase the property to expand the hospice. The older gentleman nodded thoughtfully as the younger man described his idea of having a second house where those in the final stages of recovery (and more comfortable having visitors) might live while finding work.

Churchill himself suggested that perhaps a parlor might be outfitted almost like a club, providing a place where other military men could drop by for a visit with old comrades, discuss battles past and present, play cards, or merely rest for a time in a place where empathy abounded. "I often think of them as the walking wounded—men who finish their service with all their limbs intact and few visible scars, but who have seen too much of pain and suffering to fall easily into their old lives. The family and friends that you dreamed of returning to…" The older man trailed off, staring unseeing into the distance and sighing deeply.

After some moments, the Commander's thoughts returned to the present. Blinking, he looked up at the younger man and noted the question in his eyes. "Battle of Lagos," he said simply, referring to one of the great naval battles of the Seven Years War. "It was a great victory and Admiral Boscawen a great commander… but to this day I can still hear the screams of those French sailors when the Redoubtable was driven up on the rocks off Gibraltar. Then I was given command of the Intrepid and made it to Quiberon Bay just in time to follow Admiral Hawkes into the shoals.

Jonathan nodded quietly, having heard stories from sailors who had survived the terrifying naval battle in which French and British fleets had fought desperately while dancing around reefs and shoals, buffeted by stormy winds.

Sir Paul grimaced toward his leg and cane. "Caught shrapnel. I'll never forget that day; storm waves crashing on the rocks and reefs popping up where you'd never expect it. I thought we were pulling in around an island to sneak up on the French flagship when out pops this frigate with guns ablaze. It would have been quite a sight if I was a painter, but as a young officer trying to rally a green crew…" He shrugged, sighing.

"Well, we got ourselves put together and took that frigate after some fancy sailing, but about a minute after they ran up the white flag I looked down to see why my right boot was squishing more than the left. There was a splinter as big as your thumb sticking out the side of my leg. Didn't even notice it in the heat of the battle but by then, I'd leaked enough that my boot was full of blood and I nearly keeled over in the arms of my boson's mate."

"I was young and stupid—thought I could just get the ship doctor to pull it out, bind me up and get me back out to finish up the surrender. Made it another five hours before collapsing again. Teakwood—went septic." He grunted, cringing at the painful memory. "Didn't lose the leg, but spent about a month in fevers and surgeons, then another six months recovering at home with my mother fussing about." Jonathan smiled gently.

"Spent another six months at my father's house wandering through my old life like a fog." Sir Paul continued. "I knew I didn't want to try for another command at sea—I'd been a good officer but not a brilliant one—but wasn't sure of much else. I'd been affianced to a girl two years before—our families were close and she was a sweet little thing—but it seemed to me that we had nothing in common after I returned. We broke it off amicably enough and I was happy when she got engaged to some lord a few months later."

"I had just about convinced myself that going out drinking every night with my old mates wasn't doing much for me when my uncle came for a visit. He'd been an army man—talked to me enough to understand that he'd seen some ugly things while serving in America when the colonies revolted. Then he did something that probably saved my life—suggested I take myself up to Scotland and spend some time at the family's hunting lodge, getting myself together. Mother fussed quite a bit but he was her elder brother and she trusted his advice.

"So, I packed my kit, saddled my horse and headed north. Mother had insisted I take my valet but Abbot had served me through my recovery and I knew he could use a bit of time to himself, so I dropped him off in Surrey to visit his family. When I got to Scotland, the elderly couple that kept the property had the lodge opened up and got me settled before going off back to their cottage.

"I spent a couple months barely speaking to another person. The McGills came by now and then to do the cleaning and keep my larder provisioned but largely let me keep to myself. I went on some long hikes through the hills and slept rough when I'd walked too far. Did some fishing but could barely even look at a gun, let alone think about hunting for sport.

"McGill's collie adopted me in my roving and we had some good long talks about philosophy and civilization. It was only years later that I realized that his camaraderie was much less spontaneous than it seemed. Turned out that McGill was my uncle's batman in the army and my family had settled him and his wife as caretakers of the lodge when Uncle Thomas retired as thanks for his service. That dog was smart as a whip and as well-trained as a twenty-year master sergeant. I have no doubt at all that he was sent along to keep me out of trouble.

"My uncle had clued in his old comrade to my situation when he wrote to McGill to have the lodge opened. They gave me my space when I needed it, and after a few months I found myself dropping by their cottage more and more often for Mrs. McGill's scones and a spot of conversation. By September I found myself ready for a bit of society and curious enough for news of the world to come out of my cocoon. McGill gave me a haircut and shave to make me look a bit less of a Highland wildman and I headed down the road to town.

"I stayed with a friend in Edinburgh; Meriwether had been a few years ahead of me at school and then we'd served together at one point or another. He'd settled as a solicitor in Edinburgh with his wife of five years and two children. Fiona Meriwether took one look at me and bustled off to plot with the cook over how to fatten me up. After a week they had me trimmed and tailored to befit a man of my standing (my valet Abbot had finished his holiday and traveled up to Edinburgh to assist in the effort) and ready to reenter the world."

Suddenly Sir Paul colored and looked down at his plate. After a moment's pause, however, he looked up at Jonathan with a bemused look. "You are an excellent listener, young man. I haven't blathered on about my life's story for years."

Jonathan immediately disagreed, assuring the older gentleman that he was indeed interested in his history. Churchill waved him off, though, after checking his pocket watch.

"No, my dear boy. You have certainly proved the talents that make you so respected as a cleric, but I have other appointments to keep. Come by our home for dinner some evening this week and I might tell you more."

When Jonathan indicated his willingness, the Commander thought for a moment before speaking; "I believe Friday would work, but I shall have to consult Evelyn. I'll send around a note and we can work it out."

When Jonathan de Bourgh arrived at the Churchills' on Friday evening for the first of many friendly dinners, he was impressed by the happy relationship that existed between the Commander and his wife, an intelligent, well-bred woman who still spoke with the soft accent of her native Edinburgh even after twenty years in London. It was soon apparent that her intellect easily matched her husband's and that, unlike some men, he embraced it. Theirs was truly a marriage built upon affection and respect in every sense, and Jonathan felt more comfortable with them than he ever had in the house in which he had grown up.

The Churchills had two children; their son Edmund was away at university and their daughter Rebecca was in Scotland visiting her mother's family.

One Tuesday afternoon, Jonathan was in his study working on the bookkeeping for St. Elmo's, a task he truly despised. He felt slightly guilty at the relief he felt upon hearing a knock at the door but still opened it with a smile. That smile grew when he found the Commander on his doorstep accompanied by a rather severe looking young lady whom he soon learned to be Miss Rebecca Churchill.

Once introductions were made, Jonathan pressed his visitors to take tea and soon they were comfortably settled in his little parlor. He watched as the young lady took a tentative sip from the cup he served her and then, having seemingly determined that it was acceptable, nodded to herself. Then she glanced at him and they locked eyes. He was not certain, but he thought that she might have blushed ever so slightly.

The curate's eyes twinkled. "Is the tea acceptable, Miss Churchill?"

The young lady showed no reaction except to blink once, slowly. "Quite, Mr. de Bourgh."

The Commander leaned back in his chair and suppressed his desire to chuckle. He had been looking forward to introducing his daughter to this young man for some weeks.

"Please, call me Reverend Jonathan."

The young lady blinked again and he had the odd feeling that every detail of the room had been catalogued with great precision. Eyes still twinkling, he continued, "I find that tea is an excellent lubricant for conversation. My parishioners often use up all their courage to knock on my door and then find themselves seated but unable to tell me their troubles. My bishop let me in on the secret and now I always keep a kettle on the hob."

Rebecca tilted her head to one side, still studying him intently. Finally, her father could no longer restrain his laughter. "What my daughter is trying not to say, knowing that it is not quite polite, is that she is surprised that you served the tea yourself rather than a servant."

The blue eyes closed tightly for a moment, clearly embarrassed. "Papa!"

Jonathan grinned. "Please, do not make yourself uncomfortable; it is not the first time that someone has remarked upon it and I doubt it will be the last. Your father has disclosed my dark secret; I keep neither a housekeeper nor a maid but do most of my own cooking. Mrs. Burke comes by twice a week to do the heavy cleaning and see to the laundry; she isn't quite sure whether to consider me unnatural or adopt me as a favorite son."

Head still cocked, the young lady spoke distinctly. "I am surprised that someone of your family would deign to suffer so."

"Rebecca!" said her father, now in an admonishing tone.

Jonathan held up his hand, stopping the Commander's apology before it was spoken. "You strike me as an intelligent young lady, Miss Churchill. Shall you judge me on that particular accident of my birth or on how I choose to live my life?"

There were several moments of silence before Rebecca nodded slowly.

"You are quite correct; I had not realized how prejudiced I was."

"I take it that you have met my family?"

She nodded curtly and could not restrain herself from speaking bluntly. "Your eldest brother seduced a friend of mine; she was but seventeen and your esteemed father deemed her too poor to marry any son of his." Her pursed lips indicated precisely what she thought of that.

Despite herself, Rebecca was intrigued to see that the young man was unfazed by her directness. Instead, he was nodding sadly and broke eye contact to rub both hands across his eyes. "I have tried..." He trailed off before looking into her eyes. "The girl, is she well? Is there anything I can do to help her?"

Rebecca noted the genuine concern in the young man's face and her features softened. "She suffered a miscarriage before she began to show at all, which some might say was the most fortunate outcome."

Jonathan shook his head, having counseled too many women grieving over the loss of a child. "That may be what Society says but I cannot believe that the loss of any child should be counted as fortunate. How is the mother?"

Miss Churchill's respect for the young curate was rising quickly. "She is grieving, both for the loss of her babe but also for the loss of her innocence. It has not helped that her parents have been less concerned with her comfort than with concealing the event and acting as if nothing happened."

She attempted to restrain her emotions but her agitation was obvious. "Not four days after her miscarriage, they made her attend a garden party at the de Bourghs' house and act as if nothing was wrong. Your brother's engagement was announced and she had no warning."

Jonathan shook his head and looked into his cup for some minutes before speaking. "How is she now? Is there anything I can do? I will speak to my father and brother but I am afraid that my words hold little sway with either of them."

"Do not bother. If Beth has her way, she will never hear the name de Bourgh again, much less see any of them."

Jonathan was oddly pleased when she referred to the de Bourghs as 'them,' implicitly acknowledging his separation from the family.

Rebecca continued, "We arranged for her to visit my mother's family in Edinburgh; I have just returned from accompanying her." She smiled weakly. "I suppose that is why I am so riled up; I hope you will forgive my harsh words earlier. After spending so many hours in a carriage with Beth... I am afraid that the only way I could find to raise her spirits was to make up stories of how your elder brothers would be punished in a just world. We were quite inventive."

The young man managed a smile. "That sounds quite healthy and I have to admit that I indulged in something similar when I was a lad, living in the same house with them."

The two young people shared a smile full of understanding. At that point, the Commander cleared his throat, deciding that it was time to remind them of his presence. "I spent some time in India, at various ports, but enough to learn a bit of their beliefs. As I understand it, rather than death followed by an eternal afterlife in either heaven or hell, they believe that one's soul is reborn many, many times and that your actions in this life determine what you will be reborn as... cockroach or king. I admit to finding the concept attractive at times; Hell seems too good for some men."

Rebecca smiled at her beloved father. "And is that why you take such delight from stomping on roaches?"

Father and daughter shared an amused look before Sir James turned back to their host. "Well then, Reverend Jonathan. As much as I would enjoy one of our theological debates, I am afraid that my visit had a far more practical purpose. Are you still having difficulties with the ledgers for St. Elmo's?"

The young man grimaced. "Indeed; I have spent the morning working on them but I cannot make heads nor tails of it. Clearly something is wrong, but for the life of me I can't work out what. I should hate to spend the parish's funds to hire a bookkeeper but I may well be forced to do so."

The Commander smiled. "Well, I have brought you someone who will donate her time for free." He turned to grin at his daughter. "Well, she may require a few cups of tea and a biscuit or two."

Jonathan turned to the young lady and she noted genuine delight in his face, quite free from the derision that she was usually met with when men discovered her abilities at what was considered to be a most unfeminine subject.

"Truly? Miss Churchill, if you have the talent and are willing to look over my accounts, I should be most grateful."

Rebecca blinked at him and her father chuckled. "What my daughter is unwilling to say is that she is surprised that you accept her ability so readily." The Commander looked proudly at his offspring. "The truth is that my Becky is a veritable genius with numbers but we have been met with only close-minded prejudice from the academicians that she has approached." He grunted with irritation. "They seem to think that mathematics is wholly the province of the masculine mind and that no female could possibly have such a capacity."

Miss Churchill reached over and patted her father's arm. "Do not upset yourself, Papa. Their idiocy is not worth bothering ourselves over." She turned back to the curate; "My father is my greatest advocate."

Jonathan could see that the young lady was slightly guarded and could easily imagine the prejudice with which she had been confronted. "Such talent is a gift from God and it is to your credit that you have embraced it in the face of such opposition," he said before grinning. "I myself have the gift of baking excellent biscuits, so perhaps we can both ply our talents this afternoon?"

The little cottage was filled with laughter and soon the plan was agreed upon. The Commander departed on an errand while Rebecca settled at the curate's desk and was soon deep in concentration. Jonathan arranged himself in the kitchen, dividing his time between the stove and his sermon for the following Sunday; his discussion with the Churchills had inspired him and he rapidly scratched out a text on why they should embrace all the Lord's gifts, regardless of the vessel.

He was deep in thought when a movement at the doorway caught his eye. Looking up, he smiled at the young lady. "Miss Churchill! Please, come in. Would you like another cup of tea, or perhaps a biscuit? These are made with oats and raisins and are still warm. I admit that they are my favorites; when I moved out of my father's house, I begged his cook for the recipe."

Rebecca nodded and took a seat at the table, accepting a biscuit. "I hope I am not disturbing you, sir."

"Not at all." Jonathan was pleased when she nibbled on the biscuit and then took another. "Our discussion gave me an idea for my sermon this Sunday. I find that I must write down my thoughts as soon as I can or I lose them." He smiled. "I've taken to keeping paper and pencil in my pocket so that I may jot down notes wherever I am."

His admission was greeted with the first open smile he had coaxed from Miss Churchill. "I do something very similar! Really, it was my father's idea; one morning I doodled equations all over his newspaper before he had a chance to read it." She smirked at the memory and Jonathan laughed out loud.

Their conversation turned to her success with the ledgers and Jonathan was relieved with her results. The missing funds had not been pilfered but were merely the result of an accidental duplication in billing caused by the short month of February.

There was a pause in the conversation as Jonathan took the moment to check on a roast in the oven. He returned to the table and found the young lady watching him. Checking the teapot and finding the tea to be properly brewed, he strained the leaves and poured two cups.

After taking a sip and smiling with pleasure, Rebecca looked up at the young man. "You have another great talent here, sir. I wish I was as capable with a kettle but I find I always lose track of time and the tea ends up stewing. My mother quite refuses to allow me near a teapot anymore."

Jonathan grinned. "My Aunt Madeleine taught me. She never married and was forced by economy to make her home in my father's house toward the end of her life." His eyes showed his fondness. "Her rheumatism became quite debilitating when I was still a lad so she made certain that I would be able to prepare her tea as she liked it."

"Do you visit her often?" Rebecca regretted her question the instant she saw the sadness that flashed across the gentleman's face.

"She passed away several years ago, not long before I moved to this cottage, in fact."

Rebecca nodded with understanding and he found himself speaking of his most beloved relative as well as the emptiness he was left with upon her death. Eventually he paused, hearing the mantel clock in the sitting room tolling the hour and amused to find himself talking so much.

"You are a remarkable young lady, Miss Churchill. It is not often that I encounter someone with such ready empathy."

Rebecca turned her dark blue eyes on the young cleric and he was struck with the feeling that she could see straight into his very soul. "If we are being honest, I must say that I was quite surprised by your youth. Papa has said a great deal about your work at St. Elmo's and you are not at all what I pictured," she replied.

Jonathan shrugged and tucked his chin. Normally he would brush aside comments on his age with a joke about the naïveté of youth making him the only one stupid enough to attempt such an endeavor, but he was somehow certain that anything but the absolute truth would be detected instantly by those intent blue eyes.

After a moment of quiet, Miss Churchill seemed to realize that she had embarrassed the young man and instantly began to apologize. "I am sorry, I did not mean to make you uncomfortable…"

Jonathan tried to force himself to speak, absently wondering what it was about this girl that seemed to destroy his usual composure.

Meanwhile, Rebecca was still attempting to apologize. "I did not mean it as a criticism at all…"

Finally, the curate was forced to interrupt. "Miss Churchill, I admit to being somewhat embarrassed, but rest assured that I did not take offence at your comment."

The young lady met his eyes and seemed reassured by what she saw there. She nodded slowly. "It is just that… I sometimes think it unfair that the world is controlled by those who are older, but so often it is the young people who have the energy and the desire to change things."

Jonathan leaned forward, instantly transfixed by the fire he glimpsed. In that moment, he recognized Miss Rebecca Churchill as a kindred spirit, though she kept her true self hidden under tight control in most society.

He grinned, and Rebecca was left blinking at how the expression of heartfelt joy transformed the young man's face. "I completely agree, Miss Churchill. When we are young and just learning, we see all that is wrong or illogical… but everyone tells us that we must keep our heads down and not offend our elders… that we will have our chance someday, but I fear that by that time, we will no longer feel such energy… such zeal… to reform. Does that sound right?"

But Rebecca was already agreeing with him. "Yes!" For some minutes, she spoke about her love of mathematics; how it was so easy for her, how the numbers and symbols seemed to dance in her mind some nights until she got up and wrote out the derivations; equations as beautiful to her as any David or Mona Lisa.

Then she spoke of the shock when her father had taken her to the university and attempted to introduce her to some faculty in the maths department. Those men had dismissed her; some assumed her father was attempting to play some sort of prank on them while others openly jeered her as 'unnatural' and told her to go home and practice her embroidery.

Rebecca had reentered their carriage in tears with her father fuming by her side. However, once she had cried her fill, she had curled up at his side and begun to plot. With her father's permission (and often his connivance) she had begun corresponding with mathematicians at St. Andrews, leading Mrs. Churchill to comment that *her* countrymen would recognize their daughter's brilliance, even if the English would too hidebound with prejudice to do so.

Jonathan was fascinated by the young lady's description of how she was managing to consult with other mathematicians on her work by correspondence, signing herself only as 'R. A. Churchill.' She had put aside her anger and disappointment and now appeared only somewhat amused at how her correspondents all assumed she was a man.

Their conversation continued for the better part of the afternoon and only ended when the Commander returned to the parsonage to retrieve his daughter. The older gentleman was pleased to see the pair enjoying each other's company. Jonathan was invited to dinner at the Churchill residence and they parted in laughter when he offered to bring a pudding.

The two young people spent a great deal of time together over the following months and their mutual respect and affection continued to deepen. When the engagement of Mr. Jonathan de Bourgh to Miss Rebecca Churchill was announced not four months after their first meeting, several girls in his parish church burst into tears even as the Commander boasted to his wife that he had made the match himself.

The ceremony itself was held at St. Mary's and, though conducted by Jonathan's mentor, Bishop Annesley, it was delivered in the style of a small, neighborhood church. Lady Harriet sniffed, displeased that one of her sons would be married with so little pomp and circumstance. Lord Maxwell fell asleep five minutes into the service and Jonathan's two eldest brothers did not even bother to attend.

The bride and groom hardly noticed; their own joy was fueled by their mutual certainty of a happy alliance and the presence of so many friends who did support them. Edmund Churchill returned some weeks before the wedding and Jonathan was pleased to find his bride's younger brother to be a quiet, serious young man who was studying law with the intent of entering politics.

After a short honeymoon to the seaside, the newlyweds returned to London and settled into the parsonage at St. Mary's. Although a larger stipend came with his elevation in position, the couple continued to live simply, albeit unconventionally. He did much of the cooking while she continued to publish on her mathematics, and their greatest expenditures tended to be on parchment and books.

Jonathan and Rebecca de Bourgh lived and worked together in his London parish for five years after their marriage. Their first child, Madeleine, was born two years after they married. Two years after that, a baby boy was welcomed into the family and named Paul, after his maternal grandfather. Sadly, sickness swept through the slums and their son died before he reached his first birthday. Husband and wife grieved deeply and decided to seek a parish in the country where the air was cleaner and their daughter could enjoy more of nature. Jonathan felt he had done good work with St. Elmo's and the framework he had set in place would sustain itself without his presence.

So it was that, in the summer of 1784, Jonathan and Rebecca found themselves preparing to spend two weeks at a house party at Wolfram Manor, the primary de Bourgh estate in Essex, despite their mutual distaste for his family. Lord Maxwell's health had been poor recently and he had decreed that all his offspring would attend the celebration of his seventieth birthday.

The morning after their arrival, Rebecca and Jonathan rose at dawn as was their habit. Over their seven years of marriage, they had worked out a schedule beneficial to all in the family. Both loved early mornings for the quiet—a time with few interruptions from the outside world. They would breakfast together as a family, discussing the coming day. Then Jonathan would spend time with their daughter, reading to her or going on walks while Rebecca would take some time for herself, usually for her mathematics.

On this morning her mind was still rather fuzzy after a day spent traveling so she decided to find the music room and spend time on a new piece she had recently begun learning. Rebecca was careful to close the doors tightly—she had no desire to disturb the other houseguests—and finding the pianoforte to be well-tuned, began warming up with some scales and simple pieces. For her, music was like mathematics for the ear—the organization and division of the notes was as beautiful as any calculus. She smirked to herself—she had long since given up trying to explain such things to the young ladies she met—their primary interest in music seemed to be as a necessary skill to exhibit themselves to gentlemen.

Fingers limbered, she decided to move on to her goal of the morning, a piano concerto composed by the young Bavarian prodigy, Wolfgang Mozart. She worked her way through it slowly the first time, noting fingerings and stopping several times to work out the trickier passages. After an hour, she paused and stood, walking to the windows while stretching her arms over her head to relieve the strain that had built up in her shoulders.

In her youth, Rebecca had often played with such focus that she would spend hours practicing without break, finally stopping to find her back aching and fingers cramping. Looking out across the gardens, she smiled to herself. Having children had undoubtedly enhanced her ability to do multiple things at once. She wondered what the academicians lauding her recent work would say if they knew much of it had been done when she had been up in the night, holding a babe to her breast with her right arm while writing with her left.

With the help of her friends at St. Andrews, she had submitted her most promising works to the Royal Society and it had been presented with acclaim. She would not lie about herself but knowing that the prejudice against women was still too great, she always submitted her work as "R.A. Churchill" and did not correct those replies she received as "Mr." She turned down invitations to meetings or lectures, citing a "family situation" that did not allow travel.

After working out the tension in her shoulders, Rebecca decided that she was ready to try the concerto again. Settling at the bench, she arranged the music so that page turning would be the least bother and then, taking a deep breath, poised her fingers over the keys and threw herself into the music.

Lady Anne Fitzwilliam had enjoyed her eighteenth birthday two weeks prior. The youngest of the three Fitzwilliam children, she had a quiet warmth and desire to see everyone around her happy. She loved the light of mornings and often rose before the rest of the house to spend time sketching or painting with her watercolors. This morning she rose early as usual and ventured downstairs with the idea of spending some time practicing on the pianoforte before the other ladies arose.

As she approached the closed door of the music room, she heard the opening notes of a concerto she had only recently begun to learn. Curious, she cracked open the door to see a woman, handsome rather than beautiful, dark auburn hair pinned up in a simple style and wearing a simple green muslin frock. Most noticeable was the woman's focus—there seemed to be nothing else in the world but her and the instrument. Lady Anne slipped into the room and quietly seated herself in a chair with a clear view of the woman's hands as her fingers flew up and down the keys.

Meanwhile, Rebecca was completely unaware of her audience. When she finally reached the end of the piece, she sat motionless for a moment as the last notes echoed through the room. She was recalled to the present by the sound of clapping and turned to see a young lady with a warm smile rising from a chair by the door.

"Oh, that was so lovely! Your fingering is so precise! I've been working on that piece for weeks but I still end up slurring my way through the difficult passages."

Rebecca was still working her way back to reality and could only stare for some moments. "Thank you."

"Oh, I'm so sorry, I've interrupted you. I woke early and was thinking of practicing myself when I heard you from the hall and couldn't resist. Please forgive me; I'll leave you to your solitude."

By then Rebecca had recovered her wits and smiled at the younger lady whose sincere apology was belied by the disappointed look in her eyes. "Oh, no— please stay. I've been here for two hours and it is high time for me to break."

Observing the young lady's happy smile, Rebecca continued, "That was actually the first time I've made it through the entire piece without a stop— I thank you for your praise, but there are a number of sections where I fudged my way through the timing. This arpeggio on the second page keeps tripping me up." Pulling out the appropriate page, she demonstrated, groaning at the end when, once again, she stumbled over the final triplet.

"Oh! I had trouble with just that passage, but I think I've finally worked out a fingering that works. May I?" Anne had drawn closer to the piano and bent to place her fingers on the instrument even as Rebecca shifted on the bench to give the younger woman room.

Lady Anne worked her way slowly through the notes to remind herself of the piece, then started at the beginning of the section that was troubling her new friend, her long, slender fingers dancing fluidly through the arpeggio. As she reached the end, Rebecca clapped her hands with pleasure "Yes, you've got it! Would you go through it again, more slowly this time so that I may follow the fingering?"

The two women were still in that same position when Jonathan de Bourgh and his daughter entered the music room with a new acquaintance of their own. Lady Anne observed her new friend's face transform from exacting focus to pure pleasure when the older lady noticed her little family. Holding out her hands with a smile, Rebecca laughed as her daughter ran into her arms, kissing the little girl on the cheek and smirking at her husband who seemed to have forgotten the crown of daisies on his head.

"And how are you, my dear? Did you have a nice morning with your papa?"

"Oh Mama! It was lovely! We saw the kitchen garden and Papa found a mint he wants to try growing! And then we met Mr. Darcy and he showed us the pond and told me what kinds of fishes live there! Are you playing a duet? May I learn?"

Little Madeleine de Bourgh might be only four years old (going on five) but she had a good mind and an inquisitive nature that was nurtured by both parents. Walks with her father were often occupied with identifying plants, birds, and insects that they encountered. While her mother had taught her numbers and encouraged her interest on the pianoforte, her papa had taught her to make her letters and she was deeply proud that she could write her name. A happy evening in the de Bourgh home was one with her parents settled in comfortable chairs by the fire, each with their nose in a book. For as long as she could remember, little Maddy had joined them, usually lying on the rug between them, paging through an atlas of maps or a monograph illustrating plants and animals from England and abroad.

Lady Anne smiled softly at the little girl. Her own parents had followed the traditional path of leaving her and her siblings' care to a series of nurses and governesses; she was struck by the simple joy of this mother and daughter. It had never occurred to her to regret the rather distant relationship with her own mother, but clearly Rebecca de Bourgh saw children as a joy, not merely a duty and Anne tucked the thought away for future consideration. At that point, Lady Anne's mind suddenly registered the presence of another gentleman in the room.

Mr. George Darcy was a tall, handsome man with an ease in society that gained him a large circle of friends. In her first Season, Lady Anne had noticed him immediately and was embarrassed at how often her thoughts returned to the one dance that they had shared. Her father's estate in southern Derbyshire ensured that the families saw each other occasionally in the country as well as in London and although Mr. Darcy had never paid her any other notice, she could not help but wish for his attentions. Her elder sister warned her not to aim so high; the Darcys might not have a title but their wealth and history made them one of the most powerful families in northern England if not all the British Isles.

To be honest, Mr. George Darcy had paid scant attention to the youngest Fitzwilliam girl. He had asked her for a dance out of respect for his old school chum, Lord Henry Fitzwilliam (the girl's elder brother). To himself, he had acknowledged her to be pretty enough but she had been so quiet during their dance that he was left with no sense of any personality at all. In addition, the Fitzwilliams were still *nouveau riche* by Darcy standards and he was well aware that his own father was currently hoping to broker a marriage for him to one of the Duke of Norfolk's daughters.

For the next fortnight, young Mr. Darcy chose to spend some significant time with Jonathan de Bourgh; the living at Lambton had recently fallen vacant and Darcy's ailing father had given him the responsibility of appointing a new cleric. By default, Mr. Darcy also found himself spending time with Mrs. de Bourgh (or rather, Mrs. Rebecca, as she insisted she be called in all but the most formal of situations) and that lady's new friend, Lady Anne.

Although on the surface it might appear that Anne and Rebecca had little in common, they found a great deal to admire in one another. Both had a sincere love of music which separated them from the dilettantes so frequent in society They also both enjoyed the freedom that riding gave them and the week saw the pair often exploring the Essex countryside on horseback. Lady Anne was sweet and innocent, wishing all around her to be happy. Rebecca was clever and far more cynical, but knowing so much about the world's evils made her appreciate her new friend's sunny optimism all the more.

Unfortunately, Jonathan and Rebecca's enjoyment of their stay at Wolfram was quite ruined in the second week when the Reverend overheard his eldest brothers arguing over billiards. Barely containing his disgust when he realized that they were already drunk at barely two in the afternoon, he confronted them. When he came to understand the terms of their wager, he lost his temper entirely.

Lewis de Bourgh had bet his elder brother that he could seduce a certain young lady by the end of the house party but George was dismissing Lewis's claim of success because he had not arranged to be observed *in flagrante*.

When Jonathan railed against their behavior, his elder brothers dismissed him as a prude. He went to his father but Lord Maxwell brushed him off, hinting that if the girl's father could not keep her under control, then there was little hope she would have remained chaste, wager or no. "Boys will be boys," he grunted and dismissed his youngest from his presence, not at all sorry to see the girl's family brought down a peg or two.

In later years, Jonathan and his wife would look back on that summer party at Wolfram with deeply divided feelings. After discussing the situation with Rebecca during the coach ride back to London, Jonathan made an appointment with the lady's father to inform him of the situation. The girl was found to be with child and never again seen in London, although the circumstances surrounding her removal were kept quiet.

Thoroughly disgusted by his family's lack of morals, Jonathan and Rebecca severed all connection with the de Bourghs. This was made easier when, in less than a year, they found themselves settled in Derbyshire at the Lambton parsonage. One of Jonathan's first duties was to marry the newest Master of Pemberley, Mr. George Darcy, to Lady Anne Fitzwilliam.

Father Jonathan and Mrs. Rebecca, as they were known in their parish, settled happily into their new life. Rebecca visited Pemberley House regularly and servants and guests alike were often treated to duets by the new mistress and her friend. With Mr. Darcy's blessing and occasional assistance from Lady Anne, they organized a ragged school, teaching the children of the poorest tenant farmers, miners, and villagers their letters and numbers.

Young Madeleine found herself perfectly content with their move to the country. Her greatest pleasure, however, arose from the appearances of two little brothers and a sister named Ruth. She embraced her role as elder sister and Maddy's parents were often treated to impromptu spelling bees or recitations of psalms. As she grew, her role in the school grew from pupil to tutor and, perhaps not surprisingly, she informed her parents that she wished to become a teacher, or, if that was not possible, a governess.

Understanding the harsh realities of such positions far better than their daughter, Jonathan and Rebecca recognized that the young lady's great capacity to love would be better served as a wife and mother, but opportunities to find a well-matched beau were limited by the size of the neighborhood. Thus, when Madeleine turned eighteen, her parents arranged for her to visit her mother's Churchill relations in London for several months and enjoy a proper Season.

Although Sir Paul Churchill had passed on several years before, his widow was still active and retained her good nature. In addition, Rebecca's brother, Edmund, had married a delightful young lady named Agnes and the couple had several children, including a daughter who would be entering society that very spring. Though they expected to miss her dreadfully, her parents were content that exposure to a broader society would serve their eldest daughter well.

Madeleine departed Derbyshire just as the arrival of spring triggered a faint veil of green to fall over the landscape. She had no doubt that she would miss her family and friends immensely but the young lady could not ignore the excitement that stirred in her breast. Her memories of London were those of a little girl; she returned with the eyes of an adult and was looking forward to seeing and experiencing all that she might see.

Her sojourn was everything that she might have dreamed. In addition to parties, balls and shopping, her mind was edified by visits to museums, exhibitions, and the occasional scientific demonstration. Sooner than seemed possible, the family was rising early to take breakfast at Vauxhall Gardens in celebration of her last Saturday in London.

For years Madeleine would be unable to think of that idyllic day without falling prey to a paralyzing guilt. After a decadent meal of pastries and ices, they had wandered the paths to be entertained by tightrope walkers and clownish jesters. Madeleine had even convinced her cousin Emma to ascend to the clouds in a hot air balloon while holding on to each other's hands tightly.

The happy group had returned home tired and dusty but full of good cheer. Maddy had climbed the stairs to her room and just tucked away her ticket stub and program in a box she was using to collect mementos. She was about to ring the bell for a maid when a knock came at her door. Deep inside, she had known immediately that something was desperately wrong when she looked up to find both her aunt and uncle standing there with miserable looks upon their usually good-humored faces.

"What has happened?" she asked with more composure than any eighteen year old should have.

Her Uncle Edmund opened his mouth twice but was too overcome to speak. He finally held out an express from Derbyshire that had arrived while the family was out. As Madeleine began reading the letter from George Darcy, she barely registered her aunt guiding her to the bed and wrapping her arms around the sobbing girl.

The letter was brief and the words not at all what Madeleine would usually have expected from the jolly Mr. Darcy. In the instant before her own grief crashed down upon her, Maddy sensed the intense heartache and guilt that the Master of Pemberley was suffering.

Dear Miss Madeleine,

In the month of May, a pox epidemic swept through Derbyshire and claimed the lives of many at Pemberley as well as the surrounding villages. It is my sad duty to inform you that both of your parents were taken from us. The sickness also claimed the lives of your sister and brothers. I do not know if there is anything I can say to adequately express my sympathy for your loss. Please know that Father Jonathan and Mrs. Rebecca's good works shall be remembered as long as there are Darcys at Pemberley. Although your parents' lives were cut short, they have left a legacy that will endure.
Please contact me immediately if there is anything that I may do to assist you.

With greatest sympathy,
George Darcy

16 SISTERS AND DAUGHTERS

Thomas Bennet sat silently at his desk. Certainly there were duties to which he should be attending; even a relatively small estate such as Longbourn was constantly generating work for its master. Of course, he had become particularly adept at ignoring all but the most critical over the last two decades. However, ever since a particularly intense discussion with his second daughter earlier that spring, he was attempting to mend his habits (to varying degrees of success).

"*My dear Lizzy,*" he thought wistfully, eyes drifting to a letter that he had tucked under the corner of his blotter, hoping to remove it from sight if not his mind. She had sounded happier in that letter than she had in months but his melancholy had increased with every line. His favorite daughter was coming home to Longbourn that afternoon, but she was not coming alone.

His favorite daughter was bringing home a man.

Elizabeth's letter had described the various dinners and outings that she had enjoyed while staying with her Aunt and Uncle Gardiner in London. Usually he would have been amused by her witty observations of the audience at the opera or the odd young man who had guided them around the botanic gardens.

Her descriptions, however, were peppered with mentions of a certain gentleman from Derbyshire. In April, Mr. Bennet had comforted his daughter after she had rejected Mr. Darcy's marriage proposal and then discovered that much of her ill opinion of him was based on misconceptions and misinformation. He had even encouraged her to give the young man another chance should she ever meet him again.

However, that had been when Mr. Fitzwilliam Darcy was merely a signature on a letter and a vague memory of a tall, serious young man standing in the corner of a drawing room. In truth, Thomas had felt exceedingly virtuous after counseling his daughter and that feeling had

219

buoyed him through the past month. He felt that he had improved his relationship with his wife, and his two middle daughters had required surprisingly little effort on his part to diminish the worst of their silliness. Mr. Bennet had to admit to feeling a certain degree of pride in their improvements.

Mary still held what he considered to be an overabundance of enthusiasm for theological tracts, but she had expanded her interests to include the memoirs of various missionaries and their experiences with the natives of distant lands. She had taken to studying his atlas of maps so often that her father now left it out on the side table in his book room so that she might refer to it at her leisure.

Catherine had devoted herself to drawing with a passion that had amazed her father, although he had had to reassure her repeatedly that he really didn't mind if she used up paper, as long as it was in an honest effort. The solution had proven remarkably enjoyable for both; each Sunday afternoon, father and daughter would sit together and she would show him her week's progress in her sketchbook. Her trust in him had increased apace with his pride in her.

Mr. Bennet's reveries were interrupted by the sound of what he could only describe as loud female noises in the hall. He frowned. For all the improvements he saw in Mary and Kitty, he had yet to reach Lydia. To prevent her from following the regiment to Brighton, he had enlisted the help of her mother. The unfortunate byproduct of that action had been the deterioration of that woman's relationship with their youngest daughter.

Lydia seemed to regard Mrs. Bennet as some sort of turncoat from her cult of personality. She alternated between coaxing and lashing out at her mother and had lately taken to spending more and more time visiting her Aunt Phillips in Meryton. Now that Lieutenant Wickham and the militia were removed from Hertfordshire, Mr. Bennet was not particularly concerned that his youngest could get into any trouble worse than overspending her allowance on lace and ribbons. He could proclaim any number of rules (and he felt he was becoming better at enforcing them), but nothing seemed to reach Lydia.

The rumble of approaching carriages trickled through his open window with the summer breeze, bringing Thomas back to the present. Sighing heavily, he attempted to put on a happy face before leaving his study.

When Mr. Bennet reached the front door, most of his family already stood outside, waiting for two large coaches to come to a halt. The first was one which he was moderately familiar with; a modest four-wheeled chaise that the Gardiners rented whenever they traveled beyond London. Thomas was amused to see his youngest nephew leaning half out of the open window to wave madly at his cousins before being pulled back to safety by his mother.

The Gardiners' carriage was followed by a larger, closed coach pulled by four matching Cleveland Bays. There was nothing ostentatious about the vehicle but to a knowledgeable eye it was obviously of superior quality and extremely well-maintained. Mr. Bennet was intrigued when its owner opened the door himself and hopped down before the footman could do his duty. Intrigue was succeeded by amusement when the gentleman turned just in time to catch the youngest Gardiner daughter when she launched herself straight into his arms.

Although Elizabeth's father had not yet convinced himself that he was happy to see Mr. Darcy at Longbourn again, he could not help but be charmed by the man's easy manner with the children. Having caught Amelia, Darcy swung her around before setting her gently on the ground, only to turn and bow deeply to her elder sister in the manner of a courtier to a grand lady. Of course, the moment Rebecca's foot touched the ground, all pretense was forgotten and she raced her sister to hug their cousins.

Mr. Bennet was forced to divert his attention from the Darcy carriage for a moment when his nephew and namesake, Tommy Gardiner, ran over to greet his uncle. When he finally turned back, it was to see an unknown young lady emerge, followed by Elizabeth.

Longbourn's master watched as his second eldest went directly to Jane. When the two sisters clung to each other for many minutes, he was reminded of just how much time they had spent apart since Christmas. Mr. Bennet was distracted from this train of thought when Mr. Gardiner was finally able to extract himself from his own sister's fluttering embraces. The two old friends shook hands, saying little but still managing to express how happy they were to see one another.

"Well, Edward; I'm glad to see that you've all arrived safely. Lucky you have two carriages— this is quite a circus that you and Madeleine are traveling with."

The other man smiled indulgently. "Yes, indeed. We were most appreciative when Mr. Darcy volunteered his carriage—I suppose we might all have fit in one, but it would not have been a particularly comfortable voyage!"

Gardiner had just determined that Mr. Bennet should be reintroduced to that gentleman when Elizabeth finally reached them. Accepting her kiss on his cheek, Bennet squeezed her hand and found himself blinking rapidly to suppress the tears he felt welling up.

"My dear Lizzy... it is good to see you home, daughter." He stepped back but retained hold of one of her hands. "Well, let us get a look at you. No great changes that I can see... still mud on your petticoat, I see."

"Oh, Papa," said Elizabeth with a slight blush, but even as she brushed at her skirt she rolled her eyes. "Just a bit of dirt—it will come out in the wash. Nothing a good country girl should worry about!" She caught her father's eye and they both laughed easily.

Mr. Bennet caught the hint of amusement on both of the visitors' faces just as Elizabeth turned and gestured for them to come nearer. "Speaking of country girls, may I introduce you to Miss Darcy, Papa? And you remember Mr. Darcy, of course? We have spent much of the coach ride from London speaking on their home county of Derbyshire."

Thomas made the appropriate noises but all the while he was observing the Darcys carefully. He was about to speak when the high-pitched tone of his wife's agitated voice reached him.

"Mr. Darcy's carriage? But why didn't you come with Mr. Bingley? We've all heard that he has returned to Netherfield but it has been three days and none of us have seen him!"

Mr. Bennet was uncertain whether to be diverted or disturbed when Elizabeth squeezed Miss Darcy's hand and winked. He decided to be amused because the action seemed to ease the shy girl's anxiety. He turned toward his wife without looking at the girl's brother, feeling that he was not sufficiently calm to endure that gentleman's unspoken opinion of Fanny's impropriety.

"Mrs. Bennet, shall we thank Mr. Darcy for his generosity? I cannot imagine that the Bingley carriage could be in any way superior. Now, have you met Miss Darcy?"

After the appropriate greetings were exchanged, Mr. Bennet exerted himself. "I am certain that all of the travelers wish to clean up and rest, but perhaps Mr. Darcy and his sister would like to return to Longbourn this evening and join us for dinner? Mr. Bingley is welcome as well, of course."

Mrs. Bennet began twittering about soups and fish before the words were out of his mouth. Even as he noticed Jane's blush and Elizabeth's pleased smile, Mr. Bennet watched the two Darcy siblings. He suspected that the young lady was good-humored beneath her timidity and was gratified to see her brother shield her slightly from the view of the others and speak to her quietly.

Seemingly reassured by his sister's response, Mr. Darcy turned to Mr. Bennet. "Thank you, sir. We would be delighted to dine with you if our host does not already have plans for us. I shall ask Mr. Bingley as soon as we arrive at Netherfield and send a note."

Thomas nodded agreeably and then began herding his small flock indoors, leaving Mr. Darcy to help his sister back into their carriage. The dust from their wheels was still hanging in the air as Bennets and Gardiners flooded into Longbourn. Its master paused a moment in the foyer and for once found enjoyment in the sounds of his house filled with a happy, bustling family.

Some time later, Mr. Gardiner found his brother-in-law contentedly reading in his book room. After the two exchanged greetings again and spoke for some minutes about everyday subjects—conditions on the London road, the state of Mrs. Gardiner's health, Mr. Gardiner's procurement of a volume containing some of Voltaire's more polemic essays—Elizabeth's uncle brought the conversation around to the topic he most particularly wished to discuss.

"As you know, we had to alter our travel plans somewhat. Madeleine's illness forced us to delay our departure and I must still return to London by the end of July; we have a shipment coming in from the Orient and I must be there to check it over before it goes into the warehouse," Mr. Gardiner began.

Bennet merely nodded, most of his attention still on his new book. "Yes, yes. You are for the Lake District, correct?"

Edward smirked; some things never changed. His old friend was never so distracted as when he had a new book in his hands.

"Actually, we changed our itinerary somewhat. Did Maddy's letter not reach you?"

Thomas looked up distractedly. "Fanny may have spoken of it. Something about taking the children on a pilgrimage to her childhood home, was it not?"

"Lambton," Mr. Gardiner agreed, his eyes twinkling in amusement—clearly Elizabeth's father had not yet made the connection. "In northern Derbyshire."

Mr. Bennet squinted at the other man, wondering why that should mean anything to him. "Yes?"

Edward suppressed the desire to laugh out loud. "When we met Mr. Darcy and his sister in London, we discovered that we had a most surprising connection." He paused, letting his explanation draw out.

In a flash, Thomas made the link between the Darcys and Derbyshire... and his favorite daughter... who was accompanying the Gardiners on their trip. He grunted in irritation. "Speak plainly, Gardiner. What connection?"

This time, the other man allowed himself to chuckle out loud. "Oh, 'tis quite astonishing, really. You know that Madeleine's father cut ties with his family before he died? She was living with her mother's brother when we met."

"Yes, yes— the Churchills. Your letters were full of them for months; I am not likely to forget the name." Mr. Bennet was feeling decidedly tetchy.

Gardiner smiled. "Well then, you may also remember that when Maddy was still a lass, her father resigned his parish in London to move the family to the country... to Derbyshire, in fact. They were tempted north by the offer of a living in a small market town called Lambton. The offer was made by Mr. George Darcy, our acquaintance's late father; Lambton is but five miles from Pemberley, the Darcy family's estate."

Bennet was beginning to suspect what was coming. "How...

coincidental. And did young Master Darcy condescend to acknowledge her?"

Elizabeth's uncle knit his brows at the sarcastic tone. "Indeed, there was no condescension involved; he greeted her as an old family friend. He has fond memories of her parents; they died in the same epidemic as his own mother when Mr. Darcy was ten and Madeleine was eighteen."

Mr. Bennet did nothing but grunt.

Edward decided to stop stringing his friend along. "In short, when Mr. Darcy heard that we were planning to travel to the north but would not have time to tour the Lakes as we'd hoped, he invited us to stay at Pemberley."

Mr. Bennet's mouth opened and shut several times before he was able to frame any words. "Are you telling me that my Lizzy shall be staying in that man's house? For how long—a week? A fortnight?"

"Actually, we are planning on a month entire."

"A month!" Mr. Bennet burst up from his chair and began pacing his study while Mr. Gardiner sat watching him.

"Thomas, she shall be chaperoned by myself and Madeleine, not to mention our four children who will, no doubt, trail at her heals even should they wish to be alone."

Bennet returned to his seat and collapsed into it with a huff. "Mr. Darcy has expressed an... interest... in my Lizzy."

Edward thought it safe to smile. He had two daughters himself and was not looking forward to the years ahead when men came calling. "Bennet, the gentleman is completely besotted with your daughter; observe him at dinner if you do not believe me. And Elizabeth has begun to realize that he is just the sort of man who could compliment her in temperament and understanding."

Thomas sighed and rearranged himself in his chair though it did nothing to relieve his discomfort. "She did not think very much of him during the winter," he grumbled, still feeling peevish.

"I understand that there were some misunderstandings."

When his brother-in-law only grunted, Mr. Gardiner continued, "Really, Thomas! I had understood from Elizabeth that she spoke to you about her association with Darcy even before she came to us in London— she said you yourself encouraged her to revise her opinion of the gentleman!"

The two men were silent for some minutes until Gardiner's confusion was lifted by a spark of intuition. "Ah... You did not expect her to see him again."

Mr. Bennet shrugged and settled further into his chair with a petulant look on his face.

Edward chuckled. "Oh, Thomas. If I didn't dread my own daughters coming out, I would find you quite amusing. Do you know of any specific flaws in Mr. Darcy's character? Not his personality, mind you; he is a quiet man and has developed a rather forbidding mask to protect himself from unwanted attention. Having seen the ton's attention to him in person, I cannot say that I blame him."

Thomas was forced to shake his head. When it was clear that he was not going to speak, Mr. Gardiner continued, "I have seen a good deal of the young man over the last fortnight. Mr. Darcy is clever, well-educated, and cares deeply for his responsibilities. Really, Thomas, I should think that you would find a great deal to like in him! Just show him your library and the two of you shall be lost from the rest of us for the remainder of the day!"

Elizabeth's father shrugged.

"Oh, come now, Bennet. Have you even had a conversation with him? He is very uncomfortable in large groups, especially when he is the center of attention (which he often is, as a single gentleman in possession of a large fortune). Really, I would think that you should have a great deal of empathy for the young man; losing his mother at a young age and then his father when he was barely of age. He has not had it easy, for all his wealth and connections, and he is not the sort to rattle around like some I could name."

Finally Elizabeth's father was prompted to speak. "Yes, yes. I have heard all the praise; Mr. Darcy is an intelligent, honorable gentleman, a sterling character, highly regarded by peer and servant alike. But she is *my* daughter and *I* am not ready to give her up."

"Bennet..."

Thomas gestured at a letter sitting at the corner of his desk. "When Lizzy wrote to me of meeting him again, I made some inquiries."

Gardiner's eyebrows rose.

Thomas chuckled sardonically. "Nothing terribly strenuous, I assure you. I merely asked Mrs. Hill to find out what the Netherfield servants had to say of their former guest..." He looked slightly embarrassed. "And I wrote to Tristan Beverley— he's teaching at Cambridge now, you remember?"

Edward nodded and encouraged his friend to continue.

"You will be happy to know that he had nothing but praise. Young Master Darcy was clever and diligent in his studies, not even a hint of any disciplinary problems He was even in the chess club— Beverley actually encouraged me to challenge the lad to a match."

When Bennet looked up, he found his old friend considering him thoughtfully. He shrugged. "I have had my eyes opened to the perils that threaten my daughters at this age... I am attempting to become a more attentive parent."

Mr. Gardiner's expression had become entirely serious. "I must say that I am happy to hear you say that, Thomas. I admit that Madeleine and I were worried when we left after Christmas. We both love Fanny, but her enthusiasm for marrying off our nieces seemed to have reached a fever pitch."

Thomas grimaced. "It is my own fault. I should have set aside a monthly sum to provide for her and the girls after my death, but, well… you know the story. We expected to have a son who would inherit Longbourn and support his mother and sisters as necessary. By the time it became clear that he was not going to appear, it seemed too late to begin making economies." He sighed. "I cannot tell you how much I despise the idea of Wilberforce Collins' son inheriting Longbourn."

Mr. Gardiner's face matched his brother-in-law's. "I have not met the young man but I will admit that Lizzy's description was not encouraging."

The two men sat silently for some minutes, both remembering the elder Mr. Collins with distaste. Finally Edward blew out his breath. "Well, let us remember that this William Collins is the son of your dear sister, as well." He forced a grin. "And we may still hope that perhaps *you* shall outlive *him*!"

Bennet smiled bleakly. "Yes, and even if he does manage produce a son, I cannot imagine any child with Charlotte Lucas as a mother would not have at least a smidgen of sense."

They chuckled for a few moments before Mr. Gardiner commented, "Well, I should go check if Madeleine and the children have settled in." Levering himself out of the comfortable old armchair, he paused a moment before speaking in a more serious tone. "Thomas, give Darcy a chance; speak with him. I do not think you could find a man better suited for Elizabeth in all of England, and you understand me well enough to know that I am not referring to his wealth or consequence."

Seeing that Elizabeth's father had become grim again, Gardiner grinned. "And if you are worried about him being too forward in his courtship, perhaps you should take advantage of the fact that he himself is the very protective guardian of a sixteen year old sister!"

Mr. Bennet blinked and then a pleased and, to be honest, mischievous smile spread across his face. "Thank you, Gardiner."

Elizabeth's uncle left Longbourn's study laughing.

Dinner that evening was interesting, not so much for the food or conversation, but for the undercurrents among its participants. Mr. Bennet could not help but appreciate it when Mr. and Mrs. Gardiner seated themselves on either side of Fanny. With the ease of long practice, they kept Longbourn's mistress chatting on appropriate subjects and minimized her interference with the rest of the table's conversation.

In the middle of the table, his younger daughters seemed pleased to speak quietly with Miss Darcy. Well, Mary and Catherine were talking, gradually drawing the shy girl out with questions about her studies in music and art and experiences at school and in London.

Lydia was sulking; she had tried to dominate the other girls' attention but had been admonished sharply by Kitty to stop interrupting Miss Darcy. The youngest Bennet daughter was now scowling at her plate, mashing her food together with her fork and sticking her lower lip out. She only became more peeved as no one noticed.

Thomas sighed. Something would have to be done with Lydia, but at the moment, he had no idea what. His attention was drawn back to the present by a deep voice at his right elbow.

"Mr. Bennet; Mr. Gardiner mentioned that he had sent you a volume of Lord Byron's latest verse. What did you think of it?"

Bennet was about to make some quip and return to his observation of the table when he noticed Elizabeth's expression. She was seated at Mr. Darcy's other elbow and clearly pleased to see him attempting to know her father better. Thomas sighed to himself and rapidly revised his words.

"I've not finished it but I liked what I read well enough. I know the man is somewhat hedonistic in his personal life, but that does not diminish his obvious talent as a wordsmith."

Darcy nodded, taking a sip of wine. "I agree. We are none of us without fault. Lord Byron's talent is irrefutable and, although I cannot approve of his lifestyle, I dislike the idea that his work could be entirely dismissed because of it."

"The baby thrown out with the bathwater, so to speak?" Mr. Bennet chuckled.

"Papa," Elizabeth inserted; "Mr. Darcy and his sister have been reading Mrs. Wollstonecraft's essays."

Thomas' eyebrows rose, impressed in spite of himself. "Ah, that takes courage these days. Another example of Society getting on its high horse. Have you read any of those reviews condemning her? Clearly not a one ever bothered to actually read any of her tracts— they just added to the rumor mongering and now the ton has decided to condemn her and her ideas because she did not manage her personal life according to their strictures." He smiled at Elizabeth. "I wonder how many live in glass houses?"

Before Elizabeth could respond, however, her elder sister spoke up. Jane disliked controversy and was concerned that the conversation was becoming too improper for the dinner table. "Papa, did you not once say that our Aunt Jane went to hear Mrs. Wollstonecraft speak in London?"

Mr. Bennet turned his attention to his eldest. Jane had been fidgety all afternoon and barely spoke when Mr. Bingley finally arrived with the Netherfield party. Elizabeth had stayed at her side, holding her hand reassuringly while the young gentleman had greeted his hostess. Once the Gardiners had successfully distracted Mrs. Bennet, however, he had moved directly to Jane's side and they had spoken quietly until the butler announced dinner. Jane had blushingly accepted Mr. Bingley's arm and he had escorted her to sit immediately to his left.

Knowing what Jane was about, Mr. Bennet smiled gently and allowed her to shift the topic. "She did indeed." He went on to summarize some of his sister's comments on the feminist icon and then conversation shifted to a scientific lecture that Lizzy had attended with the Gardiners while in London.

Elizabeth's father couldn't help but be impressed by Mr. Darcy. The younger man's contributions to the discussion were well-reasoned and insightful; though he had not attended the particular lecture in question, he had read several of the scientist's papers and was obviously comfortable discussing the issues.

While Mr. Darcy debated some point of logic with Elizabeth, Mr. Bennet sipped his wine and observed the two young couples. To his left, Jane and Bingley sat smiling and, although they made some small, pleasant comments, they did not contribute anything substantive to the discussion. In direct contrast was the couple to his right; Elizabeth and Darcy were energetically debating some of the professor's finer points and referencing other works. They clearly derived pleasure from their disagreement. At one point the gentleman even laughingly accused the lady of espousing an opinion which couldn't possibly be her own.

There was a hint of flirtation, but on the whole, Mr. Bennet could not fault them. Obviously the young man from Derbyshire had discovered Elizabeth's fine mind and was reveling in it; something that her father could certainly appreciate. Elizabeth herself was glowing with happiness and Mr. Bennet saw that her heart had been touched, even if she did not yet realize it.

He sighed and Elizabeth turned to catch a flicker of sadness in his eye. "Papa?" she asked softly, breaking off her conversation with Mr. Darcy.

Luckily, Mr. Bennet was saved from making up an excuse when Mrs. Bennet announced that it was time for the ladies to withdraw. Thomas smiled weakly and waved a hand at his favorite daughter. "Nothing to worry about, Lizzy; run along."

He pushed out his chair and stood. "Well, gentlemen; if you will accompany me to my study, I shall see if I have any libations that might tempt you."

Mr. Gardiner laughingly protested that Longbourn's master couldn't possibly have finished all of the port that he had been given by his brother-in-law at Christmas. Chuckling, the two old friends led the way.

After pouring the port and passing out the glasses, Elizabeth's father stood quietly, listening to Bingley chatter on to Mr. Gardiner about various business matters. He gathered that the younger man had discovered his brother-in-law's excellent business sense and was implementing some advice he had been given when they met in London.

Mr. Bennet's attention wandered and he noted that his other guest was examining the bookshelves. He moved in that direction with a determined air. "Do you see anything that you like?" Thomas took a certain amount of perverse satisfaction when the younger man started.

Mr. Darcy turned serious eyes on Elizabeth's father and reminded himself to be as open and amiable as he was capable. "You have an excellent collection, sir."

Mr. Bennet nodded agreeably at the compliment.

Rather than fall into silence, Darcy exerted himself to continue the conversation. "You have the complete series of Linnaeus' *Systema Naturae*... I've not seen all the editions together outside of a university library."

Mr. Bennet couldn't help but be pleased. "I found them at a bookshop in Oxford when I was a student; apparently a professor had passed away and his widow needed the money." He smiled and pulled the first volume off the shelf and showed it to the younger man. "Many only read his tenth edition because, of course, that is where he introduced the binary naming system which has become all the rage."

Thomas was even more pleased when Mr. Darcy indicated his understanding of the reference and added, "I must admit that these theories on the classification of living organisms are not as interesting to me as studying how the man's mind worked. By publishing thirteen editions, Mr. Linnaeus has provided me with windows on the progression of his thinking across several decades."

Mr. Darcy was clearly intrigued. "I never considered it in such a way. I remember first learning of his binomial system; I appreciated its logic— the grouping of morphologically similar organisms together as 'species' and then the grouping of similar species as a 'genus,' and so forth."

Bennet nodded. "Yes, his final system is elegant in its simplicity, yet I believe that every student should read all of his revisions from first to last. It gives you an excellent sense of how even the most brilliant mind did not produce such a complex theory fully formed. Take the whales for example; in earlier editions, Linnaeus considered them to be fish, yet subsequent studies of their anatomy prompted him to remove them to the mammals in his tenth edition."

The two men continued to speak on the subject for some time until Mr. Bennet noted that his guest's glass was empty. After offering refills to all his guests, he returned to stand by Mr. Darcy. There was a moment of silence while both men sampled the wine but eventually Elizabeth's father cleared his throat. "Mr. Darcy, I find myself in an odd position. My daughter shall be spending several weeks at the home of an unmarried gentleman, yet I know very little about him except from... letters."

Mr. Bennet was rather pleased to see that he had immediately captured the young man's complete attention. He also caught a flicker of what might have been amusement in Mr. Bingley's eye before that man turned back to his conversation with Mr. Gardiner. Thomas decided to tuck that observation away for future consideration and continue on with his current purpose.

"I wonder if you might like to come riding with me tomorrow morning? Should Mr. Bingley not have a horse for you to use, I'm sure that we could arrange something."

Mr. Darcy was looking at him with the sort of absolute focus that always made Elizabeth's father wish to do something entirely improper, such as jump up on his desk and imitate a rooster. Luckily, the other gentleman responded before Thomas gave into the imp whispering in his ear.

"Thank you, sir. I would enjoy seeing more of the area. While I appreciate your offer of a mount, I have my own."

"You brought Icky? Oh, of course—you shall be riding back to Derbyshire and leaving the carriage here for Miss Darcy..." Bingley's attention had been caught at the mention of his own name. It took him a moment to figure out why his comment had been met with a grimace from his friend and bemused curiosity from Mr. Bennet and Mr. Gardiner.

Charles suppressed his natural laughter with mock formality and bowed slightly toward Fitzwilliam. "I beg your pardon, Darcy; of course I meant to inquire about the great *Icarus*."

Bingley could no longer quell his chuckles and Mr. Gardiner and Mr. Bennet both turned inquisitive eyes upon the other young man.

After a baleful look at his friend, Darcy rolled his eyes. "As a colt, he would run madly about the pasture, kicking and bucking as if trying to launch himself into flight... then he would fall to the ground and sleep like the dead until he was rested enough to go at it again. Also, he is a dapple grey and when he sheds in the spring it looks like ash floating away in the wind; I was reading Greek mythology at the time and Icarus seemed an appropriate name. Unfortunately, he also enjoys rolling in mud; once he nuzzled dirt all over my sister's new frock. She declared that he would be called "Icky" forevermore."

Darcy joined the others in laughter and Mr. Bennet was pleased to see that Elizabeth's admirer did indeed possess a sense of humor.

After several comments from his other guests, Mr. Bennet contributed; "I had a similar experience many years ago. When Jane turned ten, I decided that we needed a nice, gentle pony for my daughters to learn to ride on. I consulted with Mr. Brady— Netherfield's former owner— and we found a lovely little chestnut mare with what I considered to be the rather elegant name of 'Eunomia.' However, within a week, the girls had nicknamed her Nelly, and Nelly she remains to this day."

Mr. Gardiner chuckled— it was a story that he had heard before and he had perfected the accompanying punch line. "Ah, Thomas... did you really believe that you could keep the goddess of good order at Longbourn for any length of time?"

They laughed and when the four gentlemen returned to the ladies some minutes later, all were in an excellent humor.

When Darcy entered the drawing room, he shared a smile with Elizabeth but also saw that Georgiana was fighting fatigue. After a few quiet words with his sister, he signaled Bingley that it was time to depart.

Mr. Bennet was distracted for a minute by Mrs. Gardiner and when his attention was returned to their departing guests, he was somewhat irked to note that Jane and Elizabeth had accompanied the gentlemen outside alone. He made a mental note to speak to Fanny about chaperoning their daughters properly.

When he joined them, Jane stood with Mr. Bingley by the carriage, her eyes downcast as he spoke to her quietly. Some yards away, Elizabeth was listening to Mr. Darcy, Miss Darcy at her side. His daughter looked to be equal parts amusement and concern. When she shot a look at her father, Thomas guessed that her admirer had relayed their plan for the next morning.

He cleared his throat and his two eldest daughters moved obediently to his side. Gratitude for the Bennets' hospitality was repeated by the guests and farewells exchanged by all. When Mr. Bingley's carriage finally pulled away, Mr. Bennet turned to his second daughter. "Well, that was an entertaining evening. I suppose that your young man informed you that we are going riding tomorrow morning?"

Elizabeth smirked and, taking Jane's arm, led them toward the door. Speaking over her shoulder, she called to her father; "He did indeed; I informed him that he was lucky it wasn't hunting season."

Chuckling, Thomas followed the pair into the house. It was only later when he was readying himself for bed that he realized his favorite daughter hadn't protested his reference to Mr. Darcy as 'hers.'

The next morning, Mr. Bennet sat down to breakfast with three of his daughters. Lydia was still abed and Elizabeth had departed at dawn for an early morning walk. He was just reaching for a second cup of tea when she blew into the room with pink cheeks, wind blown hair, and sparkling eyes. He couldn't help but smile.

"Good morning, Lizzy. Have you been reacquainting yourself with all your favorite trees and rocks?"

She grinned back. "Oh yes, Papa! I walked up to Oakham Mount; there was a beautiful sunrise— all oranges and pinks with mist rising up off the fields… Oh, and I found a patch of wild purple orchids in bloom!"

Mr. Bennet was pleased when Catherine responded to her sister's enthusiasm. "Oh, that sounds lovely. Are they far? I would love to try to sketch them!"

Elizabeth beamed. "Not far at all—perhaps a fifteen minute walk. They are just beyond the fork in the path to Oakham Mount, the one that leads to those old plum trees near the stream? I would be happy to show you, if you'd like."

Jane and Mary had just agreed to accompany Kitty and Elizabeth on their walk when Hill announced visitors.

Mr. Darcy had arrived precisely on time and the Master of Longbourn was not terribly surprised to see him accompanied by Mr. Bingley.

Kitty peered beyond the two gentlemen. "But Mr. Darcy; where is your sister? You've not left her all alone at Netherfield, have you?"

The gentleman looked slightly embarrassed. "She said that she wished to spend the morning practicing the pianoforte."

"Hmmm…" Elizabeth arched an eyebrow at her sister. "Perhaps Miss Darcy felt that she should not visit us so soon again without a specific invitation?" The look on the gentleman's face confirmed her guess.

She smiled and turned back to her sister. "Kitty, why don't you write a note inviting Miss Darcy to spend the day with us; perhaps she might like to join our little expedition this morning?"

The younger Miss Bennet looked her question at the tall, intimidating gentleman. She blinked when he smiled broadly.

"I believe that my sister would appreciate that very much, Miss Catherine."

Kitty nodded faintly and left the room, thinking that she might need to revise her opinion of Mr. Darcy.

Perhaps unsurprisingly, Bingley had seated himself beside Jane during this exchange. As soon as he confirmed that she was planning to walk out, he voiced his enthusiasm to join the ladies.

Just then, shrieks could be heard from another part of the house. Those who called Longbourn home pieced together the words fairly easily. "He is here?!? Oh, Hill! Hill! Why didn't anyone tell me!?! Where is Jane?!? Lydia— my dear girl! What are you doing still in bed?!? The *gentlemen* are here!" Fortunately, Lydia's response was too low to be distinguished by those in the breakfast room.

Quickly ascertaining that Mr. Darcy had already broken his fast, Elizabeth's father set aside his teacup and stood. "Well then, sir. Shall we be off?"

Understanding what he was about, Darcy followed suit. While Mr. Bennet was waiting for the maid to retrieve his coat and sending word to the stable for his horse to be brought around, Elizabeth spoke quietly with her sisters. After giving Mr. Darcy an encouraging smile (which warmed the young man's face considerably), she stood, intending to go upstairs and check on the Gardiner children.

However, at that moment Mrs. Bennet swept into the breakfast room.

The matron appeared significantly calmer than her earlier tumult might have suggested (probably due to the presence of her brother just behind her). Calm or not, she looked like a cat presented with a bowl of cream when she caught sight of Mr. Bingley at Jane's side.

After a look from Elizabeth, Mary claimed her mother's attention, offering to prepare her tea just as she liked it. While Mrs. Bennet was effectively distracted, Lizzy spoke quietly to her uncle. It was quickly arranged that the Gardiner children would spend the morning with their cousins while he and Mrs. Bennet visited their sister, Mrs. Phillips, allowing Mrs. Gardiner to rest.

When Mr. Bennet finally extracted Mr. Darcy from the breakfast room, the two men made their way to Longbourn's stables in a companionable silence. While the stableman was saddling Mr. Bennet's gelding, Elizabeth's father inspected Darcy's grey.

"So you are the mighty Icarus, are you?" he said, letting the horse sniff his hand before patting him on the shoulder. "Or do you prefer to be called Icky? Not quite so mighty, that!" The big grey snorted and shook his head, causing his long mane to flop about and prompting both men to chuckle.

Darcy rubbed the horse behind one ear affectionately. "He's a big clown; sometimes I think that he's more canine than equine."

Mr. Bennet chuckled, watching as the horse shut his eyes in ecstasy as his master scratched just the right spot. "Well, as long as he doesn't try to sit on my lap, I can't fault his temperament."

True to form, Icarus pricked up his ears when the stableman led out Mr. Bennet's bay. Darcy smiled, "I've never seen the attraction of flighty horses that spook at the slightest noise. It's one of the reasons that we've been cross-breeding thoroughbreds with other, calmer breeds at Pemberley for the last decade."

As Mr. Bennet stepped away to take possession of his own horse's reins, he glanced back at the other man's gelding. "Larger breeds, as well, by the looks of him. What is he, sixteen hands?"

Fitzwilliam smiled and adjusted the girth before mounting. "Seventeen hands, two inches at the withers. Icarus came from crossing an Irish hunter that I bought from my cousin—he had been given the mare in payment for a debt—to one of Pemberley's thoroughbred stallions."

In a few minutes, both men were mounted and headed out of the paddock.

They rode silently for some minutes, Mr. Bennet following his usual route to check over Longbourn's more distant fields and pastures. Thomas made some slight comment, pointing out the hedges that marked Longbourn's boundary to the adjoining estate.

Darcy nodded but remained silent. When he finally did speak, Lizzy's father was immediately concerned by the younger man's solemn tone. "Mr.

Bennet, I can go no longer without expressing my most profuse apologies to you. Miss Elizabeth has indicated that she has spoken to you about our... interactions... at Kent. As I am sure you already know, your daughter's behavior was impeccable in every way; I am wholly to blame for our misunderstandings."

When the man paused to take a breath, Thomas sighed before responding, "Mr. Darcy, I had hoped for a pleasant ride with a bit of easy conversation, but I see that you are not one to put off a matter simply because it is likely to be uncomfortable."

"Mr. Bennet, I..."

"No, no— that was not meant as a criticism; quite the contrary, in fact." The conversation faltered for few minutes as the two reined their horses to maneuver through a gate. Once it was latched behind him, Mr. Bennet turned his attention back to the original topic.

"I don't know if Lizzy told you, but Lydia was going to travel to Brighton with the regiment as the companion of their Colonel's wife. I don't know what I was thinking; Mrs. Forster is worse than a featherhead."

Thomas considered his next words carefully, wishing to keep some details private. "Lizzy came to me and counseled against it. I'm afraid that I still think of my girls as, well, girls... not young ladies; the thought fairly curdles my blood, to be honest."

Darcy nodded gravely. "I feel the same about Georgiana; she is ten years my junior and I still remember holding her in my arms for the first time as if it were yesterday."

Bennet eyed the man appraisingly, but then nodded; "Yes, but just wait until you have daughters of your own— it is far, far worse." He chuckled at Mr. Darcy's look of abject horror.

"Well, you should know that Lizzy shared your letter with me." His eyebrows rose at Darcy's unsurprised expression. "She informed you of that, did she?"

Mr. Darcy nodded, adding, "I was glad to hear that she did so. It was completely improper of me to have written her."

The older man eyed him. "Do you regret it?"

Darcy looked discomfited, but replied honestly, "No, sir. I am perfectly aware that in handing that letter to your daughter, I disregarded your authority and put Miss Elizabeth's reputation at risk, but... I..." He took a deep breath and fiddled with his reins before continuing in a rougher voice. "I admire your daughter a great deal, sir, and it leaves me inarticulate at the best of times."

Thomas couldn't help but snort slightly, causing the younger man to glance at him and redden. "You have heard of my many offenses, obviously," he sighed. "For much of my life, I have been selfish and overbearing, caring for none beyond my own family circle; thinking meanly of all the rest of the world and desiring to think meanly of their sense and worth relative to my own. As an only son (and for many years an only child), I was spoilt by my parents and not taught to correct my temper."

He sighed again, though more softly this time. "My parents taught me good principles but lately I have come to see that I was left to practice them in pride and conceit. Your daughter taught me a lesson, hard at first, but most important."

The two men rode in silence for several minutes until Darcy recalled the point he still needed to make. "In truth, I left Kent expecting that I would never see her again. I was taken by surprise when she refused my offer and then furious when she told me why. Although I believed myself to be perfectly calm when I wrote that letter, I now shudder to think of how bitter I must have sounded."

Mr. Bennet shrugged. "It sounded remarkably calm to me, given the preceding events."

Darcy only shook his head. "I cannot agree, but regardless; I was awake all night, trying to understand what had gone so horribly wrong... how I could have so completely misconstrued her opinion. I had no hope of being able to explain myself in her presence; I... I felt too much to speak easily. So I attempted to write it out, and you have seen the results."

Bennet's bay startled when a pheasant burst out of the grass by his nose. Once the horse settled down, some time passed during which the only noise was the creaking of saddle leather and the jingle of the horses' bits. Finally, Elizabeth's father stirred himself to speak.

"The reason I mentioned Lydia was that I feel I should thank you, Mr. Darcy. Had you not shared the information of Lieutenant Wickham's perfidies, I would have allowed her to go to Brighton, and God only knows what trouble she could have gotten into there. I am afraid that living in the country has dulled my sense of the dangers that face my daughters as they grow up and enter the world."

Darcy nodded. "I cannot criticize your preference for the country over town. I myself would spend all my time in Derbyshire, if I could."

Mr. Bennet caught the younger gentleman's wistful tone and they spent the remainder of their ride discussing the northern countryside and comparing stories of Pemberley's management to that of Longbourn.

When the pair eventually rode back into the stable yard, they were met with the pleasant sight of Mrs. Gardiner sitting on a stone bench, enjoying a bit of sun and knitting. Even as she greeted the two gentlemen, her sharp eyes noted the companionable air between them. Her husband had told her of his conversation with Elizabeth's father and she was pleased to see Thomas making the effort to know the younger man better.

Mr. Bennet handed the bay's reins off to the stable boy and smiled at his sister-in-law. "You look to be very happily situated, Madeleine!"

Mrs. Gardiner returned his merry greeting with a contented look. "You find me all alone, sir. I had difficulty knowing what to do with myself!"

Longbourn's master chuckled. "So the merry band is still out botanizing?"

She smiled back. "Yes, though I expect them back soon; it is almost time for luncheon and Tommy and Jonathan seem to have clocks in their tummies that keep perfect time." Madeleine turned to the other gentleman who had just joined them after seeing to his horse. "Good day, Mr. Darcy! Did you have an enjoyable ride?"

Fitzwilliam replied agreeably and after they had discussed the route that the two men had ridden, he inquired after his sister.

Mrs. Gardiner smiled again. "Ah, yes; the two of you absconded before her note came. Miss Darcy shall be joining us for luncheon and staying the afternoon, as will Mr. Bingley. We hoped that you would be amenable to such a plan; Mrs. Hill is preparing a picnic so that the children may join us."

Mr. Darcy had just confirmed his willingness when the three turned at the sound of voices.

Jonathan and Tommy burst from the shrubbery and came running across the yard toward their mother, trailed by Amelia who was making a valiant effort to keep up despite her shorter legs. The boys brought flowers for their mother who fussed over them while ignoring the somewhat bedraggled appearance of the blooms. Amelia added her own to the bouquet but then turned to peer up at the tall gentleman from Derbyshire.

Without a thought, Fitzwilliam dropped down to his knee so that he was at eye-level with the little girl. "Did you have a nice morning, Miss Amelia?"

She grinned. "Oh, yes! Lizzy told us the names of ever so many flowers. Spring is so much prettier at Longbourn than home. Is it spring at your home, too?"

Darcy smiled. "Indeed it is, and we have many flowers there. Perhaps your cousin shall like them as well?"

The little girl nodded with great seriousness. "Lizzy likes all flowers—but I'm sure she'll like yours special." She held up a daisy; "Would you like this one? I can put it in your button hole—Papa says I do it just right."

"Thank you very kindly. I should be honored if you would do me such a service; I must admit that I don't know the proper method."

With absolute focus, little Miss Gardiner carefully threaded the daisy through and arranged it at a precise angle upon his collar.

Such was the sight that met Elizabeth's eyes when she emerged from the shrubbery, Rebecca at her side. Fitzwilliam blushed slightly at her warm glance even as her father rolled his eyes and muttered something acerbic about "young lovers" before Mrs. Gardiner shushed him.

When Bingley appeared, Mr. Bennet noted that Jane was walking at the gentleman's side and seemed significantly more comfortable than she had on the previous evening. Once the children's eager descriptions of their walk dissolved into yawns, Mrs. Gardiner gently herded them all upstairs to wash up and have a short lie down.

While the ladies went to wash up, Mr. Darcy tracked Elizabeth's father to his study. Longbourn's master had retreated for a moment of quiet and, although he had come to rather like the younger gentleman after their morning ride, he was not particularly pleased to have his peace interrupted. His mood deteriorated even more when he saw Darcy's serious expression.

The younger man stood before him, eyes on the rug and hands clasped behind his back. Thomas settled back in his chair and let the silence stretch out. Finally Mr. Darcy appeared to reach a resolution; he squared his shoulders and looked Mr. Bennet dead in the eye. "Sir, I wish to ask for your permission to court your daughter." The sentence came out in a rush.

Although Thomas should have known it was coming, he still felt like pulling out his shotgun. "I suppose you have already spoken with Lizzy?" he asked eventually.

The young man's smile was enough to confirm it. "Yes, sir. I asked Miss Elizabeth if her... feelings... had changed while we were in London, before I invited the Gardiners to stay at my estate. I did not wish her to be made uncomfortable and I feared that if her opinion of me was unchanged since Kent..."

"And she agreed?" Thomas had to ask, although it was painful to him.

"Yes, sir." Darcy's tone indicated that he appreciated the second chance he had been given. He was about to speak further but Mr. Bennet waved him off, not interested in hearing the ranting of a young lover.

"I shall have to speak with Lizzy, you understand." The young man's confident nod made her father feel very old. He stood and turned to stare out of the window. "Well, then. She should be in the drawing room by now. Please send her in to me."

"Of course, sir." Darcy stood and studied the older gentleman's back for a minute. He was tempted to feel affronted by such a curt dismissal, but reminded himself that Elizabeth was this man's favorite daughter. Before leaving, he spoke softly, "Should your daughter ever accept my offer of marriage, I would consider it to be the greatest honor of my life."

Mr. Bennet could not speak, but a slight nod acknowledging Darcy's words was enough. When Elizabeth knocked on the door some minutes later, he had himself under better control and their interview was conducted expeditiously.

Lizzy agreed that, now that her misconceptions had been put aside, she found that the effort of getting to know Mr. Darcy to be very rewarding indeed. "I find that I like him very much, Papa, and I should like to know him better." She paused and Mr. Bennet gave her the time to frame her thoughts.

"I know him to be a very good man, Pap, but I still feel as if there is much I do not understand about him. When he speaks of Pemberley, it is almost as if it is a part of him, like a leg or a heart, not just some grand estate to brag about. Somehow, I feel that if I can see him there, at his home, I may finally understand him... see him complete and unmasked." Elizabeth flushed slightly. "I'm sorry, Papa. Am I speaking nonsense?"

Mr. Bennet sighed and took both of his daughter's hands in his own. "No, my dear. I believe that you are very sensible, indeed." He kissed her forehead before stepping back. "Now then, run along; I am certain that your mother has much for you to do for our picnic this afternoon!"

After exchanging a few more affectionate words, Bennet shut the door behind his favorite daughter before she noticed the tears that threatened to leak from his eyes. He treated himself to a small glass of port and sat in the chair by the window, sternly reminding himself that Elizabeth would be loved and respected, should she continue along her present course.

When Miss Darcy arrived an hour later, her carriage deposited her on Longbourn's front steps but she was drawn toward the gardens before she had even set foot in the house. When she rounded the corner, the sound of voices that had drawn her was revealed to be the entire Bennet-Gardiner-Phillips clan bustling about, carrying things to a little copse. Georgiana was particularly amused to see her brother carrying two chairs and being directed as to their placement by Mrs. Bennet.

"Ah, Miss Darcy. I'm glad that you were able to join us."

Georgiana turned to find Longbourn's patriarch approaching. She curtsied and managed a small smile. "Mr. Bennet." She had not quite figured the older man out, yet.

Thomas nodded back pleasantly, reminding himself that the girl was probably not accustomed to the rambunctious tenor that characterized his own household. "Come, come, no need to stand on ceremony. As you can see, the girls have organized a picnic so that the children may join us. You met the Gardiners in London, I understand?" Mr. Bennet had exchanged little beyond greetings with the young lady and was curious to know Mr. Darcy's sister better.

Georgiana exerted herself to respond. "Yes, sir. We spent the day at the Kew gardens together." She smiled when little Amelia Gardiner came running out of the house in a flurry of skirts and launched herself at Mr. Darcy. "My brother has always had a way with children."

Thomas had turned in the same direction and could not help but be amused when the tall, serious young man from Derbyshire bent over so that he might converse with the littlest Gardiner.

Soon after, Miss Darcy's arrival was noticed by Catherine and she found herself drawn into the happy rabble. There was no ceremony or artifice and Georgiana found herself relaxing as she would never have imagined possible in a crowd of relative strangers. When her brother caught her eye and raised an eyebrow, silently inquiring after her welfare, she broke into a sunny smile that he had not seen since before Ramsgate.

The party was soon happily settled in a grassy corner of the gardens; the Bennets had obviously done this before and there was an easy order to their chaos. Lawn chairs were set beneath an old oak tree for Mrs. Bennet and her sisters. The others arranged themselves on blankets around them while the servants set out the food on a simple trestle table low to the ground. There was no ceremony, just a great deal of good food, happy laughter and comfortable teasing.

The children were full of energy after their nap and it was not long before their attention wandered. After being pelted by a poorly aimed grape, Mr. Bennet recruited Jonathan and Tommy to help him bring out the cricket bats and wickets. Once Mr. Bingley and the Darcys had been educated as to 'Longbourn House rules' (which seemed to consist primarily of dire consequences should a fielder step off the lawn and stumble into the flower beds), a pleasant afternoon was had by all. Darcy was amazed to see his own sister step up to bat and cheered as loudly as any when she scored a run on her first try.

The remainder of the afternoon was spent in relaxed amiability. Even Lydia was convinced to join in the cricket game and showed that, when her energy was focused in a more positive direction, she was quite an exceptional wicketkeeper.

When the Darcys and Mr. Bingley finally returned to Netherfield, it was nearly dark and they stood for a few minutes on the front steps, admiring the colors of the twilight sky. Georgiana squeezed her brother's hand and looked up at him with eyebrows raised.

Fitzwilliam glanced over to see a similar expression on Charles' face and couldn't help laughing. A happiness that he had never felt before seemed to settle over him like a warm blanket. "Yes; Mr. Bennet has given me permission to court his daughter."

17 GETTING TO KNOW YOU

Fitzwilliam Darcy was not having a good day, which was odd because he had every expectation that the next would bring one of the very best of his life. Tomorrow, Elizabeth was to arrive. The very thought of having her at Pemberley made his chest tighten with hope. Today, however, was not turning out as he had wished. Long before dawn, he had been woken with news of a fire at one of his tenant's cottages. He had ridden out immediately and then spent hours with the men, hurling buckets of water and sand to put out the flames and keep them from spreading.

The family had escaped with their lives but Mr. Greene had been badly burned attempting to save some of their possessions. Darcy had immediately sent for the apothecary in Kympton; that man had taken one look at the distraught farmer's shoulder and hustled him off to clean and bandage his wounds.

The structure itself was a complete loss. Pemberley's master spent some time reassuring the family that it would be rebuilt promptly and making arrangements for them to stay in an empty pensioner's cottage in the meantime.

When Darcy finally returned to Pemberley House, it was nearly mid-afternoon. He had dunked his head in a water trough before leaving the scene of the fire but was still grimy from the smoke. Exhausted, he slid down out of the saddle and handed the reins to the stable boy who met him. Patting the equally exhausted horse on the neck, Will said quietly, "Give him a double measure of oats, Jack, for he surely earned it today."

After the boy led his horse away, Darcy stood for a moment by the stable, staring out across Pemberley's lake at two ducks swimming contentedly, sun glinting off the ripples of their wake. It seemed surreal that such serenity could exist not five miles from where he had so recently witnessed such destruction and misery.

After a few minutes of contemplation, Darcy's attention was brought back to his present situation by the sound of voices. Not wishing to be caught in such a grubby state by tourists visiting Pemberley, he turned and was about to head toward the kitchen door when a wholly unexpected voice froze him in place.

"Mr. Darcy?"

Rounding the corner of the stables was, horror of horrors, the very lady whom he most wished to impress; Miss Elizabeth Bennet, herself, accompanied by the two Gardiner boys.

"Mr. Darcy, are you well?"

Her worried voice reminded Fitzwilliam of his manners. "Miss Bennet," he said gruffly and bowed correctly, although such formality seemed a farce given his current state. For an instant, he considered trying to put his coat back on, but as it had been dunked in a dirty pail of water after catching fire itself, he decided absently that it probably wouldn't do much to improve his appearance.

Vaguely, he heard Elizabeth send the boys inside to tell Mrs. Reynolds that the Master had returned and would need a bath and food immediately. He was still standing in exactly the same place when she turned back to him and took his hands to examine them.

"Are you hurt? Mrs. Reynolds said that there was a fire and you had gone to help."

Though exhausted, the sound of Elizabeth's concern sang in his ears. He smiled and the resulting expression was almost goofy. "I am well, just tired." He squeezed her hands in his. "When did you arrive? This is not quite the welcome I had planned for you, I am afraid."

Elizabeth studied him for a moment, dark eyes searching. Seemingly reassured, she nodded and then tugged his arm to begin walking toward the house. "We arrived just after noon; the roads were good and we made excellent time. We considered stopping for an extra night in Nottingham but Georgiana assured us that it would not be a problem if we arrived a bit early." She did not add that Miss Darcy's eagerness to return to her ancestral home had been equaled by her obvious desire to see Elizabeth reunited with her brother. "Was anyone hurt?"

It took Darcy a moment to realize that she was asking about the fire. He summarized the situation and she nodded, asking a few questions about the family's circumstances that he found himself oddly pleased to answer. By the time they reached the front steps, he was feeling less overwhelmed and more certain than ever that if the woman beside him should ever agree to become Mrs. Darcy, he would be the happiest man in the world.

Elizabeth delivered Mr. Darcy to the housekeeper who bustled him off to his rooms before he even had a chance to greet the Gardiners. "They are perfectly well, sir. Miss Bennet has the right of it—you need to let Hawkins clean you up and see to that cut."

Will touched his forehead and found his fingers smeared with blood from a scrape of which he'd been unaware. They reached the door to his rooms and he stopped for a moment, hand on the doorknob.

"I assume you will wish to come down and take tea with your guests?" Mrs. Reynolds eyed the young master with a sharp eye. She'd known him since he was four years old and the moment she'd seen him looking at Miss Bennet she had known who would be Pemberley's next mistress. From what she had seen thus far, the young lady was polite, kind, and intelligent, all of which made for a promising beginning. Her unaffected actions in looking after Mr. Darcy just now, however, had done the most to win the old housekeeper's heart.

After a pause, Fitzwilliam looked up at her and smiled, tired but happy. "Yes, but could you send up a plate of sandwiches? I haven't had anything but an apple for breakfast and it might be embarrassing if I left nothing for our guests to eat at tea."

The housekeeper assured him that she would arrange it immediately and departed, her serious demeanor breaking into a smile the moment his back was turned.

When Darcy descended the stairs nearly an hour later, there was no hint of his travails except for a bit of sticking plaster on his forehead and a tiredness around the eyes. His eyebrows rose at the site of Mrs. Reynolds scolding two young maids in the hall. When she caught sight of him, the girls were sent on their way with a final remonstrance.

Mrs. Reynolds turned to him, hands still on her hips, but Fitzwilliam could now tell that her lips were tight to keep from laughing rather than from irritation.

"Problem, Mrs. Reynolds?"

She couldn't quite stop a laugh. "Fighting over who is to look after the youngest Gardiner lass. One would think that none of the staff has ever seen a child, the way they are all a flutter! Hauling out all the old trunks of toys and cleaning the schoolroom…" She paused, intrigued by the soft look on the Master's face.

"It has been a long time since there were children at Pemberley," he said quietly.

"Yes, sir," she replied in a similar tone, understanding that he was thinking of the times before his mother had died, when the Darcys had often entertained other families and Pemberley had been full of the sound of laughter and young voices. Both of the Darcy children had become quiet and serious beyond their years after the death of their parents.

Fitzwilliam sighed before looking up at the woman who had been much like a surrogate mother. "Well, let us hope that this is a sign of times to come."

Master and housekeeper smiled at each other in perfect understanding. "Yes, sir. I shall make certain that everything possible is done to make our guests comfortable."

"I know you will; I have every faith that they shall love Pemberley." He sighed slightly and, looking at the floor, muttered under his breath, "If only I had as much faith in myself."

Mrs. Reynolds studied the young man with understanding eyes for a moment before squaring her shoulders. "Miss Georgiana asked me to send the tea tray in to the rose sitting room when you were ready to join them. Shall I do so now, sir?"

Knowing just what she was about and appreciating the nudge, Darcy smiled. "Yes, and thank you, Mrs. Reynolds."

"Of course, dear." The housekeeper bustled off, unaware of the endearment that had slipped out.

Darcy watched her for a moment before squaring his own shoulders, reminding himself of a litany of things that he must do and must not do, and then heading in the direction of his guests.

When Mr. Darcy entered the sitting room, his eyes were immediately drawn to the sight of Elizabeth standing at a window looking out across the gardens, her light yellow gown looking like an extension of a sunbeam. There was no telling how long he might have stood in the doorway staring had not Georgiana jumped up from her seat to greet him.

Looking down at his sister, Will managed to gather his wits and kiss her on the forehead. "Hello, Georgie-girl." He turned to the other occupants of the room and bowed slightly. "Mr. and Mrs. Gardiner, Miss Bennet. Welcome to Pemberley. As I said to Miss Bennet earlier, I apologize for not being here to greet you properly when you arrived."

Elizabeth's aunt and uncle easily assured him that he had nothing to apologize for; their every comfort had been seen to by Miss Darcy and Mrs. Reynolds. Georgiana looked pleased at the praise of her hostessing and Fitzwilliam smiled at her proudly.

After discussing their travel for several minutes, Georgie and the Gardiners were distracted when two maids arrived with trays of tea and cakes. As they were setting things out, Darcy moved to stand by Elizabeth who had remained quiet since exchanging courtesies. Fitzwilliam bowed slightly over her hand.

"Miss Bennet."

"Mr. Darcy."

"And how do you like Pemberley?" he asked softly after a pause.

"Oh, 'tis beautiful, sir. I have never seen a place where nature has done so much and man has allowed the natural beauty of the landscape to compliment his structures." She paused, momentarily discomfited that he might think her enthusiasm mercenary. "I like it very well, indeed," she finished weakly.

Darcy beamed, love for his family's legacy shining in his eyes. "I am glad." He paused, searching for something to say that would not be too forward. "When I met you at the stables, were you coming back from a walk?"

Elizabeth's smile returned. "You understand me very well, sir. Having caught a glimpse of your beautiful woods, I could not remain inside for long. Jonathan and Tommy were wild to get outdoors after so long in the carriage and I was happy to offer my services as companion."

They spoke companionably for several minutes about the woods, the various paths around the park, and Pemberley's gardens until Georgiana called for their attention and they rejoined the group.

Once they were all seated and sipping tea, Elizabeth made some small compliment on the room. Darcy looked around for the first time, his attention having previously been on its occupants. "I cannot remember the last time I was in here." His eyes caught signs of disuse; some of the old wallpaper was peeling in a corner and there was a bit of water damage in the plaster ceiling above. Though the room was clean and neat, the furniture was outdated and there was a general feeling of desuetude. "This was Mother's favorite sitting room."

Mrs. Gardiner smiled. "Yes, I asked if we might see it; I remember Lady Anne redecorating it just after she was married. Old Mrs. Darcy had moved into the Dower House and insisted that the new mistress put her own mark on the manor, as she termed it."

The two Darcy siblings looked around at the room with new eyes. "It is very like Mother's private rooms," commented Will softly.

Madeleine smiled kindly. "She adored the new floral patterns coming from Paris—big pink cabbage roses, violets and ivy, and so forth. I can remember coming with Mama to visit her; Mrs. Darcy would have those tables littered with swatches of fabrics and wall hangings, trying to match and choose." Her eyes twinkled at the memory. "She had a very different style to your grandmother; Lady Edna always leaned toward simpler styles."

Fitzwilliam smiled. "Grandmother was always very practical."

Mrs. Gardiner laughed aloud. "I remember once early on, your mother wished to change a room but was worried that her new mother-in-law might be offended. Old Mrs. Darcy just laughed and told her to change whatever she wished; it was a relief that her son had married a woman who enjoyed such things because she herself did not!"

"Yet the Dower House is decorated much as you describe—simple yet elegant, with brighter colors than... this..." Will waved his hand around at the contrast between what he described to the pastels and florals that saturated his mother's room.

Madeleine smiled. "Yes, well... I suspect that Lady Edna was quite set in her own tastes but she was a wise woman and understood that a new wife must be encouraged."

Darcy barely kept himself from looking toward Elizabeth. Luckily, Mr. Gardiner made a comment about the architecture of the house that turned the conversation to its history. Seeing that his guests had finished their tea, Fitzwilliam invited them to view the house from the outside so that he might better explain the history of the various additions. This proposal was quickly agreed upon and the remainder of the afternoon was spent outdoors, joined by the Gardiner children who had taken tea in the schoolroom with their nurse and a coterie of Pemberley maids.

As they wandered around the perimeter of the house and the nearest gardens, Darcy pointed out particular features. "The land was originally granted to John d'Arcy in 1071 for his aid to William the Conqueror against the Fenland rebels. D'Arcy married Kate of Hartwick but spent most of his time with the troops in support of William, first on the continent and then later in Scotland, leaving his wife with an enormous tract of land but little more than a hut in which to live. Family legend says that young Mrs. d'Arcy oversaw the design and building of the first Pemberley House—you can still see the stone ruins up on the hill there. Her husband returned after several years, just in time to settle in at the new manor house, father a son, and promptly die. Kate never remarried; she raised her son by herself and kept his inheritance intact until he came of age... no small achievement for a widow in that day and age."

The party agreed that they would explore the ruins at some point during their visit. A question from Mr. Gardiner returned the conversation to the current Pemberley House. By then, they had wandered to the side of a sunken garden and could look back at the Palladian structure, limestone glowing in the late afternoon sunlight.

Darcy gestured to the stone walls of a sunken garden. "This was the site of the second Pemberley House—those walls formed the foundation. In 1605, Grant Darcy married a wealthy Scotswoman that he met in Paris. According to family legend, when she first saw Pemberley, she was shocked by the ramshackle manor house, bare of all but the most basic of amenities. She flatly refused to live there and the only way her new husband could convince her not to return to her father in Edinburgh was by offering to build an entirely new, more modern house."

The group laughed, particularly when Mr. Gardiner raised his hand to his brow theatrically. "Ah, the things we husbands do to keep our wives happy!"

Madeleine arched her brows in mock outrage and responded tartly, "If you were the one seeing to the cooking and cleaning, you would be eager for modern facilities as well!"

After some further banter, Darcy continued his story. "Unfortunately, neither ever lived in the new house. The couple were both more interested in society and politics than farming so the family split their time between London and Edinburgh— years went by before an architect was even hired. Apparently their son, Gowan Darcy, didn't see his birthright until he was fourteen years old and he accompanied his father on a visit to confer with the architect and check on the construction. Supposedly Gowan fell in love with the land at first sight and begged his father to let him stay, even if he had to camp in the woods and forage for food."

Elizabeth's eyes sparkled. "I can easily understand his sentiment, especially if he had been raised in the city."

"Indeed," Darcy grinned back. Unfortunately, his father did not share our enthusiasm and young Gowan was promptly sent back to school. However, as soon as he finished he returned to Derbyshire and took up residence in the old manor house. He began overseeing the estate and even introduced some new breeds of sheep that greatly increased its revenue."

Fitzwilliam looked out across the hills and woods, eyes shielded from the low sun by his hand. It was difficult to explain how this land pulled at him when he was away, but telling the history of his ancestors was the closest he could come to sharing it. He looked at Elizabeth and her bright eyes and intent expression told him that she understood.

"Although Mr. Darcy the elder had never spent much time in Derbyshire himself, he had made all the decisions as to site and architectural design for the new house. He was particularly enamored by the intricate Gothic styles that were so popular in France and Italy during his youth." Seeing that Mr. Gardiner looked particularly intrigued, Fitzwilliam added, "We still have the original plans in the library if you would like to see them." When that gentleman nodded eagerly, Pemberley's current master made a mental note before continuing his story.

"Gowan was not here long before he concluded that the architect's design was wholly at odds with the landscape. In one letter to his father, he described it as 'like a French nobleman in all his finery, lace and heels, stranded amidst the natural wildness of the Peaks.' He also pointed out that the new mansion was being built on the river's floodplain."

Mr. Gardiner choked back his laughter while Fitzwilliam nodded sardonically. "You may guess what happened. Mr. Darcy senior stuck stubbornly to his plans but rarely visited the place, preferring the city. The son was enamored by the more modern designs of the Italian Renaissance—Andrea Palladio, Inigo Jones and so forth. Their relations became increasingly strained. By the autumn of 1626, construction of the house was nearly complete but work was stalled by a month of heavy rains."

Realizing what was to come, Elizabeth shut her eyes and whispered, "Oh no."

"Oh yes; the River Derwent topped its banks and flooded the valley. When Grant Darcy came to view it a month later, the waters had only just receded, leaving behind a thick layer of mud everywhere. The roof and upper portions of the building had collapsed when support beams were washed away and the cellar was filled almost to the top with muck.

"Family legend has it that within an hour of his arrival, Gowan's father was back on his horse. They went directly to the nearest solicitor and Grant Darcy signed over the entire estate to his son, telling him, to 'Do what you will with the place, for I never wish to set foot here again.'

"Gowan Darcy threw himself into the project. He was able to engage Inigo Jones himself to design a house that would complement the landscape and by spring the workers had begun building the structure you see today. They salvaged much of the stone from the flooded ruin but left the foundation walls to form this sunken garden. To prevent a repeat of the flood, they enlarged the lake and raised the knoll for the new structure."

Elizabeth and the Gardiners looked around at the park surrounding Pemberley House with new eyes. The landscaping had been done with such attention to its context that the lake and its surroundings looked perfectly natural and the house, though large, seemed to balance with the surrounding peaks and woods rather than command them.

"Your ancestor did very well, indeed," murmured Elizabeth and the others added their compliments.

Though usually uncomfortable when people praised his estate, Darcy felt an unaccustomed warmth at their words. Where so many would have waxed lyrical over the mansion because of the wealth it represented, Elizabeth and her family did not truckle to him with empty tributes. They truly understood the sentiment he felt for the house and the land; a physical manifestation of his heritage that was as much a part of him as his eye color or tall stature.

Clearing his voice slightly to loosen his throat, Fitzwilliam focused on bringing the tale to its conclusion. "Being on site, Gowan Darcy was able to move along the construction much more efficiently than his father and the main building was completed within three years (it probably also helped that they used the local limestone almost exclusively). He then promptly married a local girl, Miss Margaret Manners of Haddon Hall, and they settled at Pemberley and proceeded to make the house into a home. It is said to have been a great love match— they eloped from her elder sister's wedding breakfast when she was eighteen. Her father disapproved of Gowan Darcy because he was 'rich in land but poor in everything else' and his parents disagreed with the Manners' politics."

Will chuckled— his grandmother had loved the story of Meg and Gowan Darcy and had told it often. "Naturally, the couple lived a long, blissfully happy life together and raised their eight children at Pemberley, rarely venturing beyond Derbyshire."

He turned to Elizabeth who was listening intently. "Tomorrow I hope to take you on a tour of the gallery; their portrait is one of my favorites. I would go to look at it often as a child; in the midst of all those severe paintings of my grim ancestors, they always seemed so content."

Elizabeth murmured her agreement and took his arm as the party turned and began to walk slowly back to the house. Mr. Darcy's story had affected her deeply; she felt as if she had been given a precious gift and was beginning to realize that to be Mistress of Pemberley would be something, indeed.

Mr. Darcy had said little about his parents as a couple. His memories of his mother seemed to be those of an adoring child and what little was said about his father seemed laden with a sort of distant reverence; a barely concealed desire for approval that was rarely given. The vision of young Fitzwilliam Darcy contemplating that old painting and imagining warm and loving parents made her want to hug him. It was little wonder that he had reacted so oddly to her big, bustling family

Elizabeth's thoughts returned to the present when her aunt reminded their host that the morrow would be Sunday. After some discussion, they settled on a plan to attend services at the Lambton church and Darcy offered to send a note to Mr. Jessop, inviting the rector to dinner. Mrs. Gardiner was very pleased, for though she wished to know what had happened to the people from her childhood, she hoped that the cleric would help her reconnect without devolving into unpleasant gossip.

Elizabeth listened quietly but eventually Mrs. Gardiner turned to eye her niece knowingly. "Lizzy, you must not feel required to attend us on every visit. I plan to do a great deal of reminiscing that will quickly become dull to anyone who did not share my childhood. I know that Edward plans to take the children fishing and I hope that you shall be able to find something to occupy your time, as well." The twinkle in her eyes left Elizabeth suspicious that her aunt was turning matchmaker.

"Well, dear aunt, if you do not desire my company then I suppose I might be able to find a path or two interesting enough to explore." Her smirk belied her airy tone and the others laughed, well aware that the second Miss Bennet was already itching to walk the woods and peaks that she had seen from the carriage. "And I have heard from an excellent source that Pemberley's library is among the finest in the land, for its owner is always buying books."

Darcy rolled his eyes and grumbled, "Miss Bingley has visited the estate only once, for less than a week, and spent but an instant in the library when Mrs. Reynolds gave them a tour."

"Ah, well. At least she is cognizant of its value, even if her estimation is based on a volume's purchase price rather than its content," said Elizabeth gaily. She was well pleased with her witticism when a happy giggle bubbled up from Miss Darcy. Georgiana was so pleased with the company that she was beginning to feel light-headed.

After checking their watches, it was agreed that the Darcys would take their guests on a brief tour of the first floor, ending with the library (the ground floor being dedicated to the kitchens and servants' quarters) before they all retired to dress for dinner.

Fitzwilliam guided them from the central courtyard into the north wing of the U-shaped building. He looked slightly taken aback when Georgiana commented that a proper tour should begin from the main entrance rather than a back door, but the Gardiners soon reassured him that they were perfectly pleased with his approach.

Opening one of a set of massive double doors, he waved them into a grand ballroom with windows along three walls, many opening out onto the terrace beyond. Once the Gardiners and their niece had expressed their admiration, he spoke softly. "I remember when I was a child, our parents hosted some grand balls here. I would watch from the windows of the schoolroom," he gestured toward some windows opposite. "The courtyard was lit with torches and those who were not dancing would spill outside to drink and talk in the moonlight. It was a magnificent sight."

Darcy took note of his sister listening to him with wistful eyes and reprimanded himself for not having shared more memories of their family in happier times.

When the guests were satisfied, Fitzwilliam guided the party down several halls, pointing out a large formal dining room, the red parlor, and the billiards room, among others, and eventually finding themselves back in the front foyer with its grand double staircase wrapping around above them.

Elizabeth laughed, her face full of admiration for the graceful lines of Pemberley's entrance hall. "This, I remember! I was beginning to think that I will need a ball of string in order to find my way around!"

Darcy raised his eyebrows and responded, "And do you fear finding the Minotaur roaming our halls at night?"

This quip prompted much laughter, though when Fitzwilliam led them off to explore the south wing, Elizabeth took his arm and squeezed it reassuringly. Though he had been jesting, it was still nice to know that she did not consider him to be anything like a half-man, half-bull creature searching out innocents to maul.

Walking through the south wing, Darcy showed them his study (the desk piled with ledgers and correspondence waiting to be dealt with), the mistress' study (currently uninhabited), the rose sitting room (where they had taken tea), and the music room (Georgiana's favorite). After Miss Darcy had received many compliments on the new pianoforte that her brother had given her for her birthday, Fitzwilliam guided them to a final door and opened it with a flourish. "Miss Bennet, allow me to present... our library."

Elizabeth preceded him into a room of equivalent size to Pemberley's ballroom, but with tall oak bookshelves arrayed around the room like a well-ordered regiment of soldiers.

"Oh!" she breathed. With all her concentration on the literary riches before her, Lizzy did not notice her host beaming. Her simple, unaffected enthusiasm was just what he had yearned for.

Barely hearing the keen comments from the Gardiners, Thomas Bennet's daughter walked slowly past the walls of books, running her fingertips along their spines even as her head swiveled from side to side, trying to take it all in. Several comfortable chairs were half hidden in nooks created by the arrangement of the shelves, and elsewhere there were convenient tables if one wished to spread out large monographs or examine a set of maps.

At the end of the room, Elizabeth found nirvana. A large fireplace faced with the native golden limestone was surrounded by comfortable leather settees. Several rather battered cushions and piles of books on the low table made it clear that the area was used often.

Hearing footsteps, Lizzy turned and was unsurprised to see that Darcy had followed her. Smiling up at him, she said softly, "I suspect that if we ever need to find you, this is the first place we should look."

Will returned her smile. "Perhaps you as well?"

In an easy camaraderie, he showed her how the library was organized and pointed out several books that he thought she might particularly enjoy. Lizzy restrained herself to a new volume of Dorothy Wordsworth's poetry and a copy of Hawkins' 1760 edition of the *Compleat Angler*.

Darcy grinned when he saw her pluck the latter from a shelf. "I hadn't realized that you had and particular interest in fishing."

Elizabeth smiled. "Actually, Papa would take me when I was little; with no son, he treated me as the next best thing. In fact, he recommended Charles Cotton's book to me when I told him that we would be visiting Derbyshire; he said that it was a true nature lover's description of the Peak District. I did not know that there had been a revision."

"Indeed—your father is quite right about Cotton's narration of his travels. I admit that it is an old favorite of mine; I have a copy in London that I read whenever I am longing for the country." Darcy took the book from her hand and flipped it open. "This newer edition is prefaced with a short biography of Charles Cotton by William Oldys. It is fairly well done though Oldys seems to have been more fascinated by Cotton's flair for the burlesque than his love of Derbyshire."

Fitzwilliam handed the volume back to her and their gloveless fingers brushed. His breath caught but he quickly gathered his wits and inquired, "Do you ride, Miss Bennet?"

Realizing from her raised eyebrows that his question might have sounded disconnected from the previous topic, he rushed to add, "I merely meant that, having witnessed your love of the outdoors and your interest in the written descriptions of the Peaks… there are many prospects that are too far to reach on foot and cannot be accessed by any wheeled vehicle. I would be happy to show you, or Georgiana could…"

Elizabeth smiled broadly and touched his arm. She was still unsure why such a man would be so desirous of her good opinion, but she had to admit that his occasional babbling in her presence was endearing. "Thank you, Mr. Darcy. I should very much appreciate your guidance. My sisters and I all learned to ride when we were young, but I admit that I have not sat on a horse in quite some time. Longbourn has only one palfrey in the stable— my father does not like us to ride his gelding—and old Nelly has been growing increasingly… elderly. To be honest, I feel guilty even mounting her—she groans in such agony as if she is about to collapse!"

"Well, we have several horses that might suit you. Shall I give you a tour of the stables?"

Elizabeth beamed at his boyish enthusiasm. "I should like that very much." Then she nodded toward the approaching Gardiners who were now accompanied by both Georgiana and Mrs. Reynolds. "However, I suspect that we will have to delay our outing for another day."

"Mr. Darcy?" Though phrased as a question, Mrs. Reynolds tone was one he remembered from the schoolroom.

"Ah, Mrs. Reynolds. Have I lost track of the clock again? Is it time for us to dress for dinner already?"

"Yes, sir. Cook has a special menu planned and it would be best if it is not kept sitting."

Mr. Gardiner chuckled good-naturedly. "Well friends, it sounds like we have our marching orders." He smiled at Pemberley's housekeeper. "What time are we to assemble, ma'am?"

Mrs. Reynolds pursed her lips and assumed a serious demeanor, though her eyes twinkled with amusement. "Half-past seven, sir."

With some joking, the group obediently dispersed to their rooms.

Having dressed for dinner with her usual efficiency, Elizabeth was directed by a footman to the parlor on the first floor. Her eyes betrayed her surprise when she realized that they were to dine in Pemberley's most stately dining room.

"So formal, sir? You do us great honor."

Darcy saw the question in her tease and shrugged self-consciously, explaining, "We use it so rarely… and I thought that it would be appropriate for your first dinner at Pemberley."

Not quite certain if he was using 'your' in the singular or plural sense of the word, Elizabeth blushed slightly. In a flash, the import of her visit struck her. The man standing before her wished to spend his life with her... of all the ladies he must have met in London and beyond, he had chosen her... fallen in love with *her*.

For Elizabeth could no longer doubt that the gentleman was deeply, ardently in love with her; a love that encompassed both passion and friendship, just as she had always dreamed. She sighed and a little shiver ran through her when she realized that they had been staring silently at one another for several moments.

Before either could say anything, the Gardiners were led in by Miss Darcy. After some easy conversation about the comfort of their chambers and satisfaction with the care being shown to their children, dinner was signaled. Mrs. Gardiner moved cunningly to her husband's side and, taking his arm, she was pleased to see Mr. Darcy obediently offer his own to his sister and Elizabeth.

They were served with all the pomp and circumstance possible for a party of five, none of whom had much preference for the pretensions of formal dining in general. It was clear that Pemberley's staff, having been without their master for some months, were eager to please. The food was superb, wine glasses were kept full as if by magic, and, when the dessert course was brought out, both Darcys sighed with contentment.

The guests began laughing as the siblings eagerly examined the dishes; Georgiana colored slightly but it was a sign of her comfort in their company that she also managed to smile.

Fitzwilliam grinned widely, showing his dimples. "You may laugh all you like but I shall not apologize for our eagerness. Our cook knows that shortcake with strawberries and cream is our favorite."

Georgiana added. "It is a simple, country dish but I am convinced that there are no better berries on Earth than those at Pemberley." She took a bite and sighed with contentment.

Moving his spoon towards Elizabeth's plate, Darcy offered puckishly, "I would be happy to eat your portion if you don't want it."

Laughing, the young lady slapped away his hand. "Oh no, your assistance is quite unnecessary, sir." With one eyebrow raised, she brought her hands protectively over the dish. "And do not forget that I have four sisters; I am well practiced in defending my sweets, Mr. Darcy!"

The dinner ended in good humor, the guests easily agreeing with the Darcys' assessment of the dessert. The evening ended soon after. The travelers were tired from their time on the road and Darcy was feeling the effects of his morning's travails. Although both he and Elizabeth had separately expected to lay awake thinking of the other, both fell asleep (also separately) within moments of their head touching the pillow.

Sunday passed quietly. After breakfast, the party divided among two carriages and made the scenic drive to Lambton. At Mrs. Gardiner's inquiry, Darcy admitted that Pemberley's chapel was currently vacant. "Mr. Venton passed away last year and I was not satisfied with any of the candidates who applied for the position." Seeing the question in Elizabeth's eyes, he explained further.

"Our family supports a rector at Lambton and a vicar in Kympton, a small market town to the north of the estate that you have not yet seen. There is also a chapel associated with Pemberley House. However, the curate there occupies such an intimate position within the household that I am perhaps over-careful in my requirements for a replacement." He shrugged helplessly but the other occupants of the carriage expressed their approval.

Madeleine spoke with authority; "That sounds like a perfectly reasonable course of action. You are absolutely correct; it is one thing to take on a cleric for the local parish, and another entirely to invite a stranger in who will be ministering to your servants and staff every Sunday, often without your presence."

Fitzwilliam appreciated her reassurance and was happier than ever that he had had the opportunity to become acquainted with the Gardiners. He could easily understand why Elizabeth loved them so.

After the carriage stopped at a pretty, well-kept stone church and they were handed down, Elizabeth noticed several wagons with servants that she recognized. When she questioned him, Darcy explained that arrangements had been made for the staff to be transported to town for services until a new curate was found for the Pemberley chapel. He shrugged modestly when she praised his thoughtfulness.

"They can return in the wagon directly after services, or a second is sent out at five so that those who wish to visit family or so forth can stay the day. It is nearly eight miles back to the main house; when I was a boy, I used to race my cousins to the horse chestnut tree on the green," he grinned in remembrance. "I decided that I shouldn't expect that from some of our older staff, however."

Elizabeth grinned. "Distances are rather different here. At Longbourn, it is but a few minutes to walk to the church; even Mama would not consider calling for the carriage. And of course we girls think nothing of walking in to Meryton, as you are well aware."

Darcy smiled but his sister approached with the Gardiner children before he could reply. Elizabeth turned to the younger woman. "Miss Darcy; you have become quite a favorite, it appears!"

Little Amelia tugged on her cousin's skirt to get her attention. "Lizzy! Lizzy—look! Miss Darcy let me wear her hair ribbons! Aren't they pretty?"

Elizabeth was just agreeing when Mrs. Gardiner appeared at their side, taking charge of her flock with the easy composure of an experienced mother. "Now Amelia, we are about to go to church. What does the bible say about little girls fishing for compliments?"

The youngest Miss Gardiner scrunched her face in serious concentration for a moment before brightening. "But Mama, I wasn't being vain... I was telling Lizzy of Miss Darcy's great sacrifice!"

The little girl stumbled over the last word but it only made her sincerity more adorable. Her mother swept her up and kissed her forehead. "My dear girl, I stand corrected."

In good spirits, the group walked the short distance to the church. As the foremost members of the congregation, Mr. Darcy and his sister were greeted with respect and his party eyed with curiosity. Elizabeth decided that Lambton was not so different from Meryton after all. Among the strangers filing into the pews, she easily recognized characters that she suspected were quite similar to those she knew in her home county.

When the congregation had settled and the Darcys and their guests taken their seats in the front row, Mr. Jessop stepped to the pulpit and proceeded to deliver his sermon on the importance of practicing daily kindness to one's neighbors. "For, though generosity in times of great catastrophe is certainly necessary and appreciated, we must remember that the little kindnesses that are practiced each day, to neighbor and stranger alike, may have an even greater impact."

The sermon was relatively short but it was obvious that the congregation listened closely to the elderly cleric and considered his words with great respect. Elizabeth was impressed and said so to Mr. Darcy when the service was concluded.

Pemberley's master nodded seriously. "Mr. Jessop is an excellent man and I shall be very sorry when he decides to retire, a time I fear is approaching. My father appointed him to the living soon after the epidemic that took Reverend Jonathan (Mrs. Gardiner's father) and so many others. When the bishop heard of the tragedy our neighborhood had suffered, he recognized that some young, inexperienced curate would not be adequate to the task. Apparently Mr. Jessop was an old friend of the bishop and agreed to come north from his own parish in Devon."

Mrs. Gardiner spoke from behind them. "That was a wise decision. Having lost so many, I can only imagine how much the melancholy must have weighed on the survivors."

Darcy nodded seriously, thinking of his father. After that terrible summer, George Darcy had fallen into a depression and never really revived.

Seeing that they had reached the front steps where the reverend himself was farewelling a parishioner, Fitzwilliam gestured them forward. "Please, allow me to introduce you."

After exchanging greetings with Mr. Jessop and sincerely complimenting his sermon, Elizabeth stepped back and listened as her aunt eagerly conversed with the man who had assumed her father's pulpit. As they spoke of people Lizzy had never met, her attention turned inward.

More than ever, Elizabeth was fascinated by the many sides to Mr. Darcy; he seemed like a precious gem in that the more she studied him, the more facets she discovered to be admired. She smiled to herself at the fancy; it was not a wholly accurate metaphor for he was not a hard man, whatever she had thought upon their earliest acquaintance.

She was impressed by his obvious consideration for the other parishioners; he had waited patiently while an elderly woman finished speaking with Mr. Jessop, unlike many of his position who would have taken their precedence for granted. When his turn came, his respect for the older man had been obvious as he greeted the Reverend and then presented the Gardiners.

At that moment, Mr. Darcy looked every inch the Master of Pemberley, acknowledging other churchgoers and listening carefully to two men who seemed to be discussing the need for maintenance along some local road. Yet, with little effort Elizabeth could also see the young man, very isolated since the death of his parents but determined to do all in his power to meet his responsibilities.

Elizabeth watched as a dark brown curl flopped down the gentleman's forehead and he brushed it away absently. She suddenly wished that she could tuck it behind his ear and run her hand through those wavy locks; a vision of what he might look like when he had just woken up in the morning, hair mussed and face not yet troubled by his many duties, shimmered into her mind.

Elizabeth blushed and turned to look out across the cemetery. She was struck by her intense desire to protect this man, to make him happy, to give and return his love.

She loved him. Had the sky been suddenly filled with fireworks, Lizzy would not have noticed; the fireworks in her heart were far brighter than those any black powder could manage and the revelations in her mind were equally dazzling.

When they had resumed their acquaintance in London, Elizabeth had worried that her feelings might only be a sort of gratitude; a reaction to the great compliment she felt at such a man's continued attentions as well as his assistance after her attack in the park. Once she had finally put away her old prejudices, she had easily recognized that his looks and intellect attracted her. However, it was only when she had seen him on his beautiful grounds at Pemberley that her heart had truly recognized its other half.

Hearing footsteps behind her, Elizabeth smiled and turned, unsurprised to see Mr. Darcy.

For a moment, Will forgot what he had been about to say; the soft look in Elizabeth's eyes was one he had never beheld there before. However, before either might speak, Amelia and Tommy appeared at their cousin's elbow.

"Lizzy! Have you met Mr. Jessop? He's coming to dinner, did you know? He's a very nice man—he knew our grandpapa, did you know?"

Allowing the children to draw them back to the group, Elizabeth and Fitzwilliam shared a resigned smile and thought contentedly of the coming weeks. With Elizabeth staying at Pemberley, they had every hope of spending time together.

The remainder of the morning was spent introducing the children to their mother's childhood home. As Mr. Jessop guided them to the parsonage, they passed the cemetery. Mrs. Gardiner paused briefly at the gate but acknowledged to her husband that she was not yet ready to visit the graves of her parents and siblings so soon after sitting in the church where she had listened to her father preach so often.

Mr. Jessop kindly took them all to his home and served tea. Though it was early in the day for cake, he could see that his predecessor's daughter could use a bit of comfort and he knew from experience that the two Darcys would never turn down a sweet. After discussing the neighborhood for some time, Mrs. Gardiner was able to show her children the room that she had shared with her sister and the garden in which she had played as a girl.

It was well past noon when they all climbed back in the carriages and returned to Pemberley. The adults were quiet and the children caught their mood. Little Amelia fell asleep, cuddled in her mother's arms and both were comforted by the contact.

After a cold dinner, the afternoon was spent in quiet conversation and reading. Neither the Darcys nor the Gardiners were excessively religious, but obeying the Sabbath seemed appropriate to all that day.

Fitzwilliam woke on Monday morning full of plans but one look out of the window made him grimace. He had hoped to tempt Elizabeth out for a walk that day, but a heavy rain had begun falling during the night and showed no sign of letting up.

After breaking his fast, Darcy received a note from his steward regarding some estate business that could not be delayed. Before retreating to his study, he apologized to his guests but they waved him off. Mrs. Gardiner was eagerly looking forward to spending some time with Mrs. Reynolds looking through Pemberley's attics for some old trunks of her parents' belongings; the housekeeper believed they had been stored there after the parsonage was cleared for Mr. Jessop. Mr. Gardiner was pleased to spend some time with his children and Miss Darcy happily claimed his niece as her companion for the morning.

It took several hours, but Darcy eventually finished the most critical paperwork and then went searching for his guests... for one particular guest, if he was to be honest.

Taking a guess, he made his way to the music room and was rewarded by the sound of laughter even before he stepped through the doorway. His heart was warmed by the sight that met his eyes. Elizabeth was seated with his mother's violin and Georgiana appeared to be giving her instruction. Or had been. Currently both were giggling so hard that tears were forming in their eyes.

"Ladies, am I interrupting?"

Georgiana's eyes goggled when she caught sight of her brother watching them from the doorway. She squeaked, then covered her mouth with her hands and looked toward Elizabeth. That lady's laughing eyes only prompted Miss Darcy to collapse back into giggles.

Miss Bennet shook her head in mock disapproval of the girl before carefully setting aside the violin and bow. "Yes, Mr. Darcy, you are interrupting, but it does not necessarily follow that such an interruption is unwelcome." She quirked an eyebrow at Georgiana, eyes twinkling. "I have been entertaining your sister with my exemplary musical skills."

Darcy's eyes were warm and he stepped toward her, unable to keep his distance. "I did not know that you played the violin." He looked sharply at Georgiana when his sister burst into fresh peals of laughter. Seeing that he would get no answer from that direction, he turned back to Elizabeth who rolled her eyes.

"I do not, but your sister very kindly offered to instruct me." She reached to run her fingers across the strings, creating a soft ripple of sound. "It is a truly beautiful instrument, though."

Georgiana began to regain some of her composure. "Oh, Wills, I am sorry. Elizabeth was just telling me a story about..." Suddenly she recalled herself and looked back to Miss Bennet, who rolled her eyes again.

"It's all right, Georgiana. Your brother has had the very great pleasure of seeing my cousin for himself." She turned back to the gentlemen and spoke with heavy emphasis, "Mr. Collins."

Darcy pretended to look for someone hiding behind a settee. "Here?"

As Georgiana gaped at the sight of her brother making such a joke, Elizabeth smiled broadly, pleased to see him display his wit openly. "Thankfully not, although I am sure that he would be on the first post chaise from Kent should he hear that you were inquiring after him."

Fitzwilliam pretended to cringe in horror and moved closer to Elizabeth, motioning for her to sit and joining her on the settee.

Attempting to keep her mind off his proximity, Elizabeth spoke quickly; "Actually, I've just received a letter from my sister."

"And is your family well?"

She smiled. "Exceptionally well. It seems that Mr. Bingley has been calling at Longbourn with great regularity."

"I am very glad to hear it." The two shared a warm look of understanding.

"Have you not heard from your friend?"

"I…"

Whatever Mr. Darcy was about to say was cut off by a loud crash from the next room. Elizabeth leapt to her feet and followed him to a different door than that which opened to the hall. Seeing little more than darkness beyond, Lizzy stepped back into the music room in order to retrieve a small lamp. Holding the light aloft in the darkened room, Elizabeth could now recognize Mrs. Darcy's rose sitting room, although its condition was vastly different from the last time she had been there. Apparently, some leak from above had weakened the plaster and now most of the ceiling had fallen in a gray, dusty mess all over the furniture and floor.

"Bloody hell," Darcy breathed. Suddenly realizing that he had spoken aloud, Will glanced back and colored slightly at the sight of Elizabeth and his sister. "Please pardon my profanity… it is just that I thought we had this leaky pipe fixed last fall but it appears to have weakened the plaster again. Georgiana—will you call for Mrs. Reynolds, please?"

Miss Darcy disappeared at once and Fitzwilliam gingerly made his way across the room to another door that was well camouflaged in the woodwork and wallpaper. Elizabeth followed him with the light and they carefully climbed up a narrow staircase that hugged tight to the wall of the house. When they reached a small landing, Will opened a simple door to the left and she followed, taking note that the stairs continued spiraling upwards.

Stepping into what appeared to be an unused lady's dressing room, Elizabeth lit another lamp with the one she held in her hand as Darcy examined some dampness on the floor and wall. After thanking her when she handed the second light to him, Fitzwilliam spoke absently.

"My grandfather installed a system of cisterns on the roof to collect rain water which is then piped down to basins in the primary apartments, supplemented as necessary from water pumped up from a well. He was a great believer in regular bathing and it was much more convenient than having the servants running up and down the stairs from the kitchen each time water was needed. Unfortunately, one of the pipes developed a crack last winter. I thought that it had been repaired but it appears as if the entire section shall have to be replaced."

While Fitzwilliam looked through a disguised door into the large closet set up for a lady's maid, Elizabeth opened a larger door to the left and stepped through. Holding the lamp high, she caught her breath at the sight. It was certainly the largest bedchamber she had ever seen, but its size was made comfortable by the presence of large windows along two walls and a pleasant sitting area formed around the fireplace on a third.

Elizabeth had just noticed the cabbage rose wallpaper (so similar to the sitting room below) when she felt Darcy come to stand just behind her.

"This was my mother's room." He spoke quietly but his deep voice vibrated with feeling.

Elizabeth turned to meet his eyes and shivered at the intensity in them. "'Tis a beautiful apartment." She moved slightly and her shoulder brushed against his chest. Suddenly she was keenly aware of his proximity.

Blinking, Fitzwilliam spoke breathlessly, "Father had all of her things packed up or given away after she died. I barely recognize it." Unconsciously, he shifted forward ever so slightly so that her upper arm was lightly pressed against his chest. The color in her cheeks told him as much about her feelings as the fact that she did not move away. All thoughts of leaky pipes disappeared from his mind.

"Elizabeth…" he whispered as his hand came to rest at her waist.

Looking deep into his eyes, Lizzy felt the heat of passion flash through her body, from her scalp to her toes. "Will…" she breathed and her hand rose to touch his cheek. He turned his head slightly and kissed her palm.

He gently pulled her closer as his eyes flickered between her mouth and her eyes. Elizabeth was just about to go up on tiptoes to meet his lips when a most unfortunate thing happened.

"Mr. Darcy? Are you there, sir?" The sound of Mrs. Reynolds' voice brought both back to reality in an instant and they jumped apart like a pair of frightened rabbits.

Fitzwilliam gulped a breath and closed his eyes tightly for a moment, desperately trying to pull his wits together. With an apologetic look to Elizabeth, he stepped back into the dressing room and called to his housekeeper, voice rough with emotion barely under control.

"Yes, Mrs. Reynolds. We were just checking for water damage in Mother's old chambers." He cleared his voice slightly. "It looks like the same pipe is leaking in the same spot. Have you sent for Mr. Jenson?"

The older woman reached the top of the stairs and looked around, seeing everything. "I will do so immediately, sir, although he may not be here until later tomorrow. I heard that he was working at Haddon Hall this past week when their own man fell ill."

Darcy gestured to the ceiling of the closet which also showed signs of water damage. "As long as he comes tomorrow. I'm afraid that most of the plasterwork shall have to be redone, as well."

Mrs. Reynolds nodded and after a last look around, she moved to the stairs, followed by her master and his guest. With her back turned, she commented, "It is lucky then that we did not bother much with redecorating the mistress' chambers when the dressing room was replastered last September. 'Tis a clean slate for some nice girl to make her own."

Fitzwilliam very nearly missed the next step.

Darcy and Elizabeth were still flushed when they entered the music room behind Mrs. Reynolds to find the Gardiners with Georgiana. After discussing what needed to be done immediately so as to minimize further damage, the housekeeper excused herself and headed toward the door.

Just before she departed, however, Mrs. Reynolds called over her shoulder, "If you ask me, that ceiling falling 'tis a sign from God; Pemberley is in want of a new mistress." And with that pronouncement, the venerable housekeeper sailed out of the room, leaving behind several people stifling their laughter and one couple blushing deeply.

18 YES

Mr. Darcy was in a dither. He had very nearly *kissed* Elizabeth. While that event in itself would not have been a bad thing (indeed, he had fantasized about it for months), he was not at all certain that she would not have flayed him alive had he done so without first gaining her permission.

She had not moved away from him, but was that merely a symptom of her passionate nature? He did not want to seduce her (honestly, he was not exactly certain that he could). He wanted her love. He wanted to marry her. He wanted to lock them both in his bedroom for several weeks together, alone. Preferably all in that order, although the ungentlemanly part of his brain that seemed to control his nether regions would occasionally argue that the order of the last two items was not necessarily set in stone. Of course, the educated, civilized part of his mind that had spent the last two decades desperately trying to stamp out any behavior bearing similarity to George Wickham would immediately dismiss such a suggestion (though not quite as successfully in his dreams as in his conscious mind).

Regardless, he was absolutely certain that *something* needed to be done. *Immediately.*

The morning after the ceiling fell in the rose sitting room, Fitzwilliam rose early, hoping to catch Miss Bennet at breakfast and perhaps entice her out for a walk in the park so that he might discover her feelings. However, it seemed as if everything was conspiring against him. No sooner had Elizabeth set foot in the breakfast room than a footman arrived with a message that the steward needed the master urgently.

With an apologetic look to the lady, Darcy dutifully left for his study but it took only a brief conversation with Timmons to quash any hope for a quick solution. A driver trying to reach the Manchester road had attempted a shortcut by crossing on a narrow bridge close to the Pemberley's boundary. The cart had come too close to the edge and now the whole rig

JEAN SIMS

was teetering on the brink with one wheel resting on nothing but air and a mule team that could do no more than keep it from slipping further.

"I apologize for calling you away from your guests, sir, but when Jack O'Meara came across him, the driver positively refused any help— said his boy was running to a cousin's but then wouldn't say who the cousin was. O'Meara thinks there's something dodgy about him."

Knowing Pemberley's old gamekeeper had good instincts about people, Darcy grimaced. "Very well, Timmons. Gather some men and let's see what he's about. Have my horse saddled and brought around— I'll just tell Mrs. Reynolds what's happening."

When Darcy and his men reached the bridge, he was not impressed by the man who stepped forward and immediately began to harangue Pemberley's gamekeeper. "I told you there was no need to go to the big house, you old fool! My boy's gone to fetch my cousin's team— I don't need no other help!"

Darcy eyed the two mules straining in their harness and the cart which, to his eye, was slung rather low for the load of hay it appeared to carry. He spoke quietly to his steward before stepping forward to address teamster.

"Sir," he interrupted. "We have not been introduced. I am Fitzwilliam Darcy, owner of this estate.

The man turned to him, having not yet noticed the gentleman and Darcy caught a flicker of fear in his expression. With a strained smile, he bowed, tugging his forelock. "Mr. Darcy, of course. I didn't realize that the family was at home, sir. I'm surprised you'd bother coming out for such a minor concern."

"Everything at Pemberley is my concern, Mr....?"

"Errr... Black, sir. Name's John Black. Not from these parts, sir. Just been visiting some relations and now we're headed back home."

"Indeed, that does not surprise me at all, Mr. Black. This road is rarely used by anyone who isn't local, and *we* all know the bridge isn't wide enough for most vehicles." Darcy gestured to a well-worn track leading down to a ford less than ten yards downstream.

Mr. Black looked as if he had been forced to suck on a lemon. Before he could answer, however, John Timmons called to his master from the cart. The driver's face flushed with anger and not a little alarm. "How dare you! You've no right to go poking around my property!"

When Darcy looked over the side, he was not greatly surprised to see bags of coal that had been hidden under the hay. With a nod of approval to his man, Pemberley's master turned back to the driver with a stern look. "Mr. Black (or whatever your name is): I shall ask you this only once before I have you bound and sent off to the magistrate in Kympton. Where is the coal from, sir?"

All the man's bravado collapsed and he looked as if he was about to fall

262

on his knees. Before he might begin his confession, however, two things happened in rapid succession. First, Darcy's men managed to shift the wagon's weight enough that the mule team were able to pull it back onto the bridge. Second, a man and a boy came cantering up the road on a second pair of mules.

The rider began bellowing even before he had his feet on the ground. "What the devil have you done now, Johnny Blake? I swear to God, I'll not be bailing you out of any more scrapes, married to my wife's poor sister or not!"

"You said I could have a bit of coal as well as the hay, Pete," protested Mr. Blake (formerly known as Black) weakly.

"Aye, a bit I said! Not my whole store!" Suddenly Pete recognized the gentleman standing by the wagon. "Oh, God blind me— Mr. Darcy, sir. I didn't see you, sir." Shutting his eyes in mortification, the man bowed low. "I'm Harris, sir. Pete Harris. I work in the Fernilee colliery, sir; my family rents one of your cottages in Horwich by the Goyt."

Darcy was beginning to feel a bit better about the situation. "I am glad to meet you, Mr. Harris. This is your brother-in-law?"

"Well, I guess we are that, sir. Our families are close so we've always called each other cousins, even before we married the Barker sisters. He's not a bad one, Mr. Darcy, just going through a rough patch. He lost his job when the mill at Ashbourne burned and came to see if I knew of any work. He's got three boys as well as the lad there, and his wife's been real sick, like."

"As far as I'm concerned, Mr. Harris, this matter is between you and Mr. Blake. I assume you don't want to call the magistrate?"

"Oh stars no, Mr. Darcy. I'll show him the rough side of my tongue on the way back to Horwich, right enough, and watch him like a hawk to see he doesn't run off with something else that's not his, but I don't want him locked up or nothing. He's a good worker, sir, just needs someone to keep him on the straight and narrow, like."

Darcy nodded, satisfied that the matter was well in hand. "Very good, Mr. Harris. Mr. Timmons?" He looked over to catch his steward's eye. "Do we know of any work that Mr. Blake might qualify for?"

Timmons rubbed his chin and considered the matter. "As a matter of fact, I'd advise he try the canal office at Whaley— I heard they're looking to hire on more muleskinners for the locks."

Harris thanked him sincerely, looking relieved and slapping his cousin's shoulder with a little more force than necessary, but even Blake looked a little less frightened. The extra mules hitched up and the cart turned around, this time using the ford. Timmons sent the Pemberley workmen on their way while Darcy thanked O'Meara for his diligence.

Although Fitzwilliam would have returned directly to the house (and

Elizabeth) had he only himself to please, they were near the Greene's farm and it seemed only right that they should check on progress clearing the burnt cottage. Once there, Darcy was drawn into a discussion about whether it might be better to build the new cottage on a different site, slightly uphill from the. original. By the time he was able to get away, he returned to Pemberley House with barely enough time to wash and change for luncheon.

The midday meal was a pleasant affair. Elizabeth and Mr. Gardiner had taken advantage of the fine weather to explore the gardens with the children. Georgiana and Mrs. Gardiner had many stories to tell after spending several hours poking around in the attics; Miss Darcy had become quite fascinated by all the relics of her ancestors that were stored there and the older woman was clearly happy to spend time with the daughter of her mother's friend.

Best of all, they had discovered a trunk tucked away years before with things salvaged from the parsonage before Mr. Jessop had moved in. Much had been burnt for fear of contagion, but the few mementos which remained brought tears to Mrs. Gardiner's eyes; several books (including her father's bible), a pendant of her mother's inherited from that lady's grandmother, and Rebecca Churchill's notebooks, filled with mathematical derivations and notes on their publication.

However, all of these had faded in importance when Jonathan and Rebecca's daughter discovered a flat, rectangular object carefully wrapped in clean rags. When she had freed it from its covering, the normally calm mother of four had sat down on the floor and wept, for it contained a painting of her parents and the four children, posed before the parsonage on a sunny day with roses blooming on the arbor; a painting by Lady Anne Darcy.

Clutching the canvas as if it were the most precious thing on Earth, Mrs. Gardiner had immediately gone to find her husband and children. She was finally able to introduce her sons and daughters to their grandparents and her beloved husband to his in-laws. Later, in private, she admitted to Edward that she had begun to forget what their dear faces looked like and had feared facing their graves with such guilt.

By luncheon, Madeleine had recovered enough to tell some merry stories from her childhood and by the end of the meal, Mr. and Mrs. Gardiner declared their intention to drive into Lambton that afternoon and visit the cemetery. The children would be resting and Elizabeth, sensing that her aunt preferred to visit her family's graves this first time with only her husband, indicated her preference to remain at Pemberley to write letters and perhaps explore the library.

After they waved the Gardiners off in a curricle, Georgiana gave her brother a pointed look and announced that she would be spending the afternoon at her lessons. Finding himself agreeably alone with Miss Bennet, Fitzwilliam was just about to ask if he might join her in the library when, much to his irritation, another footman arrived to inform him that he was needed. However, upon hearing that Mr. Jenson had arrived to assess the plumbing problems, Darcy knew that he could not ignore the summons.

Sighing, he turned to Elizabeth. "Miss Bennet, please excuse me." Her understanding smile went only so far toward appeasing him.

Even in his impatient state, it was nearly two hours before Darcy was free to go in search of his favorite guest. The discussion with Jenson had begun with a short list of required repairs but had rapidly escalated to advances that had been made in plumbing since Darcy's grandfather had installed the facilities nearly fifty years before. After poking around the exposed pipes in the walls and ceilings, they had climbed to the roof to inspect the cisterns that captured and stored the rainwater.

Darcy was always interested in modernizing Pemberley and found the craftsman's suggestions fascinating. However, on this occasion his desire to return to a certain guest was greater and he finally detached himself, leaving Timmons to see to the man and requesting a full proposal be prepared for his perusal.

After a quick stop in his chambers to clean up, Fitzwilliam was finally free to seek out Elizabeth. However, after checking the library, music room, and sitting room without discovering the lady, he began to feel as though he was in a romantic novel in which the author would never quite allow the hero and heroine enough time alone to reach an understanding.

By the time Will met his housekeeper in the hallway, he was done with disguise. "Mrs. Reynolds, do you have any idea where Miss Bennet might be?"

The servant's lips twitched at the half-petulant, half-eager expression on her master's face. "Yes, sir. I believe that the young lady left for a walk but a few minutes ago. I thought she might appreciate the prospect from the old stone footbridge by the willows, so I recommended that she walk around the lake towards the south woods."

Darcy's face broke into a broad smile and he impulsively kissed the older woman's cheek before turning toward the front door and calling over his shoulder, "Thank you, Mrs. Reynolds! You are a treasure!"

Standing on the front steps, Will shielded his eyes from the afternoon sun and studied the distance. Catching a flash of color from between the trees, he smiled to himself and took off at a quick pace along a tack that would intercept her.

It was lucky for Elizabeth that she noticed the gentleman well before they met, for her composure might not have survived had the focus of her thoughts appeared unexpectedly before her. As it was, she blushed when he kissed her ungloved hand and averted her eyes when he straightened to look her full in the face. Preferring to walk, she tugged his hand slightly and he fell in at her side without argument. "And how was your morning, Mr. Darcy?"

As they strolled along the edge of the lake, Elizabeth encouraged him to speak of the encounter with Mr. Blake.

When he described the happy resolution, she became serious. "You did well to attend to the problem yourself."

Embarrassed, Fitzwilliam attempted to brush it aside. "I did no more than any estate owner would have done."

Elizabeth turned and, arms akimbo, looked him sternly in the eye. "No, sir. I am quite certain that my own father would never have left his study. Had this man been honest and his cart damaged, you would have assisted him, would you not?"

At Darcy's nod, she turned abruptly and began walking again, arm gestures displaying the strength of her emotions. "Papa would have avoided getting involved at all cost, and most likely made the man's misfortune into a joke."

Fitzwilliam was becoming uncomfortable, uncertain what had prompted the lady's critique against her father. "Miss Elizabeth…"

Elizabeth sighed and touched his arm. "Forgive me, Mr. Darcy. I am out of sorts this afternoon; I was reading some letters and the contrast to your devotion to your responsibilities was striking."

Rapidly sorting through what she had said, Will ventured a question. "Has something happened at Longbourn?"

Lizzy shrugged. "Nothing out of the ordinary. Charlotte— Mrs. Collins— wrote that her father had mentioned a certain ford is in need of repair. Technically it is in common land just beyond Longbourn's border, but the Bennets have always taken responsibility for its maintenance. We had a very wet spring and a flood washed out the gravel to the point that it is unsafe for horse or wheel." She sighed.

Something tickled the edge of Darcy's mind. "How is it that Mrs. Collins came to write of this to you?"

Elizabeth smiled sardonically. "It has always been so with us. Even as mayor, Sir Lucas was often too genial to press any of his neighbors and I am one of the few who has any influence over my father." She sighed again. "And if it is unlikely that I can cajole him to do it, then I simply arrange to have the work done and inform him of it after the fact. However, I have not been home very much this spring."

The couple walked quietly for some minutes as Fitzwilliam considered all that Elizabeth had said and intimated. He was amazed; every time he thought he understood her, she revealed a new dimension. Although he had observed Mr. Bennet's unenthusiastic attitude toward his estate, he had not realized quite how lackadaisical the man was, nor what an active role his second daughter took in counteracting her father's carelessness.

After thinking for several moments, Will turned to Elizabeth with an intent look and inquired, "What do you know of indoor plumbing, Miss Bennet?"

The lady laughed and admitted that she had overseen much of the installation of a new plumbing system at Longbourn several years before. Improvements at the Gardiners' house in London had caught her mother's eye and, after a month of near constant nagging, Mr. Bennet had finally capitulated. Unfortunately, he had done little other than sign the contract with the craftsman. Fearing the repercussions of a poor job, eighteen-year-old Elizabeth had stepped in and done her best to oversee the work in her father's name, writing to her uncle with questions when she needed information.

Darcy found himself eagerly explaining Pemberley's existing system and discussing the possibilities that Jenson had suggested. The pair entered into an energetic conversation that lasted until the path turned and broke from the forest.

Elizabeth stopped in mid-sentence and clapped her hands together. "Oh, how lovely!" Before them was a picturesque stone bridge that arched over a babbling brook, framed by two enormous willows.

The lady stepped to the center of the bridge and looked out upon the prospect with awe. The lake before Pemberley House currently reflected blue sky and puffy white clouds, making it appear that the edifice of creamy limestone was floating on an island in the sky.

Darcy's feet might still be on the ground, but emotionally the sight of his beloved standing so had launched his head into the clouds. "Elizabeth…" he barely breathed her name but she heard him. Their eyes met and Will saw more affection and trust in them than he had ever dared hope for.

She held her hand out and without seeming to move, he was by her side, looking into her eyes and cradling her hand as if it were the most precious thing on Earth. "Elizabeth… I… do you…" He felt too much to articulate the questions he was desperate to ask.

Fortunately, she knew precisely what he needed to hear. Bringing their clasped hands to rest on his chest, she touched his cheek, running her finger lightly against his skin.

His face seemed on fire where she touched him and he leaned closer. "Elizabeth?"

For a moment, she closed her eyes and tucked her chin. Had her hand not remained on his cheek, he might have been concerned. As it was, his patience was rewarded when, a second later, her sparkling eyes met his.

"You are the best man I have ever known."

"Do you… dare I ask…"

JEAN SIMS

Elizabeth smiled brilliantly though her eyes were glassy with unshed tears. "Do I love you? Oh yes… so much that I do not know how I could not always have felt so." Her eyes traced the features of his face. "My heart is so full that I feel I shall burst with happiness. I can only pray that your affections and wishes are unchanged."

After a moment of stunned immobility, Darcy expressed himself as sensibly and warmly as a man violently in love can be expected to do. Drawing her into the circle of his arms, he kissed her hair, her forehead, her cheek, again and again, as he had longed to do for months.

Leaning away, his eyes were drawn to her slightly parted lips but he feared that once he tasted their sweetness, he would never remember to ask the question that promised so much happiness for them both. "My love for you has only grown… the feelings I spoke of in Kent seem like such pale things in hindsight. My heart recognized its other half, but I did not know you… or myself… well enough to know what true love felt like."

Taking her hands in his own, Will knelt before her. "Elizabeth Bennet, I love you more than life itself and I cannot imagine going through this world without you at my side to share it… in good times and bad, in sickness and health. Will you grant me the very great honor of being your husband?"

By now, tears were running freely down Elizabeth's cheeks but she paid them no mind. "Dearest Fitzwilliam… the honor would be mine." She tugged at their joined hands until he rose to stand before her again. The look of heartfelt delight that diffused over his face became him and she pulled her hands from his grip so that she might rest them on his chest.

"My dearest, loveliest Elizabeth…" was all Will could say before brushing her lips with his own. Tender kisses grew heated as their passion flared and soon he could feel her hands around his neck and in his hair as his own wrapped around his waist and pressed her to him.

There was no telling how long their ardor might have lasted had not a pair of geese suddenly erupted into flight almost beneath their feet. As it was, the splashes and honking surprised the couple greatly; Elizabeth nearly leapt away from the low stone wall she had come to lean against, though Darcy would not let her leave the circle of his arms.

When they realized the cause of the disturbance, both blushed and Elizabeth giggled. "Are all of your wildlife such good chaperones, sir?"

Fitzwilliam spoke before thinking; "I sincerely hope not." Then he blushed even redder and Elizabeth's peals of laughter rang though the woods. Still somewhat stunned by the volatility of their combined passions, he took several deep breaths and attempted to bring himself under better regulation.

As much as he might like to go directly to Mr. Gardiner and present their new understanding, he knew that he was not currently fit to be seen in company. Looking more carefully at Elizabeth, he realized that she was in no state to be returned to her relatives, either. Her lips were kissed red and swollen and, though he could not remember doing it, her hair had been loosened from its pins and the maid's careful work was threatening to tumble down her back.

Elizabeth noted the direction of his eyes and reached up to discover what had caught his attention. Stepping back and turning away, she blushed slightly and began removing her hairpins. Fitzwilliam stooped to retrieve one that had fallen to the ground and then watched wide-eyed as her long chestnut curls fell down her back unbound.

"I had no idea your hair was so long," he said breathlessly.

Setting the pins on the stone ledge and using her fingers to comb out the tangles before beginning to re-braid it, Elizabeth responded, "Oh yes, I finally had to cut some inches off after Christmas. It was getting so heavy that it hurt my head when I put it up. And in summer it is so hot… I began to think of cutting it much shorter."

Fitzwilliam reached out to brush a loose curl behind her ear. "Please don't."

With an amused but affectionate look at him, Elizabeth proceeded to pin up her hair in a simple style she often favored for precisely the reason that she could manage it herself without need for a maid. "Very well, if that is your wish, sir."

As much as he wished to remain in their current position (or resume the previous one), Will recognized that they had a better chance of remaining relatively chaste if they were walking. Looking about him, he chose a direction and offered Elizabeth his arm. Accepting it, she rested her head on his shoulder for a moment before stepping off and leaving the lovely bridge behind them.

They strolled in silence for some minutes, hearts too full to speak. The path led them to a picturesque lane that curved through some woods and Darcy explained that it was little used but for some of the estate's groundskeepers and foresters.

Ambling along the track arm-in-arm, Fitzwilliam's mind had moved beyond the initial amazement that she had accepted him and begun to plan. Should he leave immediately for Longbourn to finalize their engagement with Mr. Bennet, or might he indulge himself by enjoying Elizabeth's company at Pemberley for the remainder of her visit, though it was not quite proper for him to do so?

While Fitzwilliam was busy arranging their lives, Elizabeth turned to him and spoke but the only part of her pert inquiry that he could focus on was the ending. "Is that how it is, Mr. Darcy?"

"Will you not call me by my Christian name, love?" She had long done so in his dreams and he hungered to hear the syllables pass her lips. She directed a teasing smile at him.

"Shall I call you Fitzwilliam, then? I fear that shall take some practice; at present it makes me think of your cousin, the Colonel."

Glancing around to make sure that no one was there to see them, Darcy caught her up in his arms and spun them about in a circle, laughing with the simple joy that she allowed him to do so. "Well, I certainly would not want that! My closest family has always called me Fitzwilliam or Darcy, except when my sister calls me Brother, or Will."

With her feet back on the ground, literally if not figuratively, Elizabeth looked up into his dark eyes, warm with love and devotion. "Very well, then; Will it is." And received a happy kiss as a reward.

As they turned and began to walk again, she pondered. "Fitzwilliam Darcy. So Fitzwilliam is for your mother's family?"

"Yes; the Darcy tradition is to name the heir for his mother's family. My father was lucky enough to be named after the Georges, but my grandfather was Worthington." Seeing her smirk, he laughed aloud. "Yes, another mouthful. I once heard that the boys at school called him 'Worty.' Grandmother would tease that he married her for her surname, so that his own son would not have to endure similar teasing."

"So Bennet will do quite nicely," said Elizabeth before coloring when she realized what she had just intimated.

"Yes. Bennet Darcy will do superbly, amazingly, wonderfully well," said Darcy as he again picked his fiancé up and spun them around in a circle, both laughing in the sheer joy of their new understanding. Upon setting her down, they heard noises of a cart approaching from around the bend in the road, so collected themselves and walked forward again, this time on the grassy verge so that the vehicle had room to pass.

The man was an old tenant of Pemberley, hauling hay to the stables. As he passed, he raised his cap to them. "Hullo there, Mr. Darcy. Beautiful day to be alive, ain't it?"

"Hello Mr. Martin! It is indeed. Good day to you, sir!"

Their exchange was near rote, repeated at many such encounters before, but today Fitzwilliam felt the full truth of the statement. He tucked Elizabeth's hand around his arm and smiled down at her as they continued their walk.

They wandered far and paid little attention to their direction but luckily Pemberley's park was ten miles around and its master was familiar with every inch. Had Elizabeth not noted how low the sun was in the sky and prompted them to check their watches, the new lovers might have continued walking until the moon rose.

They spoke of their past and their future, of likes and dislikes, of friends and family and, most importantly, of their mutual joy in their new understanding. Fitzwilliam was full of plans and wished for Elizabeth's input on everything. Lizzy found the realization of their love after so many obstacles and angst nothing short of amazing, and highly deserving of laughter. Will attempted to apologize again for all the mistakes he had made but she only shook her head and reminded him to follow her philosophy; to remember the past only as it brought him pleasure.

When the couple finally reached the house, they had barely enough time to return to their respective rooms and change for dinner. Before parting on the stairs, Will stole a last kiss. "Shall we inform the others this evening or keep it our secret for now?"

Elizabeth smiled up at him, wondering how she had ever mistaken Mr. Darcy for a cold, unfeeling gentleman. "My love, I do not believe we could hide our happiness from our relations tonight if our lives depended on it."

Such a statement surely merited another kiss and it was only by the sheerest luck that the couple had drawn apart before a footman appeared in the hall. Before he could distract her again, Lizzy curtsied and teased lightly, "Thank you kindly, Mr. Darcy, but I believe I can find my way from here."

If the servants had observed the Master standing frozen, watching his guest's light figure tripping down the hall and entering the chamber assigned to her, he would not have cared, for he was rewarded with a happy smile from his beloved just before she disappeared behind the door. After a further moment of stillness, he shook his head and laughed out loud; he was acting like some love-struck puppy. Even so, he turned and practically trotted down the hall toward his own chambers, already planning to skip his bath and change quickly so as not to miss any time in Elizabeth's company.

Darcy would have been glad to know that the lady of his heart was of a similar disposition. Upon entering her room, Lizzy leaned back against the door and closed her eyes, breathing deeply and trying to regain some shred of her normal composure. She feared that if she did not, she might fling open the windows and call out 'He loves me!' to anyone in shouting distance.

"Miss? Should you like a quick bath before you dress?"

Elizabeth blinked open her eyes to see the maid who had been assigned to her. "Yes, thank you, Hannah."

In short order, Miss Bennet was bathed, dressed, and her hair arranged in a becoming style. This was primarily due to the efficiency of the maid; the young lady kept drifting off into a dreamy trance and had to be recalled to the present on several occasions.

When Elizabeth descended the stairs, she was greeted by the happy sight of both Darcys happily talking to a familiar figure.

"Colonel Fitzwilliam! It is good to see you, sir!"

With a happy smile, the Earl's younger son stepped forward and, bowing with a flourish, kissed her hand before grinning at her with a twinkle in his eye. "Miss Bennet, I cannot tell you how glad I am to see you here at Pemberley."

"Have you only just arrived?"

A mischievous glint sparked in the gentleman's face and he glanced towards his cousin. "Actually, we arrived nearly two hours ago, but no one was certain where to find Darcy…"

Moving quickly before his cousin began to tease in earnest, Will directed Elizabeth's attention to an older gentlewoman who was standing just beyond. "But I *am* here now and there is no reason for us to be standing here in the hall. Miss Elizabeth Bennet, please allow me to introduce you to my sister's companion, Mrs. Annesley. She has just returned to us after several weeks in Staffordshire, visiting her niece and their new son."

Lizzy stepped forward to greet the woman who had done so much for Miss Darcy over the last year. The small party obliged their host by moving into the drawing room, although the Colonel's amused look told Fitzwilliam that he had only delayed the inevitable. While the ladies laughed over Mrs. Annesley's description of the father's euphoria upon being presented with his first child, Darcy spoke quietly with a footman who had appeared at the door.

Several minutes later, Elizabeth paused in the conversation and turned slightly to her left, somehow sensing that Will had moved to stand beside her. She raised her eyebrows inquiringly at his serious look.

"The Gardiners send their apologies but will not be joining us this evening; your aunt had a difficult afternoon and Mr. Gardiner feels it better that she retire early."

While the Colonel inquired as to the source of Mrs. Gardiner's troubles and Georgiana launched into an eager explanation of her new acquaintances' connection to Lambton, Elizabeth was flooded with guilt. Since meeting Mr. Darcy by the lake, she had not given a single thought to her relatives.

Reading her expression, Fitzwilliam touched her elbow in comfort and spoke quietly; "There was a second message to you from your aunt, saying that your uncle is being overprotective and you should enjoy your meal."

Elizabeth pondered for a moment but soon most of the worry cleared from her eyes. "My aunt is frank enough that she would call for me if she had need of my company. I shall talk to her tomorrow morning but for now I am sure that my uncle knows what is best."

Will nodded and then, after pausing, caught her eye and inquired softly, "Should we delay our announcement? I am perfectly willing…"

Elizabeth gave him an affectionate look. "No, Georgiana and Colonel Fitzwilliam are your closest family (and soon to be mine); if we do not tell them now, I'm sure they would guess it by the end of the evening."

Her fiancé flashed her a brilliant smile and then turned to nod at the footman standing by the door. The servant stepped out and then a moment later the butler himself entered with a tray and proceeded to pour out champagne in the most delicate crystal goblets that Lizzy had ever seen. His activity quickly caught the attention of the other three occupants of the room and the Colonel shot an inquiring look toward his cousin.

Darcy merely smiled and waited until everyone had a glass and was looking at him expectantly. "Sister, cousin, friends," he nodded to each in turn. "I hope you will all join me in a toast." He paused, his throat tight with emotion but one look at Elizabeth's shining eyes steadied him enough to continue. "Today, Elizabeth has done me the very great honor of accepting my hand in marriage."

Will suddenly found himself juggling two full flutes of champagne, having barely caught up Elizabeth's from her hand as Georgiana leapt across the room and threw her arms around the other lady with a shriek, "We shall be sisters! Oh Elizabeth—I am so happy!"

He caught sight of Mrs. Annesley, also with two glasses, smiling broadly just before his cousin slapped him on the back. "Well done, Darce! Congratulations—I will most certainly drink to that!" And with that, the Colonel tipped back his flute and drank his wine down in a single gulp.

Darcy managed to take a sip of his own as Mrs. Annesley congratulated him sedately. He then found a safe place to set both glasses just as Georgiana broke from Elizabeth and moved to hug her brother. "Oh Wills, I am so very happy for you," she whispered.

Richard turned to congratulate Miss Bennet in a slightly more reserved manner, allowing Will to hold his sister tightly for a moment. How had he ever thought that connecting himself with the Bennets might harm Georgiana? Her transparent joy at the prospect of having Elizabeth as a sister was all that he might have hoped for.

They were a merry party at dinner that night and dallied at the table longer than usual, though few would have been able to recall the menu. It was only Georgiana's determination to quiz her future sister that finally prompted a brief separation of the sexes.

If Miss Darcy was stunned to hear that the happy couple had discussed Pemberley's *plumbing* during their stroll prior to her brother's proposal, she was soon reassured by Miss Bennet.

With a fond look toward her future sister-in-law, Lizzy patted the girl's arm; "It may sound strange to you, my dear, but to me, it was reassuring."

Georgiana couldn't hide her disbelief. "Reassuring? Surely my brother could have thought of something… anything would have been a more romantic topic!"

Seeing that the girl was genuinely distressed, Elizabeth took her hand and leaned back in the settee on which they sat, staring into space as she tried to summarize what was in her heart.

"I know very well how much your brother loves me; it is in his eyes, his voice, his every look and touch. I do not need him to read me poetry or shower me with trinkets. His willingness to discuss estate business… to share his most intimate worries and concerns… to include me in his planning and decision making… that means more to me than any sonnets or jewels. It tells me that he wishes for a partner in life." She smiled impishly at the younger woman who was listening intently. "For I would be no fit wife for a man who desired only a lady to ornament his arm at the opera and play hostess to Society."

Georgiana giggled but still looked thoughtful when the gentlemen rejoined the ladies in the music room. Lizzy immediately noticed that Darcy was blushing and looked mildly vexed with his cousin; the Colonel trailed him with a glass of brandy, still laughing at some joke of his own.

"Mr. Darcy, you are just in time. Will you turn the pages as I play? And then perhaps the Colonel will do the same favor for Georgiana if she would agree to entertain us with a song?"

As she rose and moved to the pianoforte, the Colonel muttered something that the ladies could not hear but caused his cousin to blush even redder. Rolling his eyes, Darcy moved to Elizabeth's side with alacrity.

While she sorted through the music and chose a piece, he leaned over to whisper in her ear, "Thank you."

She smirked and moved to seat herself and adjust the bench. "You appeared to need rescuing."

He leaned down to straighten the pages before her. "As a younger brother himself but my elder, Richard seems to believe it his cousinly duty to step in as the big brother I lack."

Lizzy chuckled and played a few scales softly to limber her fingers. "Well, as both younger and older sibling myself, I can quite understand his determination!"

Darcy looked at her fondly and, though she began to believe that she might happily spend the evening doing nothing but staring into his eyes, Elizabeth remembered that they were in company and turned her attention to the music. Will would have been at a loss to remember what compositions were played that evening. However, he would always remember feeling as if they were enveloped by a warm glow of happiness

Though he might have wished for more, Darcy had to content himself with a warm look and a kiss on Elizabeth's hand when the ladies retired for the night. The loving smile that she gifted him in return made him even more reluctant to join his cousin in the billiards room.

Luckily for Darcy, Richard was sufficiently tired from his hard ride from Newcastle via Staffordshire that he was satisfied with a single game and some relatively gentle ribbing over his younger cousin's certain felicity in marriage.

That night, Will had a dream that began like one he had had since childhood. Mr. George Darcy and his son drove through Lambton toward

Pemberley in silence, looking out at the normally vibrant village, now subdued. The cottages and shops were all hung with bits of black crêpe; the cemetery was spotted with new plots and another funeral was underway even now. Mr. Darcy took a deep breath and let it out slowly, clenching his jaw as they passed and staring straight ahead with a stony, haunted expression.

Ten year old Fitzwilliam consciously attempted to imitate his father, which was difficult as his toes could not yet reach the floor of the carriage. He held his hands together so that they wouldn't tremble while he stared out of the window at the place which had always been his home but appeared to have changed so much in the last month. Sunken in his own misery, Will's father did not notice.

Normally, Will's dream extended to their arrival at a darkened, silent Pemberley House, draped in black, devoid of people, and smelling of death. (In his younger days, his nightmare had included his Aunt Catherine swooping after him like some evil black vulture, trying to grab up him and his baby sister and drag them away from their home).

This night, however, his dream shifted and the carriage pulled up just as Pemberley House and the lake before it lit up, glowing in the morning sun as if dark storm clouds had just parted. His father had turned to him and said gently, "You must get out here, son."

Fitzwilliam Darcy, the grown man, stepped from the carriage and was met with the heartwarming sight of Elizabeth standing on the steps with hands outstretched in welcome. Without a backward glance, Will ran forward, catching her up in his arms and holding her tightly, surrounded with the warm certainty that all would be well; Pemberley would finally be filled with life and happiness and *family* again.

CONTINUED IN BOOK II

ABOUT THE AUTHOR

Jean Sims was born in Seattle and currently lives in Iowa City with her two cats, Oliver and Ernest. She received a B.A. from Wellesley College and a Ph.D. from the University of Chicago, accomplishments that have left her keenly aware of just how much she doesn't know. When not chained to her computer, she enjoys running, gardening, and dreaming up new ways to evict the family of squirrels currently residing in her attic.

Made in the USA
Middletown, DE
10 December 2014